Kathryn Casey

THE
FALLEN
GIRLS

Bookouture

Published by Bookouture in 2020

An imprint of Storyfire Ltd.
Carmelite House
50 Victoria Embankment
London EC4Y 0DZ

www.bookouture.com

Copyright © Storyfire Ltd., 2020

Written by Kathryn Casey

All rights reserved. No part of this publication may be reproduced, stored in any retrieval system, or transmitted, in any form or by any means, electronic, mechanical, photocopying, recording or otherwise, without the prior written permission of the publishers.

ISBN: 978-1-83888-602-8
eBook ISBN: 978-1-83888-601-1

This book is a work of fiction. Names, characters, businesses, organizations, places and events other than those clearly in the public domain, are either the product of the author's imagination or are used fictitiously. Any resemblance to actual persons, living or dead, events or locales is entirely coincidental.

For my husband, who's been with me through all the good times and the bad. Life is a journey, an adventure. How wonderful to have a trusted companion.

PROLOGUE

Sixteen brothers and sisters perched on chairs and table edges, sat hip to hip on the cramped floor: the girls in long-sleeved prairie dresses that swept to their ankles, the boys in pants and collared shirts. All heads bowed and hands clasped, as twelve-year-old Delilah whispered, "Heavenly Father, thank thee for this day. For the rain that fell this morning and watered our crops. Please send more. Thank thee for the well the men are digging and the water it will bring."

Evening prayers. Delilah had always cherished the ritual, the calm before the chaos of helping prepare the little ones for bed. Yet she dreaded what followed. The prospect of leaving the family's mobile home and walking into the night terrified her.

The double-wide trailer smelled of the coming day's bread baking in the oven. On the couch, the women of the household huddled together, serene yet attentive, hands folded piously on laps. Delilah's smooth brow wrinkled in worry as she focused on her mother. The girl looked so like Sariah that townsfolk who saw them together remarked on the resemblance. From her mother, Delilah inherited her thick auburn curls, her startling blue eyes, and the sprinkle of pale freckles that arched across her upturned nose. Sensing her daughter's gaze, Sariah formed a cup of her palm and drew it toward her chest, a signal the children understood meant "more."

As instructed, the youngster resumed her posture, pinning her chin to her chest. "Thank thee, Lord, for my brothers and sisters, for our mothers. Bless our father and Mother Constance, who have left us to live with you in heaven." Delilah paused, and then murmured, "Oh, and if you could please tell Sadie—"

"Amen!" Mother Ardeth roared.

A snicker flitted through those gathered, the scattered teenagers rolling eyes, the adolescents glancing nervously from Delilah to Ardeth, while the youngest sensed something significant had happened but didn't understand what. Fourteen-year-old Lily leaned into Delilah and whispered, "Sis, you know my mom doesn't like any talk of Sadie. You shouldn't—"

"Enough, daughter!" Mother Ardeth snapped at Lily. A staunch woman with arched black eyebrows, Ardeth held a special place in the household. As first wife, she functioned as the family matriarch. But she'd also taken on her dead husband's roles, and these responsibilities weighed on her, in the past year turning her long black hair a steel gray.

Seated between Ardeth and Sariah, Mother Naomi made certain no one misunderstood. A softly round woman with wire-rimmed glasses, a slender nose and a pile of fading brown hair, Naomi tilted her head back. "Thank you, Heavenly Father!" she cried, as enraptured as if she gazed on heaven's gate rather than stained ceiling tiles. "Evening prayer has ended."

At that, Mother Sariah rose and clapped her hands. "It's time, children. Lily and Delilah, take the young ones out, then pajamas."

"Mom, I…" Delilah pleaded. Her stomach churned dinner's beans and tortillas, perhaps a physical manifestation of her fears. To quiet it, she pressed her hand against the wide white sash that belted her worn blue cotton dress.

Bending down, Sariah whispered in her daughter's ear, "No more, Delilah. Please, stop. You'll frighten the little ones."

The girl's bow-shaped lips melted into a frown. "Yes, Mother."

The battered aluminum door squeaked in harsh complaint as it scraped the concrete stoop. Lily and the children jostled behind her as Delilah stepped out into the night. All around her, insects chirped and burred. The double-wide rested on concrete blocks on the edge of the community cornfield, acres of pencil-straight stalks heavy with the year's harvest. In the near distance, a mountain ridge formed a solid black wave between the shadowy valley and a cloudless, navy-blue sky speckled with pinpoint stars. A golden oval, a nearly full moon hung high above Samuel's Peak. A hundred years earlier, the leaders of Elijah's People, a small fundamentalist Mormon sect that settled the valley, named the precipice in honor of its great prophet, the saint who led its people to Utah's Alber Valley.

A soft breeze carried the scent of fresh-cut alfalfa drying in the fields. As Delilah clomped down the five stairs to the dirt path, eight little ones followed like a brood of chicks trailing a hen.

Each step as loath as a prisoner's to a cell, Delilah marched forward. Wielding a neon-orange plastic flashlight thicker than her arm, she pointed a wide funnel of light ahead and followed it. The short procession turned a corner, and Delilah could no longer see the trailer.

Hastening to catch up, Lily shuffled beside her. "You need to stop talking about Sadie, Delilah. You know my mom—"

"I know!" Delilah came to an abrupt stop that left the younger children bumping into one another like dominoes behind her. "Lily, can you feel it?"

"What?"

"Someone," Delilah said, a catch in her throat. "Watching."

Lily's black hair was gathered in a topknot and puffed to frame her coffee-colored eyes. An analytical girl often in trouble for questioning her elders, she appeared doubtful. Why would anyone watch them? They took the young ones out every night, and no one ever bothered them. But as she nudged her sister forward, Lily trained her own flashlight, a twin to Delilah's, on the cornfield and searched between the rows. When satisfied, she proclaimed, "This is silly. I don't see anything. Why do you think someone is—"

"I can feel him."

"Who?"

Delilah gulped back the bile rising in her chest. "I don't know."

"Delilah, no one is—"

"He is, Lily. He watches me." She repeated, "I can feel him."

Again skimming the field, Lily craned her neck to peek between the rigid stalks. Nothing moved save the ruffle of leaves in a draft off the mountain, beginning to turn cool after a blistering late-summer day.

Impatient, Lily scowled at her younger sister. She wanted to put the little ones to bed, so she and Delilah could finish the checkers game they started before dinner. Lily felt pretty sure she had Delilah outmaneuvered.

"There's no one out there," Lily insisted. "Let's just—"

"You sure?" Three inches shorter than her sister, Delilah looked up to Lily not just literally but figuratively. She was the closest to Delilah in age, and the sisters had consoled each other through their father's death and shared the difficult days when they were evicted from their big house in town. In the past year, their lives had become increasingly difficult. Even with Father and Mother Constance gone, and the oldest of their siblings married off, that left nineteen living in a three-bedroom trailer without indoor plumbing. At night, every inch of floor became a bed.

"Yeah," Lily said. "I'm sure no one's out there."

Delilah swallowed hard.

At the metal-sided outhouse, the children took turns entering through doors marked 'MEN' and 'WOMEN'. They fidgeted and snickered in line, whispered in each other's ears. A ten-year-old girl picked a nearly closed buttercup from the weeds at the edge of the path and held it under a younger girl's chin. "If I see a reflection, you have a boyfriend."

The other children clustered around.

Wide-eyed, the smaller girl asked, "Do you see one?"

The older girl nodded yes.

Clapping her hands, the little girl bounced up and down. "Who is it? Who is it? Who's my boyfriend?"

The other children hooted, as the girl holding the buttercup giggled. "It's too dark!" she teased. "Silly, silly. No reflections in the dark!"

The minutes ticked past until all but one straggler finished in the outhouse. Four-year-old Kaylynn habitually dawdled.

Growing impatient, weary and ready to end the day, the youngsters squabbled. Two boys shoved one another, and Lily ordered them to be still.

Watching her older sister, Delilah felt ashamed. For days, her mother had assured her no one hid in the corn. *I'm not a little girl anymore. I need to be strong. I need to grow up.*

"Sis, take the children into the house," she told Lily. "I'll wait for Kaylynn."

"You sure?" Again Lily focused her big orange flashlight on the brittle stalks, heavy with ripening corn. In days, it would be ready for harvest. Then there would be canning for the girls to do and cornbread to bake for dinners. A pale moth fluttered lazily by, weaving through the beam.

"I'm sure," Delilah said, pulling up her shoulders, standing up straighter.

"Good! Hurry up and we can get back to our game." Lily waved at the children. "Let's go. Pajamas and bed." The little ones padded off toward the trailer, twittering and talking.

Moments later, Delilah stood alone in the night, regretting sending Lily away. In the moonlight, the shadows grew ever longer. The incessant hum of the insects swelled.

"Kaylynn, hurry up," Delilah shouted through the outhouse door.

PROPERTY OF MERTHYR TYDFIL PUBLIC LIBRARIES

"I'm trying," the little one called back.

Fighting a mounting disquiet, Delilah sought comfort by murmuring the verse of a familiar children's song. "God watch over me…"

At the far side of the outhouse, a patch of stalks shimmered. Delilah stiffened. The flashlight beam searched. Nothing.

"When are you coming out?" she yelled at Kaylynn.

From inside the outhouse, the little one shouted, "In a minute."

"Please hurry!" Holding the flashlight with both hands, Delilah scanned the hard dirt visible between the rows and continued her song. "God watch over me and keep me—"

Something moved. Something unseen disturbed a clump of stalks.

The flashlight held before her, Delilah crept toward the corn. Peering between the stiff green shoots and their long slender leaves, she searched. She heard a throaty purr. The flashlight's beam skimmed low. From the darkness, two iridescent gold eyes emerged.

"Ebenezer?"

A scrawny gray tabby inched forward. Relief flooded through Delilah. "You're the one watching me?" Holding the flashlight tight, she leaned into the corn. "Don't tell anyone how scared I was, okay?"

Crouching to pet the cat, Delilah didn't notice the stalks shiver a few feet to her right. She never saw the man shuffle out of the corn. By the time she looked up, he towered above her. In a single movement, he wrapped one thick arm around her waist and clamped his other hand over her mouth, muffling her screams.

CHAPTER ONE

I stared at the guy, not blinking. He said nothing, just squirmed off and on in the rickety metal chair, his handcuffed wrists resting on the battered gray metal table between us. I wished, not for the first time, that I had X-rays coming out of my eyes like the ones they show in comic books, the kind artists draw with pulsing heat rays. The truth? I wanted the guy to fry. Right there in the interrogation room.

While I watched.

The waste of DNA that held my attention was on camera at a local drinking establishment nine hours earlier, a cowboy bar on Dallas's city limits. He'd liquored up and gotten into an argument with the bartender, who cut him off. The bartender picked up a phone and started to call someone, I figured a cab for his drunken customer. The guy stood up and shouted at him, something I couldn't hear on the surveillance tape. In a final effort, the bartender made a move to grab the perp's car keys off the bar. The drunk beat him to them. Shouting back over his shoulder, the guy staggered out the door.

Ninety seconds later, he moseyed back in, this time with a pistol in each hand.

The only good news: near closing, the joint was almost empty. An hour earlier, five times the number of people could have died. As it was, we had four victims: one dead bartender; one dead waitress; one dead twenty-two-year-old college student who'd pulled an all-nighter and stopped in for a drink to unwind; and a regular at the bar, a guy from the neighborhood who spent most nights drowning his sorrows with shots and beers. That guy, lucky stiff, lived. At least so far. He was in the ICU, holding on by his fingernails.

While I stared down the guy across from me, I thought about the squad of cops spreading out over the city, ringing doorbells. Family members would answer, little suspecting that they'd receive the worst news of their lives. One family would head to the hospital, perhaps arriving too late to say goodbye. The other three vics were never coming home. Last I heard we were still looking for next of kin for the college student. His family would never see him walk across the stage at graduation, never celebrate when he landed his first real job, never dance at his wedding. The waitress? The bartender? That's where it got really sad. A total of five kids between them, the oldest twelve. What would happen to them?

I thought about the three bodies on the way to the morgue. Such a waste. Those folks woke up yesterday morning never considering that it would be their last. Life? Well, it's not always fair.

In my world, events make that clear entirely too often.

Our office door reads: CRIMES AGAINST PERSONS. Although fairly new, only a detective for the past three years, I pull the toughest cases—murders and sexual assaults. At Dallas PD, I have something of a jacket, a reputation. I work leads to death, no pun intended. The truth is, I have a lot of time on my hands, since I don't have a life outside the job.

That's how this particular shooter became the focus of my undivided attention.

My shift didn't start until eleven, but I arrived early. My calendar empty, I didn't have anything else to do on a Saturday morning. So I was at my desk dissecting a case folder when this guy shuffled through the door in leg irons and cuffs at 8 a.m., two beat cops piloting him by his elbows. Somebody heard shots and called it in. They found my companion passed out with his head on the bar, his hand curled around a half-empty beer mug.

Guns don't mix well with stupid. Guns and stupid are even more dangerous when paired with crazy drunk.

"You know, booze can make you do things you wouldn't otherwise," I said to the guy. I gave him a sociable smile. As much as I wanted to vaporize him, I needed him to cooperate and talk. "I'm sure you didn't mean to hurt those folks. Really the alcohol is to blame, don't you think?"

We had an open-and-shut case, no doubt about it. But the DA's office always appreciated not only a wrapped package but one with a well-fluffed bow. I wanted to tie the guy up with a confession on the wall-mounted video camera focused on his face. I also had a rep in the department for being able to draw confessions out of perps. As serious as the cases were, and this one certainly was, I saw it as something of a chess game. I enjoyed the challenge of working angles to convince the bad guys to talk.

In particular, I wanted no wiggle room for this one. He was going down.

"Damn it. I told you. I didn't kill those people," he said. Not a bad-looking guy—he had a mop of curly blond hair and a beard to match, deep-set smoky brown eyes and a muscular neck that spread into well-developed shoulders. I figured he worked out. He'd have a lot of time to firm up his pecs in a prison cell.

"You have someone else we should investigate for the killings? You were the only one there. Just you and the four victims in the bar," I told him. "And we have you on camera, holding up your guns like Rambo."

At that, he twisted his mouth far to the side, digesting my words.

"I don't remember nothin' about shootin' no one. I didn't do it."

"You want to see the video again?" I offered. "Happy to cue it up on my iPad. We can even order in some popcorn."

At that, the guy's eyes turned to suspicious slits. "Videos can be doctored. I see it all the time on the Internet."

I let loose a long sigh and leaned across the table toward him. He looked uncertain, but I smiled like he was my new best friend. "I really think you need to get in front of this," I advised, dropping my voice low to pull him in. "I mean, you killed those folks, and it's memorialized on a video. You're not walking out of here."

The guy scooted back, putting distance between us. "I didn't—"

"Don't give me that!" I brought my hand down flat with a bang. The table shook. The guy jumped, eyeing me like I was the crazy one.

"Lady," he said. "I don't—"

"Detective," I corrected him. "Detective Clara Jefferies."

"Detective Jefferies, I…"

He stopped talking, I figured unsure of what to say. I waited a bit, let him stew, and then I offered, "Let's figure out your best option." I sat back in the chair, appearing to relax. "Like I said, my bet is that the booze made you do it."

The guy thought about that. "Well, I guess…"

Almost have him, I thought. *Almost there.*

"If you hadn't been drinking, you wouldn't have killed those folks, right?"

At first nothing, but then, just as hope faded, he nodded.

Got him.

The prosecutor, judge and jury wouldn't care that he was drunk. It wasn't an excuse. But if he thought it might give him any advantage, he might open up.

"Tell me how it happened."

The guy blew out a raspy breath. I smelled sour booze and stale cigarettes. "Well, I—"

"All I want is the truth."

The guy bobbed his head. "Okay, well, I had a fight with my old lady about our kids. She got riled up, and when she's like that, you can't argue with her."

To keep him talking, I made my face sympathetic.

"I decided I'd leave and let the bitch cool down. I was at the bar for a couple of hours. No problems. But then the bartender pissed me off, told me I couldn't have another drink." The guy's voice rose, still angry at the bartender's audacity. "I wasn't done drinking, you know?"

"I understand," I assured him. "You needed another one. The bartender really didn't have a reason to—"

"That's what I told that asswipe!" the guy shouted, grinning at me as if grateful that I understood. "I wasn't drunk. I didn't need a damn cab."

"What happened next?"

"I go outside. I'm thinking I'll go home. But then I remember that the wife was pissed. Probably still is. Probably waiting to holler at me some more. I could picture her there, sitting in a chair, mad as a loon, hoping I'd come home so she could let loose."

"So what did you do?"

"I opened the car door."

"And?"

"I remembered the guns were in the trunk."

"So you…"

"I popped the trunk, grabbed the guns, checked to make sure they were loaded, and then I walked back inside the bar…"

Hours later, I left the interrogation room rubbing the back of my sore neck. The chief and one of the assistant district attorneys waited. They'd been watching on a monitor. "Thanks," the prosecutor said. A short guy in a pinstripe suit, he had a red silk handkerchief in his breast pocket. Around the cop shop he was known as Dandy. In the courtroom he put on quite a show, and juries loved him. "Great confession. When he said he checked to make sure the guns were loaded? Clear evidence of premeditation. You got everything on tape? Including reading him his rights?"

"It's all on the video, including Miranda," I said. I ran my hand through my hair. A few black strands had worked their way out of the tight bun at my nape. I tucked the stragglers in. "Do you need anything else?"

"Nah," Chief Nevil Thompson said. A wiry man with shoulders habitually pulled up to his ears and a long, narrow face, he'd ruled over Dallas PD for my entire nine years with the department. I started as a dispatcher and got my criminal justice degree in night school. I admired the chief. He'd been good to me, promoting me up the chain. Sure I worked hard and gave it my all, but it meant a lot that he noticed. Usually he'd be home on a Saturday, but the media was all over the bar shooting. "Good work, Detective."

"Thanks, Chief." I'd been in the interview room so long my morning Egg McMuffin had worn off. Emphasizing the point, my stomach growled. "Since we're all set, I'm going to grab a late lunch before I type this up."

"Make it dinner," the chief advised. When I shot him a questioning glance, he explained, "Check the time."

I looked at my watch, the brown leather strap cracked and creased. The scratched face distorted the dial, but it looked like 7 p.m. "Guess you're right."

The chief shot me a sympathetic glance. "Clara, go home. We've got the video of the confession. Someone else can write the warrant. You can file your full report on Monday."

"I've got to—"

"You've done enough. Get out of here. Unwind. Make yourself some kind of a life away from this place."

I had to admit I was tired, but nothing waited for me at home. Actually, I didn't think of my studio apartment in those terms. The space was barely furnished, my refrigerator embarrassingly empty. I'd been meaning to go grocery shopping, swear off fast food and take up cooking. Somehow that never happened. "I could put in a few more hours, finish my report and hang around. Saturday nights get busy, and—"

"We have a full shift on. They'll do just fine. Go home," the chief repeated. "That's an order."

I took a deep breath. "Okay, I'll leave. But first I'm going to type up my report."

The chief's eyebrows bunched together. "I give up. File your report."

"Thanks, Chief, I—"

"But then get the hell out of here and go somewhere. Home. A restaurant. A bar. A movie. Visit friends, if you have any," he growled.

"Chief, I—"

"Clara, tomorrow's your day off. Take it!"

My cubicle had a view of Dallas's glass-and-granite skyline, with the Chase Tower in the distance. As I finished my report on the bar killings, the city lights came on. I stood at the window and peered down at the streets. Folks drove by on their way to a Saturday night out. On the sidewalks, couples walked arm in arm. The city looked peaceful, and I considered how most people just wanted to live their lives with a bit of happiness and a minimum of pain. I thought about the small but dangerous minority who wouldn't let that happen, the ones who had no second thoughts about taking what belonged to someone else, even a life.

My neck was still sore, my lower back felt tight. At thirty-four that shouldn't happen. For the most part, I was in good shape, and I was too young for aches and pains. I considered the fine wrinkles webbing my eyes. One of my fellow detectives described them as laugh lines, but then noted that he'd never actually seen me crack a smile.

"Probably stress," I muttered. I considered the next day, Sunday, and decided I would listen to the chief and try to sleep in. I couldn't remember the last time I'd had an entire day to myself. I grabbed my suit jacket and slipped it on over my white cotton shirt. I unpinned the leather sash with my badge from my belt, stuffed it in my old black bag, the leather scratched and the strap frayed. *Maybe I should go shopping and buy a new one*, I thought. I entertained the idea for mere seconds before I decided, *Nah. This one's fine.*

Shopping malls and grocery stores made me nervous. I had a hard time with big buildings and crammed aisles. Too many options and I felt paralyzed. Maybe because I'd grown up in a world where I was never allowed to choose anything for myself.

I'd taken four steps from my chair on my way to the elevator when my desk phone rang. I stopped and looked at it. The phone kept ringing. For once, I considered not answering.

"Detective Jefferies here," I said into the receiver a moment later. Silence.

"This is Detective Jefferies, Dallas PD. Who's calling?"

On the other end, someone cleared his throat. In a low, deep voice, he said, "Clara, it's Max."

"Max?"

"Max Anderson. From Alber."

"Alber…" It felt like a lifetime ago. It felt like someone else's life.

"Clara, it's me," the man said. "Max, from home. I need your help."

CHAPTER TWO

"Clara. A detective. Working homicides, no less. I've seen your name in the newspapers. You've handled some big cases." Max had recounted the condensed version of his own story: how he'd been a cop, worked his way up to major crimes in Salt Lake City, before he hired on as chief deputy at the sheriff's department in Smith County, Utah, where we grew up. I remembered his soft laugh from when we were kids. "Heck of a coincidence, both of us in law enforcement. Don't you think?"

At first, I did. But then I reconsidered.

"With the way we grew up, maybe we just want to bring a little sanity to the world," I said, conjuring up an image of him from long ago, a shy, lanky teenager with a thatch of hair the light brown of hay, hazel eyes that nip down in the corners.

Silent at first, as if mulling over my theory, he said, "Could be."

Our shared history aside, this wasn't a social call, and Max quickly got to the point. "Clara, I need you in Alber for a day or two."

The strength of my reaction surprised me. I reared back, and said louder than I'd intended, "No. I can't."

I blamed it on work. I had obligations. Yet I sensed that Max understood the real reason. The prospect of returning to Alber flooded me with dread. I'd left a life behind there, painful memories that haunted me. A decade ago, I promised myself that I'd never return. And the day I left, I knew that I'd never be welcomed back.

"Let me tell you about the case," he said. In that morning's mail, Max's boss, Sheriff Virgil Holmes, had received an anonymous note that claimed a young girl had disappeared two nights earlier. "I tried to talk to the family. They refused to cooperate. The Alber police chief gave it a shot after I did and he got the same result. We're making no ground."

The day ended without a lead, without any confirmation that the note was genuine. "I need someone the family will talk to, Clara. To find out the truth. That's you. You're the only one."

"Me? Why would they talk to me?"

"Clara, because—"

"I'm not part of that world anymore. I'm an outsider," I pointed out, my voice high and strained. "Max, I'm sorry. I'd like to help you, but…" I lowered my voice and tried to regain control. "You can't ask me to go back there. You just can't."

For a moment, he was silent. Then Max said, "Clara, the missing girl is Delilah."

In a whirl, my memory played a reel from my past, snippets of little girls in prairie dresses running through the fields. One had red-gold hair and a smile that tugged at my heart. "Delilah?"

"Yes."

I pictured her, little more than a toddler when I'd left Alber, jumping on still-bowed legs when she tried to play hopscotch with the older children, her bulky skirt bunching around her knees when she barreled head-first down the slide. The family Max had gone to see, the one that turned him away, was my own.

Delilah Jefferies was my half-sister, the oldest daughter of Sariah, my father's fourth wife.

"Delilah must be a teenager now."

"Almost. She's twelve," Max said.

"You think she's been taken?"

"No one has filed a missing person report," Max admitted. "But yes, I do."

I didn't ask any more questions. "I'm on my way."

CHAPTER THREE

Max stared at his cell phone for a moment before he placed it on his desk. He leaned back in his chair and looked out the window. His small corner office overlooked the field behind the courthouse, the mountains in the distance. It was dusk, and the sun's last rays painted the sky rose gold as it dipped in the west.

Clara's coming, he thought.

He pictured the girl he'd known. Tall, slender, the blackest hair, thick brows like her mother's that arched up when surprised or annoyed. As a teenager, Clara had worn her feelings on her sleeve, as the old saying went, and he wondered if she was still so easily read. Then he shrugged off the thought. Time had passed. Clara was a different person. She was a detective, a cop, not the girl he knew.

We all change. Life chews us up and spits us out. Stuff happens in an instant, and nothing's ever the same.

He wondered why Clara fled Alber.

The teenage girl he remembered appeared content in their world. While many struggled under the tight constraints, she'd flourished. Something bad must have happened. *Maybe, when we have time to really talk, I'll ask.* But then he shook his head. *Too personal. We don't really know each other anymore. It's been too long.*

When he told her that he'd moved back to their hometown, Clara had sounded shocked. He wasn't surprised. It wasn't anything he could have predicted he'd do. Those like him, shunned and forced out, those like Clara who turned their backs on the faith and fled, rarely returned. If his life hadn't taken such a painful turn, he would have stayed away as well.

Back in Alber for a little more than a year, Max wondered every day if he'd made the right decision.

Sixteen years living in Salt Lake, he'd built a life. He'd owned a brick bungalow just outside downtown with his wife, Miriam. Their daughter, Brooke, went to a good school. He'd turned his back on his past, done everything he could to put Alber behind him. In Salt Lake, his neighbors and friends were mainstream Mormons: members of the Church of Latter Day Saints, which had renounced polygamy in the 1800s. Those he met were good people who easily accepted him as one of their own. No one asked about his six mothers, dozens of brothers and sisters, or his father, who advised the children every morning to "Be right with God! For the End of Days is upon us!"

Behind a locked door, he kept an arsenal of guns and rifles, enough to supply a small army.

"Crazy old man," Max muttered.

To be fair, Max had to admit it wasn't just his father's teachings. When the world ended, the sect's leaders preached that the good families in Alber would have to fight off hordes of sinners. In the end, only the virtuous members of Elijah's People would repopulate the earth.

"The End of Days is upon us, and we need to be judged worthy." Max pictured his father, one of the church elders, his disheveled stark-white hair and his wrinkled face snarled into a twisted frown. The old man raised an index finger, pointed at the sky and proclaimed, "On the day of reckoning, God will take retribution and condemn the sinners to hell." When the old man prophesized a date on which the world as they knew it would end, Max, nerves on edge, had waited for the sky to open, to see God descend on a glowing cloud surrounded by the great prophets.

"We weren't worthy!" his father had shouted, when the appointed day passed without earthquakes, floods, or hurricanes. "God has found us lacking in faith and fortitude!"

After each predicted Day of Atonement came and went, his father hibernated in seclusion. When he emerged, wild-eyed and scruffy, he whispered of revelations and announced the date of a new day of reckoning. Again, Max nervously waited for what felt inevitable but never came.

Despite it all, Max was devoted to his father, and he believed the old man loved him, right up until the day Max became one of the lost boys, the young men forced out of Alber to change the ratio of men to women and free up the town's girls to be married off as second, third, fourth, even sixteenth wives.

Looking back, Max realized that he probably should have seen it coming.

On Max's seventeenth birthday, a town elder called his father and informed him that Max had to leave Alber. At home that night, the sister-wives all avoided him and Max saw his mother crying, but first thing the following morning, she threw his clothes into a duffel bag. The old man drove Max to St. George, took him to the center of town, handed him two hundred dollars, kissed him on the cheek, and left. Max stood, clutching the money in his hand, while he watched his father drive away. Nowhere to go. No one to help him.

Years passed. He returned to Alber only once, for his father's funeral.

Good riddance, Max thought.

Would he have returned without the accident? Miriam dead. And Brooke. Dear little Brooke. What happened to them was his fault, he judged, and it ate away at him every waking moment. Guilt stalked him at every turn.

After the accident, the practicalities of life had overwhelmed him. Brooke's doctor and hospital bills overflowed in each day's mail. Tortured by crushing regret, Max knew he'd made mistakes. He'd lost his job and their security. Sheriff Virgil Holmes's call had saved him.

"I've got a big county to police, and it includes a handful of these polygamous towns," the sheriff told him that day on the phone. "Listen, Anderson, I hear you grew up in Alber, and that you were a hotshot cop in Salt Lake, a lead investigator. I know you've hit tough times, but I'm willing to give you a chance to turn it around."

"Sheriff, I can explain what happened with my job in Salt Lake. I'm a good cop. I—"

"No need. Just sign on and come help me," the sheriff had said. "I need a chief deputy who can head up investigations, and I need someone like you who can talk to these polygamous folks. Someone who speaks their language."

It was more than Max could have asked for: a good salary, health insurance and a means to support Brooke. He couldn't undo all that had happened, but this, perhaps, could enable him to repair some of the damage.

Unfortunately, it hadn't been easy to start over.

Alber had always been clannish and that hadn't changed. Max had history with the people, but not the kind that opened doors—this case was a vivid example of that. He'd spent most of the day investigating and no one would talk to him about the note. He couldn't even find out if it was real or a sick hoax.

I better tell Sheriff Holmes that Clara's coming, Max thought.

The sheriff should have been home with his family on a Saturday evening, but earlier Max had heard a familiar voice in the building. When Max peeked in the sheriff's open office door, he had his phone propped up to his ear and was slipping files into his briefcase.

"Yeah, yeah, I'm ready," Sheriff Holmes said. "I'm getting everything together right now. I'll work on it tomorrow."

The sheriff gave Max a nod.

"You know, I think this is going to work. The whole area's excited about it," the sheriff told whoever was on the phone. "Sure, I'm in. No problem. Got the money set aside for my contribution. Let's talk next week."

At that, the sheriff hung up, and Max noticed that his boss looked particularly pleased. "Good news?"

"Yeah. On the ski resort. The governor found a group of investors out of Salt Lake, and they're drawing up plans. It looks like this might come together." A slight man with a round belly, Sheriff Holmes had big cheeks and bushy gray sideburns, but a bald head that glistened under the overhead lights. He wore his politician's smile as he peered at Max from behind a pair of aviator glasses. "You sure you don't want a piece of this? Those who get in early, throw in a bit of cash at the start, all goes well, we'll make a fortune."

"I can't afford it," Max said, turning down the offer for what wasn't the first time. "There's not a lot of extra money these days."

"Tough break. This could be a gold mine." Sheriff Holmes gulped a healthy dose of air. "Speaking of that, how's your girl?"

"Hanging in there." Max didn't like to talk about Brooke. He changed the subject. "Sheriff, I'm working on that missing person case, the Jefferies girl, Delilah, and—"

The sheriff furrowed his brow, decidedly unhappy.

"Didn't I tell you to turn that case over to the local PD?" From the beginning, Sheriff Holmes had been dubious about the tip. A missing twelve-year-old, one would expect the parents would be begging for police help. As the day went on without any cooperation from the Jefferies family, the sheriff became convinced it was a ruse. Earlier that day, he'd ordered Max to refer the case to Alber's chief of police. "I told you not to put any more resources into it. We had that talk, right?"

"We did. And I did as you asked. But the chief tried and couldn't get anywhere either. The family wouldn't let him in the door."

"Those damn polygamists. They're a cult, I tell ya. They keep everything so hush-hush," the sheriff snarled. Once he started complaining about the polygamous towns, the complications of having the communities as his responsibility, Max's boss could rail on for hours. Max had tried to explain the realities to the sheriff, to help him understand why towns like Alber were so resistant to law enforcement, but to no avail. The reclusive towns were a testy thorn in the sheriff's side. "Always hiding something. Won't talk—"

Rather than listen, Max cut in. "Chief Barstow offered to give it another shot tomorrow, but I decided not to wait on him. A young girl like that. This could be bad. So I put in a call to Clara Jefferies. Delilah's sister."

The sheriff looked even more displeased. "You told me about her. She's a cop? A detective?"

"In Dallas."

"She agreed to come?"

"On her way."

The sheriff stuffed a few more files into his briefcase. "I wish you hadn't done that," he said. Max shot him a questioning look, and the sheriff said, "Chief Barstow won't like it, you going past him when he offered to keep working it. We need to maintain good relations with the locals."

"I know," Max said. "But we're losing time. If the girl has been abducted, time is important."

"That's the crux of your problem, having to say *if*," the sheriff said. "A day into this, it shouldn't be *if* the girl is missing."

"You're right. We should know," Max admitted. "But while I can't be certain, I think this is real. Like I said, I'm convinced Delilah is—"

"You told me what you *think*, but where's the evidence?" the sheriff snapped. His brow puckered with concern, and he shook his head. "Not the way I would have played this, Max. I would have held back and made sure I had a case before I locked horns with the local PD."

Everything the sheriff said was true, all of it standard procedure. Max knew that, but what choice did he have? A young girl could be missing. "Sheriff, I—"

"What's done is done," the sheriff said. "But in the future, when I give you a direct order, you obey it."

Max's right eye twitched just slightly. He thought about how he couldn't afford to lose his job. With his past, there weren't a lot of others waiting for him. "Of course. Absolutely."

"Glad we've got that settled." Sheriff Holmes grabbed his briefcase and walked toward the door. "Now, let's both head home for the night. And let's hope this Dallas cop has some sway with these people."

CHAPTER FOUR

My roll-on waited in the closet. I'd lived in the studio apartment for five years and hadn't used the luggage since the day I'd moved in, but had never bothered to put it in storage. I folded shirts and slacks, and lined them up on the bed. It was the end of August and it would be searing hot in Utah. Then I heard my mother's voice. "Clara, a virtuous woman is modest. Only a loose woman exposes her arms and legs. Only brazen women tempt men by showing their skin." I pictured the prairie dresses of my youth.

While I'd never return to those days, I needed to fit in enough to make the townsfolk, my family in particular, feel comfortable around me. I removed the short-sleeve shirts I'd packed and added two with long sleeves. I took out a knee-length pencil skirt in favor of a second pair of tan slacks.

Almost done, I packed my black leather holster and slipped my Colt .380 Mustang Pocketlite into my bag's side pocket. With my credentials and badge, I'd bypass TSA and carry onto the plane. Just in case I needed it, I added a seven-round backup magazine to my luggage.

As the suitcase filled, I replayed Max's phone call in my head. Was Delilah really gone? Over the years, I'd worked enough child abductions to know that when a kid disappears, the reasons can be terrifying.

A year earlier, a ten-year-old Dallas boy hadn't shown up for dinner. His parents called his friends—no one had seen him. Searching the neighborhood, they found their son's bike abandoned near a playground. The chief asked me to lead the task force, and we jumped on it fast. We sent out an Amber Alert and plastered the news stations and Internet with the kid's face. I called in a forensic team, FBI profilers, and helicopters. We collected and analyzed video from every camera we could find in a two-mile radius.

Despite our efforts, the case spun out of control. Media crawled all over us, circling the kid's house and the neighborhood with drones. False leads poured into my office, and we had to investigate all of them. We had no idea if one could be legit.

Then we got a tip. A grocery store manager reported that she saw a guy act strangely, staring at the headlines on the newspapers in the rack, talking about the case to another customer standing nearby. "The guy gave that lady the creeps," the manager told me. "Something about him was off. He looked excited about the case."

We had a list of every sex offender in Dallas, and we zeroed in on those who lived or worked near the store. I took driver's license photos of all of them to the grocery manager and she identified the man. Minutes later, I knocked on the door of a well-kept ranch house.

Just in case this lead was the right one, I had a SWAT team back me up.

The guy answered, looking like any other homeowner, wearing a T-shirt and shorts. At first, he couldn't have been more cordial, but that changed when I tried to talk my way into the house. Visibly agitated, he'd slammed the door and shouted at me that he had a gun. He ordered me to stand back and threatened to kill the kid.

I worked for hours trying to talk him out, and finally convinced him that he had no other option that brought him out alive.

Hands in the air, he'd strolled through the front door, but I knew the moment I saw the grin on his face that the boy was dead.

As hard as I'd tried, I couldn't save that boy. I wasn't going to let that happen to Delilah.

I was hoping to fly out that night, but there was nothing available and a twenty-hour drive from Dallas to Alber wasn't a reasonable option.

I texted to tell Max I'd arrive on the first flight in the morning and tried to get some sleep. The day had been long, and the one to come promised to be tough. But as I crawled into bed, memories of Delilah kept me from drifting off. I saw her as a baby in her mother's arms, Sariah beaming at her, so proud. My father and mother, Mother Naomi and Mother Constance stood around them, all welcoming our new baby. I remembered Delilah's softness on my lap, the sweet smell of her neck as we cuddled on the couch. I remembered her at one, newly walking, tottering with my sister Lily and the other children, singing "Ring Around the Rosie," giggling when they all fell down.

At 2 a.m., I gave up and turned on my computer. I surfed the web, skimming newspapers and missing person articles, searching for cases of missing children in Utah, any unexplained disappearances of minors, but found nothing recent. After that, I logged on to NCIC, the National Crime Information Center, and searched the files on missing persons. There were dozens, but none anywhere near Alber—I kept looking until I eventually fell asleep.

The plane touched down in Las Vegas at ten, and I rented a black Nissan Pathfinder for the three-hour trek northeast into the mountains. After I entered Utah and passed St. George, the worn asphalt highway cut through great valleys covered with spindly pines and low brush. For the first half of the drive, campers and tourists, tankers and eighteen-wheelers drummed past, but as I swung southeast, the road became nearly deserted. I wound between mountain ridges, past grass-covered fields and through thick pine forests that were crisscrossed by thin streams and dry creek beds.

The drive gave me ample time to consider what waited for me, but I pushed back memories, held them at bay. I'd never intended to return to Alber, never thought that I would even consider it. I'd put my past behind me—the prairie dresses, the cinder block school where I taught kindergarten, all of it.

"I'm a cop, a detective," I said out loud. "Ten years on the outside. Nine years with Dallas PD. I'm a different person."

Yet at the same time, I pictured our rambling house, my sisters and brothers running through the yard, our mothers sitting on the porch knitting and watching us play.

As I drove, the towns became smaller. They were spread farther apart, surrounded by wilderness, and I considered the isolation of living in the mountains, especially in the winters, when icy roads became nearly impassable. The town elders liked the solitude, and the separation served as a barrier to protect them.

I crossed a bridge over the Virgin River and, a short distance ahead, a brown and white sign greeted me:

ALBER, UTAH
ELEVATION 5,841 FEET
POPULATION 4,346

Tucked into a notch at the base of a pine-covered mountain ridge, Alber spread across a sloping valley. At the far end, Samuel's Peak guarded the town, a silent sentry keeping watch. Glowing against the clear blue sky, the afternoon sun glistened off the summit's stark gray wall of stone. I remembered how in sunset's dwindling light the mountainsides sometimes shone a burnished gold. When I was a kid, my mom told me the spirits of our founding fathers lived on that peak. She said our dead ancestors protected us from the dreaded outsiders, those who condemned our way of life and our faith.

In Alber, we trusted no one outside our sect. Other Christians, including mainstream Mormons, we labeled Gentiles. They were not of us. Only Elijah's People were the chosen ones. Those held up as the greatest sinners were people like me—ones who had once been part of the faith but willfully turned their backs on the teachings. We were labeled apostates, and the townsfolk, even our own families, considered us traitors. The sect's prophet ruled it a sin to eat at the same table or converse with an apostate.

On the road into town, I pulled to the side, sat on the shoulder and considered the view. I thought about driving Alber's streets and seeing familiar faces. Many of those I knew, old friends, family, would turn away when they recognized me. Only thoughts of Delilah kept me from turning the Pathfinder around and retracing my route to the Las Vegas airport, or to begin the long drive east back to Dallas.

A semi hauling a load of massive tree trunks rumbled past, dust clouded and the SUV shook. Ahead I saw the truck pull through the gates into my father's sawmill.

Father.

It had been nearly a decade since I last saw him. That crisp fall afternoon I stopped at the house and visited with him and my mother. The sweet smell of apples filled the air, and we made plans for a gathering the coming weekend. I said nothing about my visit being a goodbye. As I strode away, I'd passed my brothers and sisters hoeing the garden, the younger ones playing tag in the yard, and I'd waved.

How would they react when I walked back into their lives? I pictured the frown on my mother's face when she first saw me, the judgment in my father's eyes.

Yet I wanted to see him, and Mother. The years had passed, but they were still my parents. Despite all that had come between us, what my father had done, I loved them.

I considered following the lumber truck into the mill.

Once it parked in the receiving dock, Father would emerge from his office to examine the load. I pictured him in his white dress shirt and black trousers. As a young girl, he let me help measure the logs and check each for splits, fissures that rendered them unusable. How proud I'd been.

At the thought of seeing him again, I felt not only an overwhelming sense of trepidation, but something else-a fleeting pang of remorse.

I should have said goodbye, I thought. But I knew that if I had, Father wouldn't have let me leave.

Instead of driving directly into town, I put the Pathfinder back in gear and continued down the highway. Thirty minutes later, I entered Pine City, the county seat.

In the center of town, I parked in front of the Smith County Courthouse, an unremarkable, low-slung, cream brick building with a tarnished bronze statue out front—a ten-foot rendering of a battle-weary soldier dedicated to the area's World War II dead. I showed my badge, walked around the metal detectors, and asked for directions. At a door marked SHERIFF'S OFFICE, I asked for Chief Deputy Max Anderson. A young deputy in uniform buzzed me in.

When I walked up, I found Max reading a report. I noticed framed photos on his desk of a pretty blond woman and a little girl who looked just like her. I waited, watched. I thought about how he didn't look so terribly different. Back in the day, the sight of him made my heart flutter.

"Uh-hum," I coughed.

He looked up. "Clara."

"Hi, Max."

"Thank you for coming." Max walked around his desk and raised his hand to shake mine. "I didn't think I'd ever see you again."

I took his hand in mine and was close enough to smell his musky aftershave. "I *never* thought you'd return." He'd told me how he'd been offered the job, but I still wondered why he'd taken it.

"I decided it was time to come back," he said. "And I'd heard that the area was changing. Towns like Alber were opening up. I wanted to be part of that."

Nearly eighteen years older than when we'd parted, Max's hair had sprinkles of gray at the temples. I thought about touching the familiar dimple in his chin, brushing my hand across the day's stubble. I remembered when I first noticed he shaved. He was sixteen and I was fifteen. I'd convinced him to hike to the river west of town, to run off for an afternoon. That day I cupped his smooth cheek with my hand and pressed my lips against his, soft and tentative. That was how Father caught us, in the midst of our first kiss. Mother had grown suspicious and sent Father to find me. A year later, Max became one of the lost boys.

I've always wondered if he was forced out because of us.

The town leaders, as it would turn out, had other plans for me.

"Alber, changing?" I scoffed. "Max, Alber never changes."

"Haven't you been following the headlines?"

I had been reading the newspapers. Over the past years, authorities had moved in on some polygamous towns and arrested the leaders for marrying off young girls to grown men. The raids made headlines and monopolized the news. One day at Dallas PD headquarters, I stood with the others watching a breaking news report on the raid of a polygamous commune in Texas. The detectives around me chuckled, amused by the women in prairie dresses, their long hair falling to their waists, being led away with their children to buses, transported to an area for processing.

"I need the names of their hair stylists," a woman had said, running her hand over her highlighted bob. "My husband would love that look. Early cavewoman."

I never volunteered that I once looked like the women they jeered at, that I'd once been one of them. I wasn't sure why I did, but I turned to the others and said, "In their own way, I think they're beautiful."

I'm sure none of them suspected why I'd said what I did. A decade in Dallas, and I'd never confided in anyone, never admitted where I came from. I told no one about my roots. As a child, I grew up in a crowd. As an adult, I lived a solitary life. From the day I entered the outside world, I fought to remain disconnected. If anyone got close, I pulled back. I feared making friends. What if, in a weak moment, I confessed? Could any outsider understand where I came from?

My comment had hung in the air, making the atmosphere awkward. The others focused hard on me, appearing surprised. "I suppose they are," one detective eventually said. Before long, we wandered off to our desks.

As often as I scanned the news articles, watched the TV reports, I'd sought for but never found Alber mentioned. Standing across from him, I looked at Max and wondered what he could be talking about. "The feds came here?"

"Alber, too," Max explained. "Arrests were made. The Barstows have lost much of their control over the town. Families left. Some of the men, fearing arrest, ran off, leaving the women and children to fend for themselves. Others have moved in. Apostates like you are returning. Lost boys like me. Outsiders not living the principle are buying up foreclosed houses cheap."

The Barstows were Alber's most powerful family. For generations, no one built a home or married without their permission. The principle, or the Divine Principle as it's formally known, was the catchphrase for polygamy, the doctrine of plural marriage. For more than a century and a half, only those who believed in the sanctity of the Divine Principle were allowed to live in Alber. In my family, the practice of polygamy went back five generations.

I didn't know what to think. I'd envisioned Alber as a constant. I changed, the world changed, but in this secluded mountain town inhabited by Elijah's People, I thought nothing would ever change.

"The families we grew up with are gone?"

"Many are still here, most trying to live the old ways," Max said. "But everything around them is shifting. Clara, we have a women's shelter in town. Hannah runs it."

"Hannah?" I said, and my lips edged up at the corners. "Hannah runs a shelter?"

"In the Barstow mansion, right in the center of town."

I shook my head, disbelieving.

"I arranged for you to stay with her while you're here," Max said. "She's excited to see you."

"And my family? How have they fared?"

I thought Max might answer, but instead he said, "I really need to show you. Too much has happened to explain it all."

That seemed reasonable, but first I wanted more information on the reason I'd come. "What about Delilah? Do you know anything more than when we talked on the phone? Are you certain that she's missing?"

"That depends how you define certain. Officially, I have no concrete evidence," Max admitted. "But my belief is that the note's legit, that Delilah's in trouble."

"If you have no evidence, why do you think—"

"Call it gut instinct. Clara, you know how secretive Alber can be, how suspicious of anyone in authority from outside the community. Like I said, among the faithful, a lot hasn't changed."

"But surely, if Delilah were missing, my family would reach out for help," I insisted.

"I'm not sure," Max said. "You know what it's like in Alber. It's not unusual for no one to report a crime. All too often, the first we hear is when they have a dead body."

I winced at that, and Max apologized. "Sorry to be so blunt, but—"

"No. No. I know you're right." For generations, when secular authorities showed up in Alber, doors closed and folks became mum. "I would just hope in this instance… when we're talking about the welfare of a child, it would be different."

"Let me get the note." He grabbed a case folder off his desk and pulled out a sheet of paper protected by a plastic evidence sleeve. "The sheriff got this yesterday morning. After he did, like I told you on the phone, I went to talk to your family. Ardeth refused to open the door."

"So Mother wouldn't talk to you, but did you go to the mill and ask for Father?"

At that, Max appeared stunned. "I thought you knew," he said. "Knew what?"

Max hesitated, and I considered what he'd so dread telling me. Then I realized what it had to be. "When did it happen?"

"Clara, your father died of cancer a little more than a year ago. I can't believe no one told you."

I considered that, and I realized it could have been no other way. "There's no reason they should have. When I left Alber, I abandoned the family." I thought of Father, that I would never see him again, that I'd never have the opportunity to explain why I left. But then, I guessed he knew. After all, he wasn't blameless. He may not have known everything, but he'd been involved in much of it.

"Max, I'm here to do whatever I can for Delilah, but remember that I'm even more of an outsider than you are," I said. "You know what they're like to folks who turn their backs on the faith and leave."

Max stayed silent, perhaps thinking of his own situation. He wore a badge that said he was the law, but when he had a lead on a case, my mother, who he'd known all of his life, refused to talk to him.

"Let's see that letter," I said. "We need to figure out what's happened to Delilah."

Max handed me a single page of white paper with handwriting across it in a looping script. It looked like something a young girl might have written.

DELILAH JEFFERIES DISAPPEARED THURSDAY NIGHT.
SHE WAS THERE, AND THEN SHE WAS GONE. VANISHED.
I THINK A BAD MAN TOOK HER. PLEASE HELP!!!!

I held it close, and fought to keep my hands from trembling. I kept seeing the corpse of the boy in Dallas, the one who never returned from a bike ride.

CHAPTER FIVE

Delilah tried to guess how long she'd been there. A scratchy blindfold cinched across her eyes, she saw only a slender thread of light through a gap where it straddled her freckled nose. It had to have been days, but how many? Her tears and sweat soaked the blindfold, the salt making it stiff and coarse. She tried not to cry. If she lay still enough, she thought she might sleep. At times, she did doze off, but then the nightmares came. Always her dreams sent her back to the cornfield, to that moment when she first saw him.

I should have kicked and hit him with my fists. I should have found a way to fight him.

She'd been so stunned, she never fought back. Now she had no recourse. Her hands were pinned behind her. When she twisted her wrists and tried to free them, metal cut into her skin. A chain attached to her handcuffs trailed the length of her body, to where a set of leg irons encircled her ankles. They were so tight that they made her toes tingle.

Delilah felt caged, caught in a steel web. The chain was somehow anchored to the wall behind her, and she could move only a dozen feet or so before it pulled taut.

At times her horror, her panic, built until it threatened to explode. She had no choice other than to scream—high-pitched, wounded animal cries.

In response there was only silence. No one came.

The thin lumpy pad beneath her smelled of urine and worse. Unable to see the room around her, she listened for clues. Old pipes groaned. At times, she heard scratching, like rats scampering across the room or a squirrel foraging in the attic. An old house, she thought. But where? Nowhere the man worried that someone would hear her.

"Help! Please, help me!" she shouted. "Someone come! I need help!"

Off and on, a lock clicked and she heard a door open. The man entered. Most of the time, he came alone. Delilah felt queasy as she sensed him standing a few feet away, staring at her, silent.

"I want to go home," she pleaded. "Please, let me go."

He said nothing.

Other times, he brought someone to feed her. While the man paced the room, a woman with a soft voice whispered, "Open up."

Delilah felt a straw on her chapped lips. The cool water soothed her dry throat. The gruel the woman fed her was thin and tasteless, but Delilah greedily sucked it down.

In the background, the man encouraged Delilah. "Now, that's good, isn't it? Eat up."

She wanted to refuse the food, but her stomach cramped in emptiness.

"Please, mister. I have to go home. My mom is really worried about me," she'd told him, doing her best to hide her terror. "My family is looking for me. If I don't get home quick, my mom will send my brothers. Once the men in town find out, they'll search for me. They'll call the police, and they'll be looking for me, too."

The man had said nothing but, "Eat."

Another spoonful of the gooey mush had touched her lips, and she took it. When Delilah finished, the woman had gently wiped her lips with something soft.

The bowl empty, they left.

Once again alone, Delilah rolled on the mattress as far as the chains allowed. She searched with her fingertips, her legs, felt for something, anything that might be of use. When she lay on her side and stretched out as far as she could, her bare feet brushed over a rough wooden floor.

Delilah considered the temperature. Three times she'd felt the room cool, stay cool for a long time, before the heat gradually built. Those must have been nights, she decided. That meant she'd been in the room for three nights.

He took me on Thursday night. This must be Sunday.

How could nearly three days have passed and no one had come to rescue her? "Momma must be so worried about me," she whispered.

As Delilah had the evening she was taken, she fought to stay calm by singing church hymns and lullabies. "*God, watch over me and keep me safe / Keep me sweet and help me to obey,*" she began, her voice trembling. "*Lord, guide me to salvation.*"

Her parents had taught her that if she followed God's law she'd be rewarded. Delilah questioned what she had done to deserve such punishment. *Where am I? How long will he keep me here?*

One thought above all others couldn't be silenced. *What will he do to me?*

CHAPTER SIX

My hands felt clammy even in the heat, as we set out to talk to my family. When Max pulled into Alber, I stared out the windows at the town where I'd been born and spent the first twenty-four years of my life. On the surface, Alber didn't look markedly different. A wave of emotion flowed through me when we passed the familiar faded sign outside my family's sawmill, sensations so confusing I couldn't parse them out.

JEFFERIES LUMBERYARD

OPENS SUNUP

CLOSES SUNDOWN

"With Father gone, who's in charge?" I asked Max.

"Your brother Aaron," Max said. "The ones who continue to live the principle keep to the prophets' teachings. Oldest male inherits."

"I would have hoped, with the leaders gone, that maybe they wouldn't be holding on so tightly to the past," I said.

"In some ways, they've closed in tighter." Max hesitated for a moment, then tried to explain. "Clara, these people saw their way of life attacked, their leaders arrested, put on trial and sent to prison. The lesson they learned is that the prophets were right. Outsiders, all nonbelievers, are enemies to be feared."

We passed a big box of a house surrounded by a high picket fence. Through the slats, I saw women playing with their children. The day had turned into a sizzling one, but home-sewn dresses covered the women and girls neck to ankle. Long-sleeved shirts and trousers sheathed the boys. I recognized one of the women from my high school science class. We'd once blown up baking soda volcanos together. I raised my hand and waved, and there was a glint of recognition in her expression, but she didn't acknowledge me. Not even a nod. Instead, she shooed the children inside.

In seconds, the yard yawned empty.

The streets we traveled cut a checkerboard through town, and Max's car kicked up dust. I remembered how in hard rains the dirt roads flooded and transformed into fast-flowing drainage ditches. Much of Alber was pale brown and gray, matching the mountain ridge towering over it. A thick pine forest covered the lower mountainsides. In town, people had planted maples and oaks. Some, decades old, had grown massive. Branches dangled rope swings, and boughs held crudely built treehouses. Infrequent rains collected in cisterns watered the sparse grass, the corn and alfalfa fields, and the vegetable gardens. Locals reserved precious well water for drinking, cooking, washing clothes and bathing.

After years in Dallas, I appreciated how different Alber truly was from the outside world. The homes sprawled, large by the standards of most middle-class neighborhoods.

My memory unearthed a family dinner. I must have been six. Father at the head of the table, glowing with pride. "Today it's been revealed to me through the prophet that I am to be given a third wife," he'd announced. There were only eight of us children at that time, and we looked one to the other, questioning. My mother and Mother Constance rose and ran to our father, circling arms around him and shouting praise to the Lord for such good news. He undoubtedly saw the confusion on our young faces. "The prophet has chosen a new mother for our family, a woman named Naomi."

Too young at the time to understand, years later I learned the grave importance of that announcement. Elijah's People held that a man needed at least three wives to cross into heaven's highest spheres. When Mother Naomi joined us, Father and his wives entered a blessed circle, the elite eligible to enjoy the afterlife's greatest rewards.

So many wives. So many children.

Years passed. As a child of my father's first wife, I lived in our six-bedroom house with my parents, Mother Constance, and my many brothers and sisters. Moments of solitude were rare and quiet a luxury. The house rang with the constant chaos of children, crying babies our jarring background music. At night I slept with my three oldest sisters.

When Mother Naomi arrived, our father purchased a used but well-kept double-wide and moved it onto the back property. Six years later, Mother Sariah joined her, and soon the trailer overflowed with their combined children. Most afternoons, our backyard resembled a schoolyard playground, children everywhere.

That was the setting of my last memory of Delilah. While the others played tag and ball, we had a book opened between us. Delilah and I shared a deep love of fanciful stories—tales of clever bunny rabbits, spider villains and silly pigs.

"Clara, when I'm growed, will you read to me?" she asked.

"Sis, you won't need me. You'll read yourself." Her lower lip formed a heart-twisting shelf. "But I'll always be with you. Sisters are forever friends."

Two tender young arms encircled my neck, and Delilah rewarded me with a peck on my cheek.

A week later, I abandoned Delilah along with the rest of my family.

Where was she now?

Max drove past what had been the home of Emil Barstow, the president of Elijah's People, the religion's greatest living prophet. He'd wielded incredible authority in Alber. Based on his revelations, he gave men wives and property. And he took them away.

If the prophet judged a man unfit, not a true practitioner of the faith, he had the power to reassign the man's entire family, wives and children, to another. The town elders had families that made ours look small.

A red-brick colonial that marked the center of town, Barstow's mansion had a command spelled in white brick on the side visible from the street: OBEY AND BE REDEEMED.

"What happened to old man Barstow?"

"In prison," Max said. "Since he's in his eighties, my guess is he'll die there."

That's when I noticed a sign nailed onto the wall beside the Barstow mansion's front gate.

HEAVEN'S MERCY SHELTER
A HOME FOR WOMEN AND CHILDREN

"It's hard to believe that Hannah stayed through it all," I said.

"She did go into hiding for a while," Max said. "Clara, things got tense for Hannah after she helped you leave. Those in charge weren't happy."

"How tense?" I'd always wondered what consequences Hannah had suffered. I knew there were influential forces in Alber who wouldn't ignore what we had done. There were so many times I'd wanted to contact Hannah, but I worried that would bring her more trouble. Instead, I cut all ties.

"I don't know. And I don't know that she'd tell even you. Hannah's never been one to cower. At the same time, she understands what she has to do to live here, who she can piss off and who she can't," Max said, shooting me a sideways glance. "Things have changed in Alber, Clara, but not completely. Too many hold onto the past. Some hope to reclaim it. It's good to keep that in mind. Hannah has to be careful. We all do."

Max's words weighed heavy.

We drove past the old meeting place, where religious ceremonies and weddings took place, and town affairs had been discussed. Now a sign hung over the door that read "Danny's Diner."

"The town has a restaurant?" I remarked.

"The food's not bad," Max said. "The Lawler house is a bed and breakfast."

A restaurant. A B&B. For more than a hundred years, those were unheard of. The women cooked. No one ate out. Visitors weren't offered a bed because they weren't welcome to stay overnight. At dusk, the local police made it known to outsiders that they had to be on their way.

Some would have seen such circumstances as inhospitable, but for much of my life, I'd viewed Alber simply as home. The town was all I knew, and I was part of it.

On the surface, we were a community. Neighbors banded together and helped one another raise homes, build their spreads. At summer picnics, the children played while our parents relaxed on lawn chairs and talked of the prospects for the year's crops. Yet at times I felt or saw signs that all wasn't as I wanted to believe. Scratch the surface, and there'd always been a hidden tension in Alber.

A few blocks west, we approached my family home, a wood-sided structure with a large front porch. The closer the car brought us, the faster my heart beat. Max remained silent, and I stared resolutely out the window. I felt the dread I expected, the nervousness of knowing that in a few minutes I would see my mother, my family, for the first time in a decade.

My childhood home ever closer, I drew a deep breath. The opening words to a familiar prayer popped into my head, but I pushed them out. That, I reminded myself, wasn't something I did any longer. I wasn't the Clara who'd walked these streets.

We reached the house. I expected Max to pull over and park, but he drove past. I didn't see the double-wide where Naomi and

Sariah lived with their children. Max kept driving and the house I grew up in disappeared behind us.

"Aren't we stopping to talk to my family? Isn't that why I'm here?"

"Your family doesn't live in town anymore. A couple from Salt Lake bought the house – computer programmers who telecommute. One husband. One wife. Five kids." He glanced over at me, his lips stretching into a straight line. "After your father died, your mothers lost the house to taxes. Ardeth had the mobile home moved. They're living in it at the foot of Samuel's Peak. There's a community of true believers like them—ones displaced from their homes—squatting on public land out there."

We drove on, but a short distance later he looked over at me. Something must have telegraphed that I was struggling against a chaos of conflicting emotions. "You okay?"

My chest tightened. I lied. "Yeah. I'm fine." I thought about Max. "What's it like, living here, interacting with the people you grew up with, after what they did to you? You were just a kid when they forced you out."

Max stayed quiet for a moment, and I wondered if I shouldn't have asked. Then he raised his eyebrows and cocked his head in something of a half-shrug. "I have good memories as well as bad." His deep voice grew gravelly with emotion. "This is my job. I'm lucky to have it. To do it, I have to put the past in the past."

"I don't know if I can do that," I confided.

"It's an art I'm still attempting to perfect," he admitted.

As we continued toward the mountains, Samuel's Peak drew closer. We turned at the edge of the town toward what had once been open farmland. Someone had erected a cyclone fence and partitioned the area off from the town. I recognized the arch over the gate, topped with an angel blowing a horn. It used to mark the entrance to Alber's cemetery. Behind the fence stood a dismal settlement made up of shacks, single- and double-wide trailers. It had the look of a place without hope.

"How are the women making ends meet?" I asked. "With so many children."

"Most rely on the little government assistance they qualify for. Some take in sewing and sell vegetables from their gardens. One group quilts and sells what they make through the gift shop in town."

"There's a gift shop?"

"In the old Johnson house."

As we drove the dirt roads, dozens of dilapidated trailers spread out around us. I'd never seen poverty like this in Alber before, and it saddened me to think that the families I'd known, so proud of their homes, now had so little.

"Where's my family?"

"At the back, near the cornfield." Max glanced at me, and I sensed that he understood how hard I was fighting to stay calm. "It's a lot to take in," he said.

"I'm fine," I insisted again, this time betrayed by an emotional catch in my voice.

We drove by a drilling machine, men with shovels chiseling away at the earth. "There's no sewer or water back here," Max explained. "Some of the men are putting in a well."

On the final narrow road, the one that ran parallel to the mountain, under the peak where legend said the spirits of our forefathers lived, the cornfield spread out in front of us. Max signaled a right turn where the rows met the road, allowing no shoulder. The stalks were a thick, vibrant green. The car rounded the corner, and a figure leaped onto the road directly in front of us. Max slammed on the brakes, and the car skidded to a stop. I braced myself on the dashboard as someone darted back into the cornfield.

"You okay?" Max asked. He looked shaken. It had been close. A second later on the brake, and he wouldn't have been able to stop in time.

"Yeah, but who…" I coughed hard and cleared my throat. "The belt knocked the air out of me."

"I nearly hit him," Max said.

"Him?"

"Whoever it was," Max said, spitting out the words. Angry. "Where'd he go?"

The edge of the corn shimmered as something hidden moved inside it. A man, six foot or more, broad at the shoulders and narrow at the waist, emerged slowly, tentatively. He wore heavy-rimmed glasses. Once out on the road, he wiped off his brow with his shirtsleeve.

"Who is that?" I asked.

"Jim Daniels," Max whispered, reaching over for the car door handle. "He manages the cornfield for the settlers."

"You okay, Jim?" Max shouted, as he climbed out of the car. I swung my door open.

"Thought you were going to run me over!" Daniels shouted back. "Don'cha look?"

"Shit, Jim. I don't expect folks to run out of the corn onto the road without looking. Couldn't see you until you were right in front of me." Max said, irritated. "You'll get yourself killed if you're not more careful. What are you doing in there?"

"Checking the crop. It's near ready to pick," Daniels said, his face weather-beaten from years in the sun. He scrutinized me, curious but distant. I'd gotten out of the car and stood on the passenger side. His eyelids hung heavy, and his gaze felt cold. "Who's that with you, Max?"

"A visitor," Max said, sidestepping the question.

Daniels didn't ask anything more, but he continued to size me up—my city clothes, my trim bun. "I better get back to work. Got a lot to do before we harvest."

"Next time check for cars first, okay?" Max advised.

"Yeah. Sure, Max," Daniels said. He nodded at me. "Have a good visit."

"Strange guy?" I asked, when Max and I were back in the car. Daniels seemed just a touch off. The way he looked at me, it felt as if there were a disconnect there.

"Yeah," Max said. "Jim's kind of an odd one—inordinately quiet, not very social. He moved to town eight years ago. Never any problems with him, though."

A hundred or so feet farther down the road sat a white-sided, double-wide trailer, more battered than I remembered it. Perched on cement blocks and anchored to an electric power meter on a wooden pole, it had five cement steps leading to a rusted screen door. Behind the trailer, as far as the eye could see, row after row of corn stalks spread, leaves reaching up like hands splayed out to praise the bright mountain sun.

Max pulled off the road and stopped. He waited.

"Do you want me to walk up with you?" he asked.

I hesitated. "No."

The sound of the car door echoed in the air. Gravel pricked the worn-thin soles of my black loafers as I took deliberate steps toward the trailer. My heart pounded as if I'd stopped running mid-sprint. At the foot of the steps, I paused. I glanced back at the car. Max had gotten out. He stood at the passenger-side door, arms folded across his chest.

I took the first step. The second. No doorbell. I rapped. The door clattered loose against the jamb.

Silence.

I knocked again. Harder.

Moments later, a teenage girl, long dark hair like mine, wide-set dark brown eyes like my own, stared out at me. "Who are you?" she asked.

"Lily! Come here, girl!" a familiar voice bellowed from inside.

"L-Lily, is it you?" I stammered. I routinely stared down criminals, hunted killers, but my kid sister gave me a suspicious glare, and my voice cracked. I managed a smile. "I'm Clara. Your big sister. You were young when I left. Four, maybe five? Do you remember me?"

"Lily! Inside! Now!"

As ordered, my sister stepped back and was swallowed by the trailer's darkness.

In her place, a tall woman appeared. Ardeth. My mother. Her hair formed a soft crown around her lean, hollow-cheeked face. Her dark brows arched in irritation. She looked as I remembered her in a high, ruffle-necked calico dress that ended at her ankles. I took a breath and smelled something reminiscent of a pungent cheese, realizing it had to be valerian. I must have interrupted her at work.

Many in town relied on Mother for the herbal remedies she concocted in her kitchen: tinctures, poultices, compresses and salves. She brewed potions for colds, flu, gallstones, bladder infections, even heart disease. It was rumored in Alber that Mother once conjured up a particularly potent mixture that cured breast cancer. Knowing that the patient probably never had a mammogram or biopsy, I had a few doubts.

"Mother, how good to see you," I said. She wiped her hands on her apron and stared at me as if I'd materialized from on top of the mountain. "It's been a long time. How are you?"

Her lips turned down, never threatening to edge up into a smile. "Clara? Why are you here?"

I fought back my emotions. This woman with the dour frown was my mother, true, but she was also a source I needed to cultivate, someone I had to win over. I took it slowly, not to come on too strong. "To see you and the family. I heard about Father, all that has happened. I'm concerned for all of you."

Mother opened the door, and I hastily backed down the steps, making room for her. She took the steps quickly, one after another. She hunched slightly forward at the shoulders. She was in her mid-fifties, but looked a decade older.

Feet on the ground, we stood eye to eye. Mother methodically inspected me, looking at my face and hair, my clothes, and my dust-covered shoes. She examined me as if I were a specimen on a glass slide. Although she hadn't seen me in years, she made no move toward me. She didn't reach her arms out to offer an embrace. I saw no joy at my return.

Max walked toward us, his uniform and marked patrol car conspicuously undermining my attempt to portray this as a social call. Mother looked over at him. Her lips pulled tight, an expression that brought back difficult memories.

She turned back to me and fury dripped from each word. "You just show up, after all these years, dressed like that, in city clothes. You act like you never left? And you bring the authorities?"

I held back. I hadn't come to argue. I had one purpose—to find Delilah. "Mother, you remember Max Anderson, I'm sure. He's the chief deputy for the county sheriff. I don't know if you've heard, but I'm a police officer, too. A detective in Dallas."

"And why have you come here, knocking on my door? Are you here to repent? To fall on your knees and beg forgiveness?"

"No, Mother. You know that's not why I'm here."

"Then why?" she challenged.

"We're here about Delilah," I said, narrowing my eyes, returning all the intensity in hers, knowing there was only one way to play this. "Max called me after he tried to talk to you yesterday. We're following up on a tip that Delilah's been abducted. Is she missing?"

My mother didn't answer. Her frown compressed, pinching tight at the corners.

"Clara, you have to leave," she finally said, her gravel voice rough with years of disappointment and anger. "You have to leave and never come back. You aren't welcome."

Her words cut into my heart, but I stood straighter and did my best not to let her see me bleed. "I am happy to do exactly what you're asking. Do you think I wanted to return? After you and Father…" I pulled back. No matter the grievances I harbored, I couldn't let this become about me. "I need to know—where's Delilah?"

"I don't have to tell you, of all people, anything about my family."

That one word stung more than any of the others; it wasn't our family but hers. "Show Delilah to me. Bring me to her. Prove that she's safe. Then I'll leave. But not a moment sooner."

"Delilah is…" Mother started, but then she eyed me. She glanced at Max again. Her expression chilled winter cold. "Clara, I am the mother, not you. I will not take your orders. You must obey mine. And I tell you to leave."

"No!" Shouting that one word at her quickened my pulse. I had rarely defied Mother, only the once, the day I ran. But Delilah could be in danger, and I had to know the truth. "There's a simple way for you to get what you want. Show me Delilah or tell me where I can find her, Mother, and I will leave. And you won't have to worry about me returning. Not ever again."

Instead of answering, my mother shook her head, as if in disgust, and then nodded toward Max. "I told him to stay away. We don't need the likes of him around here."

Max edged forward, until he stood at my side. "Mrs. Jefferies, I—"

"Get out of here, Max Anderson," Mother seethed. "Get out and don't come back."

My hardline tactics weren't working, so I changed them. That helped sometimes. A different approach threw people off guard. My voice a whisper, I implored her, "Mother, please—"

"You, too, Clara. We don't need the likes of you." My mother stared at me, as if I were the source of all her troubles. An angry rasp in her voice, she insisted, "We take care of our own. We don't need Max Anderson's help. Or yours."

Enough of this, I thought. "Mother, we need to see Delilah. Now."

My mother glared at me as if she didn't know me. I had truly become one of *them*, the strangers she'd warned me about as a child.

Behind Mother, the screen door banged. Lily stood on the porch with tears rivering down her cheeks. "Tell them, Mother. Please tell them. Tell them that Delilah is—"

"Lily, go inside!" Mother ordered, her voice so shrill it felt like a slap.

"Finish what you were saying, Lily," I begged. "I am here to help Delilah."

Lily stood her ground, but looked at my mother as if stricken. Then her voice became small, frightened, pleading. "Mother, tell them. Tell them that Delilah is—"

"I am your mother. You will obey me!" Mother commanded, her face twisted in rage. My sister fell silent. "Go inside, Lily!"

"Mother, let Lily talk!" I pleaded.

"Mrs. Jefferies, we're trying to help," Max pushed. "Please, where is Delilah?"

Mother scowled, and I turned back to my sister still standing on the stoop, staring down at us with a look of unabated fear. "Lily, tell me," I said. "Where is our sister? Where is Delilah?"

Mother didn't speak, but she glowered up at Lily. I remembered how I felt as a girl when Mother sized me up that way, as if she saw inside me. I felt exposed. Unworthy. Lily turned, her shoulders heaving. The screen door banged behind her as she ran inside, sobbing.

Mother gave me one last frigid glance before she turned her back and trudged up the stairs toward the trailer.

"It's true. Delilah is missing, isn't she?" I shouted.

She said nothing.

"Please, Mother. Tell me what happened."

My heart pounded, hard and angry.

My mother's hands shook on the door handle as she shot me a warning glance. Then the screen door rattled shut behind her. The inner wooden door slammed.

CHAPTER SEVEN

"I shouldn't have come with you. It might have been better if you'd gone alone," Max said. Disappointment hung heavy in the car as we drove back to his office. "Without me, maybe Ardeth would have talked to you."

"It wouldn't have mattered. From the moment Mother saw me, she was seething. She's not a woman who opens her arms to an errant daughter."

"I wish she'd let Lily talk," he said. "The way it is, we don't know any more than when we got here."

He was right that we didn't have anything concrete, but the fear on Lily's face said all I needed to be convinced. "Max, we do know more. Lily looked terrified. All Mother needed to do was show us Delilah. She's hiding the truth. Something grave is wrong."

"Something, but—"

"It has to be that Delilah is in trouble."

"Maybe, but—"

"But what?"

"But that's nothing more than a guess. What if Lily was going to say something else? How do we know?" he said, his voice firm yet a bit wary.

Max had a point. I couldn't predict what Lily wanted to tell us. But all my instincts told me that it would have been that Delilah needed help. "Max, we need to start looking for Delilah."

Max shook his head. "We need more information. We know nothing that will help us look for her. Where do we start? And we can't jump to conclusions."

"We can't ignore our suspicions either," I said. "You and the sheriff need to…"

I stopped talking when I saw the glum expression on Max's face. As soon as I'd brought up the sheriff, Max shook his head. "Clara, you need to understand, Sheriff Holmes is dubious about that note. He didn't want me to call you."

"Why wouldn't he—"

"My boss is a good guy, but he doesn't know Alber like we do. He doesn't understand how guarded this town is. He can't fathom that Delilah could be missing if no one has filed a report." Max glanced over at me and frowned. "Clara, if Lily had actually said Delilah was gone, I might be able to convince the sheriff to let us run with this, but without that…"

I had a hard time listening to Max. I didn't care what the sheriff thought. I knew without question that my sister was in grave danger. The entreaty in Lily's eyes when she begged Mother to tell us the truth was enough for me. "Delilah's in trouble. I'm certain of it," I said. "We need to issue an Amber Alert. List her as missing on NCIC. Get the word out to the media and start people looking."

Max shook his head. "Clara, I need to talk to the sheriff. He's not going to like—"

"We need to go door to door in the trailer park, find someone who saw something," I insisted. "Maybe we can find someone with information we can use to get a search warrant, to bring my mother and the rest of the family in for questioning."

Max stared straight ahead, the muscles on the right side of his jaw working. I needed Max. This wasn't Dallas, not even Texas. In Alber, in Utah, I had no authority to force anyone to do anything. He had to take the lead. "We're going to do all that, right?"

Max raised an eyebrow. "You know as well as I do that the Amber Alert system won't take any action without solid proof a child has been abducted and is in danger. Clara, you're a cop. You know they don't accept unsubstantiated reports. They want facts. The whole system is set up to block questionable reports."

"I know, but—"

"No buts," Max said, his patience fraying. "The system won't take a vague report like this one, and you know it. We haven't got a missing person report, no information on how or where Delilah was abducted. Not even when. All of that's mandatory."

I sat back and stared out the window. Max was right. The Amber Alert system was set up to only take concrete cases, not suspicions. It required information on how, where, and when abductions occurred. We didn't even have solid evidence of a crime. "Okay, but we can list Delilah as a missing person on NCIC," I said. Those guidelines were looser. It would only go out to law enforcement, but it was a place to start. "That's possible."

"How much interest are you going to get without even a photo of her or a description of how she disappeared?" he questioned.

"Max, you brought me here because your gut told you something is wrong. I agree. You're right. And we have to do something," I said.

"Clara, we can't—"

"Any chance you know a friendly judge who might be willing to give us a search warrant? If we could get into the trailer, maybe talk to Lily…"

Max scoffed. "Is that the way you do it in Dallas? Judges sign warrants without probable cause? We don't have enough to justify a warrant."

"We have the note. We have Lily worried about Delilah. We need to do something. Delilah could be…" I saw the boy from Dallas again, his face in the photo his mother gave me, and I pictured his mutilated body. That couldn't happen to Delilah. I couldn't let it.

"I know. I'm worried about her, too." As resistant as Max sounded, he didn't disagree with anything I'd said. "Give me a couple of hours. I'll find the sheriff and talk to him. I'll do my best to get him on board."

Two hours. That could be forever with Delilah in trouble.

"Max, I—"

"I can't go off half-cocked on this, Clara," Max snapped. "I went out on a limb to bring you here. Don't make me regret it."

The sun setting after a long day, the car filled with an uncomfortable silence, while outside Alber passed by. We reached the highway, and I thought about the photos of the woman and little girl in Max's office. "You must have a family to get home to," I said.

Max focused on the road, and his voice changed, growing suddenly weary. "My wife, Miriam, passed away a couple of years ago. Car accident."

"I'm sorry. I didn't know," I replied.

"No way you could have."

"You have children?" I asked.

"I have a daughter. Brooke is eight. My sister Alice watches over her."

I noticed Max's jaw tighten, and I had the sense that he wanted to say more but held back. We were childhood friends, and once there'd been the promise we might be much more, but time had made us strangers.

I thought of Max's daughter. I thought again of Delilah. "Max, if it were Brooke missing, you would…"

"Move heaven and earth," he admitted. "But this decision isn't mine. I need the sheriff to agree. I'll work hard to get that done. I promise."

I sensed he meant it. "Okay. I'll wait."

"Thank you," he said.

Still, I couldn't just sit back with Delilah in danger. "While you track down the sheriff, I'll go through the case file. Maybe there's something in there you missed. You must have looked at similar cases in the area, abductions, sexual assaults of minors. I can get a handle on—"

Max didn't wait for me to finish. "I wish there was a file to consider. There's nothing in there but the note. That's all we have."

"Why didn't you run reports?"

"I tried, but there aren't any. No reports of sexual assaults showed up in the Alber area in the past five years." Max sounded defensive. "Clara, you of all people know how private the town has always been, how little ever gets reported to anyone in authority."

Everything Max said was true. From an early age, we were taught that our religious leaders handled what happened in the town. They held all the power, not secular institutions. I thought of what Mother had said, spitting out the words like an indictment: "We take care of our own."

I turned to Max. "Of course. I should have realized we would have that complication. So there's nothing there? Nothing to look at?"

"No. No reports. Nothing about any missing girls or sex crime convictions, even accusations against any of the locals. Nothing I could find."

As we approached his office, I realized that Max looked drained. I would have felt sorry for him, if I wasn't so worried about Delilah. "Clara, go to the shelter and I'll call you as soon as I talk to the sheriff, okay?"

Reluctantly, I nodded.

"Remember what I said about being careful. You shouldn't drive around Alber alone at night. Get in the car and drive directly to Hannah's. Wait there for me to call."

"Max, that's silly. No one would bother me."

Max frowned. "As I said, there's a lot that hasn't changed around here, and you're not an insider anymore. Once you get your car, head over to Hannah's. Stay there. I'll call as soon as I'm able to talk with the sheriff."

Everything Max said made sense, but I couldn't stomach the idea that we would do nothing. "I hate to let this go until then," I said. "What if—"

"Clara, I explained. I need to talk to the sheriff," he said, his voice worn as thin as his patience. "This is my job. I need to follow protocol."

"I know," I said. "But—"

"As soon as I know anything, you'll be my first call."

I'd never been inside the gates of the Barstow compound, never set foot in the sprawling three-story mansion. When the front entry opened into an expansive hallway and Hannah Jessop, the woman who'd once saved me, waited arms outstretched, I fell into them, and for the first time that day, I felt as if I'd come home.

"Welcome, Clara," she whispered.

When I had to leave everything and everyone I loved behind, Hannah showed me a way.

I hugged her, not wanting to let go.

"What's it like being back here?" she asked.

"It feels… I feel foreign. I thought I'd come to terms with this place. I thought I'd worked it all through. But now, I don't know that I have."

Hannah released me, but wrapped an arm around my waist. "You're asking too much of yourself. You can't figure all this out. There's enough here to wrestle with for a lifetime."

I pulled back to look at her.

Hannah was in her late forties, thirteen years older than me, a slender woman with faded denim-blue eyes feathered with a pale brown. Wearing jeans and a pale pink T-shirt, she was sockless in moccasins, letting her ankles show, a provocative choice in these parts.

Hair is a big deal in fundamentalist Mormon teachings. My mother and I, all the women and girls I knew, grew our hair to our waists or longer. We tied it into poufy buns, looped it into braids, and shaped it in pompadour-type crowns around our faces. This wasn't a style choice but a mandate. Our leaders called a woman's hair her crowning glory and taught that we must keep it long in preparation for the hereafter. In heaven, we were told, we would use our hair to wash Christ's feet.

Hannah visited my home often when I was a child, our fathers close friends. As a teenager, she wore long, rope-like dark blond braids. At sixteen, the prophet married her off to a church elder with a harem of wives. For a while, I didn't see Hannah. Then one day I walked to school with Mother Constance and my brothers and sisters. Hannah marched past in her prairie dress leading a flock of children. She'd chopped her hair off just below her earlobes. I waved to her. Mother Constance pulled my hand down and hustled us away.

From that point on, Hannah became an outcast in Alber, a troublemaker who refused to comply with the teachings. Since the upheaval in town, in what I assumed was an even bolder act of defiance, Hannah had cropped her light hair close to her head.

"This shelter, how wonderful," I said. "When you told me a decade ago that one day you would have a place like this for women and children in need, I didn't believe you. And here you are, and it's in the Barstow mansion. You're a real stalwart of the community."

"Ironic, isn't it? I can't say that I'm totally accepted, but I think they've come to tolerate me," she chuckled and whispered as if we shared a secret. "Who would have thought that I'd ever live in the biggest house in town?"

All around us children played, running room to room. A group of women sat in a circle near the main room's fireplace, sewing and talking. I heard high-pitched laughs, the sounds of happiness. Upstairs, on the second floor, a baby cried.

A woman slipped past us, chasing a tow-headed boy. "Zachary!" she shouted. "When I catch you…"

The house smelled of simmering soup, and the dining room chandelier cast a soft glow.

We walked toward the kitchen, teeming with Hannah's residents, their ages spanning from infancy to elderly, all in clean but often tattered clothes, and I lowered my voice. "Everything here is so different, I can't process it all. But Hannah, did Max talk to you about Delilah?"

"He did," she said.

"Do you think she's missing?"

Hannah took a deep breath, then hushed her voice to suggest, "Let's go to the restaurant in town and have dinner. It's never busy on Sunday evenings. We can talk there. I don't want to discuss this where anyone can hear."

CHAPTER EIGHT

Delilah grew weary. Her head throbbed, and she had a constant ball of fear in her chest. Her body ached. She rested her back against the wall for support, but that pinned her arms and hands behind her, hurting her shoulders. The filthy blindfold made her eyes itch.

When she drifted off, she dreamed she heard her mother call her. When she finally slumped to the side and slid down, she jerked awake with a start.

Trying to calm her fears, Delilah imagined her home, her family. She wondered what they were doing, if they were looking for her. She knew they'd be worried. She wondered if her brothers and sisters were frightened. The way the man came for Delilah reminded her of the stories their mothers told, the ones about the boogiemen who took bad children away.

Her mother would cry, of that Delilah felt certain. Mother and daughter had always been so close.

The day before the man took her, Delilah had helped Sariah comb through her long hair. "Yours is just like mine," she'd said, holding a strand of Delilah's and comparing it to the cascade of ginger curls flowing down her back. So many of the children, especially Lily, looked like their father, with his black hair and dark eyes. It made Delilah feel special that she resembled her mother, her blue eyes the color of the hydrangeas that bloomed in the early summer.

Lily. She particularly missed Lily. Delilah wondered what her sister thought of her disappearance. Delilah worried that Lily would be especially upset. *I bet she feels bad that she didn't believe me about someone watching me.* But then, Delilah's mother hadn't believed her either.

The door creaked opened. The man and woman came with food, the same slushy mixture of milk and grain. She tried to make conversation, to get one of them to say something. She thought that if they talked, she might be able to convince them to release her. "I really want to go home," she said. "When are you going to let me go home?"

Neither the man nor the woman answered. After the last spoonful, they left.

The hours dragged. Sometimes Delilah thought she heard muffled voices somewhere in the house. When she did, she listened hard, hoping to make out what they were saying, but the voices were too soft to understand and gradually fell silent.

The room cooled. Evening came. Another day had passed. If no one had arrived to rescue her, tomorrow would be her fourth day.

Delilah again tried to sleep. Just as she thought she might drift off, the lock clicked in the door. Someone pushed it open and walked in. From the heavy steps, like boots pounding against the floor, she knew the man had returned.

Frightened, she sat up and pressed her back to the wall. She waited for something, only she didn't know what.

The quiet grated on her. She felt his eyes on her. Her breath grew shallow, and her pulse fluttered. All the while, he said nothing. The waiting made Delilah's nerves stiffen. "Why don't you let me go home?" she asked, her eyes behind the blindfold again spilling over with tears. "My mom's probably crying. My whole family is sad." She paused, but he didn't answer. "Sir, I want to go home now," she said as nicely as she could. "I don't think you should keep me here like this."

A heavy stillness filled the room. She heard the man stand, a chair squeaking against the rough wood floor. His boots made a shuffling sound toward the door.

Delilah's panic built. She didn't want him there, but she didn't want him to leave either. She needed to persuade him to let her go. Delilah struggled, uncertain what to say, how to convince him to release her. She thought of her father. If he'd been alive, the man wouldn't have done this, of that she felt certain. What did the man want? "My father owned the sawmill." Her tears soaked her eyelashes and puddled thick in her throat. "My brother Aaron runs it now, and he has some money. He would pay you to let me go."

She waited. Hopeful.

The man approached the door. She heard the knob twist.

"Please let me go," she begged. If she could just move her hands and arms, she'd at least be able to brush off the falling tears. "I'm a good girl. My mom… My family, they… I'm a good—"

"No one can help you, little one. No one knows where you are." His voice reverberated in the room, low, hoarse, and gruff.

"My uncles and my brothers will be mad. They'll—"

"Do nothing!" the man's voice boomed. "None of you people do anything but pray. And that won't bring you home."

"They will—"

"No!" he said. Then his voice grew quiet. "They will look, but they won't find you. I hear that your sister Clara has come all the way from Dallas. She's a big-city cop, and she thinks that she'll save you. But she won't."

"My sister?" Delilah asked. "I don't have a sister named Clara."

"You do." His voice grew louder but he spoke as if only to himself. "She's come to butt her nose into Alber's affairs. She'll be turned away."

"A police officer? Clara? I don't—"

"She has no idea what she's up against," the man said. "She has no idea who she's up against."

"Mister, I…" Delilah couldn't go on. She didn't know what to say. Who was he talking about? What sister? She had many brothers and sisters, but none she knew of named Clara.

Delilah heard the man walk toward her. He stopped. She felt his rough hand under her chin. Her body shivered like it did when she stood outside on a frigid winter night. She smelled his stale breath as he tilted his face toward hers.

"No one has any idea where you are, girl, and they never will. You live here now," he sneered. Then his voice grew so deep and harsh that her whole body trembled. "Remember this: If you try to escape, I'll kill you. And then I'll go to that run-down trailer your family lives in and, one by one, I'll kill them all."

CHAPTER NINE

Townsfolk had gathered in the Alber Meeting House for more than a century. The men met regularly in the white clapboard building to discuss town affairs and mete out punishment to anyone who violated our prophets' rules. For the most part, their gatherings dealt with the pettiest of infractions, as on the day the Binghams' sheep broke through their fence and trampled a corner of the Smiths' vineyard. Then there was the uproar when Jim Call's oldest son, Orson, was spotted drinking a forbidden iced tea.

The building looked the same, but as Danny's Diner a chalkboard leaned against the outside wall touting the evening special—pot roast with a yogurt dill sauce. I felt as if I'd entered an alternate universe when Hannah suggested, "You need to come for breakfast and try the lattes. I always get mine with almond milk."

Inside, the place looked like it had been transplanted from a Dallas suburb. Rectangular tables spread across the main room surrounded by trendy black metal chairs. On each tabletop, a clear glass vase held white daisies. At the far end, a cash register sat on a black granite counter. The blackboard menu hung on hooks behind it, and positioned there was a man who greeted Hannah warmly and introduced himself as Danny Bannion, the restaurant's owner. I ordered the pot roast, and Hannah settled on a hamburger and a salad. We each asked for something else that until recently would have been unheard of in Alber – a glass of red wine.

As Hannah had predicted, the restaurant was nearly empty. We sat in a far corner, at a window table overlooking the street, a good distance from the other diners. I placed my cell phone screen up on the table next to my plate, waiting for Max's call. I wondered if he'd talked to the sheriff yet, if they'd decided how we'd pursue the case. With every breath, I thought about Delilah and what might be happening to her while I did nothing.

As a distraction, I looked about at the other patrons.

Across the dining room sat an elderly couple who could have been the models for *American Gothic*, white-haired and dressed in traditional garb. The man looked familiar, and before long I recognized Michael Johansson, whose family owned the big bison ranch on the outskirts of town. She'd changed, but I pegged the woman as his first wife, Reba. She stared at me, and I smiled. She stood up and took another chair at the table, one with her back to me. When Mr. Johansson recognized me, he scooted over next to her.

Heads together, I had no doubt I was the topic of their conversation.

The restaurant's other customers—a young woman in tennis whites and her children—weren't familiar. The mom had bare legs, concrete evidence that she hadn't grown up in Alber, and the three children—all elementary school age and in shorts and T-shirts—nibbled on chicken nuggets and sweet potato fries.

"There's a tennis court in Alber?" I asked.

"Not that I know of." Hannah shrugged. "But there may be. The town is transforming faster than I thought possible. It's hard to keep up with the changes."

"And yet the attitudes of some are still the same."

"Absolutely," she agreed. "In fact, there are a substantial number of people fighting tooth and nail to return Alber to its roots."

I thought of my family, of the scowl on my mother's face when I surprised her at the trailer door. "Mother's in that group, I'm sure."

Hannah sighed. "I'm sure Ardeth regrets much of what's happening. And I can't fault her for that. Her world is changing around her. This is no longer the cloistered town our ancestors founded, the one she grew up in, the one she raised her children to live in."

Hannah's words rang true. I thought about my mother, how frightening the town's metamorphosis must be for her.

Our dinners arrived as I watched the tennis mom eyeing the Johanssons across the room. When the old-timers moved to avoid eye contact with me, they'd positioned themselves directly across from the young mother and her children. Both stared suspiciously at the family, and the old woman whispered to her husband.

I picked at my food, hungry but too worried to eat. I could think of little else other than Delilah. Where was she? I took a notebook and pen out of my bag, and I lowered my voice to be sure no one else heard. "Hannah, I need to know what you know about Delilah."

To my surprise, Hannah appeared reluctant to answer. She took a sip of her wine, paused as if considering, and then admitted, "I'm usually pretty good at confronting reality, I know, but this is difficult."

"I'm listening," I said.

She hesitated again, perhaps deciding what to say. We had a lot of history, but this side of Hannah I hadn't encountered. I'd always thought of her as something of a superhero, one of the few people I knew who was never fearful, or at least never showed it. Something, perhaps simply life in this strange town where there were so many rules and so many secrets, had changed her.

"There've been a lot of bad things in Alber over the years, Clara. We both know that."

"Absolutely." I waited.

"But there's something different now. I'm worried that there's something truly bad here."

"What?"

"Something evil." She stopped talking, and I felt her resolve wavering. That she hesitated chilled me.

"Hannah, you need to tell me what's wrong."

"I'm afraid to," she admitted.

"Why?"

Hannah took another sip of wine. "I know this sounds irrational," she whispered. "But talking about this makes it feel real, and that it might be terrifies me."

"Tell me what you know," I said.

Hannah swallowed hard, and then shook her head. "I… Give me a few minutes."

"If I'm going to help, I need to know," I pushed.

Again, Hannah sighed. "I understand that."

I checked my phone. Max hadn't tried to call. I watched Hannah warily, eager for her to open up. Rather than catch up like the old friends we were, talk about all that had transpired in our lives since we'd last seen each another, neither one of us spoke. Hannah looked as tense as I felt. Danny collected our plates, mine covered with the barely eaten pot roast.

"You didn't enjoy it? It's my wife's special recipe."

"It's great," I said. "Just not hungry."

Bannion tarried for a few minutes making small talk, oblivious to the tenseness at our table, or attempting to defuse it. He explained that he and his wife, Jimi, found the old building listed for sale on the Internet. They decided to move from Salt Lake to Alber after he heard about the bargains on foreclosures. "I think it's going to become a popular resort area, family vacations."

"If all the rumors come true, you'll have a gold mine here, Danny," Hannah predicted. "I heard today that there's talk of building a ski resort."

Looking pleased, Danny wandered off. The Johanssons had left, but the tennis mom and her kids pecked at the remains of their dinners. I again checked my phone. No calls from Max.

I couldn't wait any longer. "Hannah, we're wasting time. I need to find Delilah."

She gave me a strained look but nodded. "Well, first let's talk about what happened in Alber. Things worsened after you left, Clara. The girls the prophet married off became younger and younger, until they were in their mid-teens. He sealed them to men anywhere from twenty to eighty. Some of us in town complained, but nothing changed until the authorities moved in and made arrests."

"Max explained that," I said, trying not to sound impatient.

"For some families that changed little. Their men had nothing to hide. They stayed and kept their houses, supported their families. Everything was good," she said. "But other husbands fled, afraid that they could be the next arrested. That left a large number of families with no means of support. Many of the women lost their property and their homes. Those in the worst shape brought their children and moved into my shelter. Others salvaged what they could and relocated to the trailer park, where they're homesteading on county property—hunting and farming in the foothills."

"Still intent on living the principle."

"Of course. It's part of their religion. It's all they know," Hannah said. "This is what I'm trying to get to: the conditions here are dire, so many have moved on. The biggest exodus has been the teenagers, mainly boys but some girls. They know there's nothing for them here. They left their families for the outside world, hoping to find jobs and start new lives."

"I can relate to that," I said.

"Yes, you can," Hannah paused a moment and gave me a wan smile. I noticed the web of wrinkles around her lips and thought about how hard she'd fought for so many years. "I remember that day."

"As I always will." We had shared memories, but I needed to move the conversation along. "Hannah, you were telling me about the teenagers leaving."

"Yes. I'm laying this out for you so you understand why there's doubt. Why I can't say for sure what's happening here. If there's anything happening… to the girls."

The anxiety I'd strained to keep under control ever since I'd heard about Delilah's disappearance swelled in my chest. "Girls? Plural?"

Hannah expelled a deep breath. "Yes. Girls."

At that moment, I wished I hadn't eaten any of the pot roast. It wasn't sitting well with the conversation.

"There are two I'm worried about. Two girls I suspect something bad happened to."

I dreaded where this was going. "Delilah isn't the first to disappear?"

"I don't think so. Do you remember Eliza Heaton? You might have had her at the school, as a student."

"I do. Her dad runs the hardware store. She must have been seven or eight when I left."

"Eliza's dad did run the hardware store," Hannah said. "He passed away a couple of years ago. Eliza lived in a trailer with her mothers, brothers and sisters. A tight family, despite the dad being gone. Eliza's mom, Alma, and her sister-wives keep those kids together. They work hard. A little more than a year ago, they opened a quilting business. They sell to the shop in town, plus a couple of high-end gift shops in St. George."

"Tell me about Eliza." I needed to keep Hannah on track.

"It was five months ago. Early spring. Eliza was seventeen, a good kid, smart as a whip. Dedicated to her family. I never saw that girl when she wasn't carrying one of the little ones on her hip, a brother or sister. She loved to read. I've got a library at the shelter, one filled with a lot of the books I used to funnel to you when you were a girl. Eliza loves Jane Austen, just like you did. She called her 'my dear Jane.' I was searching the used book stores for *Mansfield Park* for Eliza when it happened."

"What happened?" I had my notebook open, and I wrote down the gist of our conversation, putting stars in the margin next to those things I considered of possible importance.

"Eliza was gone."

"Gone?"

"Disappeared," Hannah said. "She stopped coming around. I asked about her around town. No one seemed to know anything. Some of the folks looked numb to all the teenagers leaving and shrugged, like, well, another one's moved to the city."

"Did you talk to her family?"

"Yes. Her mothers claimed that Eliza ran off to Salt Lake. They said I had no reason to worry." Hannah smoothed out her white paper napkin and began absentmindedly folding it, once then twice on the diagonal, turning it into a small triangle. She looked at her handiwork, and then tossed it on the table.

"You don't believe them?"

"No."

"Why not?"

"For the past year, I saw Eliza at least once a week, most times twice." Emotions tended to embarrass Hannah, but she didn't wipe away the tears pooling in her eyes. "She wouldn't have left without saying goodbye."

"But maybe—"

"I don't think so," Hannah said, leaving just the slightest room for doubt. "I know that girl like I knew you at that age. I don't believe she ran away."

Our talk went on, and Hannah recounted a second mysterious disappearance, that of sixteen-year-old Jayme Coombs. This girl I didn't know. The Coombs family had come from another rural town and settled in Alber the year after I left. Like Eliza, Hannah befriended Jayme, loaned the girl books and hired her to work around the shelter. "I didn't need her help. The women who live in the house do chores and make repairs. But Jayme's family is dirt poor, and she needed money. Jayme organized shelves, helped with the canning. Once I hired her to dig a section of yard and put in a pumpkin patch. If I couldn't afford to pay her with money, I gave Jayme canned goods, soap, a bottle of shampoo. She was grateful. They had nothing."

"This time, too, you suspect something because she didn't say goodbye?" I prodded.

"There's more than that." Hannah bowed her head. "Jayme and I had plans."

"Plans?"

"Like you and I had plans a decade ago, Clara."

"You were helping her escape," I said.

Hannah nodded. "Based on my conversations with her, I became concerned that Jayme was being abused."

"Why didn't you move her into the shelter?"

"I did at one point, but her mother, Genevieve, came for her. Jayme gave in and went with her. Mrs. Coombs promised me she'd watch over Jayme. But things Jayme said suggested that the abuse had started again."

"So you planned her escape."

"Yes. Jayme wanted to go, and I believed she had no other choice," Hannah said.

"So you…"

"I made arrangements. Jayme was supposed to leave May eleventh. We had everything worked out. A ride to Salt Lake and a family to take her in. But then she didn't come to work at the shelter on the tenth. I went to their home and asked to talk to her. I was told that she'd run away."

"But you don't—"

"No, I don't believe it," Hannah said, sounding more sure than she had about Eliza Heaton. "Not when we had a plan to start her new life. It made no sense."

"Did you tell Max all of this?" I asked.

"I did, and we had something of a difference of opinion," Hannah said. "We actually had a rather heated conversation about it. Max appeared interested at first, but then he called me and said someone had talked to their mothers. Like they told me, the women said the girls had run off."

"And he believed them?"

"Yes."

I wondered about Max. Something seemed off. Hannah's accounts were persuasive. It seemed that Max should have taken them seriously enough to pursue them, not immediately taken the word of their families. Why didn't he? I looked at my phone again. No call. What was taking so long? "Do you know anything about Delilah?"

Hannah picked up the napkin again, this time opening the folds and smoothing it out as if trying to erase the creases. "No. But something strange happened last Friday afternoon."

I turned to a clean page in my notebook. "What?"

"I was in the grocery store, at the back near the post office window, when Ardeth came in with Lily. They looked upset."

"In what way?"

"Nervous," Hannah explained. "Lily looked like she'd been crying. She had a fistful of mail, looked like bills and such, she put in the box. Ardeth stood back to wait for her."

"No doubt watching her every move."

"Of course," Hannah said. "You know, your mother doesn't like it when the children talk to me. She guards them when I'm around."

As dark as the conversation had become, at this I smiled. "She thinks you're a bad influence."

Hannah reached across the table and covered my hand with hers. "She always blamed me for you."

"I know," I said. "Tell me what happened at the grocery store."

"Not much," Hannah admitted. "But I bought my stamps, and when I turned around, Lily was standing directly behind me. I thought she might say something."

"Mother stopped her?"

The worry lines across Hannah's forehead deepened. "All Ardeth had to do was give Lily one of her stone-cold stares, and the girl dutifully slunk back and took her hand."

I grimaced, thinking yet again of my afternoon encounter with my mother. Then, too, she'd kept Lily from speaking. "Mother should trademark those. She's exceptional at them."

"I didn't think much about it until Max stopped at the shelter this morning to tell me about Delilah, and to say that you were on your way from Dallas," Hannah said. "I told him what happened in the grocery store. We weren't sure what to make of it. There's a lot of tension in the town. Things aren't easy for the families. He seemed interested, but not convinced that it meant anything."

Our conversation stopped, both of us lost to our thoughts. No longer thirsty for my wine, I glanced at my silent phone yet again, willing it to ring. The pot roast soured in my stomach.

Across the restaurant, the young mother collected her children to leave. The oldest, a girl with a long blond ponytail that bunched at her neck, grabbed the diaper bag to help. As they walked out, I heard the soft jabbering of a parent and children. I thought of my father and mothers, my brothers and sisters, of home. It had been years since I'd considered all I lost on the day I fled.

"The anonymous note said Delilah disappeared on Thursday. If it's true, that could have been why Lily and Mother appeared upset on Friday afternoon," I said. "You said Lily put a handful of mail in the box?"

"Yes."

"One of those letters may have been the note, the tip that came to the sheriff's office. Lily tried to talk to me today. It wouldn't surprise me that she wrote to the sheriff. She could have slipped it in with the family bills."

Hannah folded her arms across her chest, as if to ward off a sudden chill. "That may be."

"But there's no way to be sure."

"Not unless Ardeth has a change of heart and talks to you, or lets Lily talk to you," Hannah said.

I thought about Delilah, tried to decide what to do. I blinked, blocking the thin tears collecting in my eyes from falling. "Three days then," I said.

"Three days?"

"According to the note, that's how long my sister has been gone."

CHAPTER TEN

I'd had little sleep the night before, and it had been a long day. During dinner, a headache had taken root, but the main problem: I had a hard time holding back a growing sense of panic. If Hannah was right, Jayme Coombs and Eliza Heaton were missing. My sister Delilah was gone.

And no one was looking for any of them.

At that moment, my phone rang. I turned away from Hannah and lowered my voice as I spoke into the mouthpiece. "What did the sheriff say?"

Max cleared his throat. He sounded upset. "Sheriff Holmes called Alber PD and talked to the police chief a little more than an hour ago. I argued against it, but the sheriff turned the matter over to him. I've been ordered to stand down."

"What?" My voice carried through the nearly empty restaurant, but I didn't try to quiet it. "That's ridiculous."

"It's an order, Clara. From my boss," Max said, carefully enunciating each word. "The sheriff assures me that the chief or someone from Alber PD will talk to your family this evening. I waited to call you, hoping for news. But I just got word that the chief will personally get in touch with you when he has something to report."

"When he has something to report?" I heard the rage in my voice but didn't hold back. "You're kidding. I'm supposed to just sit back and wait?"

"Clara, I'm sorry I've dragged you into this, but don't make this any harder than it is," Max said. "I'm out on a limb here. As

I said, the sheriff was against my calling you in the first place. We need to let the chief do his job."

"This is my sister we're talking about, Max."

"I know." Max's voice grew stern, as if warning me.

"Hannah told me she talked with you about two other girls, Jayme Coombs and Eliza Heaton. She's worried—"

"We checked up on those girls. Their families say that they're fine." Max sounded angry that I'd questioned him. "Listen, Clara, Sheriff Holmes told me to remind you that you have no authority in Alber. This isn't your investigation. Any interference won't be tolerated."

"Max, I—"

"I have to go, Clara. Good night." At that, Max hung up.

My conversation with Max kept playing in my head as I paid the bill and Hannah and I left the restaurant. We were the Bannions' final customers of the evening, and they locked the door behind us. I decided to drive directly to my family's trailer, but then I thought better of it. The police chief or someone from the department could be there when I arrived. If they were making any headway, and I hoped they were, my showing up could stop the conversation cold. If any chance existed that someone might break through my mother's wall of silence, I couldn't interfere. At least, not yet.

But I had to do something. I couldn't just wait.

We got in the Pathfinder, and I turned to Hannah. "Should we go to the Coombs' house first or the Heatons'?"

"Tonight?" Hannah said, her voice rising in alarm.

"Yes, tonight."

"They'll be getting in bed. You know how folks here go to bed early."

"Hannah, I don't care if it's midnight, I need to—"

"No. Clara, you've been gone a long time," Hannah said, the worry lines across her forehead and around her mouth stretching. "You've changed. But this town hasn't, at least not that much. Not yet. This isn't how things are ever done here."

All that was true, but it altered nothing.

"Hannah, Delilah is twelve years old," I said. "After everything you've told me, I feel certain that she's been abducted—perhaps the other girls too. I have to wait on the police chief to talk to my family, but in the meantime I can at least try to figure out what's going on in this damn town."

"Clara, you need—"

"What I need is to figure out what happened to Eliza and Jayme. I need to know if all three of these girls are pieces to the same puzzle. Because if they are, you're right."

"I'm right?" Hannah asked.

"There's something truly evil here."

Hannah closed her eyes, as if collecting her thoughts. When she opened them, she said, "Let's go to the Heaton house first. We can talk to Eliza's family."

It turned out that the Heaton and Coombs families both lived in the trailer park. I drove through the quiet town, the street lights glowing and the mountain ridge barely visible in shadow. Above us, the skies shimmered dark and clear, peaceful.

"How long's it been since it rained?" I asked, trying to make conversation and cut through some of the strain in the car. We were both on edge, unable after all this time to be truly comfortable with one another. Perhaps I'd changed too much. Plus, neither one of us knew what would happen once we knocked on the Heatons' trailer door.

"Thursday morning, just a brief shower," she said. I looked over and she gave me a brave smile. "A lot of the farmers are worried about the crops. Not much rain again this year."

PROPERTY OF MERTHYR
TYDFIL PUBLIC LIBRARIES

The road continued straight north and then turned east and ran parallel to the mountains. I thought about the old white double-wide my family lived in. My father dead a year. There would be young children, brothers and sisters I'd never met. I wondered if anyone talked of me, if my younger siblings knew I existed. I decided they probably didn't.

Suddenly, headlights glared behind us. I glanced in my rearview mirror and saw a black SUV behind us. I noticed a light bar across the top. It looked like the Chevy Suburbans the SWAT teams drove in Dallas.

Alber's streets were nearly deserted, my rental and the Suburban the only two vehicles visible on the road. That left a lot of room to work with, but the Suburban tailgated, practically attaching to my Pathfinder's back bumper.

"Is that a cop car?" I asked Hannah.

She looked in the side mirror, but couldn't get a clear bead on it, so she turned around and peered through the back window. "I don't know. I guess it could be."

"I'm going to pull over and see if whoever it is will pass us," I said, but before I could, Hannah put her hand on my shoulder.

"No. Keep driving."

"Why?"

"It may not be police. There have been some problems after dark in town," she said. "One night a man who moved here with his family from Salt Lake was found beaten along the side of the road."

"Bad?"

"Bad enough. Broke his jaw," Hannah said. "There's a lot of anger around here. People… some people are upset. During the day it seems calm, but sometimes at night things boil over."

"Max warned me not to drive around alone after dark."

"Things are tense here," Hannah said. "We just need to be careful."

In Alber, certain families historically controlled various aspects of town life. Our family ran the sawmill, the Heatons had the hardware store and as the ruling family, the Barstows controlled city hall and manned the local PD. Old man Barstow was gone, but I wondered about his sons and brothers. Max had hung up before I could ask any real questions, like the name of the police chief I should expect to hear from.

"Who's in the local police department these days? Is a Barstow still chief?"

"There are a few of the old-timers and some new officers, people from outside. I don't know the new folks well. Gerard Barstow is the chief."

I had an image of a guy I'd grown up with through high school. Gerard had been a big kid, not terribly bright, who played football. My brothers liked him well enough, although my father had never had much respect for any of the Barstow boys, and there were dozens of them. Dad always said that the Barstows thought they owned the town. But with their father as the prophet, perhaps they did.

"You think that's Gerard behind us?" I asked.

"I don't know." She looked back at the SUV's headlights again. "It could be."

"I'd like to talk to him," I said. "I'm going to pull over."

This time, Hannah put her hand over mine on the wheel. "Clara, you're from outside. I live here. I'm asking you to please keep driving. We can't be sure who that is."

Grudgingly, I did as she asked. If it was Gerard Barstow, it would only be a short delay. One way or the other, I would talk to him before the end of the evening. If not now, after I talked to the Heatons about Eliza. I eased off the gas, thinking the Suburban would pass. The SUV slowed down and stayed on track behind me.

"Why would someone follow me?" I asked.

"I don't know. But if it is Gerard, it's nothing. He follows everyone off and on. Doesn't usually bother anyone. It's like he's keeping guard. Just keep driving."

I glanced over at Hannah and noticed that she was biting her lower lip. "He makes you nervous?"

"This is silly. He shouldn't," she said. "Gerard is always pleasant enough. Seems pretty level-headed. Not like some of his brothers. The chief before him, his brother Evan, was a piece of work. Mean. Lots of rumors about him."

"What kind of rumors?"

"That he liked young girls. Very young girls. Evan used to hang around the school a lot," Hannah said. "He left town as soon as the turmoil began. I heard he moved his family to a small town not far north of here. Hitchins. He's police chief there now. God help those people."

"I remember Evan. He was an officer when I lived here, became chief a year or so before I left." Mainly what I remembered was Evan Barstow railroading the boys in town targeted by the leaders for expulsion, harassing and pushing them until they left. "But you look like you're not sure about Gerard?"

Hannah released a soft, nervous laugh.

"Clara, no offense, but growing up here the way we did, the police working for the church leaders, doing their dirty work, all cops make me nervous." Hannah paused, as if mulling that over. "Gerard has always seemed pretty harmless. I don't know if you know this, but he was one of the lost boys."

"I didn't." That made little sense. None of the Barstow boys was ever forced out. That just didn't happen.

"Yeah. They pushed Gerard out when he was eighteen, maybe a little older. It was really ugly. His own father and grandfather wanted him gone," she explained.

"Why?"

"I don't know, but I always figured he didn't fall in line the way they wanted."

"So Gerard wasn't really tied to the establishment? He wasn't here when the authorities arrested his father?"

"No, he's like Max—a lost boy who's come back now that the town is opening up."

I thought about Gerard and Max. How frightening it must have been to be driven from home as a teenager, leaving behind family and everything they knew. I drove carefully, watching the speed limit.

If that wasn't a police officer in the Suburban behind me, who could it be? I thought about what Hannah had said, about the man found beaten on the side of the road. I had my handgun in my bag, on the backseat. "Hannah, grab my bag for me, will you? Put it on the floor in front of you."

"Why?" she asked, as she did as I requested.

"No reason."

We continued on, working our way through town, driving past the big houses, most dark for the night. Some had lamps scattered about, shining in the windows, and up ahead, at the trailer park, lights hung behind the fences and cast a yellow glow. The gate to the park was closed, so I pulled over, grabbed my bag and got out.

The Suburban parked directly behind me. I kept walking, but slipped my right hand into my bag's gun pocket. Once I reached the gate, I grabbed the handle, but it wouldn't budge. The gate was locked.

"Shit," I murmured.

Out of the corner of my eye, I watched a man walk toward me. I turned toward him and poised my index finger over the trigger as he moved forward slowly.

"Who's there?" I called out.

The man entered the glow from an overhead spotlight aimed at the gate. He wore a wide-brimmed cowboy hat that cast his face into shadow. I felt an overwhelming sense of relief when I saw his khaki cop uniform and a badge just above his left shirt pocket.

"Clara Jefferies? Is that you?" the man shouted. He raised a flashlight and shined it in my eyes, blinding me.

"It is. Who are you?" I raised my left hand to shield my eyes from the glare. "And can you aim that someplace else?"

He let loose a curt laugh and dropped the hand holding the flashlight to his side. "Gerard Barstow. You probably don't remember me. It's been a long time, but I'm the police chief in Alber. I was on my way to the station when I saw your car. I was going to call you once I got there."

"I do remember you, Gerard. Nice to see you," I said. He moved closer, and the spotlight illuminated the lower half of his face. He looked pleased to see me.

"I wondered who was driving around town this late in the evening. Usually folks are tucked in by now. I thought it must be you when I didn't recognize the SUV." He sauntered closer and offered his hand. I unwrapped my fingers from my gun and shook it. "What're you doing out here at this time of night?"

"Hannah and I just finished dinner at the diner." I gave him a warm smile.

"So that's Hannah with you?"

"Yup."

"That woman," he said, shaking his head. "That shelter she's pulled together is really something, don't ya think?"

"I do," I said, intent on keeping my voice light.

"Why are you two out here at the trailer park gate so late?" he asked again.

Everything seemed fine. Gerard seemed fine. Perhaps it was just the darkness, the solitariness of the town at night that made me uneasy. Perhaps my nerves rebelled because of Gerard's family connections, the rumors of trouble in town, my concern over Delilah's disappearance, or all I'd heard from Max and Hannah about the troubles in town. Whatever the reason, I was reluctant to tell him where I was going, and made an instant decision not to mention the Heatons. "I heard that someone from your office was talking to my family. I thought I'd see if I could catch up with them at the trailer."

I wished he'd take his hat off, so I could get a good look at his eyes. He had generous cheeks, a long nose that formed a ball at the end, and thick, meaty hands.

"Yeah, that was what I was going to call you about." But then instead of talking about Delilah, Gerard said, "I bet this old town seems real different to you. You know, Salt Lake money is flowing in. A group of big-time investors is looking into building a ski run west of town on the mountain. If they go through with it, Alber could be like Vail or Steamboat Springs someday."

"Big news," I said. The truth was that I didn't care. I just wanted to hear what he knew about Delilah. "Were you able to find out—"

Barstow leaned closer and stage-whispered over to me, "Kind of a secret, but I've got some cash in the project. Figuring I'll make a killing."

"Good for you. I hope it works out." I'd had enough small talk. "But, Chief Barstow, what I need to know is if you or one of your officers talked to my family? Do you have any news on Delilah?"

Barstow finally took off his hat, which left an indentation in the fringe of thin brown hair coating his head. He held the hat across his substantial midsection, looking as pleased as someone about to hand over a longed-for gift. "Clara, like I said, I was on my way to the station, going to call you from there. But this is better. This way, I get to deliver the good news myself, which is always more enjoyable. You agree?"

"I do," I said, wishing he'd get to the point. "So what do you know?"

"Delilah is fine," he said, his grin stretching wider.

I shot him a questioning look. "How do you know?"

"After the sheriff called and asked me to take over, I stopped to see your mom and the others. They invited me in, and we had a long chat."

"Max Anderson said you'd tried earlier and they'd turned you away," I said. "What was different this time?"

"Ardeth was home. Last time, she wasn't there and Naomi and Sariah were scared, I think. You know how that mother of yours rules the roost. The sister-wives do what she tells them, and letting a cop inside the house isn't done much around these parts."

"Sure. I understand," I said. "What did you see?"

"Things looked pretty normal. No one acted worried. Only thing was that Ardeth was madder than a cat tied by its tail to a clothesline. Your visit upset her, Clara. Upset all of them."

"Chief, I—"

"Oh, I know you were just trying to help. But I think you need to understand that your mothers, well, they weren't happy to have you knock on their door," he said. "The folks round here, enough of the kids are leaving. Seeing you, Ardeth and the others feared the kids at home, the ones still there, might get ideas."

I thought about the angry look on my mother's face. I wasn't surprised that she saw me as a threat. "Okay, Gerard, I get that," I said. "Just tell me about Delilah."

"Ardeth says she's off with another one of the families, on a mission trip to Salt Lake City."

"On a mission? Delilah is only twelve." It wasn't unusual for folks in Alber to take trips to talk up the faith and try to attract new members to the sect, but kids didn't usually join in until fifteen or sixteen.

"I was surprised, too," Gerard said. "But Ardeth said Delilah wanted to go, and the family offered to take her."

On the surface, it all seemed believable. It made sense that Mother would talk to Gerard. Despite being one of the lost boys, he came from an important family. He was a member of the establishment who'd run the town for decades. So I should have been able to accept his account, but I didn't.

"Chief, did you see my sister Lily? Was she there? Fourteen or so, dark hair, looks quite a bit like me."

"I don't know the kids by name, there are so many of them," Gerard said. "But there were a bunch, big and small, standing around listening to us talk. Plus Naomi and Sariah."

"No one spoke up, objected at all?"

"To what Ardeth told me?" he asked, and I nodded. "Nah. Everything seemed good. Before I left, Sariah got me a piece of apple crumb cake she'd baked that day, and she said she was looking forward to Delilah coming home in a few weeks. She misses her."

I wasn't sure what to say, except, "So you're sure about this?"

"I'm sure." He lowered his voice. "I'm sorry that your mother turned you away, Clara. In Alber, the people here, they're not always forgiving. You know how apostates are considered."

"As the worst of the outsiders," I said. "Yes, I know."

Gerard stopped smiling and gave me kind of a deadpan look. "You know, I'm surprised Max bothered you with this, when there was a good chance nothing was wrong."

"He was worried about Delilah. The note and all."

"The note?" He dismissed it with a wave of his heavy hand. "It looked to me like it was written by a kid."

The simple language, the short sentences. It made sense that Lily wrote it. But she would only have done that if my instincts were right and Delilah was missing.

As if he heard my thoughts, Gerard speculated, "Maybe whoever wrote the note didn't know Delilah had the trip planned. Or the kid played a prank. Not sure, but the bottom line is everything's fine."

I looked over at Hannah, who'd gotten out of the car and stood a few feet behind Barstow. She shrugged, as if uncertain.

"I'm having a hard time believing this, Chief," I said. "The reaction I got from Lily today at the trailer, the note. I wouldn't be candid if I didn't say I'm still worried about Delilah."

"You can stop now. She's most likely enjoying Salt Lake, seeing the big city," Gerard said. "You know what it's like growing up in this Podunk town. You get outside it, and there's a big world out there."

"There is," I said.

Everything Gerard Barstow said made sense, but as eager as I was to get back to Dallas, I couldn't shake the belief that Delilah was in danger. Chief Barstow's vague assurances weren't cutting it. I needed to be absolutely sure nothing was amiss. To do that, I had to talk to the Heatons, Jayme Coombs' family, and eventually my family, whether my mother wanted to see me or not. I thought again about the locked gate.

"Gerard, I appreciate all you've done. I understand that my mother's not happy that I'm here, but I don't know when I'll be in Alber again. I'd like to see if I can patch things up with her before I leave in the morning," I said. I reached over and pulled on the handle, rattling the gate in its frame. "I would appreciate it if you'd unlock this for me."

The police chief glanced at his watch and his smile faded. His voice dropped an octave. "It's nearly ten, Clara. Everybody inside there's dreaming dreams by now. You know how our folk go to bed early. Up at dawn to greet the day."

"Surely you can—"

His smile melted into the slightest frown. "I'm sorry, but I can't do that. I'd advise you to stay away, Clara. Like I said, your family doesn't want to see you. Ardeth and the others were crystal about that. If you knock on their door, they'll send you away."

I stared at him for a minute. Too much seemed odd. I wasn't ready to chalk it all up to a mistake and leave town. "I don't understand why this gate is locked."

Gerard shrugged. "It's only at night. There have been some problems in town after dark. One assault and a few burglaries."

"Isn't this a bit drastic?"

"I agree. It's not something I was in favor of. But the folks in the trailer park came up with the idea. They have keys to get in and out if they need to. This way no one bothers them."

I thought of the trailer park behind us with its run-down homes, no indoor plumbing. Little to steal. "Seems strange to lock things up all the way out here," I said. "So you had one assault in town? A few burglaries? And they locked the gate?"

"That's pretty much it." He turned off the flashlight that had been dangling in his hand, throwing a spot of light onto the barren, rocky ground.

"Gerard, what would it hurt to let me in?" I tried again. "It would mean a lot to me."

The police chief's lips curled up into a smile, but the rest of his face looked cold, wooden. "Clara, I know you're a cop and all, a detective I hear, but I'm gonna say no. Those folks in there, they put that lock on that gate to keep out strangers. I respect their wishes."

"I'm not a stranger," I started, and then I saw the look on his face. He didn't have to answer. In Alber, in my family, that was what I'd become. "You're convinced Delilah's safe? You're not planning to look for her? To follow up on this?"

Gerard Barstow looked me square in the eyes. "Your mother and the rest of your family tell me that Delilah is fine. I believe them. You should too."

CHAPTER ELEVEN

The phone woke Max a few minutes after eleven. For the sixth night in a row, he'd fallen asleep on the living room lounge chair. Ever since Miriam died, he didn't like sleeping in a bed. Too many memories.

If he was honest, the whole house made him sad. A different house in a different city than the one they'd shared, but Miriam had picked out everything they owned, from the furniture to the potholders. Max had never been one for domestic concerns, and that suited Miriam. She thrived on it. Of course, the way he grew up, six mothers in the house, there'd never been a need for him to worry about making beds, washing dirty laundry or cooking dinner. This past week, he'd thought often of the peach tree in the backyard. The thing was heavy with ripe fruit. He'd wondered if he should try to figure out how to can at least some of it. The prospect had made him tired.

Max grabbed the phone before the second ring, hoping it wouldn't wake Brooke. She'd been antsy that evening, and he'd let her stay up until past nine, her summer bedtime. She needed the sleep, but he gave in easily, happy for the extra time with her.

"Gerard here," Barstow said. "Did I wake you?"

"Not a problem, Chief," Max answered mid-yawn. "What's up?"

"I thought I should bring you up to date, in case you see Clara Jefferies in the morning before we have a chance to chat."

"Oh." Hearing Clara's name, Max became instantly apprehensive. He'd brought her back to Alber knowing not everyone would be happy to see her. The sheriff had been furious with him that afternoon, irate about how Clara was stirring up trouble. Max felt responsible, and he'd begun to regret that he'd called her. He'd been looking forward to seeing her again, but they weren't the same people they'd been in high school. Everything was different, including that he had a daughter to care for, and to do that he needed to keep his job. After Miriam died, he'd failed Brooke. He couldn't do that again. It wasn't an option.

"Is everything all right? Did Clara cause any…"

"Trouble? No. I just wanted you to know that I found her trying to get into the trailer park tonight. She wanted me to unlock the gate. Said she wanted to talk to her family," Gerard said, his voice friendly. "I told her she didn't need to do that. I explained that her family didn't want to see her, and that the matter of Delilah's whereabouts was settled."

Fully awake, Max focused on the phone call. He plopped the recliner's footrest down and sat up straight. He'd never liked the way Gerard talked around things, not really getting to the important points first. Sometimes Max wondered if the police chief did it on purpose, to confuse matters. But then, Gerard was a vast improvement over Evan Barstow. That man had been cruel. Twisted. Gerard had his faults, but Max thought he cared about the town, that he did his best. "You got news about Delilah?"

"Yeah, good news," Barstow said. "Like I explained to Clara, I found out everything's fine. No reason to worry."

"How do you know that?"

"I went back out to the trailer, like Sheriff Holmes asked me to. This time Ardeth was home and she opened the door. She says Delilah's in Salt Lake. She's staying with a family there while she does a mission."

"Isn't she awfully young for a mission?"

"Clara mentioned that, too, when I told her. A little, yeah, but Ardeth said the girl wanted to do it. She's staying with a family friend."

Max thought he remembered a couple of the boys who went on missions in junior high, thirteen-year-olds. It wasn't unheard of. Maybe that was all there was to it? "Ardeth is sure nothing bad has happened to Delilah? She knows where the girl is? That she's safe?"

"That's what she says."

Max digested the information, considered what to do. Something still needled at him about the note, about the circumstances. "Chief, I don't want to make you do any extra work on this, but I'd feel better if you went back out to the Jefferies trailer in the morning. Ask Ardeth for a phone number for the folks Delilah is staying with in Salt Lake. Let's confirm that the girl's okay before we close the case."

Max heard Barstow's reluctant sigh over the phone, a long drawing-in of air expelled in a huff. "Listen, Max, I understand your concern. I know Clara's worried, too. That's understandable. But my pull with these families only goes so far. If I push too hard, they clam up. We both know how closed-off these folks are."

"Sure. Of course," Max conceded, but the sense of foreboding he'd felt since the note arrived hadn't left him. Over his years as a cop, he'd learned to pay attention to the clues his intuition gave him. "I understand what you're saying, Gerard, but I'd feel a whole lot better if one of us talked to Delilah or at least the family hosting her."

"Max, why would Ardeth lie to me? She says the girl's fine. If Delilah was missing, why wouldn't Ardeth tell me? I can't think of a single reason. Can you?" Gerard asked.

"No, but—"

"The sheriff asked me to look into the girl's whereabouts and I did," Gerard said.

"Yeah, but—"

"I'm sorry that note got everyone riled up. But this has obviously all been a mistake," Gerard said. "Let's face it: we've got no reason not to believe Delilah's family. It makes no sense that they'd lie. I'm not going to bother them again. As far as I'm concerned, this investigation is over."

CHAPTER TWELVE

The room was cool, the summer's heat not yet building, and Delilah lay on her side, as she had for a very long time, awake and trying to decide what to do. She needed to find a way to escape. She wondered where the man had taken her, how far from home. When she thought it through, it seemed most logical that they were in one of the houses perched on the edge of the valley, at the foot of the mountains. The night that he snatched her, the man carried her blindfolded and bound for what seemed like a long time. His breathing became ragged, and she thought she felt him walking up, as if scaling a slope.

Yet she knew nothing for sure. Everything that had happened in the past few days defied understanding. Delilah felt sure of only one thing—that the man had no plans to release her. When she begged him, his voice sounded gruff and unmoved.

Then she thought about the soft hands, the gentleness of the woman who helped her. Who was she? If Delilah attempted an escape, would she help?

Maybe. But Delilah decided that she couldn't count on anyone else. She could only rely on herself, and she needed a plan.

So far, as hard as she tried, she had none.

The chain kept her anchored to the wall. The man was strong. She remembered the force of him coming at her in the cornfield, the way his arms encircled her as if she were a baby doll. He'd picked her up as if she weighed nothing. She thought about the creaking and complaining the old wood floor made under the force of his boots. She'd chided herself for not fighting back when he grabbed her, but even if she had she wouldn't have been able to fight him off. She had to get free of the chains and find a way to slip past him. Or find a way to escape while he was gone. But how?

If she did, if she managed somehow to escape, then what?

Would he come after her and kill her? She decided that even that would be better than living as a prisoner. But then she considered the rest of his threat, that he would murder her entire family. Her mothers, her brothers and sisters, even her baby brother Jayden, only two and still in diapers.

Could the man really do that?

When she thought about how easily he'd taken her, plucked her up not far from her own back door with her whole family inside the house unaware, she feared that he could.

I have to protect my family. I just have to.

Yet being confined to the room, chained to the wall, was torture.

Off and on she'd wondered about the sister the man told her about, the one who'd come all the way from Dallas to look for her. He'd said her name was Clara, but Delilah didn't know of a sister with that name. Who could she be?

She couldn't think about those things, she decided. More than anything, Delilah hated the blindfold. No matter what he did to her, she needed to get it off. Her dried tears saturated it and made it rough against her skin. She tried to turn her face and angle her right shoulder up to push it, but she couldn't reach far enough to make any progress.

Despite the awful smell of the cushion beneath her, Delilah pushed her face into the rough fabric, bringing her nose down toward her chest. At first, nothing. But she kept at it, even though it scraped her skin. After four such attempts, the blindfold budged. Not a lot, maybe half an inch. But it moved.

Resting on her knees, she reasoned that to nudge the blindfold farther, she needed something to hook it on. Over the time she'd been held captive, Delilah had sometimes felt something round like a button attached to the cushion beneath her, something that dug into her skin.

Delilah scrunched forward and used her cheek to hunt for it, but felt nothing. She shimmied to the right, searched and again failed to find anything that might help. Finally, on her sixth attempt, it happened. Something hard pressed into her cheek.

Delilah sat back and thought for a moment, then crouched. Pushing as hard as she could, she ground her face into the unforgiving fabric toward the button. On the third try, the lower edge of the blindfold latched on just above her right cheek. Once she had it secure, she rolled her chin toward her chest. As she prayed it would, the blindfold edged up. A few attempts and she had her right eye uncovered.

After days of darkness behind the blindfold, it took a moment for Delilah's eye to adjust to the dim light. When it did, she realized the cushion beneath her was about two inches thick, about the width of a twin mattress but shorter. It was filthy—dirt and grease were ground into the beige fabric. In one corner, a stain had cured a nasty-looking brown. Whatever caused it had dripped over the edge and onto the side.

Delilah sat back and stared at the stain. The color reminded her of a time when she sliced her right thumb while chopping onions. Mother Ardeth washed the wound with something that stung and then pressed a salve made of feathery yarrow leaves on it. That usually worked, but that time the cut wouldn't stop bleeding. Mother Naomi retrieved the sewing kit and threaded a needle she dipped in alcohol. Holding back tears, Delilah held Sariah's hand as Mother Ardeth pierced the soft, delicate skin and pulled the thread through, tugging the cut closed. Still the wound oozed. By morning, the white gauze bandage had cured that same ugly shade of brown.

"Blood?" Delilah murmured, staring at the stain. The air suddenly felt chill, as if someone had opened a refrigerator door. "That's blood."

A sinking feeling deep within her, she turned away from the cushion, not wanting to look any longer. Instead, she gazed about the room.

The walls, the floor—everything was a dull gray, dirty and bare. One wobbly-looking bent willow chair sat in the center of the room. That, a bucket the man had given her to use as a toilet, and the pad beneath her were the only contents. She turned her head to the right and saw the outline of a long narrow window, a sheet of plywood nailed to the frame to cover the glass. Daybreak seeped in around the edges.

As Delilah turned to her left, the blindfold threatened to slip back down over her eye. Hurriedly, she crouched back down. Again she hooked the cloth on the button and pulled. Once she had the right side fairly secure above her eyebrow, she swiveled her head and repeated the maneuver with the left side. Tighter and more difficult to maneuver, it eased up slowly. She had both eyes uncovered when the button's thread snapped. Caught in the blindfold, the plastic button dug into her forehead. Delilah didn't care.

For the first time in days, she could see.

Delilah sat up again and looked around. She stared at the door waiting for the man to return.

"Now I can see your face," she whispered.

CHAPTER THIRTEEN

The inside of the house hazy, I didn't recognize my childhood home until I saw the stone fireplace in the living room with my great-grandmother's hand-quilted banner hanging above it. Against an abstract background of gold and blue stood a pair of disembodied silver wings. Mother, young the way I remember her when I was a girl, rested in the old brown high-backed rocker. I watched from the floor beside her as she placed a wooden egg inside one of my father's worn black socks. She positioned the fabric's hole at the top, and began darning, one stitch through, another and then another.

"Clara, when you're a wife, you'll do this for your husband and children, so pay attention. Socks are expensive, and holes can be mended. You'll want to take good care of your family."

In my dream, I was Lily's age, a young teenager, innocent and naive. That day, for some reason I didn't understand, Mother had insisted I wear my best dress—pink and white plaid with bows at the neck and the wrists. I bunched the full skirt around my legs. My black hair so long it passed my waist, Mother had meticulously braided the crown and coiled it in a topknot.

Even then I'd been a matter-of-fact child. "I'd rather work with Father at the mill," I said.

Eyebrows rising, Mother appeared impatient. "Clara, I've told you, that is man's work. The mill is where the men work, to support our family. Women's work is in the home. If you keep pure, God will bless you with a worthy husband and through you, your father and me with many grandchildren."

"Mother, I—"

"Be sweet, Clara," Mother cautioned. She put down her darning and leaned forward. She took my chin in her hand and tilted my face toward her until our eyes met. "If you give yourself over to God and obey the prophet, you'll have great glory in the next world. The highest honor for a woman is to be married to a righteous man, like your father. Remember that, always."

"Yes, Mother," I said. She released me and picked up her work. I watched as Mother carefully repaired the damage wrought by wear and time.

As Mother darned, Father entered the room. Happy to see him, I jumped up and ran to him. He smiled down at me.

"Are you finished for the day?" I asked.

"Yes, Clara. It's been a long, busy day, but I'm home and looking forward to supper," he said. At that, he bent down, and I wrapped my arms around his neck. It was then that I glimpsed someone walking in behind him.

A gray-haired man emerged from the shadows, and Father said, "Look who has come to visit you."

I woke with a shudder.

For hours after we returned to the shelter the night before, Hannah and I talked, dissecting what Gerard Barstow had said about Delilah, trying to decipher if it was true. Hannah believed him. "I've never known Gerard to lie," she said. "His brother Evan, yes, but not Gerard."

"I'm not buying it," I said. "Why would Lily have been so upset if Delilah's not in trouble?"

"I don't know," Hannah said. "But isn't it possible you're reading too much into what you thought she might say?"

Hannah had eventually gone to bed. Once alone, I'd plugged in my laptop. I logged on to the NCIC website and clicked on

MISSING PERSONS. On the ADD A REPORT screen, I typed in DELILAH JEFFERIES. I'd had little to enter, just her age, a physical description, and the few details in the note: that she'd disappeared the prior Thursday evening and was believed abducted from the small town of Alber, Utah.

For a contact number, I'd listed my cell phone.

After a restless night in one of the shelter's seven master bedrooms, I woke before dawn, my head filled with images from my dream and thoughts of Delilah. Still dark outside, I showered and dressed, put on khakis, loafers, and a pale blue button-down shirt. I ran a brush through my wet hair, thinking about the innocent young girl I once was. I recalled mornings in our house, children milling about, pushing past one another as we dressed for school. I could almost feel Mother Naomi working her fingers through my hair, pulling the tangles out, crooning in my ear about the blessings that awaited me when I became a mother. "You and your children will be jewels in your husband's heavenly crown."

A last swipe of the brush, and I secured my shoulder-length hair into my usual tight bun.

That done, I pulled my bag off the closet shelf and double-checked to make sure my gun was fully loaded. I clicked the magazine back in as a familiar sound, a screech, drew me to the window. I pushed back long beige drapes and discovered double doors. The sun had come up. I flipped a lock and stepped out onto a second-floor balcony.

Below me spread an immense yard surrounded by cottages, the center taken up by a primitive playground and a vast vegetable garden. As early as it was, a dozen or so children played in a sandbox and spun each other around on a wooden merry-go-round. Three girls on swings pumped hard, their feet pointed toward the sky.

Nearby, half a dozen women and the older children shuffled systematically through the garden, harvesting what appeared to be green beans. Others were on their knees digging out potatoes and pulling carrots. Near the back, a cluster of women ripped corn off stalks and piled the cobs still in their husks into their aprons. When full, they dumped the corn into barrel-size wooden baskets with rope handles.

I remembered working with my mothers, brothers and sisters during the harvest, the sweet smell of the ripening corn, the insects buzzing my face, the hard ground beneath my feet, the way the corn stalks scratched through my clothes, the leaves sharp as I grabbed a cob and pulled down, snapping it off with a crack.

From the balcony, I watched the work below for a few moments, until I heard it again—the same high-pitched shriek that had drawn me to the window.

At first, I couldn't find the source, but eventually I focused on a dark object sixty feet away on the limb of a massive oak. Perched on a twisted branch halfway up the tree, I saw the distinctive white head and tail, the curved golden beak. The eagle let loose another series of cries, and I breathed in the sweet mountain air. I pushed up my T-shirt's sleeve, uncovering the three-inch tattoo I had inked on the inside of my right arm a year after arriving in Dallas. At the time, I told myself the tat was a symbol of strength, but looking at it while listening to the eagle's cries, I acknowledged the truth.

My eagle had always been a reminder of home.

Before leaving the room, I put in a call to Chief Thompson in Dallas. It was Monday morning, and he had me on the schedule to start in three hours. "I'm taking some time off. Maybe a few days," I said, bracing for an argument.

After all, I should have called in sooner.

To my surprise – or perhaps I should have expected it – he sounded pleased. "Well, Clara, it's about time. You've got enough vacation and sick days accrued to take a few months." Then he sounded as if he had second thoughts. "This isn't like you. Is everything all right?"

"I went home for a little while."

"Where's that? I don't think you've ever talked about home."

I hesitated, reluctant to open that door. "Utah. I'm helping a deputy friend with a case."

"I should have known this was a working vacation," he said, disappointment in his voice. I didn't respond, and he offered, "If you need more time, just give me a heads-up."

"Great."

"And Clara, while you're there…"

"Yes, Chief."

"Try to relax some," he said. "At least one day of real R and R."

I found Hannah downstairs, seated at the kitchen table, a half-empty mug of coffee in front of her. "About time you got up, sleepyhead."

I glanced at my watch. "It's barely six."

"You've forgotten what it's like in Alber," Hannah chastised. "Our days begin before sunrise."

Heaven's Mercy had been busy when I arrived the evening before, but this morning it bustled. Like the garden and playground, the house hummed with activity.

The mansion had been built to serve a family of more than a hundred, so the kitchen had three refrigerators and a ten-burner stove. Five women gathered in front of a bank of four restaurant-size stainless steel sinks washing vegetables then handing them off to a second group of women, eight of them, congregated at one end of a long banquet-type table. Wielding a hodgepodge of knives, they cut cucumbers, tomatoes, zucchini, green beans, and carrots. They cracked peas out of pods. With the exception of Hannah in her jeans and a T-shirt, all the women wore their traditional garb, the long dresses and sandals over white socks.

"Our crop is coming in from the garden," Hannah said.

"I saw the action from my balcony." I made an educated guess: "Today's the first day of canning?"

"Come take a look," she offered.

I followed her down the back stairs. In the massive cellar, white shelves lined the walls and others, free-standing, filled a ten- by twenty-foot section. All the shelves held rows of gallon-size jars, those in the front filled with vegetables, but the ones to the back empty and waiting for this year's crop. "We'll have to bring these up and sterilize them soon," Hannah said. "Many mouths to feed."

"How do you do it?" I asked. She gave me a puzzled look. "How do you keep the doors open?"

"Donations, fundraising—most of our money comes from mainstream Mormon groups across the country. They've been wonderful. Such good people. Very supportive," she said. "Really, we take whatever we're offered to keep the utilities on, everyone clothed and fed. A lot of these women and children arrive like you once did, Clara, with nothing more than the clothes they're wearing."

"Are they all here because their husbands fled?"

"Not all," she explained. "Some women come because it isn't safe at home."

"I can identify with that," I said.

"Yes, I'm sure you can." Hannah put her hand on my back and gave me a soft pat. "So what are we doing today? Are you done here? Have you decided to accept what your mother told Gerard, that Delilah is safe?"

"I don't know why Mother lied to Gerard but I'm convinced Delilah is in danger," I said. "I'm going to find out what happened to the two girls you mentioned, Eliza Heaton and Jayme Coombs. I want to finish what we started last night, to talk to their families."

Hannah appeared relieved that I wanted to investigate the other girls, but asked, "What will that tell you about Delilah?"

"What I'm worried about is that all three girls are pieces of the same puzzle."

Hannah sighed and shook her head. "I think that was what worried me from the beginning."

"Why you suspected there was something evil in Alber?"

Hannah nodded in agreement.

"You'll come with me?" I asked. "To introduce me to the families? It would help."

"Of course," she answered.

But plans changed when my cell phone rang.

"Detective Jefferies, this is Gerard Barstow."

"Good morning, Chief," I said. "What can I do for you?"

"You can explain why I got an NCIC report on my town this morning, one I didn't file." I heard the irritation in his voice. I suspected he wasn't grinning like the evening before at the trailer park gate. "We need to talk."

CHAPTER FOURTEEN

Gerard Barstow offered directions, but I didn't need them. Everyone in town knew that Alber PD headquartered in the modest one-story, stand-alone building off Main Street. Growing up, I feared ever entering the place. Along with their official duties, the local police carried out the agendas of the church elders. Keeping the young ones in check, squad cars pulled up beside unchaperoned girls talking to boys on the street. Townsfolk saw, and whispers surrounded the offending children's parents at the next social gathering.

As an adolescent, my brother Fred caught the eye of the local PD.

From a young age, his twin, Aaron, had earned the reputation of an obedient son, but although identical in appearance, Fred shared none of those attributes. Instead, Fred's bicycle tires perpetually burst from popping curbs. He once smuggled a horned lizard he pulled from under a bush into school and released it in the girls' lavatory, which resulted in high-pitched screams.

I admired Fred's spirit, but my parents worried. They reprimanded him, tried to rein him in, all with little effect. By the time Fred became a teen, police monitored where he went and who he befriended. Twice that I know of, they complained to our father about Fred's attitude. At seventeen, he disappeared from our home. We children heard no explanation, other than that Fred had moved away. For months, our family grieved, especially Aaron, who'd always considered his twin his other half. I told myself that Fred would one day return. He never did.

As I grew older and saw other boys forced out of Alber, I came to the conclusion that Fred must have been one of them. After I fled, I searched for him. I failed to find him, but I never gave up. When I had time, I still combed marriage, birth, death, arrest and property tax records, hoping to find Fred. So far, without luck.

I wondered how many of my father's children, my dozens of siblings and half-siblings, had been driven off in the years since I'd left. Did any others flee as I had? And I wondered yet again where Delilah was. What was happening to her, while I was about to be tied up with a command performance at the local cop shop? I had a sister to find, and Gerard Barstow was wasting my time.

I parked the car around the corner from the station. The slots out front were taken by a line of squads, one of which looked like Max's Smith County Sheriff's car. A black-and-white from Hitchins PD parked near the front door also caught my eye – that was Evan Barstow's department.

The sun had been up for barely an hour, but it promised to be another stifling day. I opened the door and walked into a dreary wood-paneled waiting room. Someone, perhaps one of the Barstows' wives, had tried to cheer the place up by hanging curtains with yellow daisies on the only window. It didn't help. The worn linoleum floor, the smell of institutional cleaners, the dark paneling and rickety pine furniture was beyond hope.

Behind a glassed-in reception area, a woman in her early twenties watched me enter. Her skin was a deep golden brown. The first three inches of her chin-length black hair were cornrowed, at which point it splayed out in all directions. She had dark almond-shaped eyes with thick silky lashes. She didn't look like she belonged in Alber any more than I did; I'd grown up never seeing a black or Hispanic person. She pressed a button and talked into a chrome microphone. "Can I help you?"

"Detective Clara Jefferies to see Chief Barstow."

The waiting room door buzzed, I grabbed the handle and walked through into the station proper. On the desk, a plaque read: STEPHANIE JONAS, DISPATCHER.

The open area around her housed a clutter of unattended desks. "Quiet around here," I said.

"The day shift hasn't started yet. Another hour and this place will be jumping. But there's already a welcoming committee waiting for you down there," she said, motioning toward a hallway. She raised her eyebrows and gave me a look that telegraphed: be careful. "The conference room is the third door on the right."

"Thanks," I said, and I started off toward the door. I heard voices, one a low, gravelly rumble, as soon as I turned the corner into the hall. I paused to listen.

"Damn it, Chief," a man yelled. "What's going on here, all these people moving in on us like this? Are we gonna let some cop from Dallas come in here and file false reports? This ain't her department. She's got no rights here."

"Mullins, I've got this," Gerard said. "We'll get to the bottom of this. But Max, you've gotta control that woman, she's—"

"I didn't bring Clara in to take over, just to talk to the family for us." Max sounded weary, like he'd answered this attack before. "I didn't think Clara would go off on her own and—"

"Well, she's a problem now," the first man, Mullins, said. "The family says the girl's fine, and here's this cop who thinks she has a role because Delilah is her half-sister, so she logs on to NCIC anyway? Files a report? There's no common sense here."

"Mullins," Gerard said, "calm down. I had the report removed, and—"

"You had the report removed?" I walked into the room. All of the men looked up, startled to see me – including a fourth man who I hadn't heard speak. "Why did you do that?"

"And good morning to you," Gerard said, friendlier than I might have been in his situation. "We've been waiting for you."

"Actually, it sounds like you started without me." I turned to Mullins, the one railing about my intrusion, and held out my hand. "I'm Detective Clara Jefferies, and you are?"

"Mullins. Jeff Mullins. Chief detective here, Miss Jefferies." He hung onto the "Miss" a bit long, emphasizing it. The guy was squat with rheumy hazel eyes and receding salt-and-pepper hair. He had a long scar that feathered at the ends and trailed down his right cheek.

"Good to meet you, Detective Mullins." I nodded at Max, and then turned to the fourth man in the room, someone I dimly recognized. I thought of the squad car from Hitchins out front. This man was massive, and he had Gerard's jaw, one that jutted forward and came to a point. Must have been a decade or so older. "You're Evan Barstow, aren't you? The former chief here? Police chief in Hitchins now?"

"Guilty as charged," he said, followed by a gruff snicker. "I just drove to Alber today to see the family and stopped to tell Gerard howdy, when all hell broke loose. Thought I'd stay for the fireworks."

"Always looking for good entertainment, I gather," I said.

"Why not? These are small towns. Nothing much happens. Gotta have a little excitement when I can," Evan said, more of a sneer than a smile on his wide face. "But this is my town, too. I was chief here a long time, and our family lives here. I'm interested."

"So am I," I said, turning to Gerard. "And what I'm interested in is why you removed my listing from NCIC."

"Because your sister's not missing," Gerard said. "I explained last night that—"

"You explained that you didn't see Delilah. She wasn't at the house," I countered. "All you know is what my mother told you: that she sent a twelve-year-old all the way to Salt Lake on a mission, alone."

"Not alone, with a family," Gerard said.

"Yes, that's right. Thank you for correcting me," I said. "Did you get the family's name? A phone number? Anything we can use to verify?"

Gerard looked over at Max, as if questioning if he was somehow involved with my rant. Max shrugged, but then agreed with me. "I don't think the detective is wrong here, Chief. Like I said, we should ask Ardeth or Sariah—"

"Max, this isn't any of your business. The sheriff handed this case over to my brother," snapped Evan. He had been relaxed up till now, apparently enjoying the show, but Max's support for my suggestion had changed his mood. I had the distinct impression that Evan didn't support any further investigation into Delilah's whereabouts.

To my relief, Max didn't back off. "But Clara has a point. Another short meeting with Ardeth or Sariah, and we can put this to rest."

Evan ignored Max and turned to his brother. "Gerard, you gonna let this woman tell you how to run a case?"

"Detective Jefferies is just worried about her sister. I understand that—" Gerard started.

"Don't call her Detective. In Alber, she's nothing more than a private citizen." Evan's sarcasm seeped into each word. "I must be wrong, Gerard—I thought you were the chief in this town."

Gerard looked over at his brother with eyes as big as a raccoon caught in a trap, before he turned to me and said, "Clara, Evan's right. You have no jurisdiction in Alber. You shouldn't be meddling in police matters. As I said before, I need you to stand down on this."

"And if I don't?" I asked.

"What do you mean?" Gerard looked at me blankly, as if he truly didn't understand.

"Are you going to look for my sister? Will you make sure Delilah is safe?"

Mullins piped up this time. "The chief's in charge here, not you, Miss Jefferies. You need to head back to Dallas. We'll let you know if there's anything in Alber that needs your attention."

"That so?" I commented, looking over at Max. A moment earlier, he'd been my only supporter. But this time – no help. Instead Max focused on his phone, and he appeared to be reading something that wasn't making him particularly happy. In fact, he looked upset. Gerard cleared his throat and reclaimed my attention, and I noticed his lips were pinched in distaste.

"Clara, it's time for you to go home to Dallas," he said. "You don't belong here. This is our town. We're in charge."

I shook my head. "You told me last night during our little talk at the trailer park gate that this isn't the old Alber."

"Yeah, but—"

"I'm counting on that being true, and that this isn't the same police department that used to run young boys, including you and Max, out of town. The same police force that harassed the girls."

"It's not, but—" Gerard started.

I didn't wait for him to finish. "I know one thing for sure. I'm not the same woman who fled from Alber frightened for her life."

"Clara, stop," Max interrupted. Off his phone, he appeared troubled. Where before he'd backed me, he walked over and stood next to Gerard. "The chief is right. Like the sheriff said, you have no jurisdiction here. You know that. You might as well leave and—"

"You, too, Max? Telling me what to do?" He seemed confused about what to say, so I picked up where I left off. I intended to leave no room for any misunderstanding. "Gentlemen, this you can believe: I'm not leaving Alber until I'm sure my sister is safe."

As I turned to go, Evan Barstow glowered at me, his eyes filled with hate. I thought about the rumors Hannah recounted, that he favored young girls. Maybe it wasn't a fluke that he'd chosen this particular morning to drop in to visit his younger brother, the police chief.

I couldn't know how much, if anything, Stephanie Jonas had heard, but she was standing at the end of the hallway when I walked out. The men were quiet behind me; I assumed they were waiting for me to clear the area before dissecting my performance.

As I brushed past the dispatcher, she whispered, "Detective Jefferies?"

I turned and looked at her.

"If you need anything," she said, and slipped me a card. I took it. I heard something and turned back toward the conference room. Evan Barstow stood in the doorway watching us, his eyes bristling with rage.

"Thanks," I whispered to Jonas.

When I got outside, I glanced at the card. Jonas had written her cell phone number on the back. I slid it into my pocket.

In the car, I called Hannah.

"If you're still willing to go with me to talk to the Heatons, I'll pick you up on the way."

CHAPTER FIFTEEN

Hannah ran out and got in the car when I stopped in front of the shelter. The gates to the trailer compound stood open when we arrived, but we still couldn't get inside. An aging red tractor pitted with rust and pulling a dilapidated wagon lumbered ahead of us. I assumed it must have been heading to the cornfield at the back of the settlement to start the harvest. Unfortunately, two-thirds of the way through the gate, the arch caught on the tractor. The fence rustled and groaned as the driver tried to push through. When I got a good look, I realized it was Jim Daniels, the guy Max almost ran over coming out of the cornfield the day before.

I waited anxiously as Daniels revved the engine, only to have the fence jangle forward and lean precariously, threatening to crash to the ground. Complicating the situation, the gate's ornament, the horn-blowing angel, had somehow been dislodged, dangled down and wedged onto the tractor's antenna. I pulled off the road and Hannah and I watched as four industrious-looking men scrambled onto the tractor, intent on freeing it.

Daniels glanced at me, and then hastily back to the task at hand. I thought about how odd the man had seemed the day before, the way he burst out of the cornfield. Max had said he'd always struck him as a bit strange.

"Tell me about that guy driving the tractor."

"Jim Daniels?" Hannah asked.

"Yeah. That guy." By then Daniels straddled the tractor seat, personally tugging on the angel.

"I don't know much," she said. "He's been here a while. His family came from a neighboring town. Someone told me that he has an agriculture degree from someplace in Iowa. Maybe five or six years back, the town co-op hired him to manage the community fields, the corn and alfalfa. Sometimes he works on private gardens. Gives advice, helps if there's a bug or a blight problem."

"He seems okay?"

Hannah looked stunned. "I never thought about it. Jim's kind of standoffish, maybe. But he's so quiet, he's always just blended into the background."

"Never any talk about him?"

"Not that I know of. Why?"

"Just wondering." I pointed at the gate, the men still trying to jerk the arch off the tractor. "This could be a problem."

"They'll get it," Hannah dismissed. "You know, Jim's family of yours."

I shot her a curious look and she explained, "His second wife is your younger sister Karyn. Well, half-sister. Constance's youngest."

I thought about Karyn, all the others. My family, people I hardly knew.

The clock ticking, my nervous energy built as I worried about Delilah. "Let's walk around the tractor."

"The Heatons live on a far back lot on the west," Hannah protested. "It doesn't make sense to leave the car here. We would have to walk back and get it to drive to the other end of the trailer park, to the Coombs' house."

"Shoot," I said.

"Patience," she urged.

"Does this happen often?"

"No, but we had a lot of wind last Thursday, came with that morning rain. It must have loosened the arch."

Moments later, Daniels, a man I now knew was my brother-in-law, sprung the antenna free and pushed the arch back up, righting the angel. The men cheered and threw victory punches toward the sky. As the tractor lurched forward, the wagon rattled behind it like a burlap bag of loose bolts.

Hannah and I followed in the Pathfinder, passing rows of trailers. Crumpled cardboard boxes, abandoned tools, old furniture and worn-out children's playground gear cluttered the yards. When we reached the cornfield, the tractor veered to the right toward my family's double-wide, but Hannah instructed me to keep driving straight back on the field's western edge, heading toward the mountains.

"There it is," she said a short time later, pointing at a single-wide with a small camper beside it. The blue-sided trailer looked decades old, but it was clean and well-tended. It faced the road, and the cornfield spread out behind it.

I parked a bit down the road.

"That was the Heaton place back there," Hannah said.

"I don't want to telegraph that we're here. This gives us a few minutes to walk around unnoticed," I explained. I grabbed my bag, and Hannah and I swung the Pathfinder's doors open. "Let's go."

As we approached the trailer, I motioned for Hannah to continue on toward the back. Hidden behind the single-wide sat a rickety, three-door outhouse, and off to the side in addition to the camper stood a half-dozen good-size tents, large enough for three or four people to sleep in, bordering the cornfield.

"For the older kids," Hannah whispered. "This isn't unusual. Not enough room inside for beds. The camper is their quilting shop, where they keep the sewing machines."

A lean-to on one side had an opening to store hay beneath a corrugated tin roof, and a frail-looking bay greeted us, shaking its head and ruffling its mane. The horse was tied up next to a water trough. Most of the families in Alber had horses when I lived there, and I suddenly realized this was the first one I'd noticed since my return. "Where did the horses go? Why haven't I seen more of them?"

Hannah shrugged. "Most had to be sold. The women can barely feed their kids, much less a horse or two. Looks like the Heatons managed to keep one."

A small tribe of goats in a pen elbowed to get past one other, attempting to greet us, kicking up dust and bleating as we walked by. A black-and-white one with short horns threw his head back and let out a throaty call as something rustled past us overhead. I looked up and saw three young girls trampling across the trailer's flat roof as if playing a game of chase, the metal quaking under each step.

I couldn't help laughing, and one apparently heard me. Six or seven, she shook her head in surprise, no doubt unaccustomed to intruding strangers. She jerked back and pointed at us, while the other two rumbled to stops beside her.

The tallest girl, perhaps ten, looked warily from Hannah to me and yanked the other two back. In seconds, they'd vanished. I assumed they must have scurried down a ladder on the trailer's rear, when one of the girls rounded the corner and ran past us to hide a dozen feet away, behind an ancient oak. The other two copied her, and before long all three peeked out at us from around the tree's thick black trunk.

Hannah shot me an amused glance, and then walked gingerly toward them, stopping a few feet from the tree. She bent closer to their heights and asked, "Well, hello. Are your mothers home?"

At that moment, the screen door burst open, and a haggard-looking woman in a long beige dress appeared, drying her hands on a dishtowel. "You children stay on the ground and stop all that noise, you hear?" she shouted, searching the top of the trailer for the small offenders. "You'll crack the roof and let the rain in, and this thing is all we've got to live in!"

Suddenly noticing us, her feet stopped before her body did and she nearly fell forward. She looked from Hannah to me, and her face blanched. "Hannah Jessop, what're you doing here?"

"Grace… You remember Clara Jefferies," Hannah replied.

The woman turned to me. She took me in head to toe, questioning, and then appeared to piece it together. I didn't know if she'd address me directly or not, but after she carefully assessed me, the woman said, "I heard you'd come back, Clara, but I couldn't believe it. What nerve you have."

"Word gets out quickly," I said, ignoring the barb.

"Where's your badge? A cop too, I hear." Not giving me time to answer, her words tumbled out. "Another reason you're not welcome."

I remembered a girl named Grace, a classmate of mine, plump with delicate features. In the eighth grade, we sang together in the school choir. I wondered if this could be the same girl, grown into a woman. I didn't remember my friend having a jaw so hard set, the twin indentations between her eyes making her appear angry.

Life had taken a heavy toll.

Grace moved closer and scowled. "Those who descended on us, harassing our community, had badges, too. They worried our husband so, he had a heart attack and died." She pointed at the Pathfinder a short distance down the road. I sensed her fury building. "You're not one of us. Get back in your car. You don't belong here."

I approached her slowly, calmly, shortening the distance between us. "Grace, I'm not here to cause any problems. I'm here to help you—"

"We don't need your help. You need to leave!" she commanded.

"Please, let's just talk," I pleaded. I had no desire to linger any more than she wanted me to stay. I'd come for information. Then I'd be gone. "I'm not here to hurt you. I'm—"

"Get out!" Grace screamed, her face inflamed with a seething rage. "Leave now. Everything of value we had has already been taken from us."

Hannah stepped forward to intercede. "Grace, please, Clara came to help. I asked her to. I told her about my concerns, about Eliza."

At that moment, two other women emerged from the trailer wearing threadbare but clean, carefully pressed dresses and stern expressions. The older one I recognized as Alma Heaton, the family's first wife. Her hair had turned a yellow-gray, one that matched her pallid complexion. A look of incredible sadness on her face, Alma took Grace gently by the arm and pointed her toward the trailer door. Then she called out to the little girls watching wide-eyed from behind the tree trunk.

"Inside," Alma ordered. When they didn't immediately react, she demanded, "Children. Inside, now!"

The others vanished inside the trailer, and left Hannah and I alone with Alma. A slight, frail woman, she had the look of someone who'd been chronically ill for a very long time. Turning to Hannah, she seethed, "You have no business bringing police here. I told you Eliza left of her own free will, abandoned us like all the others."

"Alma, please," Hannah pleaded. "I'm worried that Eliza may not have left willingly."

"Eliza ran off, I tell you," she hissed. "Can't you leave us alone?"

"That girl loved all of you."

Tears formed in Alma's red-veined eyes. "We thought she did. We were wrong."

Hannah's voice became soft, urging. "Eliza wouldn't have left you. In your heart you know that, Alma. What can it hurt to answer some questions? I asked Clara to—"

"My daughter is no longer one of us. I will not speak of her." Alma ran the back of a hand gnarled by decades of hard work over her cheek to wipe away tears. "Making things worse, you bring a police officer to this house, after what the Gentile police did to our family and our town."

"How can you be sure that Eliza is safe?" I tried to redirect the conversation.

"My daughter abandoned us," Alma hissed. "Like all the other teenagers, the ones who turned their backs on their families and faith. Like you did, Clara Jefferies."

Alma Heaton glowered at me, but addressed Hannah. "You have no right to bring her here." She stalked toward Hannah, pointing at her face with one rigid finger. "This isn't a grand palace, but it is our home. We say who is invited. *She* is not."

"Alma, please," Hannah implored.

"I want you, both of you, to leave, now."

"No, Alma," Hannah whispered. "Talk to Clara. We only want to help Eliza. If you know where she is, tell us. Please, just tell us."

"No! I will not speak of Eliza. Never again!" Alma's denial erupted from deep within her, carrying with it the grievances of a life gravely damaged.

"What if she's not?" I countered.

Alma turned toward me. "What?"

"What if Eliza isn't safe?" I asked. "Would you turn your back on her suffering?"

Ever so slowly, Alma Heaton shook her head, nearly imperceptible at first, then harder and stronger. Her breathing turned hoarse, her eyes stared sharp. "You question me, a mother, challenge my love for my child?" she taunted. "You, who have no children, a barren woman who rejected her people?"

Her words hit their mark, a wound deep within me. I willed my face calm. I knew this world. Here a woman without children was an embarrassment, a failure, an empty shell. "This isn't about me. It's about your daughter. I'm asking how you can be so sure Eliza is safe." My heart beat hard against my ribs. I was being judged again as I had years earlier. Discounted as less. Even though I knew I wasn't that person any longer, that I didn't need anyone's acceptance except my own, it hurt. "If you are truly sure that Eliza is safe, tell us where she is. What can that hurt? Once you do, we will leave willingly."

Alma bit hard on her lower lip. Her eyelids became heavy, sagging over her eyes. She didn't answer.

Instead, she whispered one last command, "Leave!"

With that, she walked back to the trailer, disappeared inside, and slammed the door behind her just as my own mother had the day before.

Hannah and I tarried for a moment, frustrated that we'd been turned away.

As we reluctantly left, I felt only regret, not any anger toward Alma. She was a good woman. My mother was a good woman. They lived by the rules they were taught as children. They lived lives they'd been assured would bring honor to their families, lives that guaranteed great rewards in heaven. Then the world invaded and changed the rules, and they lost much of what they held dear.

Alma Heaton and my mother were left adrift in a town where they'd once belonged. As the world continued to intrude, they would increasingly become the strangers, the outsiders.

And me? I had failed again. I knew no more than when I'd arrived in Alber. I had no grounding on what was truth, or what were lies.

"What do we know now? Anything that can help us?" Hannah asked when I turned on the Pathfinder's engine. "What are we going to do?"

As sympathetic as I was toward my mother, toward Alma Heaton, toward all the women of Alber, I had no choice.

"We're going to drive to the Coombs' house to ask about Jayme," I said.

"It'll be the same." Hannah sounded resigned. "Last time I was there, there was a terrible scene. Jayme's mom screamed at me and told me never to return."

"If they send us away, we'll drive back to the Heatons' and try again. And if that doesn't work, we'll go back to the Coombs' house. We'll keep pushing until we wear someone down. I'm not leaving until we know where Eliza and Jayme are."

Hannah hesitated, and then asked, "Clara, what if Alma is telling the truth? Maybe my mind fashioned this terrible theory out of nothing but suspicion."

That was something I'd considered. "You have reasons to suspect there is something very wrong. If this is all an innocent mistake, why didn't Alma simply tell us what she knows?"

"I don't know," Hannah said. "But I worry that I'm wrong, and that we're putting ourselves and them through all this for no reason."

"That's the hope, isn't it?" Hannah shot me a questioning glance, and I explained. "That would be the best possible outcome: that we're wasting our time, because all three girls, Eliza, Jayme and Delilah, are safe."

"But you don't think they are?"

"No, I don't," I said. "There's something very wrong here."

CHAPTER SIXTEEN

By the time the lock clicked and the door creaked open, Delilah had fallen asleep. She woke with a start. Early-morning sunlight sent fingers of light into the room from around the boarded-up window, and Delilah looked up to see the man staring down at her. In his hands he held her breakfast, another small bowl of gruel, a curious look on his face.

"How did you get the blindfold off?" he asked.

"I—"

She couldn't decide how to answer. Maybe it didn't matter. He didn't look angry, only intrigued by how she'd managed it with her wrists chained behind her. She stared at him, his jowls, his thick neck, and his slicked-back hair. She noticed a single vein pulsing in his neck, a thick, rope-like cord that came out of his shirt collar and disappeared behind his right ear.

"I asked you a question." He clomped toward her, his heavy boots creaking the worn wooden floorboards. "How did you get the blindfold off?"

"I rubbed it off," she said.

"Rubbed it off?" he repeated, and she nodded.

"Hmm," he said. "I haven't had any of them do that before."

He put the bowl down on the chair, then leaned over and pushed her face toward the wall with one rough, meaty hand while he yanked at the chains on her wrists and ankles with the other. Satisfied, he picked the bowl back up and announced, "Those seem okay."

"They're…" She stopped, tried to clear her throat. Her empty stomach painful from hunger, bile again worked its way up her chest. "I didn't do anything with those. They're tight. Too tight. They hurt."

"I bet they do," he said. He pulled the lone chair toward her. Once he had it positioned in front of her, he sat down. "You hungry?"

She nodded.

First he leaned toward her and pulled the blindfold off her head, threw it in the corner. When he did, the button fell out.

While he spooned the meager offering into her mouth, giving her barely time to swallow, she tried to decide if he looked familiar. She felt certain he wasn't anyone she'd ever actually met, but he could have been someone she'd seen around town, maybe when she was with her parents, or at school. She wasn't sure. Before the troubles, the exodus where so many of the fathers left, there were a lot of big men like him in town. They were her friends' fathers, the loggers her father catered to at the mill.

She'd never paid much attention to any of them.

While Delilah ate, the man said nothing, just brought one tablespoonful after another to her lips and waited for her to take it. When she finished the last of it, he wiped her mouth with a paper napkin covered with cheerful pink and green flowers.

"Where's the lady who usually feeds me?" Delilah asked.

"I decided to do it myself today," he said. "Didn't need her."

Delilah curled her mouth into a worried knot. "When will you let me go?" she asked.

"I won't." He shook his head. "You belong to me."

Delilah gulped hard. Her voice thin with fear, she asked, "But I don't want to be here."

The man snickered at her, as if she sounded foolish. "What you don't want? That doesn't matter. I chose you. That's a great honor. You're mine."

She coughed to clear her throat, trying to dislodge a lump of fear. "What are you going to do to me?"

He sat back in the chair and looked at her. "Nothing right now, little one."

She thought about that. "Later, will you let me go?"

This time he pursed his lips. When he did, the vein on the side of his neck stood out more. "No."

Delilah took a long breath. "Please. I want to go home."

The man examined her, unblinking. "Delilah, you won't ever leave this house. You will live here until the day you die." He leaned forward, closer to her, and lowered his mouth until it met hers. She smelled his stagnant breath as he pushed his rough, weather-worn lips against her soft ones. Her eyes flared wide with panic, as his closed and a look of pleasure softened his face.

Terrified to move, she froze and waited. When he finished, he pulled away.

"When I judge it is time, you will become sealed to me forever. We will be man and wife." He stood and returned the chair to the center of the room, then began to walk away.

"Sir," she whispered, and the man stopped. He looked back at her. "Please, take the chains off. They hurt."

"Not until you prove you can be trusted."

"How do I do that?"

"You do what your parents taught you to do," he said. "You obey."

CHAPTER SEVENTEEN

From the Heatons' trailer, I drove south on the road that traced the cornfield. When we reached the first intersection, Hannah instructed me to turn left. I did, and we drove east, following the road along the cornfield's southern edge, the sun still low and in our eyes. We passed my family's double-wide, and I saw my mother and Mother Naomi hanging sheets on ropes suspended from two spindly trees. My mother had on her wide-brimmed straw hat, the one with the flowered sash I remembered from when I was a kid. Behind them young brothers and sisters I didn't know played. Hannah noticed me watching them.

"Should we stop?"

I'd been considering it. I didn't see Lily. If I had, I would have answered differently. "No."

"They might—"

"It will only cause another scene. Mother won't let them talk to me," I said. "Since she's there, the others will follow her orders."

A dozen or more trailers later, we slowed to pass the tractor pulling the wagon along the edge of the cornfield. The pickers had grown to a small army of women and children; some looked as young as ten or eleven. They worked their way through the rows of corn, snapping off the cobs and throwing them into cloth bags they dragged across the field. A dozen or more men collected the full bags and lugged them to the tractor, dumping them into the wagon. They'd been busy. At least twenty rows had been harvested, but another eighty or more needed to be cleared.

In their wake, a second battalion of men and teenage boys followed, using machetes to cut down the empty stalks. They left behind a carpet of debris, a thick thatch that would be turned into silage.

Hannah motioned. I turned left and drove north, continuing to outline the perimeter of the field, heading toward the mountains. As we approached the road's end, Samuel's Peak grew closer, and then loomed nearly overhead. Hannah pointed at not a trailer but a ramshackle cottage. Little of the structure's last coat of white paint remained, leaving the wood exposed. Over the decades, Utah's harsh sun had turned it silver.

I pulled over and parked.

The trailers were old and weary, many pockmarked with rust, but they looked like palaces in comparison to the house before us. A substantial branch, twisted and rotting, had fallen off an oak in the front yard, blocking the path to the house. Rather than cut it up and dispose of it, someone had removed a section of fence, making a second way to get into the yard. A large hole in the front wall had been repaired by nailing boards across it, big gaps between the wood letting the elements in. Jagged-edged screens tacked on with staples covered broken windows missing panels of glass. I wondered how the family fared during the winters, when instead of letting in mountain breezes they needed to keep out harsh cold.

"Even before the troubles, the Coombs family was among the poorest in Alber," Hannah whispered. "But now, with just the wives and children, no husband to work, they have nearly nothing."

As we had at the Heatons', I led Hannah around the side of the house toward the back. The yard was covered with refuse, broken toys, rusty sheets of metal and pipes, and piles of boards and logs that struck me as a good place for rattlers to breed. An old outhouse with a hole in the wooden roof that had to let in rain stood to one side, the odor emanating from it nearly overpowering. The cornstalks behind the house had already been mowed down fifteen feet deep. To our left, in the distance, the crew of harvesters worked their way back toward the house. I heard the murmurs of the women and children talking as they snapped off the cobs, the men shouting at each other as they cut the stalks. The sun rising ever higher, the heat had begun to build.

I again motioned for Hannah to follow, and we made our way to the front door.

On the porch, I had to dodge a dinner-plate-size hole to get close enough to knock. I rapped once, twice, then stepped back to wait. No one came. I tried again. This time I heard footsteps from inside the house, squeaking floorboards. Hannah and I stood back and waited. The door creaked open far enough for one eye to look out, the height of someone young.

"Well, hello," I said. I bent down a bit. "I'm Clara Jefferies. This is Hannah Jessop. We're looking for your mothers."

A tiny voice said, "They ain't here."

"Where are they?" I asked. "It's important that we talk to your mothers. Someone older."

"My momma, my whole family's working in the field. Every one of them. But I gets to stay home, cause I'm too little to reach the cobs," the child said. Gradually the door edged farther open, a bit at a time, until we saw a young boy of eight or so staring at us with saucer-round pale blue eyes under a sparse fringe of blond hair. "What'd'ya need my momma for?"

"We need to talk to her about Jayme."

The boy frowned.

Hannah moved forward. "I think we've met, haven't we? The time you came to the shelter with Jayme to pick up her earnings. Isn't your name Samuel?"

The boy appeared to have reservations about answering, but eventually, he nodded. "Yeah, like the peak. My momma named me after it."

"What a wonderful name," I said. "And we're Clara and Hannah, as I said. We've come to talk to your mom. Or better yet, we'd like to talk to Jayme."

"'Bout what?" His face cocked to the side, he looked up at us out of the corners of his eyes.

"About…" Hannah hesitated, and then said, "To tell Jayme that she still needs to pick up the rest of her pay for helping me at the shelter."

That seemed to make sense to Samuel, and he swung the door the rest of the way open. His ragged and soiled clothes drooped on his reed-thin frame, and he had a faint swath of dirt across his left cheek. From inside, the house emitted the mingled odors of sweat and rotted meat. Since Hannah seemed to be making a connection with the boy, I stepped back and let her move closer.

"We'd like to make sure that Jayme gets her money, Samuel," she explained. "But to do that, we need your help."

"We needs that money." A spark of excitement in his eyes, Samuel suggested, "You could give it to me, and I'll give it to Momma." He appeared to think that through for another moment, and then he said, "But you was here before to see about Jayme, weren't you? How come you didn't tell Momma about Jayme's money?"

"That's right, I was here," Hannah said, taken a bit aback. I was rather enjoying her predicament. The boy and his questions were giving her pause. "You must have been listening that day I came to your house to try to find Jayme."

"You told Momma that Jayme was in trouble," he said. "Momma said Jayme weren't in any trouble at all."

Hannah beamed at the boy as if he'd answered a difficult test question correctly. "What a smart boy you are."

"Momma told you to leave," he said, giving her a doubtful frown.

Hannah hesitated just a moment, and I decided to take over. "She did. But you see, Samuel, Miss Jessop needs to talk to Jayme, to get her okay to give your mother the money. Miss Jessop can't just hand out your sister's money unless Jayme agrees to it."

Samuel thought about that and his smile wilted with disappointment. "Jayme's not here. So how's my momma gonna get the money?"

"Well…" Hannah began.

"We don't have to talk to Jayme in person," I suggested. We had an inroad. This was working. "We could talk to her on the phone, assuming you know how we can reach her."

At that, his small face brightened. "Momma gots it," he said. "Wait here."

The door slammed, and I heard footsteps again, this time running away from the door.

From the cornfield, the clatter of the harvesting crew grew ever closer. I thought about the boy inside, the prospect that he could help us. The arrival of his family, among the workers, could prove our undoing. Once they reached their house, one might spot us. His mother could come and send us packing. I opened the door a few inches and called out, "Samuel, please hurry. We need to be on our way soon."

"I am," he shouted.

Seconds later, he stood at the door holding onto his britches with one hand, trying to keep them from sliding down his scrawny frame, and clutching a scrap of paper in his other.

"What's this?" I asked.

"That's where Jayme is," Samuel said, pride at his great accomplishment shining on his smudged face. "You can call her and give us that money now, right?"

Hannah and I looked at the note.

"Are you sure she's here? That this is where we'll find her?" I handed the scrap of paper back to the child.

"My momma says it is. The man told her that she could find Jayme there anytime she wanted. He said she could call and talk to Jayme if she wanted. But Momma said she had no reason to talk to a daughter who runned away," Samuel said.

"I see," Hannah said.

The boy bunched his lips up as if he didn't approve. "The man said there's a lotta kids there from Alber, the ones who runned away."

"What man gave your mother this information? Do you know his name?" I asked.

Samuel appeared apprehensive. "Do you need to know that to give us the money?" he asked. "'Cause I don't know no name or anything. Momma just said it 'twas a man."

"No, it's okay," I said. "This is what we need, Samuel. A way to reach Jayme. Thank you."

"How long till my momma gets the money?" he asked. "We could use it quick, 'cause we ain't got any electric right now. Momma couldn't pay the bill."

I'd noticed the house was dark inside. A nonfunctioning refrigerator could account for some of the smell. I looked at the child's face, the dilapidated house, and I opened my bag. Hannah gave me a sad frown, the kind that said she understood. Out of my wallet, I pulled $160 in twenties, leaving forty to tide me over until I found an ATM. I wondered briefly if the bank in Alber had ever installed one. "Tell your mom that Miss Jessop stopped by and this is your sister's pay," I said.

He looked doubtful. "You don't have to talk to Jayme first, like you said?"

"When we tell her you needed it to pay the electric bill, she'll understand. We'll give her a call and explain," I said.

The boy grabbed the money in his dirty little hands and held it before him as if I'd handed over a fortune. "Thanks," he said.

We turned to leave and were nearly back to the Pathfinder when he shouted at us to stop. "Lady, tell Jayme something for me, okay?"

"Sure," I said.

"Tell her that Samuel wants her to come home. I miss her. We needs her here."

"We will, Samuel," Hannah said. She turned and we started off, but then she stopped again. The boy lingered at the door. "Samuel, if you need anything, if you need help, you know where the shelter is in town?"

"Where I comed with Jayme and saw you?" The harvesters drew closer, and I saw a woman splinter off and stride toward us. In a few minutes, she'd be upon us.

"Yes," Hannah said.

"Yup," he said. "I got good direction sense. Momma always says that. I can find anything."

Hannah laughed, as I urged her to move. She started walking, but she called back over her shoulder, "Samuel, if you need anything, you come see me. Don't forget."

Worried, I motioned for Hannah to hurry. The woman from the field stormed toward us. Moments later, we passed the house in the Pathfinder. I saw Samuel run to the woman, holding my twenty-dollar bills and grinning as wide as I'd ever seen a child smile. The woman took the money and dropped to her knees, my guess to question the boy.

As the house disappeared behind us, I handed Hannah my cell phone. "You know the place? Where Jayme is supposed to be?"

"No, but there can't be more than one Salt Lake Youth Crisis Center."

"Get someone on the phone," I said. "Let's give this a shot."

A brief web search yielded the organization's phone number. Hannah clicked onto it, it rang, and a woman answered. "Salt Lake Youth Crisis Center. May I help you?"

Hannah handed the phone back to me.

"I'm Detective Clara Jefferies. I need to talk to your director."

"He's not here right now."

"Is this a shelter? Do young people live there?"

"We place homeless youth," the woman explained. "We find temporary housing with foster homes and shelters. Help them find jobs."

"We're looking for a young woman. We need to verify that she's used your services. Who would you suggest we talk to?"

"I'll get Samantha for you," the woman said. "She's our program admittance officer. She should be able to help."

As we drove down the road, I noticed the workers had expanded their reach into the field. More corn had been harvested and mowed down. The crew had turned the corner and headed back, spreading out to tackle the next row. Down the road, Jim Daniels pulled the tractor out in front of us, filled with the bags bulging with corn cobs.

"Where is he taking it?" I asked Hannah.

"The park across from the Meeting Place. Or I guess I should call it the diner now," she explained. "They divide it up and parcel it out. Last year each family living in the trailer park got one bag per person. They expanded the field and planted more this year. I heard they were hoping for a bag and a quarter."

As Hannah predicted, across from Danny's Diner, the tractor pulled off the road into the old city park. It stopped in the shade of three aged oaks. There, families gathered with hand trucks and children's wagons. Someone had a gator—an ATV with a cart on the back. It looked like they used anything they had with wheels to haul home their shares of corn. Once there, they'd dry it and grind it into cornmeal, or cook and can it.

My phone was silent, and I assumed the receptionist hadn't yet found the admissions officer.

Something needled at me. "You know it's odd," I said to Hannah.

"What?"

"All three of the homes with missing girls—my family's, the Heatons' and Coombs' houses—all back up to the cornfield."

Hannah appeared to consider that for a moment. "I hadn't thought about that. It is odd."

I thought again about my brother-in-law, Jim Daniels, the man who managed the cornfield.

On the phone, someone said, "Samantha here."

"Hi, Samantha," I said, putting her on the car's speaker system. "I'm Detective Clara Jefferies. I'm looking into the cases of some missing girls in a small town called Alber."

"I've heard of that place," she said. "We get kids from there. Mostly boys, though."

"Well, I'm hoping you can help me. Jayme Coombs' mother says that her daughter is at your center. Can you tell me if Jayme is there? If she was there? If she's left, where you referred her? This is a welfare check."

"Sure," Samantha said. "Describe her. It'll make it easier."

I whispered to Hannah. "Tell her what Jayme looks like."

"Jayme is about five foot two, long dark-blond hair, kind of wide blue-gray eyes. Slight build."

"How old?"

"Sixteen," Hannah said.

"Okay. I'll ask around, get back with you," Samantha said. "It may take a while. I need to check with the shelters."

"Don't you have a list you can check?" I asked. "Just run the name through the computer?"

Samantha chuckled. "The kids from those mountain towns rush through here like flash floods. They're here one minute, on their way somewhere else the next. We try, but we can't stay on top of record-keeping. Our staff is small."

"How are you going to look for her?" I asked.

"We've got other kids from Alber in the program. We'll ask around. Some of them live at the shelters. Odds are if Jayme is or was there, they'll know."

It sounded like the best we could do. "Okay, but one more thing."

"Sure," she said. "What?"

"While you're doing this, check on a couple more girls for me. They're all from Alber. The first one is Eliza Heaton, age seventeen."

I looked at Hannah.

"She's taller," Hannah said. "Maybe five foot six or seven. Green eyes. Long dark hair. Pretty girl."

"Got it. And the third?"

"We're also concerned about the whereabouts of a twelve-year-old."

Samantha let out a soft whistle. "That's pretty young for us. I don't remember seeing anyone that young in a while. But I'll give it a try. What's her name?"

"Delilah Jefferies," I said.

"Description?" she asked.

"Auburn hair, turned-up nose, freckles. Cute kid," I said based on old memories.

"Height? Weight?" Samantha queried.

I felt a pang of regret and even shame that I couldn't better describe my own sibling. Thankfully, Hannah jumped in to answer. "Delilah is just under five foot tall, maybe ninety, something less than a hundred pounds."

Samantha paused, and I assumed she was writing it all down. "Jefferies? Isn't that your last name, Detective?"

"Delilah is my half-sister," I said.

"Oh. I'm sorry," Samantha said. Her voice dropped an octave. "Tough."

"Take a look and get back to me as soon as possible?"

"You've got it," she said. "And detective…"

"Yes?"

"Try not to worry. Most times, these kids show up."

I wanted to, but I didn't believe her.

CHAPTER EIGHTEEN

After the meeting at the Alber police department, Max headed back toward the highway. At the stop sign before he turned onto the main road, he reread the text from the sheriff:

> *Heard from Chief Barstow early this a.m. about NCIC report. That woman is off base. You brought her here. You need to get rid of her. Report to headquarters, ASAP. We need to talk!*

"Shit," he said, shaking his head. "Damn it, Clara."

Rather than setting a course straight back to the office, Max drove around for half an hour, eventually making a left off the highway and heading toward the river. He turned onto a dirt road he hadn't taken in years, not since his return to Alber. Minutes later, he arrived at a path that wound into the trees. He parked the car and trekked through the woods, stopped along the riverbank and looked out at the scenery.

This is it, he thought. *This is where we were standing when Clara kissed me.*

How many years had it been? Half his life ago, a bit more. That one kiss changed everything. He was on a path, planning to stay in Alber, near family. Then Clara kissed him. He didn't pull back, sure, but she was the one who suggested they skip school that day and go to the river. He'd been attracted to her for a couple of years, and dreamed of being alone with her. He remembered the excitement deep in his soul as they planned their escape. His first crush. His first love.

To Max, it had seemed predestined that one day they'd be together. He didn't object when she took his face in her hands and moved closer until their lips met. He'd never been kissed like that before, but he'd fantasized about what it would feel like to be so close to her, to meld into her, to touch her.

As their lips met, Clara's father had broken the spell.

"Stop!" Abraham Jefferies had shouted, as he stalked toward them with the determination of a man on a mission. Max saw outrage burning in the older man's eyes.

That day changed his life, but not in the way he'd hoped it would; because of that kiss, the church hierarchy sent him away.

When his father drove off and left him standing alone on the street, Max had nowhere to go. No one to rely on. For the first time in his life, he was truly frightened. He'd faced difficult, dangerous years when he feared he'd lose his way. Then he'd found Miriam. They had Brooke. Life was perfect.

The accident ended all that.

The grief nearly killed him, sent him reeling to the bottle while Brooke fought for her life. When she'd needed him most, he was barely rational. Overcome with guilt and regret, he'd almost lost her. She'd pulled through but never to be the same. By the time he'd fought through the pain enough to see what he was doing to his daughter, by the time he'd walked away from the booze and tried to reclaim his life, he'd lost his job, their security, and their health insurance, the very thing Brooke needed most.

His phone rang, his sister Alice calling. Max let it ring four times before he picked up. "Sheriff Holmes called. He's looking for you," she said. Alice knew about the booze and the depression. She sounded worried. "Are you okay?"

"Sure, no problem," he said. "What did the sheriff want?"

"Said he was waiting on you."

Max thought about the text: *Report to headquarters, ASAP. We need to talk!*

"How's Brooke today?"

"Like every day, working hard. The therapist is here. She has Brooke on the floor exercising," Alice said. She lowered her voice and whispered into the phone, "Sometimes it makes me want to cry. You can see the pain in her eyes. The girl's got grit going for her."

"That she has," Max agreed.

"I think you'd better check in with the sheriff," Alice said. "I wouldn't say he sounded mad, but he didn't sound happy."

"I'll head over to the office. Don't worry."

Back in the car, Max thought about Delilah. His gut hadn't settled down about the girl. He still worried about her safety, but Ardeth and the others had told Gerard Barstow that Delilah was safe. And the sheriff had given an order. This wasn't Max's case any longer. *I can't lose this job. I failed Brooke before. I can't fail her again.*

When Max considered their history, Clara Jefferies had sent his life tumbling into a free fall once before, and he'd paid a stiff price. As much as he'd yearned to see her, he wouldn't let her do it again. As he turned onto the highway, Max pressed the voice command button on his car's steering wheel. "Call Clara Jefferies."

The buzz of the phone filled the car, but no one answered.

Clara's voicemail picked up.

CHAPTER NINETEEN

"Can you hear me?"

Delilah thought she had to be dreaming. The faint, disembodied voice drifted into the room seemingly from nowhere. It sounded high-pitched, young and feminine. She thought about responding, but stopped. The man could be behind it. He said she had to prove that he could trust her. Maybe the voice was a test.

She hadn't been able to put out of her mind what he said earlier, when he saw that she'd managed to push her blindfold off: "I haven't had any of them do that before."

Any of them? Other girls? Girls he locked up in the house before her?

The man hadn't told her not to talk to anyone, but she instinctively knew he wouldn't like it. Although he'd fed her maybe an hour earlier, her stomach growled near empty. Delilah stared at the stain on the mattress and wondered whose blood it was. She thought about the voice and the woman who helped her. Could she be another prisoner?

"Can you hear me?"

"Yes, I'm—" When she heard the voice the second time, Delilah began to answer but abruptly stopped. She longed for someone to talk to, but was it worth taking the risk? What if it was some kind of sick trick?

"Say something if you can hear me."

The third time she heard the voice, Delilah thought about what she had to lose if she responded and the man heard her. She'd asked him to unlock the chains that pinched her wrists and ankles, the bonds that kept her from moving about the room, of stretching out to sleep. To use the bucket he gave her for a toilet, she had to inch over, her legs cramping beneath her. Her arms throbbed every time she nudged up her skirt.

As meager a victory as it would be, the ability to walk around the room shined like a beacon.

Then she heard it again.

"It's me. The girl who was in your room. Answer me."

Delilah knelt and looked about the room, searching. Her eyes settled on a heating vent cut into the baseboard where the floor met the wall, to the right of the boarded-up window. That must be where the voice came from. Delilah stared at the vent, waiting to hear the voice again. She decided that the next time, she would take a chance. She would answer.

Minutes passed. Hours ticked by.

Only silence.

CHAPTER TWENTY

As I hung up with Samantha at the youth center, my phone vibrated and I clicked onto voicemail. Max's voice came over the SUV's speaker. "Clara, I'm sorry the meeting didn't go better this morning, but I want to make it clear that I agree with the chief. It seems that I've brought you here for nothing. I never should have called you. It's time for you to go home to Dallas. I'll keep you posted if anything develops."

In the passenger seat, Hannah turned toward me. "What's Max talking about? Did they tell you to go home?"

There were a few things I hadn't mentioned to Hannah. No reason to make her worry. "The men agreed that I need to leave," I said. "I disagreed."

Hannah gave me a knowing frown. "So we're all alone in this?"

"It looks like it," I admitted. "I'm sorry for dragging you into it."

At first, Hannah appeared apprehensive, but she said, "No, it's okay. I understand how worried you are about Delilah. And I was the one who told you about Eliza and Jayme. But Clara, this isn't what I do. I'm not a cop. Do you have a plan?"

"Sure," I said, only partially lying. "While I wait for Samantha to get back to me, we're going to the shelter. I know you need to get back there, and I have things to do on my laptop. I'm curious about someone. I want to know more about him."

"Who?"

"I'd rather not say."

Hannah's frown grew deeper, but she didn't press for more information. "I'm surprised Max sided with the others. It doesn't seem like him."

"At the meeting, he took my side at one point. I don't think he's convinced that Delilah is safe," I said. "The old Max, the boy I knew when we were kids, would have backed me up all the way, but he's changed."

Hannah looked hesitant, like she wasn't sure she should respond, but then said, "Clara, I've always suspected that Max never got over you. He's asked me about you often in the year or so since he moved back, wanted to know if I'd heard from you. When he asked you to come back, I wondered if it was only about Delilah – I thought maybe there was still a spark there. You two were close. It's not impossible that you two would…"

My nerves kicked up full throttle, an automatic reflex when anyone suggested anything could happen between me and a man. I focused on the road. Until the previous day, we hadn't seen each other in years, but Hannah apparently still had the ability to decipher my body language. "You know, there are a lot of good men out there," she said, her voice soft, coaxing.

"Absolutely."

"But you're…?"

"Looking for Delilah," I said. I shot her a glance that said I didn't want advice. "This is what I do. I'm a cop. And to me, this makes sense. Things get personal… my experience is that if you let anyone get too close, they disappoint you."

"You're really talking about men," Hannah said.

We turned the corner and drove along the diminishing cornfield, row after row harvested and chopped down. "There have been times when I've felt like one of those cornstalks," I said.

"I don't understand."

"The only things of value I had were taken from me, like the cobs torn from their stems. Then my life was cut down and mowed under."

A look of incredible sadness washed over Hannah. "Clara, all men aren't the enemy."

"I know, but this is the best I can do," I admitted. "It's hard to forget. It's hard to trust anyone when the man I should have most been able to trust above all others betrayed me…" Hannah gave me a knowing look, and I finished my sentence, "my own father."

"Maybe you don't need to forget," Hannah offered. "My guess is that what you really need to do is find a way to understand and forgive."

We drove on in silence. I thought of the tattoo on my arm, the eagle I carried with me, my reminder of home. Yet Alber had always been a complicated memory. Here I'd had the love of family, and I'd seen harsh judgment. Perhaps more than anything, Alber was a place where dark secrets flourished in the shadows.

As I drove past the big houses, I thought of ever-watchful eyes peeking out from behind heavy curtains. Eyes that saw me, recognized me, and turned away.

Minutes later, I pulled over and parked in front of the shelter. As we walked inside, I looked again at what fifty years earlier old man Barstow had permanently bricked onto the side of his mansion:

OBEY AND BE REDEEMED

I thought about the word obey, and how those who do it can unthinkingly give over control of their lives to others.

A cluster of women congregated at the front door when Hannah and I walked into the shelter. One woman, young, maybe early twenties, held a baby bundled in receiving blankets. A toddler in worn-thin coveralls clutched her leg, as if to let go risked his life.

He looked up at me, his face twisted in fear. One small black, suitcase—the old-fashioned kind without wheels, a bright red belt wrapped around it to keep it closed—rested beside them. The woman whispered to the others between sobs. "I can't stay anymore. It was bad enough with him there. Now that our husband's gone, the other wives don't want me or my kids. If I can't stay here, I don't know where I'll go."

Hannah angled over to talk to her. As I climbed the stairs, she slipped her arm around the woman's waist. "Of course, you'll stay. We're tight for space, but there's always room. For the time being, you'll bunk with another family, two little ones about your little boy's age."

"I can't pay," the woman said.

"No one pays here, but you'll be expected to help with chores," Hannah said. "Let's get you three settled."

I stopped on the stairs and looked down at them. "She can have the room I'm in."

Hannah shook her head. "We'll move someone in there when you move out. We'll manage for now."

Once in my room, I sat on the bed and logged on to my laptop. I wanted whatever information I could find on Evan Barstow. Our encounter in his brother's office that morning bothered me. It seemed personal to Evan, when he pushed Gerard to get rid of me.

First, I looked up Hitchins, Utah, and discovered it was a small farming community of 1,936 folks thirty miles west of Alber. On Google Maps I traveled up and down the few streets. I suspected Hitchins was another polygamous town. A review on TripAdvisor verified that. "We drove through and saw folks dressed like extras for *Little House on the Prairie*. Don't plan to stop here. No restaurant or hotel. The locals don't want visitors! A cop car followed us through town and made sure we left."

When I read that last bit, I thought of my after-dark drive with Hannah the night before, Gerard falling in behind us and trailing us through Alber all the way to the trailer park gate.

I wanted to know more about the man. On Google, I typed in EVAN BARSTOW UTAH. Pages of articles and websites appeared, all having nothing to do with the Evan Barstow I was interested in. Hitchins and Alber both being fairly off the grid, I didn't find any articles about the police in either town. Nothing about big arrests, no photos of either of the Barstow boys handing out plaques to faithful officers or awards to residents who distinguished themselves by helping the local cops. None of the normal cop stuff.

From there, I opened usacops.com and scanned lists of Utah law enforcement agencies. That brought basic information on the departments, addresses for their headquarters and the names of those in charge. The Hitchins PD page listed Evan as chief. A link took me to the department's rudimentary website, where I found a small headshot of Evan and a department list with phone numbers and email addresses.

I snipped the photo of Evan, saved it, and then sent it on an email to my cell. I did the same with the phone number list.

That done, I logged on to my account with Dallas PD and went directly to a database the department pays for, one that compiles public records, including property and driver's information, voter registration, criminal indictments, convictions, and civil suits. I plugged in Evan's name, but little came up. I thought about how folks in law enforcement often hide their information, getting special permission from state and local governments to keep it off the Internet. This wasn't going to be easy. I had no better luck when I looked for property and driver's license records, nothing that included an address.

Then I had another thought.

I found Hannah downstairs in a bedroom with two sets of bunks and three twin beds, all laid out side to side. The new woman leaned over one of the beds, changing her baby's diaper. Her boy had finally let go of her leg and sat on the floor playing with an old wooden Thomas the Tank Engine.

"Can we talk? I only need a minute," I asked, peering in the doorway.

"Sure." Hannah turned back to her new boarder. "You and the children settle in. I'll find something for the baby to sleep in."

"What do you need?" she asked as soon as we were out of earshot, but she kept walking, going door to door, knocking, and looking in. "I know there's an extra crib in one of these rooms. If not, there has to be a playpen."

"Do you know the family names of Evan Barstow's wives? Not the first wife, but the others."

Hannah stopped. She closed her eyes and dropped her head. When she looked up at me, her mouth sank at both corners. "Clara, you're not investigating him, are you?"

"I just need the wives' names," I said. "That's all."

Hannah put both hands on my shoulders and stared at me. "Tell me it's not Evan Barstow you're researching. He's not someone you want to fool with. Believe me when I say that it would be a mistake."

"I understand. But I need his wives' maiden names."

"Why do I feel I shouldn't do this?" she asked.

I shrugged. "I don't know. It's a simple question."

Hannah shook her head. "I think there are three wives. The second and third are Jessica Bradshaw and Flo Jenkins."

"Thanks." I turned to go, and when I looked back Hannah watched me, her face a mask of worry.

Back on my laptop, I searched for information on Evan's second and third wives. The thing with polygamy is that it's illegal in the United States. It has been since 1862. That makes living the principle a somewhat complicated lifestyle. Over the decades, the problem has been solved by a technical maneuver: husbands only legally marry their first wives. Successive women are sealed to the men in religious ceremonies, but by no civil records filed at county courthouses. While in their day-to-day lives Jessica and Flo went by the last name Barstow, for legal matters most plural wives used their maiden names.

Half an hour later, a search of driver's license records revealed an address shared by a Flo Jenkins and a Jessica Bradshaw, my guess the house where Evan Barstow's family resided. When I looked up the property on Google Maps, it was a sprawling ranch near the mountains.

Mission accomplished, I turned off my laptop, just as my phone rang.

"We couldn't find out much, Detective," Samantha said. "There's a boy in one of the group homes who remembers Eliza Heaton, but only from growing up with her in Alber. He hasn't seen her in Salt Lake."

"What about Jayme Coombs and Delilah Jefferies?"

"Nothing. But that doesn't mean the girls didn't go through here at some point. Like I said, our files are pretty sketchy. They may have stopped at the center, had a meal or two, picked up some materials, and moved on. If they didn't ask for help finding shelter, we won't have records."

"Okay. Thanks."

Another dead end.

I shouted at Hannah on my way out the door. "Not sure when, but I'll see you later."

"Clara!" Hannah bellowed. I glanced back at her. "Be careful!"

CHAPTER TWENTY-ONE

It was still only 9.30 a.m. when I set a course for the Barstow family residence, reasoning that with any luck Evan wouldn't be there. It was hours before lunch, and I assumed he'd have gone to his office after our early-morning confrontation at Alber PD. I thought again about the way he glared at me as Stephanie Jonas handed me her card. One thing was clear: my presence upset him.

Why? Was he involved in Delilah's disappearance?

On the drive, I debated what I was looking for and how to find it. I really had no idea. I was playing a hunch. Evan Barstow had caught my interest, and I needed to know more about him. Reasoning it through, I didn't believe that if Evan had Delilah he would hide her on the farm, surrounded by his family. Evan was smarter than that. Even if he thought he had control of the women, the children might talk. Secrets known by too many are hard to keep. Still, I couldn't be sure. The thought that my sister could be hidden somewhere in Evan's house pricked at my nerves.

Reflecting on my situation I also considered that, in a strange twist of fate, being a regular citizen worked to my advantage.

As the sheriff and the Barstow boys had pointed out, I had no jurisdiction in Alber. I certainly had none in Hitchins. Making an official visit, I would have had to abide by the rules and identify myself as law enforcement. Under the current circumstances, I had no more status than any interested party. That meant more freedom.

Yet, I'd embarked on the ultimate fishing expedition. I had no idea what to look for. My only hope: that if there was something on the property tied to Delilah, I'd notice it. But for that to be possible, it had to stand out enough to attract my attention. Admittedly, that was a long shot. After all, I'd had no contact with my sister in a decade.

Evan Barstow's spread, between Alber and Hitchins, looked like a typical farmhouse—peaked roof, bluish-gray siding, and a broad front porch with four rocking chairs. A circle of pines, maples, and a few oaks buffered the house from the sun creeping higher in the east.

I drove past twice, sizing up the situation and formulating a plan. I didn't see Evan's official car, leading me to believe that, as I'd hoped, he wasn't home. A woman in a long dress rode a mower through the yard, cutting the grass. Children milled around, playing ball and pushing each other on swings, while a second woman watched from one of the chairs on the porch.

On my third pass, I turned my phone off and rubbed my eyes to get them a little red. Cattle and horses grazed on both sides of the long driveway. At the sound of my SUV hitting the gravel, the woman supervising the children stood. Immediately, she shouted at the little ones to rush into the house. The woman on the mower wore headphones to block the engine noise, and apparently didn't hear my car or her sister-wife's shouts.

I parked the car, scrambled out, and made a beeline toward the woman on the mower. At that precise moment, she made a 180-degree turn. She jerked a bit in surprise to see me, pulled the mower to an abrupt stop and flipped off the engine. I wasn't surprised when she scanned the yard for the children and her sister-wife. Families who live in the shadows hide from the outside world. She had to wonder who had come unannounced and what I intended.

To defuse the situation, I deployed my most sociable smile. I waved, as friendly as a next-door neighbor dropping in for cookies and tea. She slipped off her headphones.

"Ma'am, I'm wondering if you can help me. I'm in a pickle," I said. With that, I brushed at my eyes with the back of my hand, as if wiping away tears. "Maybe you saw me drive past a couple of times? I'm trying to find my way to St. George. I'm lost. I don't know how, but I took a wrong turn. And I need to call my sister to tell her that I'm going to be late. I need to get her to the doctor for her treatments. I promised. I just can't let her down." I gulped, like I was trying to hold back sobs. "She must be worried sick that I'm not there."

"Oh, dear, that's terrible." A tall woman with a rawboned face and clear blue eyes, she smelled of sweat, dust, and grass as she walked toward me. "Why don't you use your cell?"

"That's the problem," I said, holding up my phone's blank screen. "I do such stupid things sometimes. I didn't bring the cord, and it's out of power. And the car's navigation system hasn't worked in more than a year."

"Well, I…" she said. "I don't have a cell phone. My husband has one, but he's not home. All we have is the house phone, but he wouldn't like it if I let you in."

"Oh, it would just be a minute. If I could use any phone, it would be such a blessing," I said. In this world, I understood what people wanted to hear. "I was praying for help when I saw you."

"Well…"

"Any map would work. My sister lives a few blocks from the downtown temple. If I get there, I can find her house."

The woman paused, I guessed assessing the situation. I was a woman alone, in my scenario lost on the road. She smiled ever so slightly. When she spoke, she sounded pleased that she could help. "My husband has a map in the kitchen. I think it has a blow-up of St. George. Let's go inside, and we'll get you taken care of."

On the front porch, the screen door rattled, and I was inside. The furniture was aged and worn, the house conspicuously clean. "I'm Jessica," the woman said.

"I'm Jane," I said, looking around. I stared at the staircase and wondered about the rooms upstairs. Could Delilah be confined there? Did she see me arrive? Of course, if she had, she wouldn't know me, or realize that I'd come looking for her. "It's nice to meet you," I said to Jessica.

"Stay here," she said. "I'll bring the map. It may take me a few minutes to find it."

She hurried from the room. I waited until she disappeared through a doorway, and then walked toward it. I paused when I heard another woman whisper, "You shouldn't have brought her in here. If Evan finds out, he'll be mad."

"We won't tell him. Then there isn't a problem. Take the children upstairs, and don't come down until I tell you. She'll be gone in a few minutes," Jessica said.

A herd of footsteps ran up a back staircase. Frustrated, I realized I couldn't risk sneaking up the stairs to the second floor to look for Delilah, not with Evan's wives and children peering from the shadows. *Oh, Delilah, where are you? Are you here?*

I heard rustling from the kitchen—Jessica rifling through drawers, looking for the map. If I couldn't get upstairs, I still intended to see as much of the house as I could. Quietly, I stepped back and turned to the right, into the living room. Over the fireplace hung a family portrait, a photo with Evan Barstow in the center, three wives including Jessica beside him, surrounded by thirteen children. The room had couches against three walls and a bulky recliner in one corner, lamp tables and a barren pine coffee table.

I glanced over the room, looking for something, anything out of place, while I listened for Jessica to return. Nothing. From the living room, I turned into the dining room, a long table encircled by seventeen chairs, including two high chairs, a wooden bowl of bright red apples in the center.

"What are you looking for?" Jessica asked. She stood in the doorway with a confused look on her face. She held a folded map.

"The phone," I said, smiling broadly. "I thought I could call, to tell my sister what happened and that I'm on my way."

"Oh," she said. "Well, okay. I'll take you to the phone. But let's get the directions figured out first."

I followed her into another room, a man's study. Evan had a large carved maple desk in the center, the legs ending in claw feet. Behind the desk a hunting trophy stared down at us—the long-snouted head of a bull moose, its bulky rack of antlers nearly four foot across. Shelves lining the walls strained under the weight of encyclopedias, religious books, math and science texts, and children's chapter books. Evan's wives, it appeared, homeschooled.

Jessica spread the map across the desk. I stood a step back, hoping she wouldn't notice that I wasn't following her finger as she traced the route from the house to St. George. "It's really easy," she said, "You just have to…"

Framed family photos and a stack of bills sat on the desk. I saw a computer hookup where Evan must have plugged in his laptop. Everything looked maddeningly ordinary.

"Do you have it memorized?" Jessica asked. "Can you get to your sister's house?"

"I think so," I said, focusing my eyes back on hers. "That's such a great help. I don't know what I would have done if you hadn't helped me. Thank you."

"You still want to call your sister?"

"Yes, please," I said. "I'm just so worried. I need to get there fast. But yes, I need to call. I'm sure she's frantic."

"Follow me," Jessica said.

We walked into the kitchen.

"It's right there," Jessica said, pointing at an old-fashioned wall phone.

I picked up the handset. She watched while I listened for a dial tone and punched in a Salt Lake area code, 801. Then I turned my back and pushed random keys. I pressed the hang-up button to disconnect. "It's me. I got lost and my phone's out of power," I said into the dead phone. "But a wonderful woman helped me. I'll leave her house in a minute. I'm about…"

I looked at Jessica and mouthed "an hour?" She held up two fingers.

"I'm about two hours from your house. I know it'll be tight, but please don't worry. I'll be there soon." I acted as if I listened to someone else talk, and then said goodbye and hung up the phone.

"Thank you again," I said to Jessica. To stall, I asked, "I'm so dry. May I trouble you for one more thing? A little water?"

"Of course." Jessica grabbed a glass and filled it out of the faucet. She handed it to me, and I sipped slowly, buying time, while I looked around the kitchen. More children's books were stacked on the kitchen table, and on the wall hung a whiteboard with simple math problems, addition and subtraction.

As I emptied the glass, I noticed a flashlight on the counter— long, heavy, and neon-orange. The color reminded me of the warning cones I put out at car accidents during my early years as a cop when I worked patrol.

"All set now?" she asked, as I handed her the empty glass. Jessica had been kind, patient with me, but she wanted me to leave.

"Yes. Thank you."

Once inside the car, I looked back at the house. Jessica stood on the porch, arms folded across her chest. I saw no one else, but in nearly every window curtains were pulled back. Hidden behind them, the sister-wives and their children waited for me to leave. Did anyone else watch? Could Delilah be looking out from behind one of those windows as I pulled away?

"If you're there, help me find you," I whispered, as I continued down the driveway. I glanced back one more time in the rearview mirror, but I saw nothing to justify my suspicions. Frustrated, I realized that my quest had been a waste of time. Half a mile up the road, I turned my phone back on. As soon as it booted, a text message popped up from Max.

Clara, come to the sheriff's office ASAP.

CHAPTER TWENTY-TWO

The monotony wore on Delilah, leaving her feeling disconnected and weary. She wished he'd unchain her arms. Her legs and chest itched, and it was torture not to be able to scratch. She'd counted four days since he'd taken her, and all she wanted was to be home with her family. When the panic built inside her, she envisioned her mother's face. That became her safe place, the memory she called on to blunt her terror.

"I'm here. Can you hear me?"

Although Delilah had hoped to hear it again, when the voice floated up the vent into her room, it startled her.

"Yes," she whispered. "I can hear you. Where are you?"

Delilah worried that she'd been right and it was all a trick, that the man would come screaming into the room to rebuke and punish her. The prickly lumps her mom called goosebumps erupted on her arms. Delilah waited, dreading the sound of his boots on the floorboards. She tried to think of an excuse to use, so he wouldn't be mad.

Time passed. Nothing happened. He didn't come.

"Where are you?" Delilah asked, this time louder.

"Downstairs, locked in the room below you."

"Who are you?"

"That girl who fed you. I came with the man."

"Thank you, I—"

"Did he take you?" the downstairs girl asked.

"Yes, I—"

"He grabbed me when I was outside working. My mom had me picking through rags, finding ones to sew into rugs. She sells them."

"I was outside, too, waiting for my sister by the outhouse."

"Oh," the girl said.

"I think he watched me from the cornfield," Delilah said.

"He watched me, too."

Delilah thought about that, how they'd both been abducted so close to their homes.

"I'm Delilah. What's your name?"

The girl didn't answer. Instead, the next thing Delilah heard came in a whisper.

"He's coming."

CHAPTER TWENTY-THREE

I made good time on the drive to the sheriff's department until I passed Alber and got stuck behind two trucks, their beds stacked five high with bags of silage. The harvest must have been going well. They'd accomplished a lot in less than half a day, snapping off the cobs, cutting and chopping the stalks. For some reason, an unusual amount of traffic clogged the road. After three attempts, I passed the trucks and sped up.

Fifteen minutes later, I arrived at the Smith County Courthouse. I felt a pang of concern when I saw Gerard's black Suburban parked crooked out front, taking up two spaces. It looked like the chief arrived in a hurry and hadn't paid attention. Of course, he probably didn't worry that anyone would write him a ticket.

At a quarter past eleven on a Monday morning, the sheriff's department buzzed with activity, every desk taken. Deputies milled about, and two women worked the phones. I started back toward Max's office, but one of the women rushed to stop me. Grandmotherly with a silver-gray French twist, she had the manner of an agitated canary. She introduced herself as Helen Jamison, the sheriff's personal secretary.

"This way, Detective," she said.

"Isn't Chief Deputy Anderson's office over there?" I said, pointing in the opposite direction.

"The sheriff wants to talk to you," she said.

It felt like a replay of my meeting at the police station. Perhaps I would have to get used to being greeted by angry shouts. I heard raised voices before I made it down the hallway. I hesitated before walking in, wanting to hear the discussion. This time Gerard was on a rampage.

"Max, why would you send Clara Jefferies into my town to rile those folks up?" Just a few hours earlier, Gerard had been the calmer of the Barstow brothers, but he sounded spitting mad. He must have heard that I'd dropped in on the Heaton and Coombs families and wasn't pleased. "I have a hard enough time convincing those polygamous folks to talk to me. Now they think I sent in some outside cop, an apostate to boot."

"I told you, I didn't send Clara," Max said. I sensed he was struggling to keep his voice level. "But she's a seasoned investigator. Let's just wait and hear what she has to say before we get all bent out of shape. Sheriff Holmes, Clara must have had a reason to—"

"What reason? Those parents aren't worried about their girls," the chief roared like a referee shouting over the crowd to call a foul at a ball game. "Then some woman cop shows up, bribes a little kid with a fistful of bills and demands the kid tell her where his sister is. Dragging Hannah Jessop with her. Stirring up trouble in Alber, when we all know the town's a powder keg with all the strangers moving in. What good could—"

Max tried to calm him. "Gerard, I don't think Clara meant to stir anyone up."

"No matter what her intentions were, we can't have that Dallas detective barging in on people. We can't tolerate it," said a voice I assumed belonged to the sheriff.

I'd heard enough.

"Max is telling you the truth. He didn't send me anywhere. I didn't consult him on my plans," I said as I entered the lions' den. "That said, I guess you could say that I did bribe the Coombs kid, although I saw it as more of a donation."

"Clara, let's talk about this. Please explain what's—" Max started.

"I got two complaints about you this morning, Detective," Gerard said, holding up the sausage-size index and middle fingers on his right hand to drive his point home. His anger raised his round cheeks until his eyes were slits. "First Alma Heaton calls, upset because you demanded information on Eliza. Then Mrs. Coombs gets lathered up about you giving her kid money and asking questions about Jayme."

"Come on, Chief." I tried to defuse the situation. "Mrs. Coombs couldn't have been that upset. Not when she needed money to turn her electricity back on. She didn't give the cash back, did she?"

Gerard didn't answer. "What my brother Evan said this morning is right. You've got no right to push your nose into my town. I want you gone."

Max moved forward, looking as if he wanted to interrupt, but unsure what to say. I'd admittedly crossed lines, and I knew I'd become hard to defend, but I felt a wave of disappointment when the sheriff put his hand on Max's shoulder. Max took two steps back and said nothing. Just the sheriff's touch was enough to silence him.

"I may not have jurisdiction, but I have rights," I insisted. "I'm Delilah's sister."

"No matter what crazy ideas you have, that's over. Your mother said Delilah is fine," Gerard said, spitting out the words. "But we're not talking about Delilah anyway. This is about the Heaton and the Coombs families, Eliza and Jayme. There's no reason to think there's anything wrong with those girls."

"Some people in town find the girls' disappearances troubling," I said.

"Hannah," Max whispered. He looked as if I'd opened a box he'd closed. "She mentioned it to me, but I didn't think… Are you worried that they could have been…?" His voice drifted off.

"Maybe all three girls are safe. Maybe there's no problem here. But what Hannah describes is strange. The girls left too abruptly,"

I said. "Hannah was close to both girls, and neither one confided in her that they were leaving."

"Clara, kids take off. They run away," Max stammered. "After Hannah talked to me about Jayme and Eliza, the chief talked to their families. Both told him that the girls left on their own, that they ran away."

"They did tell me that. There's not a lick of evidence that there's anything wrong here." Gerard shook his head, as if in astonishment. "This is getting more ridiculous by the minute."

"What if the families are wrong? What if all three girls are missing, and no one is looking for them?" I asked. "Sometimes, disappearances are connected. One perpetrator, multiple victims."

"You think Eliza Heaton and Jayme Coombs have been abducted, don't you?" Max asked.

"This is ridiculous!" Gerard looked at the other men as if asking for help. Max had a worried expression, perhaps thinking through my scenario. The sheriff? He appeared uncomfortable enough with the conversation to want to order us all from his office.

"The Heaton and Coombs families say their daughters ran away, not that they were taken," Gerard said. "And I told you last night that your mother told me Delilah is on a mission."

"All three girls disappeared under questionable circumstances. Eliza and Jayme without notice, and with Delilah there's the note," I said.

"That damn note. They didn't—" Gerard started.

"And Gerard, I remember other things, too. Things that make me question how cases like these are handled by your department."

"What the?" he sputtered. "You can't talk to me like—"

"Alber PD has never had a good reputation. For decades it was under the thumb of the church hierarchy and the police haven't always been on the right side."

At that, Gerard's eyes focused hard on mine. "The town's changed. You can see that. The police department has changed," he bellowed. "And I'm not part of the old establishment. I'm like Max. I got railroaded out of Alber when I was a kid."

That had been bothering me. "Why?"

Barstow looked baffled. "What do you mean, why?"

"No Barstow boys were ever run out of Alber. Not in my memory, and I bet no one else can recall an instance. For decades, your family ran this town, including city hall and the police department. No one dared cross the Barstows."

"What's your point?" Gerard gave me a look that challenged me to answer.

This was becoming personal. "Detective Jefferies, this isn't productive," the sheriff said. "Let's not dig up old history."

"I want an answer," I said. "I want to know why Gerard was the only Barstow boy ever forced out of Alber." I turned to the chief and asked, "What did you do?"

Gerard Barstow tracked toward me, as angry as I've ever seen a man. But at that precise moment, the phone on the desk buzzed. The sheriff latched onto it, perhaps pleased with the distraction.

Not ready to let up, I prodded, "I think you should answer, Gerard. Tell me why you were forced out."

Gerard turned to the sheriff, I supposed to enlist his aid. But Sheriff Holmes had refocused his attention on the phone call. We all stopped talking and stared at him, as his face blanched pale.

"I'll be right there," he said, and then he hung up. "Chief, we need to put this to bed, at least for now."

"Sheriff, I shouldn't have to tolerate—" Barstow started.

"Max, round up everyone you can find and the CSI folks," the sheriff ordered. "We need to head over to Alber. Someone found a body."

"That's my town," Gerard objected.

"Not the back of the trailer park, Chief," the sheriff said. "That area below the mountain is outside the city limits. It's in the county. It's mine."

Without asking a single question, Max rushed from the room.

The trailer park. My family. My mother. Delilah. A body.

"A man's or a woman's body? A child?" I asked. "How long dead?"

"I don't know," the sheriff said. "They found it hidden behind the cornfield."

CHAPTER TWENTY-FOUR

I trailed the caravan of squads and the crime scene unit's mobile base, fashioned out of a converted horse trailer, to Alber. We passed fields planted with alfalfa and wheat, herds of cattle and bison. I wondered whose body had been found, if it was Eliza or Jayme. If it was Delilah. My mind wandered back to Dallas. *As hard as I'd tried, I couldn't save him.*

Driving past the trailers, I flashed back to the boy's body, dismembered, nearly destroyed. I tried to blot out the image. At least his parents had been held back, not allowed inside the house where they would have seen the horror of what remained of their son. His mother dropped to her knees when I told her the boy was dead. I knelt beside her and held her. I tried to soften the blow, but there is pain that it's impossible to lessen.

As well as horrors that are impossible to unsee.

Overwhelming dread flooded through me, as I wondered what waited for us in the cornfield. My grip on the steering wheel tightened as the grisly vision refused to leave. The blood. The slaughtered child. In seconds the image transformed from the body of a young boy to that of a girl—ivory skin, long auburn hair. When I saw freckles on her upturned nose, I fought to stifle a scream.

We reached the two dozen or so remaining rows of corn, and the cars at the lead pulled over, the deputies and officers hastily disembarking and advancing on foot. I grabbed my bag with my badge and gun inside. Behind the cornfield, we picked our way around and over rocks, the mountain looming above us. Boulders, some as tall as we stood, had fallen from the mountaintop over the millennia. I guessed townsfolk discarded many of the smaller rocks a hundred years earlier when they first cleared the fields to plant.

Up ahead, the troopers congregated at the far east corner, below Samuel's Peak.

"What've we got?" I shouted as I walked up.

Apparently everyone was still trying to figure that out for themselves and no one responded. I found Max talking to a man with two dogs on leashes standing separate from the rest, a black Lab and a small gray-and-beige fellow that looked like some kind of terrier mix.

"A body, no description yet. It's buried under a layer of rocks," Max pointed to a mound fifty yards away. "Not sure how long, but it sounds like whoever it is has been dead for some time."

"Looked like that to me at least," the man told Max.

I knew him. His name was John Proctor. A mechanic, he used to repair my father's saws at the mill. In my decade away, Mr. Proctor had acquired the heavily lined face of a man well into his eighties. His bushy hair had turned stark white, and he carried a wooden cane with a carved stag's head at the top.

"Somebody notify the coroner?" I asked Max.

"Yeah. I did before we left the office. Doc Wiley from Wilbur. He's been ME for the county for the past four or five years. He's on his way. Should be here soon."

"I remember him," I said. "He trains the midwives in town."

"That's him," Max said.

That settled, I turned to our companion. "Mr. Proctor, tell us what happened here."

The old man looked at me warily. I'd pinned my badge on my shirt during the walk to make sure I wasn't stopped from entering the scene. Proctor recognized me. I saw it in his eyes. His jaw worked as he undoubtedly considered what must have struck him as an untenable situation. If he didn't answer me, he'd be refusing to talk to a cop. If he did, he broke his prophet's decree and spoke to someone who'd turned her back on the church.

The situation was uncomfortable. Max pulled me to the side and whispered, "Clara, I don't think the sheriff would approve of your being here."

"You know what, Max? I'm not leaving. If you want me gone, you'll have to haul me away." I wondered why he'd sold out, when he'd stopped following his best judgment to kowtow to his boss. "That could be Delilah out there. So I don't care what the sheriff wants."

Max glanced around. In the distance, the sheriff and Gerard talked on their phones, most likely calling in help. Max gave me a look I couldn't interpret, but I knew he was worried. He nodded at me and walked back to the old man. I stayed glued to his side. "John, you remember Clara Jefferies. She's a detective in Dallas," Max said. "We invited her here on a consult. You need to tell us what happened."

Mr. Proctor was missing his lower teeth, and his chin crumpled so flat it nearly disappeared as he apparently considered how to respond.

Not far away, the forensic unit cordoned off a semicircle around the body with yellow crime scene tape. A deputy started to draw a map of the area. Another had a video camera rolling. I saw Jeff Mullins, the Alber PD detective who'd railed against my presence that morning, circulating with a pad of paper, recording the names of everyone who'd made the scene.

Mullins saw me and immediately tracked toward us. "Max?"

"Yeah," Max responded.

"It's okay that she's here?" Mullins said, giving me a sideways bob of the head, frowning.

Max heaved a sigh. This was the second time since we arrived at the scene that he'd been asked to vouch for me. "Yeah. It's okay,

Mullins." He shot the guy a look that signaled him not to protest. "I'll take responsibility. Put Detective Jefferies on the log."

Mullins gave me a sour look, wrote down my name, and walked off. Max turned back to John Proctor and said, "We're still waiting. Tell us what happened."

If the moment wasn't so tense, the reason for our meeting so serious, it could have been amusing. It appeared that Proctor had figured out a way to cooperate, while technically keeping in line with the prophet's decrees. Max was one of the lost boys, not a traitor to the faith.

The old man could talk to Max; he just couldn't talk to me.

"Well, you see, Max, I was watching the women pulling off the cobs, the men felling the stalks, when it was time to take Bruno and Jazzy out for a walk. I take them on the same route every day and let them run along the front of the field. But today, since it was so congested and noisy with the work, I took them behind the field. I let them loose, so's they'd get a good run. And that's when they found it."

"Describe what you saw," I said.

Still refusing to look at me, he focused intently on Max. "The dogs did it. I let them loose, like I was telling you, and they took off. We'd never been this far back before, so close to the mountain. No one comes back here. It's hard to walk, too rocky. But the dogs had a great time, jumping over the rocks, chasing each other. Then Bruno, the Lab, got interested in that pile of rocks over there."

At that, Proctor pointed at the mound in the center of the section being cordoned off.

"Pretty soon, Bruno started nosing in between the rocks, pushing at them with his paws, his nose, like he was after something. Jazzy angled over and joined him, did the same thing. I walked over and…"

"And what?" I asked.

"Max, that was when I seen it."

"Describe what you saw," Max nudged.

The old man's head bowed and his eyes focused on his tattered tennis shoes. For a moment, he appeared too overcome to say anything. Proctor wasn't being evasive. It's not unusual for witnesses, after seeing something traumatic, to have to have information dragged out of them. He hadn't assimilated it yet. The experience fresh, he needed time to make sense of it.

"What I saw, I'm not positively sure about. But it kind of looked like something that used to be a face," Proctor said.

I thought about his choice of words: *used to be a face*. I considered what I knew about decomposing bodies, how bacteria causes them to bloat and turn different colors: reddish-purple from lividity where the blood settles, then a nasty greenish-yellow, before they finally darken. These changes suggested a timeline, by giving an indication of how long a body had been dead. Delilah had been missing four days. If that was her...

"What did the skin look like?"

Apparently wrapped up enough in his story to forget he was violating the rule of God, Proctor turned to me. His bushy white eyebrows bunched the skin between them into vertical rows. "I don't know. I didn't take a good look. I never saw anything like that in my life before. I got scared. I rounded up the dogs, ran and called for help."

Max took notes, writing everything down, including Proctor's contact information, while I walked away a bit. Once I reached the crime scene tape lying on the ground and secured with rocks, I stopped. I stared at the rock pile and thought about the body hidden inside it.

Was it Delilah?

I approached the sheriff and Chief Barstow standing back, arms folded, watching as the video tech recorded the scene. A cameraman taking still shots followed him. "We're going to wait for Doc Wiley before we uncover it, right?" I asked.

"Yeah," the sheriff said. "Not that it's any of your concern, Detective."

I didn't argue with him. "You have them looking for shoe prints, too, I bet. So they're not wiping out evidence? Any tire prints."

The sheriff frowned, but shouted to one of the techs. "Y'all are looking for shoe prints and tire marks, right?"

"Yeah," one of the men called out. "Nothing yet."

"Probably won't find anything. The ground's too hard and rocky," I said. "Also, Hannah said you had rain last Thursday morning. It most likely would have destroyed any, assuming the body was buried out here before then."

"That's what I was thinking," Chief Barstow said.

I nodded at him, not believing he'd even considered the possibilities. "Doesn't hurt to look, though."

Barstow frowned. "You know, we're not children. We've got experience with these types of crimes."

"How many murders did you have last year?" I asked, turning to the sheriff.

He thought for a minute. "One guy killed his fifth wife, murder-suicide. He thought she was messing around. She wasn't. Not much of an investigation. He chased her out into the front yard with the gun. The neighbors saw him do it. Nobody left to have a trial."

I needed to be delicate, not to come on too strong, but I guessed they had no idea what to do with a murder case. Max was the only one with experience and he couldn't do it all. If that was Delilah, any of the girls out there, I had to make sure it was done right. "As you can imagine, we have more than that in Dallas. I specialize in violent crimes, especially homicides," I said. The sheriff appeared interested, while Barstow scowled. "I personally worked thirty-six homicides last year. I cleared all of them."

Barstow eyed me, distrustful. I ignored him and concentrated on the sheriff. In his office, he'd wanted me gone. I knew that. He sounded angry at Max for even asking me to come. But in rural counties, budgets rarely covered more than the basic costs. Most sheriffs struggled to pay wages and finance expenses. Sheriffs like Virgil Holmes, with a vast county to patrol, had to work every angle to make ends meet. Investigating a murder case took time and resources, both of which he probably didn't have. It would be hard for a man in his position to turn down an experienced detective offering to work a case for free.

"I'm volunteering to help."

"Why do we want that? Not gonna happen, Detective. We don't need outsiders coming in here and—" Gerard started. "The sheriff and me, we don't—"

Sheriff Holmes cut him off. "Things have changed, Chief," he said, giving Gerard a cautionary look. "We have a dead body. I'm looking at a full-fledged murder investigation here. That's something we don't have often in Smith County. "

"But Sheriff—" the chief tried to interrupt.

Then Sheriff Holmes said something I hadn't expected. "And I've been thinking. Maybe the detective is right about those girls. Maybe they need some looking into."

"What's that got to do with her?" Gerard pressed, motioning toward me. "If that needs doing, I can do it. My men will—"

"This woman's got more experience than either one of us. Look, it could turn out that those girls were taken. If it's true, Detective Jefferies here was the only one who realized it," the sheriff said, eyeing Gerard. "The rest of us didn't put it together."

"Damn it, Virgil," the chief objected. "We don't need any help. We got this covered."

"Gerard, I got a dozen deputies and a handful of detectives to cover nearly a thousand square miles. This is my case, and I could use the help." At that, the sheriff turned toward me. "Detective Jefferies, I'd appreciate your assistance." He gave Gerard a cautionary look. "And I'm sure the chief is grateful as well."

"Thank you, Sheriff," I said.

Gerard Barstow cinched in his lower lip and didn't answer.

The discussion ended, I turned my back on both men while I fought the impulse to run toward the rock pile, to throw off stone after stone until I knew who lay beneath it.

CHAPTER TWENTY-FIVE

The day was beginning to feel like a marathon. An hour earlier I'd been hungry for lunch, but my appetite vanished once I heard about the body in the field. Still, my stomach hadn't gotten the message, and it growled in emptiness. At twelve thirty, when the medical examiner arrived, I'd been up and working for more than six hours with no end in sight. Craig Wiley MD parked his green pickup about a hundred feet from the body. Impatient, I'd hung back like the others to wait for him, careful not to contaminate the scene. But the longer I cooled my heels, the more I worried that we'd found my sister.

An internist who'd practiced in Smith County for decades, Doc Wiley sauntered over to where I stood. He hovered close to sixty, and his silver hair had thinned, the hairline receding, since I'd last seen him. I didn't remember glasses, but he wore round, brass-rimmed spectacles. A prominent potbelly strained his khaki pants and the buttons on his plaid shirt, and a patchwork of blotches from the sun speckled his exposed scalp and ears, his hands and cheeks. It appeared that he didn't take his profession's own advice to wear sunscreen.

My family didn't believe in doctors. Not many in our community did. Add to that Mother's talent for mixing herbal concoctions that she claimed could kill any infection, treat any malady, heal any wound, and our family never had much need for or confidence in Gentile doctors, as we called them.

I knew Doc Wiley because he'd once taken care of me. Hannah brought me to see him a month before she helped me escape Alber. I was bruised and bloody. I couldn't go to Mother. She wouldn't have understood. Doc Wiley put me back together.

"Good to see you, Doc," I said. "Glad you're here. We've got a situation."

"So it seems. I was surprised to hear that you'd come back, Clara. Didn't think you'd do that, under the circumstances," he said, giving me a curious look.

"Max called me to consult on a case."

"Ah. Well, that explains it, I guess. Then the rumors are right? You're a cop now?"

"In Dallas."

"Hot damn," he said, slipping his thumbs behind the straps of his black suspenders. Those and a bow tie were the doc's signature accessories. "The world is changing."

"That it is. Certainly around here." Under other circumstances, I wouldn't have minded a chat, but all my attention was focused on the pile of rocks under Samuel's Peak. "The body is over there," I said, pointing at the place. "I'll lead you and take photos with one of the CSI unit's cameras, if that's okay?"

"You bet," he said. "Have at it."

I put on shoe covers and pulled on a pair of latex gloves I'd commandeered from the CSI unit. Doc and the videographer did the same.

The others stood back, and the two of us recorded the scene as we walked toward the stone pile with Doc. When we got there, he waited while we took close-ups of the rocks in situ, as they stood.

The section of rock that commanded our attention measured about eighteen inches high and four feet wide, maybe seven feet long. As we got closer, an unmistakable, strong but not overpowering odor surrounded us. Decomp. The fact that it didn't overwhelm us suggested either a fairly fresh kill or a body that had been dead for a long time. I thought again of Delilah. It took every ounce of control I had not to throw off all the rocks. I wanted to know. I needed to know. I swallowed and willed myself calm, but my drumming pulse gave me away.

After we had the overall photos, I scanned the rocks, looking for what Proctor described, the opening Bruno made, one the old man looked in and saw a face.

About a foot from one side, I found it, a place where a rock had rolled off. I peeked in and saw leathery skin, taut, slightly translucent.

"Doc, take a look," I suggested as I snapped a couple of photos.

He rustled over and stooped down. "Well, I'll be," he said, peering between the rocks.

"Do you think it's…" I started. My pulse picking up more steam, I had a hard time spitting the question out. "Does it look—"

"Mummified," Doc said.

Relief rushed through me, so much so that I had to fight the urge to smile. "It's not Delilah then," I murmured. Doc Wiley's eyes scrunched nearly closed in a question. "One of my sisters. Half-sister. Sariah's daughter. Delilah is… missing. I was afraid it was her."

"That's the case Max asked you to consult on?" Sadness distorted his old face, drawing down his eyes.

"Yeah."

"How long has she been missing?"

"We think Thursday evening. About four days."

"You're right then," Doc shook his head. "This isn't her."

I didn't have to ask how he could be so sure. I knew.

Utah's hot, arid summers were perfect for mummification; they efficiently sucked the moisture from a body before it had time to decompose. So were Dallas's. I once worked a case with a mummified body found in an abandoned crack house. We didn't know what we had at first, a homicide or natural causes. It turned out that the guy died of an overdose. The day I walked onto the scene, the body looked just the way the one beneath the rocks did—cured a dark golden brown, rubbery, like something on display in a museum.

Even in prime conditions, a human body took at least two weeks to dry out. Delilah hadn't been missing long enough for her body to be in such an advanced stage of mummification.

My relief, however, faded quickly. The body wasn't Delilah's, but it was someone's. Eliza's? Jayme's? And what did the discovery of a dead body mean for Delilah? Wherever she was, I felt even more certain that my sister was in danger.

"Let's start here," I said. I took off the first rock and exposed a swollen cheek, a side of a nose with a slight upturn. I snapped a photo. The videographer recorded the scene, and the doc took a closer look. He motioned for me to continue. I pulled off rocks two and three, and an eye emerged, the pupil sunken into a dark orb. It looked like a Halloween mask. Rocks four and five exposed the other eye. By rock nine, the corpse had a nose and a heart-shaped chin.

The body appeared to be either a female or a young boy with delicate features.

I chose the rocks above the eyes and uncovered a forehead. At that point, we could see dark brown hair. I paused long enough for the videographer to record the moment and I took a photograph before Doc Wiley moved in for another look.

As I removed each rock, I deposited it on a piece of cardboard placed to the side, where a technician numbered, bagged and logged it into evidence. Everything would be sent to the lab. Some of the rocks were relatively smooth, holding out the possibility that latent prints might be found.

Our work continued.

As I pulled more rocks away, we could gauge the length of the hair: at least three feet. Separating from the scalp in places, it fell like a long, dark brown wig.

We were most likely looking at a woman.

The head uncovered, I took the next five rocks off the neck and chest. Each one dug into my heart. A once-white cotton collar trimmed in eyelet had cured dark and stiff from the seepage of bodily fluids. The prairie dress remained light green in scattered places with small pink flowers printed in stripes, but the majority of it had turned a dirty brown.

Once we had her completely uncovered, I looked down at the figure of a young woman. I visualized Delilah in that rocky grave, Lily, my mother, myself. If I knew the girl in the grave, I didn't recognize her. But for me, she represented every woman I'd ever known. I thought of bodies I'd seen in Dallas: men, women, children, some bludgeoned, others shot or stabbed. Each one a tragedy. Each one leaving a family in pain.

"From the clothes, she looks like a local," Doc Wiley yelled out to Chief Barstow and the sheriff. "Can't recognize her in this condition."

"When's the autopsy?" Gerard asked.

"Quick as we get her to my office," the doc responded.

I hadn't noticed, but a crowd had formed. A line of deputies roped them off near the road. Women, men, young and old, children, most probably from the trailer park, but my guess others had come from Alber proper. Some looked curious, others horrified.

"Get a body bag out of my truck, will ya?" Doc asked me.

As I walked toward the pickup, I noticed my mother in the crowd, along with Naomi and Sariah. Most of the women dabbed at tears. Mother had her strong face on, the one she used to keep the family in line. Naomi stared at me, her eyes blank, as if disbelieving. Sariah appeared stunned. Her face pale, she simply kept shaking her head, as if trying to wipe the scene away.

Next to Mother, one hand holding onto her skirt and the other covering her mouth, stood Lily.

Jim Daniels lingered a short distance away, on the edge of the cornfield he managed. A woman I recognized hovered beside him. His second wife, my half-sister Karyn, had her hands clasped, her lips fluttering as if in prayer. Daniels wrapped an arm around her shoulder. Stoic. The word described his pin-straight posture, his emotionless expression. I thought about him, how peculiar he was, distant. I recalled what I'd mentioned to Hannah just that morning, how odd it was that all three of the girls lived in houses that backed up to the cornfield.

Jim Daniels' cornfield.

I ached to go to my family, to comfort them. I needed to ask again about Delilah. Dead bodies can convince people to open up. I wanted to talk to Daniels, figure out if he was a piece of this puzzle. But I couldn't. Not yet. At that moment, someone else needed me more—the girl in the field. If there was evidence on her body, it might be the key to finding her killer. More than that, it might lead us to Delilah and the other girls. It had to be preserved.

I grabbed a black vinyl body bag out of Doc's truck. Back at the rock pile, I unzipped it and laid it out next to the body.

"I'll take the head," Doc instructed. "Clara, get the feet." Pointing at the videographer, he added, "Let's let this strapping young man take the hips."

Rigor mortis had long passed and the body hung limp, light and bone thin. As we carried it, the long skirt brushed to the side.

From the crowd, painful screams pierced the air. It broke my heart when a woman shouted, "It's one of us! One of our girls!"

I kept my attention focused on the body, moving it carefully, slowly, trying to keep the corpse and clothing together, not wanting to let anything fall away. After we had the body removed, the crime scene unit would rake the area, searching for fibers and hair, anything that might be tied to the dead girl or her killer.

I thought of what I held in my hands, the end of a life.

Sobs and screams came from the growing crowd of townsfolk as we laid the body in the bag. I glanced over and saw Mother round up Naomi, Sariah, and two young girls I didn't recognize, family of mine that I'd never met. Mother urged them away, taking them by the hands and leading them off. Jim Daniels and Karyn followed obediently behind. Her arms were around Lily, who wept, her shoulders hunched as if she'd pulled back into a shell.

I skimmed the crowd and saw others I knew, relatives, old friends. Off to the side, a group of men in work boots and carrying machetes clustered together, talking. I guessed they were the ones who'd been cutting the corn stalks.

"Max!" I called out. I walked toward him, where he stood with the sheriff. I noticed Gerard Barstow was gone.

"What, Clara?"

"Where's the chief?"

Max huffed, as if in disgust. "He threw a fit. Took off. Told the sheriff that he wasn't going to watch you run the show."

"Figures," I said. "Max, have the photographer take photos of the crowd. Send some of your men in to make a list of who's there. Maybe someone has heard or seen something that can help. Okay?"

"I've already got them canvassing the neighborhood," Max said. "But good idea about the crowd. Maybe the killer likes to watch."

"Yeah. It happens," I said.

Max raised his hand and shouted at one of his men and waved him over. I turned back to the matter at hand and bent to take a closer look at the body. The weight of the rocks, I guessed, had broken her nose, smashing it flat and disfiguring her profile. I thought about the position we found her in, laid out so straight, her hands folded one over the other across her chest. She'd been arranged in her rocky grave as if staged in a coffin.

"Look at that," Doc said, reclaiming my attention.

"At what?" I asked.

"Just above her hands."

I leaned in for a closer look. The girl's skin slacked then pinched in tight, leaving a series of indentations at the narrowing of her wrists. I scanned the body and saw similar marks above her thin, delicate feet.

"Rope marks? She was tied up, hands and legs." I felt sickened even saying it. I thought of the terror she endured before her death. How could anyone do this? What if that same person had Delilah?

"I guess." Doc moved in closer, then grabbed his battered leather medical bag. Out of it he pulled a wooden tongue depressor. He knelt down and pushed a bit at the fibrous tissue, carefully inspecting the indentation on the girl's right wrist. "From the braided appearance, I'd say a heavy rope maybe, but most likely chains."

"Whoever did this had her chained up. Chained to something?" I muttered, thinking it through. "Or to someone?"

"Guess so," Doc said.

"I wonder who she is," I said. The misshapen, dried-up face was unrecognizable, but her long dark brown hair matched Eliza Heaton's description. Jayme Coombs had lighter hair, blond, so maybe not. But I wondered if the hair on the corpse could have been discolored from blood and fluid.

"I'll pull DNA," Doc said.

"That'll take a while?"

"Maybe a week," Doc answered. "I'll put a rush on it."

"Thanks," I said.

"And I'll do the usual, look for dental work, fillings and such," Doc said. "Probably won't find any…"

I finished his train of thought. "Because most of the families don't see dentists."

"Sadly, no."

"We do have the dress. Someone might recognize it."

"Could happen," Doc said. "But the likelihood is that this girl may take a while to identify. We haven't got a lot here to work with. You got enough pictures?"

"Yes." I bent over and started zipping up the body bag. I hadn't noticed any gunshot or knife wounds. I wondered if the doc had seen anything I'd missed. "So, Doc, any idea what we're looking at here? How this girl died?"

"Nah," he said.

"Any chance this is natural causes?"

"I'll need to take a good look at her," he said. "But no. I don't think so."

"I agree," I said. "Not with those chain marks around the wrists and ankles. Not with the body buried like this, hidden behind the field."

"All true," Doc said. "Most likely a homicide."

I felt my rage building, and I fought to keep my focus, to not let my feelings interfere. I had a murder to solve. I had Delilah to find. Giving in to anger would slow me down. I couldn't risk that. "Can you give me an estimate on date of death? Just a ballpark on number of weeks?"

"Well, based on the condition of this body, the advanced mummification, I'd say we're probably looking at months," he said. "At least two or three, maybe considerably longer. But I'll know more once I take a good look at her in the lab."

Eliza disappeared five months ago, in March, and Jayme three months ago, in May. Based on Doc's estimate, it could have been either of them. Or it could have been someone else, a girl or woman whose name I hadn't yet heard, one never reported missing. I thought about my sister. I looked at the dead girl's thin figure in the body bag and felt as if the universe pointed at it and shouted: Find who did this, and you'll find Delilah.

Doc must have had similar thoughts, that this wasn't an isolated case.

We'd been in the field for two hours, and the sun loomed high overhead. In the searing heat, he wiped a thin coat of gritty sweat from his forehead with a white cotton handkerchief. As he folded it to put it back in his pocket, he scanned the lingering crowd and said, "My guess is that there's a really sick bastard in this town. The big question, who is he?"

CHAPTER TWENTY-SIX

The man came back.

Delilah heard the sound of gravel crunching under a car or truck, moments later the bang of a car door. Once before, Delilah thought she heard voices, but this time they came up clearly through the vent. The girl must have left it open.

"Please, don't," the girl begged.

"You're my wife. You'll do as I say." After that, Delilah heard ragged breathing and the girl sobbing. Delilah covered her ears and waited for it to be over.

A while later, the door slammed and she heard someone drive away. She waited for the girl to say something, but heard only silence.

"Is he gone?" Delilah asked.

At first, the girl didn't answer. Delilah thought she heard soft weeping. "Yeah." The girl's voice sounded different, hoarse and tired. "I wish... I just wish..."

"I wish he was dead and we were home with our families." Sariah had taught her not to desire that anything bad happen to anyone, but Delilah judged this an exception to that rule. "Are there any others in the house? Any other girls in this house with us, girls that the man took?"

"Not now, but when I got here there were others." She explained that when she arrived the man had two girls. One, an older girl, whose name she'd never learned. "She disappeared a few days after the man took me. I never talked to her. I saw her just once through the edge of my blindfold. She was beautiful, tall with long dark hair. The man ordered her to feed me, like he told me to feed you. She was kind."

"What happened to her?" Delilah asked.

"I don't know, but one night I heard a lot of shouting. The man was hot angry, screaming. I heard him yell that if she didn't do as she was told he had others who would."

"Did you ever ask him what happened to her?" Delilah wanted to know.

"No. But I asked the other girl. Her name was Eliza," she said. "She said the man told her that he took the older girl up the mountain and left her there."

"Set her free?"

The girl was quiet for what felt like a long time. "Maybe."

"What happened to Eliza?"

The girl didn't answer for a long time, and then said, "I'm not sure. He got mad at her one night. Just like the other time, I heard him screaming. Then, she was gone."

Delilah wondered what the man had done to the girls. "He must have killed them," she whispered. After a while, she asked, "If something happens to me, I want you to remember my name, so you can tell my family about me, okay?"

"Yeah, you said it's Delilah, right?" the girl answered.

"Delilah Jefferies."

"Would you tell my family about me? I'm Jayme Coombs."

CHAPTER TWENTY-SEVEN

Sheriff Holmes gave me his conference room to use, but not before I raised my right hand and vowed to protect and defend the citizens of Smith County, Utah. As he pinned a deputy's badge on my shirt, I couldn't help but consider the strange and unsettling fact that I'd temporarily become part of Alber again. When the sheriff officially assigned me to head up the investigation, I eagerly agreed. I intended to find the monster that had murdered the girl in the field and, I hoped, in the process rescue my sister.

"The forensic team will be on the scene for at least a couple more hours," Max announced as he walked into my temporary office.

I'd gone straight to work, setting my computer up on the large oval table and emailing Chief Thompson in Dallas to tell him I'd be gone a while longer. "What about the cadaver dogs?" I asked Max.

"They've arrived. We have them checking the entire area at the base of the mountain to make sure there aren't any more bodies buried out there."

"You think we'll find anything?" I said.

"I'd be surprised, since Mr. Proctor's dogs didn't appear interested in any of the other areas," he said.

"I agree. Who's overseeing the crime scene?"

"The CSI unit's lieutenant. He'll call if anything turns up. That way, I can work with you."

"Okay."

"Where do you want to start?" Max asked. "Since you have concerns about the Heaton and Coombs girls, we can head back out to their houses, question the families."

I'd thought about that and nixed it. "We need the upper hand. I want them on our turf. They need to understand that I'm not some renegade cop from Dallas trespassing on their property. We've got a dead body. They need to take this seriously."

"I'll round them up and bring them here then."

"Great. While they're here, we'll get DNA from Eliza's and Jayme's mothers, so Doc can compare it to the body, see if either girl is a match."

"What about your family? Should we bring your mothers in?"

"Not yet. That wasn't Delilah buried out there. My sister hasn't been missing long enough for her to be in that condition, not even if she was killed the night she was taken." I felt sick to my stomach thinking about the dead woman we'd found in the field, wondering about Delilah. "For now, let's concentrate on the other girls. That body could be one of theirs."

"Okay," he said. "You're still thinking we have a series here?"

"Yes, I am. It would be an unlikely coincidence that in a small town like this we have three missing girls and the dead one who turns up is unrelated. I'm betting that if we figure out who killed that girl, we'll find all of the missing girls, including Delilah."

"Okay. I'll get the Heaton and Coombs women and bring them here," Max said.

"Make sure both families bring photos of the girls. That could help Doc. And if we get confirmation they're missing, we can get them on NCIC and send out a media alert."

"What about Delilah? I gather we still can't do that with her?"

"Not yet. We have the same problem we've had all along – my family," I said. "You were right about the Amber Alert. We can't do anything official until they file a missing person complaint."

"What are you going to do while I'm out corralling the families?" Max asked.

"Research," I said. "I have a hunch I want to explore."

"That sounds promising. On who?"

I hesitated. I trusted Max, but I worried about how invested he was in the case. He'd brought me here and he was paying attention now, but when he allowed Gerard Barstow to sway his judgment, we wasted precious time. "We'll talk about it later."

Max turned around toward the door, but then swiveled back. "Clara," he said. I'd grabbed a chair and had my head in my computer. When I looked up at him, he seemed troubled. "It wasn't that I didn't agree with you about Delilah, that I wasn't worried about her."

"You told me to go home, Max," I said, not trying to hide my irritation. "If you had any concerns that Delilah could be in trouble, why would you do that?"

"There are things you don't know, about my situation." Max took a deep breath. "I'm not free to think of just myself. Sometimes, well, the position I'm in…"

He stopped talking and an awkward silence filled the room. When he began again, he looked at me as if confiding. "Clara, I haven't told you about Brooke, my daughter. She's…"

"What, Max?"

He seemed almost unable to form the words. "Things are complicated at home, my daughter…"

Max stopped and looked at me, unable to go on.

Weary, I rubbed my forehead. I felt overwhelmed, and it was too much at that moment to take on Max's problems. "I appreciate your explanation," I said, mustering as much sympathy as I could manage with my sister on my mind. "But we're going to have to talk about this later, because right now, every minute we stand talking, Delilah and maybe the other girls are in danger."

Max's eyes clouded with disappointment, and I immediately regretted not handling it better. Still, I needed him to get to work. "Right now, let's concentrate on figuring out who that girl in the field is and what she can tell us that will help us find the others."

"Of course, you're right," he said. As he walked out the door, I heard him whisper, "Later."

As soon as Max left, I found the storeroom and rooted around. I grabbed three sheets of poster board. Back at the conference table, I taped them together and drew a horizontal line side to side. A third of the way from the left, I made a vertical mark and noted that Eliza Heaton disappeared in late March. Six inches away, I wrote: Jayme Coombs, May tenth. Then I wrote down the date the note said Delilah disappeared, August thirteenth, three months after Jayme's disappearance, the previous Thursday evening. The final mark had the current date and BODY FOUND. I purposely left room in anticipation of more victims at both ends of the timeline, hoping I wouldn't have to use it.

I hung the timeline on the wall.

That done, I logged on to NCIC. Earlier I'd used the site to look into Evan Barstow. I still thought he was a possibility, but this time I had someone else on my mind—Jim Daniels. Ten minutes and I had a hit, not in Utah but in Iowa.

My brother-in-law was a convicted sex offender.

Daniels had been arrested at the age of nineteen for the statutory rape of a sixteen-year-old. The girl's name was Rebecca Sanders.

Nothing further came up on Jim Daniels on NCIC, so I accessed the Dallas PD database I'd used that morning to track down Evan Barstow's address. A few minutes scouting around, and I had a handful of speeding citations and an address outside Alber.

On the way out the door, I texted Max:

*Change of plans. Going out. Will bring you up to date later. I
may be back when you get here with the Heaton and Coombs
families, but if not, wait.*

On the way to the Daniels family farm, I pulled up memories
of Karyn. Coming from such a large family, one father but four
mothers, I was one of dozens of siblings, the fifth oldest and the
second of the girls. With so many to feed and care for, we all had
to work. From the age of eight, I carried babies around on my
hip and functioned as our mothers' helper. Guided by my oldest
sister, Sylvia, I sewed, cleaned, cooked, fed and diapered babies.

Karyn was Mother Constance's second daughter, my father's
tenth child.

The girl I remembered wore jeans with holes in the knees under
her dresses. She caught catfish in the river and gutted them while
our mothers lit the campfire. Karyn could outride the rest of us by
nine, bareback. Never much for studying or reading, she regularly
wandered into the back shed, where our father kept his tools. She
foraged for leftover wood she whittled into bears, insects and birds.
One winter she carved an entire chess set, the male figures on horses
or holding pitchforks and the women in long prairie dresses.

The girl I knew would rather spend the day pretending to be
a pirate high in the backyard oak tree, a rolled-up sheet of paper
for her telescope, than play baby dolls.

Mother Constance complained about her constantly. "Will
Karyn ever comb that matted mess of hair? Her crowning glory
is full of sawdust and straw!"

The tin-roofed, two-story house I pulled up to was modest,
and stood on a tract of land bordered by a split-rail fence painted
white. A woman sat on the porch shucking peas, while a smattering
of children jumped rope and played basketball.

As at every other house I'd driven up to since returning to Alber, as soon as she saw me the woman gathered the children. By the time I parked, the yard and porch gaped empty except for a five-foot-tall statue of a grizzly carved out of a tree trunk. It had the unmistakable look of Karyn's work.

I punched the bell but didn't hear it ring. I knocked. Hard. Through the door's oval window, I saw a man walk toward me.

The door opened. Jim Daniels stared down at me through his thick, black-rimmed glasses. Well over six feet with dull brown hair, his face tanned to match his hair, he looked like Karyn's grizzly. I would have guessed him decades older than the birthdate on his driver's license, which made him thirty-three.

"You looking for someone?" he asked.

"Yes, you," I said. "I'm—"

"I know who you are. Clara Jefferies. I saw you yesterday and today at the cornfield. I heard you were here, but I would have recognized you anywhere."

"How?"

"Come in." Not showing any concern, he followed me into the house, compact and crowded with furniture. Karyn's creations were scattered around us—small, intricate carvings on tabletops and whittled birds in flight hanging on a wall. I wondered if she made the log furniture in the den.

An upright piano sat in one corner, and around it hung framed family portraits of Karyn, a woman I assumed was her sister-wife, Daniels, and a pack of children. Mixed in I saw photos of our family growing up, our parents and brothers and sisters. The photos a ritual, of sorts—we took one every year. For a month or more before, we prepared, the girls sewing matching dresses out of yard goods Mother ordered from the general store.

"That's you right there, I'd guess." Daniels said, pointing at me, one of the oldest in the lineup of young smiling faces.

"You'd be right," I said.

"Karyn loves those photos."

"So, where is she?"

"Not here." I thought about what felt so odd about Daniels. He had a flat affect, a voice that could have put an insomniac to sleep, and a face that didn't register emotion. "Karyn's at your ma's trailer. They're having a family meeting."

"What about?"

"You," Daniels said. "Ardeth's upset that you're nosing around."

"Jim, I'm here because I'm helping the sheriff's office with a case. The body found in the field. I saw you there today."

"It's not illegal to watch, is it?" he asked. "It's not every day in Alber that someone finds a dead body."

"I was curious about you, and—" I started.

"And you ran a check on me. Found out that I'm registered as a sex offender," he said, his voice as unconcerned as if he'd just said that I heard he raised hogs.

"Yes."

Daniels walked over to the kitchen and shouted. "Rebecca, come here, please. This detective lady, Clara, needs to talk to you."

"Rebecca?"

"My first wife," Daniels said. "I grew up on a farm in Iowa surrounded by Gentiles. Not many of our neighbors knew we were fundamentalists, that we had what they'd think were peculiar ways. My parents hid it."

"Ah, I see," I said. "So you were nineteen and—"

"Rebecca was sixteen," he explained. "The prophet called my dad and said he had a vision, and I was to marry her. We were sealed in a meeting house in Cedar Rapids. We rented an apartment and moved in together."

"Someone found out—"

"Jim made the mistake of insisting that I finish high school," the woman walking into the room said. She had a hesitant manner, which I understood. I wasn't an invited guest. Despite that, she gave me a half-smile and said, "Problem was, I got pregnant right away. My physical education teacher asked me who the father was, and in my sixteen-year-old wisdom, I told him my husband."

A round woman with soft, light brown hair, Rebecca Daniels had chambray-blue eyes and thin lips that curled up at the corners. "Dad thought I was too young to marry and refused to sign the paperwork that would have allowed me to marry Jim legally. So Jim and I were only sealed in the church. We tried to get the charges dropped, but the prosecutor refused. Jim spent a year in jail. He got out just in time for our baby's first birthday. When I turned eighteen, we married again at the courthouse."

"Okay." This was nothing out of the ordinary in our culture, and while Jim Daniels was considered a sex offender in the outside world, in Alber he was simply a young husband. "I understand."

That didn't, however, get Jim off my radar. I wondered about him. I thought again about the coincidence that all the missing girls lived in houses that backed up to the cornfield he managed. I thought about him skulking around, hidden in the field. "Jim, Rebecca, what do you two know about Delilah?"

Their eyes met, a caution passed between them, and Rebecca shook her head at him.

"I need to know," I said.

"I'm under orders," Jim said, his voice as no-nonsense as it had been throughout the conversation. "I can't tell you anything. If you want to know anything about Delilah, you need to ask your mother."

"My mother's not talking," I said. "Delilah is in danger. I'm certain of it. I need to know what you know."

"It's not that we don't want to, but we can't tell you anything. It's not ours to tell," Rebecca said. "Like Jim said, we have orders. You need to talk to your family."

"Where were you Thursday evening, Jim?" I asked.

For the first time, he looked vaguely interested. He answered as if it were a curiosity. "You think I took Delilah?"

I stared at him, such a strange man. "Interesting that you know that was the night Delilah was abducted."

To this, Jim Daniels said nothing.

"I think maybe you're picking up on the fact that my husband is a little different, Clara. That's why you suspect him." Rebecca looked over at him, questioning, and he gave her a casual nod as if agreeing that she continue. "Jim has… he has a hard time connecting with people. He can seem rather standoffish. But my husband's a good man. He wouldn't hurt anyone. We love Delilah. She's Karyn's sister, and that makes her family."

"Then help me find her. You need to tell me what you know," I demanded, my voice rising, indignant. "A young woman's already dead, her body left to rot behind the cornfield. This isn't a game."

Daniels looked like he might say something, but his wife placed her hand gently on his arm and said, "Jim and I aren't free to discuss Delilah's disappearance. Ask your mother."

"So you admit she's missing," I pounced.

Rebecca stuttered, "I-I didn't mean to say—"

I wasn't willing to hear anything more. "I am putting you both on notice—if something happens to Delilah while all of you are playing games, you will regret it," I warned. Looking the man dead in the eyes, I said, "As for you, Mr. Daniels, if you're involved in Delilah's disappearance, now's the time to speak up. Get ahead of this while you can, before I find out on my own that you aren't being honest. Then, I promise, you will get no mercy."

Jim Daniels' expression remained calm. He showed no emotion when he said, "Clara, you need to leave. There's no help for you here."

CHAPTER TWENTY-EIGHT

On the way to the trailer park to talk to the Heaton and Coombs families, Max mulled over his latest encounter with Clara. He'd had such mixed feelings since the previous afternoon, when he'd looked up and seen her standing in his office. At times, he blamed her for what happened to him in the past and for putting his job in jeopardy. Yet he couldn't deny that he still felt the deep connection they'd shared as teenagers.

Something about Clara had never stopped touching his heart.

Max had thought about her often over the years, wanted to see her. Every time he asked Hannah about Clara, he'd been disappointed to find out that they'd lost contact. Now Clara was back, and they'd done little but argue.

Clara didn't seem to care.

Then he reconsidered. That wasn't fair. After all, Clara worried about Delilah, not unlike the way he worried about Brooke. He thought about what Clara had said, that later they'd have time to discuss it all. But what would he say? How could he make her understand?

What she's seen is that I'm a coward afraid to contradict my boss.

When he thought about it, though, sometimes it wasn't easy to know what to do. Should he have backed Clara? After all, Gerard investigated Eliza's and Jayme's disappearances, and both families insisted that they weren't worried about their daughters. That should have put any concern about the girls to rest.

Of course, the dead body in the field brought everything into question. What if it turned out to be the Heaton or Coombs girl?

"Damn," Max muttered. What if he'd sat back and done nothing while all along those girls were in trouble?

Max shook his head and made a vow: From that point forward he'd stop worrying about losing his job and concentrate on doing it, whatever that entailed. And someday when he had the opportunity, he'd tell Clara everything—that Miriam's death and Brooke's injuries were his fault. He'd been responsible, and the guilt had nearly killed him.

He didn't know if Clara would understand, but he had to tell her.

At that, he pulled up in front of the Heaton house. A pack of little girls were running circles around the trailer, and Alma Heaton sat on a garden swing, idly pushing back and forth, enjoying the view. When she saw Max walk toward her, Alma's smile melted and her face transformed, the frown lines circling her mouth deepening. He stood over her, waiting.

Alma squinted up at him and asked, "Why are you here?"

CHAPTER TWENTY-NINE

Driving away from the Daniels house, I still had two suspects, Evan Barlow and Jim Daniels. I hadn't eliminated or focused on either one. About the only thing I had accomplished was that I'd finally gotten clear confirmation that I hadn't misjudged the situation. That came with Rebecca's words: "Jim and I aren't free to discuss Delilah's disappearance."

Yet that validation hadn't changed the situation. My instincts had told me all along that Delilah was taken. The questions remained: by whom, and how do I find her?

On my way back to the sheriff's office, I thought about the business card the Alber PD dispatcher palmed me that morning. I fished around in my pocket and found it. I looked at the phone number scratched on the back and wondered why she gave it to me. I steered with one hand and punched in her number with the other. "Clara Jefferies here, Stephanie. Why did you slip me your card?"

"Give me a minute," she whispered. "A couple of the officers are here. I'll walk outside."

I did, and when she got back on, I asked again, "Tell me why you gave me your card."

"I thought maybe you could call me if you needed help," she stammered. "Maybe I could, you know, pitch in."

"How could you help?" The secretive way she handed me the card needled at me. I sensed that she had something she wanted to tell me.

"I thought maybe you'd need someone local to assist you. That's all," she said.

"I think it's more than that. What do you know that could help me?"

"Nothing, I—"

"Again, and this time please answer my question, why did you give it to me?"

"Because," she blurted out, "around here, things aren't always what they seem."

"And there's something in particular about what's going on in this town that may not be clear to me?" I asked. "What?"

The silence dragged, but I waited. I've learned that keeping my mouth shut often works better than talking when I want someone to open up. The quiet lingered, until she said, "There are a lot of secrets in this part of the world, Detective."

"For instance?" I asked. "Let's focus on the current situation."

"For instance, there's a lot that never makes it to official reports," she said, her voice lower, quieter. "For instance, sometimes doing a computer search doesn't access the really important records. Because sometimes stuff isn't entered into the databases."

"Where's it kept?" I asked.

"I'd show you if I could," she said. "But I can't. That's a private room. It's not open—"

"Stephanie, we found a body earlier today. A young woman left to rot under a pile of rocks," I said. "I can't promise you that helping me won't get you in trouble. You might lose your job. I understand that. But I can promise you that helping me figure out what's going on is the right thing to do."

I asked a lot. I knew that. I didn't have a choice. Someone had to come out from the shadows, pull back the curtains and let in the daylight. If I was right, lives depended on it. Delilah's life depended on it.

"I'll… Well… Jeez, this isn't going to be good," she said. Again, I kept mum. I heard the reluctance in her voice when she said, "Come on over to the station. The chief's not here right now. I'll do what I can."

"I'll be there in fifteen minutes."

As soon as I hung up with Stephanie, I called Max. "Where are you?"

"I just got back to the office. I've got the Heaton and Coombs women in the waiting area. They're eyeing each other, I guess wondering why I brought the others in. They heard about the girl in the field, so they're worried, wondering what we want. I think they'll cooperate. I've been waiting on you to press the issue."

"Good…" I looked at the clock again, wishing I could be in two places at once. "Separate them by family in a couple of interview rooms and let them stew. Tell them I'm on my way. I won't be long."

"Okay. You have something for me to do while I'm waiting?"

"Check in with Doc on the autopsy," I asked. "Find out what he knows so far."

"Will do," Max said.

I was relieved not to see Gerard Barstow's black Suburban parked outside his office when I pulled up. The station looked quiet, a couple of cars parked on the side, but not much going on. I walked in and Stephanie looked up from behind the glass partition and buzzed me in.

In the main room, all the desks were empty. "Stephanie, hey, where is the chief? You expect him soon?"

"Call me Stef. Everyone does," she said. "I don't know. Chief Barstow left about twenty minutes ago, right before you called. Didn't say where he was going."

"The chief often take off like this during the day?"

"Not usually. He left ticked off about you, the investigation. I heard him call his brother Evan. There was a lot of shouting."

"Where's everyone else?"

"It's three thirty. Day shift's still out on patrol, and the evening shift hasn't come in. Detective Mullins made a scene. He's taking a robbery report on a stolen bicycle. At the moment, I'm the only one here."

"Good. So what have you got for me?"

"Are you going to tell the chief about this?" she asked. The lids on her eyes shuttered, and her lips compressed into a straight line. "This could really get in the way of my plans. I'm taking forensic science classes at the community college in St. George. There aren't a lot of law enforcement jobs in the area. I was lucky to get this one. If I get fired, I may not find another."

"I can't promise we can keep it from him, but I'll do my best."

Stef didn't look happy, but appeared resigned. "This way."

We walked through the main room toward the back, and then took a turn into the hallway. Ten feet past Gerard's office, she stopped at an unmarked door on the left. Stef pulled a single key on a red lanyard from her pocket. "I found this about six months after I started working here. I worked nights back then. One night, I ran out of printer paper. I thought this had to be the stockroom. The door's kept locked. I found the key on a hook behind the chief's desk. Let myself in."

"It's not a storeroom, I take it?"

"No." She opened the door. "Take a look."

All manner of filing cabinets covered the walls of the windowless room, at least thirty feet wide by twenty feet long. Some of the metal cabinets were painted black and pocked with bits of rust, covered in thick coats of dust. They looked decades old. Others appeared brand new.

"What's in these?" I asked.

"An alternate set of records," Stef said. "I come in here sometimes, when it's quiet, and I have nothing to do. The best I can tell, pretty much forever Alber PD has kept two sets of records, public ones and private ones. These are the private ones."

"What types of cases?"

"Violent crimes, assaults, rapes and murders. Thefts. I've tried to crossmatch some with the computer. As far as I can tell, none of these are in the system," she said.

I went to the cabinets and took a look. Each of the drawers had a year inked on an index card slipped into a metal frame on the front. "Organized by date, I gather."

"Yup," she said. "Inside, they're divided by type of crime."

I pulled the most recent cabinet open and rifled through it. The tabs on the dividers read: MISSING PERSONS, SEXUAL ASSAULTS, DOMESTIC VIOLENCE, and HOMICIDES. I thought about what this meant, what it might mean, and how it could fit into the missing girls.

"We're going to pull all the sex crimes and missing persons, any homicides," I said. "I'm going to take them with me. I'll bring them back as soon as I can."

Visibly alarmed as I began taking files, Stef protested, "But if the chief finds out…"

"Then he finds out. I'll protect you as much as I can," I said.

Stef hesitated, but then rushed to help me. We stacked the files on a long table, an old dark pine one like the kind in libraries that sat in the center of the room. There were six chairs around it, and as I worked I wondered who came in this room, what kind of secret meetings took place here. I started with the current year and worked my way back. I thought about stopping at five years, but I went back ten. In the end, Stef and I had two stacks of files, each about two feet high.

"Help me get these in my car," I said. Apparently again having second thoughts, Stef hesitated. "Now, before someone comes into the station," I ordered. As I walked out carrying the first, she grabbed the second pile.

We hurried through the police station toward the front door, but I had misgivings. "Is there a back door?"

"Yeah," she said.

"Show me." We trailed down a hallway and piled the files up next to a solid steel door. "I'll drive around."

In minutes, we had the files loaded in the Pathfinder, and Stef rushed back inside the station to the reception desk. I drove out of the lot, just as Jeff Mullins pulled in. When I glanced in my rearview mirror, he strolled toward the back door. His eyes focused on the road, he watched me leave.

CHAPTER THIRTY

"Doc says the girl was strangled. There's perimortem bruising around the neck, and the hyoid bone is fractured," Max said when I walked through the door at the sheriff's office. "He can't tell how long she's been dead, but estimates that it had to be more than a couple of months. He hasn't seen a case like this before, and it's beyond his expertise. So Doc's called the ME in Salt Lake to get a consult. Doc will get back with more info as soon as he has it, but that could be a few days."

"Shoot. So will DNA. We can't wait on any of it," I said, frustrated that with limited resources everything took so long. "Did Doc have any more information on our victim? Age range? Is her hair really brown?"

"Doc says she has all her wisdom teeth, but they're not fully out. He's guessing she's late teens to early twenties," Max said. "After he inspected for fibers and such, he washed a small section of her hair. It didn't lighten. Looks like a very dark brown. He emailed us more photos of the clothes, the body, and the washed hair. They're in a file on the conference room—I mean, your office table."

"Thanks. I have files out in my car we need to bring in. I could use some help."

A few minutes later, we had the secret Alber PD files on the conference room table as well. "What is all this?" Max asked.

"I'll explain later," I said. "Where are the Heatons?"

"In interview room number three. The Coombs women are in room one."

"Let's go," I said.

"So things have changed," I said to Alma, Grace, and Savannah Heaton, the three sister-wives. "You've heard, I know, that we have a body. Doc says it's female, a teenager, perhaps up to early twenties, long brown hair."

Alma Heaton gasped, and Savannah, a thickly built woman with her hair in a messy brown bun, reached over to comfort her. "Anything else about the dead girl you can tell us, Clara?" Savannah asked.

In my prior life, I'd known Savannah Heaton. A decade earlier, when I had a desk in the town's cinder block schoolhouse, Savannah's children were my students. She stopped in my classroom to pick up one of her girls a month before I fled. She'd seen my bruises. "Who gave you that black eye?" she'd asked. I told her what I'd said to everyone else, that I'd walked into a door. Back then I was young, ashamed, and good at making excuses. Savannah gave me a knowing look, and I saw that she didn't believe me.

In my conference room office, Alma reclaimed her resolve and turned to her sister-wives for reassurance. "Savannah, Grace, we don't belong here. That's not our girl's body. Eliza ran away. We know that."

"How?" I asked.

Alma hesitated. She looked at the others. "We're not supposed to talk of Eliza. She's an apostate, like you are. Clara, you know what the prophet says about people who leave the faith. We're to shun—"

"These are exceptional circumstances," I pointed out. "Alma, you need to tell me."

Her eyes darkened and clouded over, like the mountaintops when a storm blows in. "We went on a picnic, and Eliza didn't want to come. We, she and I, had words. When we came back, the house was empty. Grace found a note, in Eliza's hand."

I stared at Grace. "Tell me what it said."

The woman who earlier had chastised me and ordered me from her yard sighed hard and shrugged. "It was short, but it left no room for misunderstanding. It said, 'I've gone to the city. I can't live here anymore. Don't try to find me.' Eliza signed it."

"And you believed it?" I asked.

Grace looked at the other two women, and I knew before they spoke that they'd feared something might be wrong, but they'd buried their suspicions.

"Well, we did think it was odd," Grace admitted, glancing over at Alma.

"Odd how?" I asked.

"Eliza didn't take her clothes. We couldn't tell that she took anything."

Moments passed. The women looked one at the other, and then their eyes closed and their heads bowed. I sensed that they each silently acknowledged the truth. Perhaps they'd always known but refused to accept it.

"Is there a way to tell if that's Eliza's body?" Savannah asked, her voice quiet with resignation.

"We're doing DNA, but that will take time. We'll need a sample from you, Alma, as Eliza's mother," I said. Alma nodded. Then I asked, "Is there anything in particular Doc can look for during the autopsy? Does Eliza have any identifying scars? Any old injuries, like broken bones?"

Alma opened her purse and pulled out the photo of Eliza we'd asked her to bring. In the image, a pretty young girl stared back at me, one with inquisitive green eyes and a self-confident smile. I hoped it wasn't her we'd found in the field. "No broken bones.

But she has a mole above her lip," Alma said, pointing at the dark, round spot on the photo.

Alma had a twin blemish on the right side of her face, half an inch north of her upper lip.

"Just like yours?" I observed.

"Yes," Alma agreed. "We… she inherited that from me."

"Max, call the doc. Ask him to look for the mole," I said, and Max left the room. "While Max does that, let me show you photos of the dress on the body. See if it looks familiar."

I'd brought the file with me. I sifted through, not wanting them to see the gruesome photos of the mummified body of what had once been a vibrant young woman. I pulled out two that I wanted them to look at. One showed the collar on the dress, the other a close-up of the green fabric with the flowered stripes. They inspected them, one woman handing the photos to the other, and put their heads together and whispered.

"No," Alma said. "We don't think this is Eliza's dress."

Minutes later, Max returned. "Doc doesn't see the mole, but the condition of the corpse, well, it's bad. So he can't be sure."

"Can you tell us anything else about how Eliza disappeared?" I asked the women. "Anything at all?"

"No. There's nothing else." Alma frowned. "Clara, can't you put our minds at ease? Can't you give us hope that it isn't our girl?"

I decided to speak in a language I knew they'd understand. "Lord willing, Eliza is healthy and well and you'll see her again soon. But we need to look at all the possibilities, Alma. I need your help to figure this out."

All the anger Alma had shown earlier in the day had washed away, leaving only sadness. "What can we do?"

"You can give Doc Wiley a sample of your DNA," I explained. "Right now, that's all you can do for your girl."

Alma Heaton nodded as tears filled her eyes.

Max left to get a DNA collection kit, and I said my goodbyes and hurried to interview room one, where Genevieve Coombs and her sister-wife waited. Their attitudes had changed as well. The finding of the girl in the field had shaken all of them.

"Tell me what you can about Jayme leaving," I asked once I sat down.

"We were worried at first, because Jayme just disappeared. She was outside, and then she was gone," Genevieve said. "But she'd run away before, to the shelter, telling Hannah Jessop crazy stories about our family. So we thought she did that again. But Hannah came to see us the next day, and she said Jayme wasn't at the shelter."

I assumed the Heatons had left, as Max walked into the room holding another DNA kit in a clear plastic bag. He stood off a bit, near the door, observing.

I didn't question Genevieve about the abuse Jayme claimed. This wasn't the time to get to the bottom of that. I needed to zero in on the girl's disappearance. "What did you do? Did you tell anyone?"

"We were worried something happened to Jayme. All her clothes were still at the house, not like she took anything. So the following day, we went to the police station," Genevieve said. "We talked to Chief Barstow. He looked worried, too. He took a few notes, and then he left us and made a few phone calls. A little while later, he came back with a sheet of paper, the phone number of some crisis center in Salt Lake written on it. He said Jayme was there. Someone saw her there. He said that she wasn't coming home."

"You reported her missing to Chief Barstow?" I asked. I looked over at Max, and he shot back a questioning glance. This wasn't what we expected to hear.

"Yes," Genevieve said. "I took the phone number home, but it made no sense to call. Jayme was gone, like so many of the other kids in town. Ran out and left us."

"We have some photos. Of the dead girl's dress and hair. I'd like to show them to you." I laid them out on the table. Genevieve and her sister-wife looked at the photos and murmured.

"Jayme's hair is lighter, more blond," Genevieve said, relief in her voice. "And the dress, it could be, but we're not sure. She had one something like that, but maybe different."

"We don't believe this is Jayme, but we want to make sure," I explained. "Would you be willing to give us some of the cells from inside your mouth, Genevieve? We want to compare DNA."

Jayme's mother agreed. Max swabbed the inside of her cheek, and we said goodbye. As she turned to leave, she looked at me. "If that's not Jayme, do you think she's safe somewhere? Maybe in Salt Lake like the police chief told us?"

"I don't know," I said. "We're going to try to find out."

As soon as the door closed behind the Coombs women, I turned to Max. "I was at Alber PD earlier. The chief wasn't in. Can you try to reach him?"

"Yeah." He pulled out his cell, dialed the number, and put the phone on speaker.

"Gerard," Max said when the chief answered. "Clara and I have a question. We just had Genevieve Coombs in here. She says she reported Jayme missing to you in May. Did she do that?"

Barstow huffed. "Max, you're questioning me?"

"We need to know, Gerard. We're trying to pin some of this down."

"Yeah, she talked to me. Told me what happened, that Jayme had disappeared or taken off. I made some calls to the usual places, the youth centers and stuff. I called a place in Salt Lake, some crisis center. A woman told me Jayme was there. So I gave the phone number to Genevieve."

"Why didn't you tell us that earlier, Chief?" I asked.

Barstow sounded furious. "I didn't see where it was any of your business, Detective. The bottom line was that Jayme wasn't missing. Like her mother told you, she ran off."

"Gerard, we have a dead body. Everything is our business." Then I thought about my own phone call with the crisis center. "How did you find that out so quickly? I've checked with that organization about the girls. They couldn't offer much help. They don't have a lot of computerized records. And the woman I talked to didn't have any information on Jayme."

"You think I'm not telling you the truth?" he railed. "Max, what the hell is this?"

"Clara's not questioning your truthfulness, Gerard," he said. "But we need to understand what's happening."

Silence, and then Gerard Barstow said, "Clara, listen. I didn't get into the particulars with the woman. But I talked to a lady there. And she said someone staying at the shelter from Alber knew Jayme and saw her at the center. This was just a couple of days after the girl left town. Maybe she moved on. But that day they said she was there."

We hung up. There was still so much we didn't know. I was frustrated that Alber PD's chief hadn't told us everything earlier, but I tried to put that to the side. All I could do was move forward. "Let's file missing persons reports on Eliza and Jayme and circulate them to the media. We have photos of both girls, the dates of their disappearances and descriptions of how they went missing."

"I'll get right on it," Max offered.

"While you do that, I'll skim the files I brought," I said, pointing at the mounds sitting on the table. "Then we're going to visit my family."

CHAPTER THIRTY-ONE

"I don't think you should keep her chained up like that," Jayme said, while Delilah listened through the vent. The man had returned a few minutes earlier. As soon as he walked in her room, Jayme turned the conversation to Delilah. "You're gonna make that girl hate you if you treat her bad, mister. Why don't you treat us better? Then we'd maybe learn to care about you."

Delilah and Jayme had come up with their plan while the man was gone. To carry it out they needed two things: to have Delilah unchained, and for them both to gain more freedom in the house. Once the chains were off and he let his guard down, they might find a way to escape.

"You girls don't need to care about me," the man said. "That doesn't matter."

"I thought you wanted us to be a family," Jayme said. "Ain't I your wife? That girl upstairs, when she gets older, you're gonna marry her, right?"

"I'm gonna marry her soon. I'm not waiting much longer. She's old enough," the man scoffed.

Upstairs, Delilah felt a wave of revulsion and her skin chilled.

"When do you think?" Jayme asked.

"Soon as I get a few things done," he said. "Some things I have to take care of came up. Gotta handle those first."

"You don't want to marry her chained, do you?" Jayme prodded.

The man didn't say anything that Delilah could hear, but there was some murmuring. She strained hard, listening. "If we was a family, you could trust us. We could cook for you, take care of you, like we were trained to take care of a husband," Jayme said. "Don't you want us to be a real family, with babies and all?"

"Babies?" he repeated.

"Yeah," Jayme said. "That girl and me could take care of you. Wives do that for husbands. If we're gonna be living here the rest of our lives, like you say we are, I think it's better if we become a family."

"How do I know you two won't try to get away?" he asked.

The girl stared wide-eyed at him. "Because we know what you'd do. You told us you'd kill us and our families. We wouldn't risk that."

"I would," he said. "Kill you all."

"If we were a real family, if you were our husband, we wouldn't want to leave," Jayme argued. "Wives take up for their husbands. Like my mom always told me, women obey their men."

The man said, "I'll think on it."

A short time later, Delilah heard a door close downstairs, as if the man had left Jayme's room. Then she heard a slight commotion outside. Somewhere a dog barked and a horse neighed. Time passed, and she heard horse hooves clomping on the hard earth.

The house grew quiet.

CHAPTER THIRTY-TWO

I divided the secret files by year. Ten stacks. I leaned over the table and opened the first file and found a photo of a woman with a cut cheek and an eye so black it was rimmed in purple. "Damn," I whispered. The notes said it was a five-month-old unsolved sexual assault. The woman was forty-six years old. I felt my anger rising, thought of my own history, the physical and emotional scars. But as horrific as the case looked, this wasn't the time.

The guy I was looking for liked teenage girls.

I set that file to the side. As I combed through the others, I found photos of men, women and children who'd been sexually abused, assaulted, raped and murdered. Not a lot perhaps by outside standards, but for a town of 4,346 souls, a substantial number. What stood out? It appeared from the files, a few scarce sheets of paper that mainly served as witness statements, that none of the cases had been investigated before being filed away.

One by one, I browsed through.

I thought about my father. Being a polygamist took planning. To keep track of which of my four mothers he slept with each night, Father had a calendar posted in the kitchen rotating their names. With so many children, he set aside one day each month for an hour alone with each of us. On my days, we hiked through the woods and talked.

"What's the outside world like?" I'd asked him once.

"Not like it is here, Clara," he'd told me. "There are bad people in the Gentiles' world. Every morning in the newspapers, every evening on the television, reporters recount horrible crimes. Here we don't hear about such things, because here we stand unified as children of God."

In my hands I held the reports that disproved his words. I looked at the victims' photos, their bloody faces, and I wondered if my father had known the truth.

We didn't live on a mountain of righteousness. Far from immune, our little town apparently had its full share of violence. The only difference: In Alber, a conspiracy of silence hid it behind a virtuous veneer. Alber took such pains to deny the truth, that I fled believing I was the only battered woman in our town. I felt responsible, believed that I'd brought the horror on myself. Looking through the files at photos of other faces like mine, bruised and bleeding, I recognized some of the victims. Others were strangers.

According to the files, none of them had gotten justice. I saw no record of anyone ever being charged with a crime.

I kept searching. In one file I found the three-year-old case of a mother who claimed a man harassed her thirteen-year-old daughter. The woman revealed the man's name. On the report, someone had used a thick marker to black it out. I held it up to the light. I couldn't see a first name, but over the second the marker thinned, enough so I could read: BARSTOW.

Evan Barstow? I wondered. I started a pile of possibly related cases. This would be the first.

Anything that didn't involve girls, teenagers, young women in their early twenties, I set aside. Many of the cases were appalling, but I couldn't consider them. I had a dead girl. Others missing. I had to find Delilah.

Then, in the files that dated nine years back, I found something of particular interest.

Fifteen-year-old Christina Bradshaw's family lived on the outskirts of the town. According to the file, she watched the younger children in the yard that afternoon. The little ones went inside for a snack, while Christina waited outside. When they returned, she'd vanished. In the week before she went missing, Christina complained repeatedly that a particular man stalked her. "This man had been warned before to stay away from Christina," the report read. "Christina's mother believes that this man has taken her daughter. An officer contacted the suspect. He denied it."

The paperwork didn't reveal the man's identity.

Bradshaw? Why did it sound so familiar? Then I remembered. Evan Barstow's second wife was Jessica Bradshaw. I picked up my cell phone. "Hannah, it's Clara," I said. "Does Jessica Bradshaw have a younger sister named Christina?"

"Let me think," she said. "It's a big family. I'm not sure. Is it important?"

"It could be," I said.

"I heard about the body. I hoped you'd call. I got worried. Is it Delilah?"

I felt a catch in my throat. "No."

"Do we know who it is?"

"Not yet," I answered. Max walked in and waited in the doorway. I needed to get off the phone. "Hannah, I'm in a hurry. I need to know about Christina."

"I don't know the girl, but hold on and I'll ask. I have a Bradshaw here at the shelter. She'll know."

I put the phone on mute and concentrated on Max. "You got the missing persons reports out?"

"Yeah," Max said. "Jayme and Eliza are both on NCIC, and I notified the Center for Missing and Exploited Children. The sheriff's secretary is sending out notices to the media in St. George, Salt Lake, and some of the smaller cities in the area. It should all be on the news tonight."

"Great," I said.

"Clara, I got one ready to go on Delilah, too. What details we know. When we get back from talking to your family, we can add a photo and get out an Amber Alert. I listed her as 'endangered missing.'"

"Good work," I said. "Just a minute, and I'll be with you."

Hannah came back on the phone. "Christina is one of Jessica's younger sisters. They're both from the same mother, their father's third wife."

"Okay. That helps."

"But there's something strange."

"Go on."

"The woman I spoke to is a cousin. She says that Christina hasn't been seen in years. They were told that she'd run off with a boy when she was a teenager."

"Did she know the boy's name?"

"No."

I thanked her and then hung up before she could ask any questions. I took the two files that caught my attention, the one on Christina and the one on the thirteen-year-old's stalker. I handed both to Max. "We're going to split up," I said. "You have two cases here, a harassment charge and a missing person. Take a look."

Max opened the files and flipped through the reports.

"Where did you get these? I don't remember seeing either one," he said. "I searched for missing persons when I first got the note on Delilah. This report on Christina Bradshaw didn't come up."

"It's a long story. Talk to their families. See what you can find out. Find out who the Bradshaws suspected in their daughter's disappearance."

"They had a suspect?"

"It says they did," I said. "And the other report, the thirteen-year-old, the family named the man they say stalked their girl."

"Who was it?"

"It's been redacted. All I can read is the last name. Barstow."

"One of the Barstows was involved?" His voice rose in alarm.

"It appears that way."

"Clara, I can do this, but are you sure you don't want me to go out to talk to your family with you?"

"I'm sure." I picked up the folder with the photos of the dead girl's dress to bring with me. "This time, I'm going alone. And I'm not leaving that trailer until I find out what happened to Delilah."

CHAPTER THIRTY-THREE

The man walked in before Delilah heard him. The light had softened and filtered in around the boarded-up window. Late afternoon leaning toward evening, she decided. Still a long time before night.

"You have a good nap?" he asked.

At the sight of him, Delilah's heart pitched so high she thought it might lodge in her throat.

"I sleep a lot," she said. "I wish I could move around."

"I've been thinking about that," he said. "You think if I unchain you, you'll keep settled down?"

"Yes." Delilah said, hopeful. "I promise."

Out of his back pocket he pulled a small ring with two keys. "Turn around," he said. Delilah did, and the man leaned toward her. She thought he'd reach for her wrists, but he paused to take her hair in his hand, feeling the weight of it. "I've always loved the look of a redhead. That's why you caught my attention."

Delilah shivered.

"You cold?" he asked.

"Maybe a little," she said.

"Come on. We're going downstairs," he said.

The old house looked a mess, with boxes and newspapers scattered across the floor and furniture. Dirty clothes heaped in piles. "This way," he said, leading her into a short hall. A door opened into a bathroom, the tub filled with water. "Git in."

Delilah moved forward, and then turned to close the door.

The man put out his hand to stop her and pointed at a chair in the hallway. "Leave it an inch open. I'm gonna sit here. I want to hear what you're doing."

"Okay," she answered.

Although uneasy with the man so close behind the door, Delilah dropped her clothes on the floor. As she sank into the water, relief flooded through her. The warmth soothed the bruises the chains had left on her sore ankles and wrists and felt better than any bath she'd ever taken. She eased her head under the water, and then came back up, her hair streaming wet down her back.

She worked shampoo into her hair and lathered it into her scalp, then grabbed a bar of soap and a well-worn washcloth. Delilah scrubbed as if she hadn't had a bath in years, scouring her skin. She wanted to wash the last four days away, the soiled mattress, the dim locked room, and the shame she felt when the man looked at her.

"Better finish up," he ordered.

"Just one more minute," Delilah shouted. She closed her eyes and leaned back to rinse her hair.

Without warning, the door opened. The man's heavy hand came at her and pushed her under the water. She kicked and flailed her arms, gasped for breath. The back of her head struck the smooth surface of the tub with a *thunk*.

Helpless, her mind flashed on her mother, the sister-wives, her brothers and sisters, as if saying goodbye to each one. She felt her father's presence and wondered if he had come to pull back the curtain and welcome her into heaven.

At the moment she gave in to the inevitability of death, the man let go.

Delilah broke through the water's surface, splashing waves across the tub. Her starved lungs sucked in air. Ragged coughing, a violent lurch deep within her, and she vomited filthy bathwater.

Shaking, she looked over at the man, who stared at her with cold, dead eyes. "Listen, little girl," he hissed. "Don't you ever cross me. You understand?"

"I-I-I…" her naked body trembled so violently that she couldn't get the words out.

"You give me any reason to doubt you? I'll kill you. Count on that," he shouted as he grabbed a towel off the door and threw it at her.

CHAPTER THIRTY-FOUR

It appeared that the family meeting Jim Daniels had mentioned was still in session. The street in front of my family's trailer was lined with cars when I arrived. I knocked on the door, and someone looked out the window on my right. The door didn't open. I knocked again. Harder. Still nothing.

"Mother," I said, pounding on the screen door with my fist. It rattled, making a loud, tinny racket. "Open this door now!"

The lock clicked. The door opened a few inches, and a man stood behind it.

"Aaron," I said. "Thank you. Now please let me inside. I need to talk to all of you about Delilah."

He eased the door open a bit farther. My oldest brother had changed over the years. His shoulders were broader than I remembered and he looked heavy and solid, his forehead wide and his chin set. He scowled at me with Father's dark eyes. "Clara, Mother doesn't want you here. She wants you to leave."

I shook my head and stared right back at him. "No. Not this time. I'm not going anywhere."

"You need to get off her property," he said. "You have no right to be here."

I held the file with the photos in my hand, and I slipped it under my right arm so that I could open my jacket to show him my badge. "Aaron, I've been sworn in by the sheriff. I'm now Deputy Clara Jefferies with the Smith County Sheriff's Office. Please remind Mother that she's squatting on public property.

Mother has no ownership rights to this land, and I have every right to be here. So open the door. I'm coming in."

"Just a minute." He started to close the screen door, but I stuck my foot in to stop him.

"We're going to leave this open," I said. "You've got two minutes."

I heard murmuring inside. It didn't take long. The door swung wide, and I entered a room filled with familiar faces—Mother, Sariah and Naomi, my older brothers and sisters, including Karyn, who I'd missed at her home a couple of hours earlier, and younger ones who looked at me, eyes wide. Wondering who I was, I guessed. For a moment, it took my breath away. I'd been on my own for a decade, and the familiarity felt both welcomed and strained.

"Hello," I said. "I'd like to talk to each one of you individually, but there's no time. Which one of you is going to tell me what happened to Delilah?"

Alarmed, all three of our mothers stood and rushed about, nudging the youngest children out of the room, pushing them to other parts of the trailer.

"Go play," Naomi urged an eight- or nine-year-old with her slender nose and light brown hair.

"This isn't a place for little ones," Mother said. "Be good, and we'll call you when dinner is ready."

Once the evacuation ended, the women reclaimed their places on the couch. Even with the children gone, the room felt claustrophobic. I wondered how so many lived in such tight quarters. But then, they didn't have a choice. I noticed Lily in the center of a group of teenagers, leaning against the opposite wall. She looked upset, her face flushed and one hand cradling her forehead as if she had a terrible headache.

"I asked a question," I said. "What happened to Delilah?"

Everyone in the room turned and looked at my mother, who had her head down, staring at her hands on her lap. "Clara, I asked you to leave. What you are doing is not acceptable. You need to go now. Staying here won't help Delilah. It will hurt her."

"I'm not going anywhere, Mother." *She can't even bear to look at me*, I thought. "And why would you say that? Why would my staying affect Delilah in any way?"

"There are things I can't discuss," she said. "But the situation is being handled. You need to leave."

"Mother, this is ridiculous. No announcement has been released about Delilah. The police aren't looking for her. I don't know who you think is going to save her, but she needs help, and you shutting down like this? Refusing to help me? You will get Delilah killed."

Beside Mother, Sariah let out a moan, like an animal in pain.

"Clara!" Mother shouted, glancing at Sariah and giving her a stern look. "Stop this. I told you, it's being taken care of."

"By who?" I couldn't accept their unwillingness to hear the truth any longer. I had to lay it out so there could be no misunderstanding. "Did you see that girl's body today? The one found in the field?"

Mother looked up at me. "I did, but—"

"Is that what you want to happen to Delilah?"

Sariah let out a sob. At that same moment, from her perch against the wall, Lily released a sharp breath that sounded almost like a muffled scream. Aaron went over to Lily and slipped his arm protectively around her shoulders. He whispered in Lily's ear. She nodded. I thought I heard her mumble, "I'll try."

"What is being handled?" I asked not just my mother but the others in the room. "That something needs handling means that Delilah is in trouble. You're not denying that now, I take it?" None of them answered, their eyes settling on either me or Mother. A few of my sisters appeared to have been crying and I saw a brother I didn't recognize, perhaps sixteen or seventeen, with his hands up to his head. He turned away, not to face us.

I walked over to him, stepping around those seated on the floor. I put my hand on his shoulder and whispered, "Why don't you tell me what's wrong? I bet you know."

He looked up at me, his eyes red. I dropped my hand, and he ran out of the room, terrified.

"What are you all afraid of?" I shouted. "Mother? She can't hurt you. And I promise you, someone here is going to answer my questions. I'm not leaving until I know the truth!"

"Ardeth, maybe Clara is right. Maybe she can help," Sariah whispered. She held a baby's pacifier in her hand, kneading it. Her hand trembled.

"Sariah, shush," Mother said. "I make the decisions for the family. I—"

"You know that dead girl we found behind the cornfield today? Maybe her family sat by and did nothing when she disappeared. I saw some of you there. You looked worried. Were you thinking it might be Delilah?"

Murmurs ran through the group as if some of those in the room agreed with me, but mother yelled over them, "No! We don't have to tell you anything, and we won't. I am protecting Delilah, whether you know that or not."

At that, Sariah brought her hands up to her face. She wept, as Naomi turned and held her. "Ardeth, please," Naomi begged. "Please, let's tell Clara. Maybe she can help us. Please."

"No!" Mother shouted. "Don't you remember what they've done to us? Clara is one of them. The ones who came and ruined us. She can't be trusted."

At that, Lily's voice rang through the room, "Tell her!"

Everyone else in the room went silent.

Her arms thrust down at her sides, ending in fists so tight that veins bulged on the backs of her hands, Lily broke away from Aaron and stood in the center of the room. Tears streamed down her cheeks, and her face had turned a faint, blood-spatter red around the eyes from rubbing. As if no one else existed, she stared at our mother. Her voice softening, Lily begged, "Mother, please tell Clara what happened to Delilah. Please."

Aaron tried to again grab Lily by the shoulders, but this time she swiveled her body and wrestled away. "Mother Sariah, how can you not tell Clara, so she can help us find your daughter? Find my sister? Please, we need to find Delilah!"

Sariah cried harder, her chest quaking.

"Tell Lily, Mother," I demanded. "Explain to her why you're not helping me find our sister."

"It is being handled," Mother said, her voice breaking with emotion but stern. "But not by you. You can't help us."

At this, Sariah stood, her face a mask of rage and trepidation. I'd never remembered any of the sister-wives defying my mother. No one dared. Glancing from Mother to me, Sariah focused across the room on Lily, whose sobs shook her like tremors.

At that moment, something changed.

Sariah stared down at Mother, who still had her hands folded on her lap, refusing to look up at us. "Lily," Sariah said, her words measured. "You and I will go outside with Clara, where the small children can't hear us. And we're going to tell Clara everything we know about the night Delilah disappeared."

Mother looked up at Sariah, as if she'd been betrayed.

Lily's tortured face pulled tight, as she attempted to harness her tears. "Yes," she whispered. "Yes, we will."

"You didn't see anything or anyone? Nothing unusual that night?"

Lily, Sariah and I sat on faded metal chairs at the back of the lot. Behind us, the cornfield loomed, empty far off into the distance until it ended at those final rows still standing. It was now a crime scene, the harvest abandoned after the finding of the body. I had the folder with the photos on my lap. I thought about asking them to look at the dead girl's dress, but I decided it served no purpose. I knew the body wasn't Delilah's.

I reached over and held Lily's hand. "Let's go through it one more time. Make sure I know everything."

Lily described the prior Thursday's evening prayers and following Delilah down the steps to the outhouse with the little ones. "She kept saying someone watched her from the field, but we shined our flashlights in and we couldn't see anyone."

The cornfield, I thought yet again. *What did it have to do with the cornfield?*

"I didn't believe Delilah. I thought she was being silly," Lily said. She teared up again, and covered her face with her hands. "Why didn't I believe her? If I had…"

Sariah wrapped her arms around Lily and held her, whispering, "I thought Delilah silly, too. We didn't know. Lily, we couldn't have known what would happen."

"I shouldn't have left her out there alone. I should have stayed to protect her," Lily said. "Why did Kaylynn take so long in the outhouse? That girl always dilly-dallies. If she'd—"

"Shush," Sariah ordered. "Don't ever say that. This isn't Kaylynn's fault any more than it's yours. If anyone is to blame, I am. I should have listened to my daughter."

"None of you are to blame," I said. "The person to blame is the one who took Delilah."

Sariah looked at me as if my words had given her the first solace she'd had in days. "Clara, I'm sorry," she said. "I'm sorry Ardeth didn't trust you. We should have—"

"Please, let's just talk about Delilah." I had a notebook out, one I filled with the details. "Describe to me what Delilah wore that evening."

"She had on a blue dress with a white collar, a white sash belt around the waist. I remember thinking how pretty it looked with her red hair," Sariah said. "Her sandals and white socks."

"And she had a white ribbon in her hair holding it up at the top," Lily said. "A thin one tied in a bow."

"Anything else she said to you that could help me? Any description of anyone you saw around that time hanging out around the trailer, watching Delilah or any of the other girls?"

"Nothing," Sariah said.

"If someone watched us, he did it hidden in the cornfield, as Delilah said. I didn't see anyone," Lily said.

I thought again about Jim Daniels.

"Is Karyn still inside?" I asked.

Sariah looked concerned. "We heard you went to her house today, that you talked to Jim and Rebecca."

"I need to talk to Karyn," I said. "Please ask her to come out."

"I'll do it," Lily said, jumping up. As she rushed off, she turned back to me. "Clara?"

"Yeah," I said.

"You won't let him hurt Delilah, whoever took her, right?"

That was a tough one. "I'll do my best, Lily. And you are doing your best, I know. Keep thinking about that night. Anything you remember, whether it seems important or not, tell me. Let me decide if it is something that can help find our sister."

"I will," she said.

Lily disappeared inside the trailer, and Sariah put her hand on my arm. "Clara, Jim's not a bad man. He's not. I know you suspect him, but—"

"If he didn't do it, I need to rule him out," I said, leaving no room for argument. "Right now, I'm wondering about him. I need to find out more."

"Okay." Sariah looked satisfied.

"Maybe you should go inside, too," I said. "So I can talk to Karyn alone."

Sariah appeared reluctant. "Clara, I need to help."

I took the hand that moments earlier Lily held. "Sariah, you have helped. You've told the truth. Now let me do my job."

Moments after Sariah left, Karyn walked down the concrete steps toward me. "It's been so long, Clara. I've wondered about you often. Did you think about us when you were so far away?"

I tried to decide how to answer, whether or not to admit that though I tried not to, my thoughts too often returned to Alber and my family. Instead, I redirected the conversation. "Karyn, I need your help. Do you know anything that could help me find Delilah?"

Grave sadness darkened the hollows around Karyn's eyes and she shook her head. "I wish so that I did. I've prayed that I would be able to help."

"I need you to tell me—"

"Where Jim was that evening?" Karyn asked.

I gave her a questioning glance. "How did you know I'd ask that?"

"Everyone in the family knows you questioned Jim and Rebecca today. They all know about the time he spent in jail," she explained. "Jim was with me that evening, with two of our children. We drove to St. George to pick up fertilizer. I have the receipt in my purse. I can get it and show you."

"Okay. Why didn't he and Rebecca tell me that?"

"I think Mother frightened them so about talking to you, they weren't sure what they could or couldn't say." With that, Karyn stood. "I'll go inside and get the receipt. I looked earlier and it has the time on it. Jim signed it."

"I'll wait here," I said.

Karyn began to walk away, but turned back to me. "You know, when we go into the city, I see cameras all over. I bet they have them at the Walmart. You should be able to see us on camera."

I smiled. "You *have* thought this through."

"I'm used to having to explain Jim to others. People often don't understand him. My husband is brilliant in many ways, but he doesn't interact well with people. Rebecca and I realize that he can come across as awkward." She gave me an unassuming smile. "I'll be right back with my purse."

At that, she turned and headed back to the trailer. Karyn hadn't made it to the steps when Lily burst out the screen door. She held something: a long, thick, neon-orange flashlight.

"Clara, Delilah had her flashlight with her at the outhouse," Lily said, rushing toward me. "Mine is just like it. This one. When Delilah disappeared, the flashlight vanished, too."

She put the flashlight in my hands. It looked familiar. Why?

"This is so strange. I have the feeling I recently saw one just like this," I whispered. "Maybe there are a lot of them around?"

"No, we just had the two, Delilah's and mine. Naomi bought them in Salt Lake, at a hardware store. They're special. The beam is strong and you can adjust it so that it's wide. It's good to use to take the little ones out at night."

Karyn looked at me. "I guess whoever took Delilah must have taken the flashlight."

I thought back to earlier that day. I remembered seeing a flashlight just like the one I held in my hands on a kitchen counter. At the time, it reminded me of traffic cones. I grabbed my cell phone. "Max, I know who has Delilah," I said. "Meet me at the sheriff's office. We need a search warrant."

CHAPTER THIRTY-FIVE

Lily sat in the seat next to me as we drove through Alber on the way to the sheriff's office in Pine City. Behind us, Sariah and Naomi followed in the family van. As Delilah's mother, Sariah needed to authorize the official missing person report. I wanted Naomi available to sign a statement, since she purchased the matching orange flashlights. As the Pathfinder bounced down the road, Lily held her flashlight on her lap, clutching it tight, as if it were a talisman with the power to bring her sister home.

"Can you explain what Mother meant?" I asked Lily. "When she kept insisting that someone was taking care of all this, handling it? Who was she talking about?"

"I don't know," Lily said. "Mother told us not to worry, that someone we could trust would find Delilah."

"But she never said who?"

"Not to me. I don't think she told anyone," Lily said. I drove for a few more minutes, and my sister turned to me. "I think I do remember you, Clara. I remember you from when I was little. That I'd go to school and you were there. Teaching."

"Lily, thank you for that." In Dallas, no one truly knew me. Since I'd arrived in Alber, almost everyone had turned away from me as if I didn't exist. Lily's recognition touched me to my core. For the first time in a very long time, I wasn't an outsider, but someone remembered: I was their teacher, their sister.

"Did you think of us while you were gone?" she asked.

After so many years separate, it felt odd to look into eyes so like mine. The moment filled me with pleasure, but at the same time it broke my heart. Since arriving back in Alber, I'd been forced to face the truth; when I fled, I lost so much more than I would have ever admitted, even to myself. "I've tried hard not to think of the past, because it hurts to remember. But, yes, I've thought of all of you. I wondered if you were happy and well. I wondered if anyone remembered me." Alber disappeared behind us as I turned onto the highway. "What this trip has taught me is that you can leave home, but you can't ever truly leave it behind. No matter where you end up, where you started haunts you. And the people you love? You carry them with you, whether you realize it or not."

It was going on six thirty and the Smith County Courthouse had closed an hour earlier. I called Max, and he unlocked the door to let us in.

"I asked Judge Crockett to wait in his courtroom to sign the warrant," he said as we rushed through the lobby. "Everything's in place."

We marched into the sheriff's office, and I said, "Sariah, I'll need the photo."

She handed me a recent one of Delilah, a rosy-cheeked smiling kid with big blue eyes and freckles, older but not much different than the way I remembered her.

"Here, I'll take that." Max handed the photo off to Helen, the sheriff's secretary. "Scan this in," he told her.

Then Max pulled a two-page report out of a file with Delilah's name on the front. "Sariah, here's the missing person report. You need to sign it so we can launch the Amber Alert."

He handed her a pen. Sariah stared down at the paper, then over at me, searching my face. Her shoulders tense, her expression pained, I understood her fear. Never before had any of the sister-wives gone against my mother. But Sariah read the document, and then scrawled her signature across the bottom. "Now you'll look for my Delilah?" she asked, her voice unsure but hopeful.

"Yes," Max said. "Now everyone will look for her."

"Send out the Amber Alert and the missing person report," Max instructed Helen. "It's all in the system. Everything's ready."

"It'll be done in two minutes," Helen said. "Mrs. Jefferies?"

Naomi responded as well, but Helen singled out Sariah. "I'll say a prayer for your girl."

"Thank you," Sariah said. "You're very kind."

"Do we need anything else from them?" I asked Max. "I brought Naomi and Lily in case you have any questions about the flashlight. Do you want them to sign any kind of statement?"

"I don't think so. Not at this point. This should do it."

At the courthouse door, Sariah turned back to me. She reached out and wrapped her arms around me. "Bring my Delilah home, Clara. Please, bring her home."

I wanted to respond, but I didn't trust my voice. As they walked away, I pulled myself together, turned and headed back to find Max.

Moments later, we had our heads together over the computer at his desk.

"Clara, I've got the affidavit for the search warrant written, but something's bothering me. How did you find out Evan Barstow has an identical flashlight? How did you get inside his house?"

I'd prepared for this question, one I anticipated I'd be asked. I needed to walk a thin line, not lie but not tell everything. "I was suspicious, and I wanted to see where Evan lived," I said. "I pulled into the driveway and asked to use the phone. One of his wives, Jessica, invited me inside. While I was there, I saw the flashlight sitting out in the open on a countertop. Then, at the trailer, Lily showed me her flashlight, identical to the one taken when Delilah disappeared. It's unusual, bigger than most, and the color, that bright, bright orange. I realized that it matched the one at the Barstow house."

"That's all that happened? You just walked up and asked Jessica to use the phone?" Max didn't believe me. I didn't blame him. "Clara, are you sure you didn't do anything I should know about to convince her?"

"Nothing to worry about," I said.

Max stared at me as doubtfully as if I'd just told him that I'd chopped the top off one of the mountains with a penknife. "Clara, you're a cop. If Evan Barstow is behind all of this, if he does have Delilah, the other girls, if he killed that girl out in the field, you do understand that it's a problem if you lie to get the warrant. Any evidence we find may not be admissible."

"Everything on the warrant is true." On the surface, I wasn't lying. And at that moment, I didn't have the luxury of worrying about a trial that could be a year or more away. I wasn't concerned about what a judge might or might not rule. Time ticked away and I cared about one thing: saving Delilah.

The arrest warrant came together easily. Making the case against Evan Barstow stronger, it turned out that we didn't just have the flashlight. While I'd been at the trailer, Max contacted the two families in the police reports I'd found in Alber's secret files. The first didn't help because the Bradshaws insisted the report on their daughter's disappearance had been a mistake. The girl's mother had told Max that Christina apparently did leave on her own. "Six months after they filed the report, they received a letter from her. In it, Christina said that she'd run away to Chicago with a boy and married him," Max recounted.

The other family, however, the parents of the thirteen-year-old who'd filed a complaint, told Max that Evan was the man who harassed their daughter. For months, he watched her in the mornings as she walked to school. He trailed her in his squad car as she traveled home in the afternoons. Frightened, the girl's mother began driving their daughter. The mother refused to let the girl leave the house alone. "They couldn't file charges because

Evan was the Alber police chief at the time. The officers refused to take them," Max explained. "But the girl's parents wrote down their complaint and turned it in. They wanted a record of what Evan was doing."

Max attached a statement from the family with a copy of the original paperwork at the back of the search warrant.

Moments later, Max and I met with District Court Judge Alec Crockett in his chambers behind the courtroom. Ready to head home for supper, the judge had his black robe hanging on a coat rack. Well into his sixties, he looked like the grandpa next door in khakis and a green polo shirt. He didn't appear to worry about breaking the law against smoking in a county building as he puffed on the scant remains of a Lucky Strike. "So this is a search warrant for the home of the former Alber police chief? He's currently the chief in Hitchins, right?"

"Yes, your honor," I said.

"And what you've got is…" He stopped talking and eyed the two of us while smashing the cigarette's stub out in an overflowing ashtray.

"That Evan Barstow has a history of stalking young girls," I recounted. "That Delilah Jefferies was abducted last Thursday evening. That Delilah's orange flashlight disappeared at the same time she did, suggesting the kidnapper took it as well. That I saw what I believe is Delilah's flashlight in Evan Barstow's home, sitting out in plain sight on a kitchen counter."

"Barstow's wife let you in?" The judge's shaggy right eyebrow rose in suspicion.

"Yes, Judge," I said. "I wasn't employed by the sheriff's department at the time, and had no authority in Smith County. I went to the Barstow home as a private citizen. I asked to use a phone. Jessica Barstow invited me inside."

"She did, huh?" His skepticism didn't appear in the least abated. "This doesn't sound like a lot of evidence. I'm not sure it's enough probable cause."

"We're not asking for an arrest warrant, Judge," Max countered. "This search warrant is limited. We want to confiscate the matching flashlight so it can be processed for fingerprints and DNA, and to see if there's any evidence Delilah Jefferies has been on the property. We'll be looking for clothes that match the description of what she wore when she was taken."

The judge seemed to consider that. I knew walking in his office door that a warrant wasn't a sure thing. We should have had more evidence, but we didn't.

"You found a body today I heard, in Alber?" the judge asked.

"Yes," Max said. "A young woman, somewhere from teenager to early twenties, Doc Wiley says."

"And we also have two other girls besides Delilah, both local teens, feared missing. We put reports on NCIC today," I added. "Judge, there are indications we may have a serial predator here. These cases have similarities, girls suddenly disappearing. The three we have IDs for all lived in the trailer park in houses that backed up to the cornfield."

Judge Crockett shook his head. "Damn strange."

The tension in the room eased when the judge picked up a pen. He handed the signed warrant to Max. "The Barstows are a powerful family. This thing could blow up on all of us," he said. "I sure hope you two know what you're doing."

CHAPTER THIRTY-SIX

At seven forty-two that evening, three sheriff's department squads and the county forensic unit descended on Evan Barstow's home. Max and I led the charge in his county car. All the way there, I wondered if there was any chance we'd find Delilah somewhere on the property. I didn't think so, but I hoped. When we arrived, we saw Evan's Hitchins PD car parked out front. I watched warily as he sauntered out onto the front porch holding an AR15.

"Shit. He's armed. How do you want to handle this?" Max asked.

"He's not a fool. He'll put it down," I said. "We'll take it slow."

We pulled over about where I'd stopped the Pathfinder earlier that day, and the others queued up behind us. Max radioed all of them to stay in their cars. He and I got out simultaneously and Max held up both of his hands, empty, while I hung back behind the car door, my hand hovering at my side over my gun. "Hey, Evan, put that thing down, will you?" Max said. He gave a slight chuckle, like it was all pretty silly. "You know it's not a good idea to have a weapon in your hands when the cops come calling."

After a slight hesitation, Evan dropped the rifle to his side. "What's going on?"

I strode over to him and handed him the search warrant. The front door opened, and all three of his wives clustered behind it. Jessica had her hands up to her mouth, appearing shocked when she apparently recognized me. Meanwhile, a dozen or more kids piled up inside the windows, jostling past each other to get a look.

"You were in my house?" Evan said, after he read the affidavit. "Jessica let you in?"

"I asked to use a phone. She was kind enough to invite me in," I said. "As you read in the warrant, Delilah Jefferies was officially declared missing this afternoon. In the report, it's noted that when she was taken the abductor also took a large, neon-orange flashlight. I believe it is identical to the one I saw sitting out in the open, inside your house."

"That's not enough to get a goddamn warrant," Evan said.

"The judge thought so," I answered. "Especially with your history."

"My history?" he jeered. "You're kidding."

"Not at all," I said. "Look at the paperwork at the back. It's the report you buried at Alber PD on the teenage girl you stalked."

At that point, it seemed that Evan remembered we had an audience, his family. "Get out in the backyard," he shouted at his wives. "Take the kids."

Inside the house, the women and children scurried about. Once they were gone, Evan turned to Max and me. "There's nothing in my house to find."

"There's at least one thing," I said. He gave me a strange look. "That flashlight. I bet it has Delilah's fingerprints and DNA on it."

"I don't know anything about an orange flashlight," he said. "Someone must have left it here. This is all some kind of mistake."

"You should really tell us what we need to know, Evan," I suggested. "It would be good to get in front of this before it goes sour on you. Taking Delilah is one thing. Murdering her is another."

"I don't have Delilah!" he seethed. "Stupidest thing I've ever heard."

"Not for someone like you, someone who has a thing for young girls," I said. We glared at each other, and his hand tightened on the AR15.

"Damn you," he seethed, and I had no doubt he itched to hold up that rifle, take aim at me and pull the trigger. "Go ahead and search the house. I don't have your damn sister. I told you that, and when this all shakes out, I'm going to bury both of you in lawsuits."

"You're welcome to try," Max said. "But right now, put that firearm away before something you regret happens. Then join your family in the backyard. You know the drill. For the time being, make yourself scarce. The forensic unit needs to get started."

"I'll need to lock this up in the gun safe," he said, holding up the rifle.

"Sure, Evan. No problem," Max said. "While you have it open, let the CSI guys take a quick look inside."

Evan frowned and stalked off, fuming.

Once the family cleared the house, the forensic unit spread out inside. Two techs splintered off to search the barn and stables.

While I listened, hoping to hear someone call out that Delilah had been found, I walked Max and the lieutenant in charge of the CSI unit into the kitchen. There the flashlight sat on the counter, just as I remembered it. "Collect that," I said. "Bag it. Then bring it out to Max's car."

"In here," the lieutenant yelled. A forensic photographer responded. He took photos of the flashlight where it sat on the counter, then he moved to the side and an evidence collection technician took over.

A few minutes later, we had the flashlight in a paper bag. Max brought it out to his squad. We kept the bag open and looked inside, while I held Lily's flashlight next to it. "Well, they sure look similar," Max said. "Same size, material, shape, design, the on-off button is identical."

"They're a match," I said. "This has to be Delilah's."

At that moment, I felt the burn of someone's eyes trained on me. Evan Barstow, his face distorted by anger, stood on the side of the house watching us, his cell phone up to his ear. "I wonder if he's calling a lawyer," I whispered to Max.

The CSI lieutenant took the flashlight from us. He folded the top of the bag down and sealed it with tape. With a black marker, he noted the case number associated with Delilah's missing person report on the bag. He jotted down that we recovered the evidence from the kitchen counter inside Evan Barstow's home. Finally, he dated and signed the bag across the tape's lowest edge.

"Give me that other flashlight," he asked, and I did. He went through the same process, logging them both into evidence.

The flashlights processed, the search of the house continued, to my disappointment no one crying out that they'd found my sister. Meanwhile, a metal-sided shed a hundred yards away caught my eye. I walked over, hoping. I knew Delilah wasn't inside when I realized the door stood wide open. I peeked in at saws, hammers, and other tools dangling from a pegboard. On the opposite wall hung a whip, horse leads, and an old buggy harness. I thought of the binding marks on the body in the field. Without touching it, I examined the black braided horse lead, wondering if it could cause such marks. My heart missed a few beats when I discovered a pile of coiled chains in one corner.

This was a sticky situation.

The warrant was tightly written. Limited to Delilah's case, we were only authorized to confiscate certain things: the flashlight and any blue dresses that would fit a girl. White hair ribbons, tan sandals and white socks. We needed a convincing reason to legally take anything else into evidence.

On my knees, I inspected the chains, looking for any signs of skin or blood. I saw nothing except dirt and rust.

"What's up?" Max asked when he walked into the shed.

"No one's seen any signs of Delilah, I gather?" I had to ask, even though I knew he would have told me.

"No, nothing indicating she's been here," he said. "Did you find something?"

"Call the CSI folks in here. We're going to take these chains and have them tested. The horse leads, too," I said, staring up at him. "One or the other might match the binding marks on the girl in the field. The lab may be able to find DNA."

Max frowned. "Every ranch in the county has chains in the barn. They're used for towing and hauling. Everyone with a horse has leads."

"I know, but—"

"Unless you see evidence that these particular chains were used in the commission of a crime, they aren't covered by the warrant," Max said softly, almost as if apologizing. "You know that, Clara. If you take them and they aren't covered by the warrant, it'll be an illegal seizure."

"I know the law, but—"

"Then follow it," Max said, an undercurrent of irritation in his voice.

I stared at him. "Max, we're going to regret this. Once we leave, Evan can throw the chains in a vat and clean them. We need to take these now."

"No," he said. "We're going to stick to the rules. I don't want to do anything we'll regret later."

I stood, simmering. Three feet away from him, I frowned and said, "While I appreciate that you don't want to stray outside the law, the overriding goal here is finding my sister while she's still alive."

Max's expression softened, but he said, "Clara, taking the chains isn't an option. We can't. Evan may end up tied to a murder. I won't let you jeopardize our case."

I knew he was right, but it didn't matter. I wanted those chains in evidence. Max stood in the way. I swallowed my anger and followed him out of the shed back to the house.

After the CSI unit finished up, Max handed Evan a list of what we'd taken, while I glanced back at the shed and again regretted leaving behind what might be valuable evidence.

"You're gonna take good care of that stuff. Those clothes belong to my daughters," Evan said, as he signed the inventory. "When you find out I have nothing to do with any of this, I'll expect everything back in good shape."

"We're getting the flashlight processed ASAP. Fingerprints. DNA," I said. "We'll be getting in touch. Until then, a squad will watch your house. Consider yourself under surveillance."

"Don't worry. I'm not going anywhere." Evan's eyes drilled into me. "I want to be available to hear you explain to the judge that you lied to get in my house. Something about a sick sister?"

Max looked over at me, not pleased.

"I didn't lie on the warrant," I said. "Everything is factual. Evan, don't leave the county. We'll be in touch."

CHAPTER THIRTY-SEVEN

Max had been in more than his share of uncomfortable situations, but the drive back to the sheriff's office ranked high on the list. The inside of the car felt like a pressure cooker cranked up to high.

"Are you going to explain to me how you really got into Evan Barstow's house? What's this about a sick sister?" he asked.

Beside him, Clara shifted in the passenger seat and stared out the window. Her voice flat, she said, "I did what I had to do."

"If you lied, this could come back and bite us," he pointed out yet again.

She glanced over at him and scowled, peeved, he felt sure. "I told you I didn't lie on the search warrant's affidavit," she said.

"But if you lied to Evan's wife, that could open the door for a defense attorney to challenge the evidence we found in the search, including the flashlight," he countered.

At that, Clara's brow wrinkled, and he had the feeling she chose her next words carefully: "Max, you need to stop worrying about your career and start worrying about finding my sister."

Max sucked in a full helping of air and felt his blood pressure rise. He knew the case was personal for Clara. He admitted that she had reason to question his motives. He hadn't backed her up when he should have. But whether Clara understood or not, he'd put any concern about his career aside. All he cared about was doing the right thing for the case.

He wanted to find Delilah just like Clara did. And he understood that with each tick of the clock, the danger the girl was in intensified. But what Clara failed to consider were the realities of the situation. It had been four days since Delilah was taken. In stranger abductions, nearly three quarters of children ultimately murdered died within the first three hours.

As much as Max hoped to bring the girl home alive, he knew he more likely faced the arrest and eventual trial of a murderer. Any shortcuts Clara took, any stepping over the line, could result in letting the monster responsible walk out of a courtroom a free man. She had to understand that her actions could have consequences. "Clara, I don't know how things are done in Texas, but Utah judges frown on law enforcement lying to get inside houses."

For a moment, she kept silent, perhaps considering how to respond. "I told you, I didn't lie on the warrant. Yes, I told Evan's wife I was lost and I had to call my sick sister," Clara confessed. "But what you're not considering, although I've mentioned it before, is that at the time I wasn't a Utah cop."

On one hand, Clara made a good point. She wasn't acting as a law enforcement officer at the time. But that didn't guarantee that a judge wouldn't rule against them in a courtroom. And when she'd wanted to take the chains although they were outside the warrant? Then, Clara wore a Smith County deputy's badge.

I have to find a way to get through to her, Max thought.

"Listen, I'm sorry. I am. But we have to be careful," he said, reasoning that they needed to talk it through. He wanted them to be in agreement, work together, instead of at odds. "We both know the consequences of not following the letter of the law. If we'd taken those chains, we might have permanently poisoned the well. Every piece of evidence we found at Evan's house could be ruled inadmissible."

"So you pointed out." Clara squinted over at Max. "I was willing to take that chance to speed this investigation up. I would do anything necessary to rescue Delilah before she ends up like that girl in the field."

"Don't you think I want that, too?" Max protested, attempting to hide a burning indignation. "I know how it is to feel helpless. Brooke was hurt in the accident, bad. And I… didn't handle it well. I let her down. She's still trying to get better, and I can't get fired. I can't do that to her. Not again."

The car's interior went silent, and Clara turned away.

CHAPTER THIRTY-EIGHT

After her bath, the man gave Delilah a clean dress and a sandwich, the first solid food she'd eaten in days. It tasted dry, the bread crumbly and old, but she dared not complain and consumed it in seconds. Once she finished, he led her back to the upstairs room.

"I need you to do something for me," he said.

Delilah gazed up at him. "What?"

He fished around in his pocket and pulled out a note card and a pen and handed them to her. "Write down what I tell you."

While unsure, she didn't want to upset the man. Delilah braced the note card against the wall, the pen poised over it.

"Write this: I ran away, and I won't be coming home. Don't look for me. Then sign your name."

Stunned, Delilah dropped her arms and blinked at the man. "Why do you want me to write that?"

"Because I want you to. Why is none of your business." He glared at her so hard the nerves underneath her skin crawled. "Don't make me regret taking off your chains. I can put them back on. I can do whatever I want to you, whenever I want to do it."

Delilah stared at the man. Unsure what he intended to do with the note, she didn't like it. She didn't want to write it. She didn't want anyone to stop searching for her.

"You do what I told you. Write that note." The man moved close and stared down at her, his eyes targeted on hers. "If you don't, you will be sorry."

Delilah thought back to her terror in the bathtub. When he trapped her underwater, the world grew hazy, and she knew he could kill her. Certain she had no alternative, her hands trembled as she printed what he'd dictated in big capital letters. At the end, she scrawled her name in cursive, the way her teachers taught her at the cinder block school in town.

"That's a good girl," he said, when she handed it to him.

"What are you going to do with that?"

"Nothing you have to worry about." He looked pleased as he ran his hand along the side of her face, lingering on her smooth, young skin. "It won't be long now."

"What won't?" she asked, trying not to let him see that she had to fight the urge to pull away from his touch.

He didn't answer. Instead, he turned and left. She heard the door lock click behind him. He came back a few minutes later and gave her a bottle of water. Then she heard faint noises from outside. She stood at the window, trying to see out. All she could make out in the thin, jagged slit of light between the board and the window frame were slices of green leaves on a tree and what looked like the mountainside in the near distance. A short time later, she thought she heard someone leave on a horse.

With the man, she assumed, gone, Delilah examined the room. The handcuffs and chains had left bruises on her wrists and ankles, but it felt good to walk about. First, she inspected the door: thick wood panels that fitted tightly. For an old house, the place looked well constructed. She planted one foot against the wall as a brace and grabbed the handle, trying to jerk it open. She pulled and pulled but it wouldn't budge. She scratched her fingertips and tore her nails attempting to pry the board off the window. Dozens of long screws held it tight. Next time he let her out, she decided she needed to find something to use as a tool. She wondered if a butter knife would work on the screws. Maybe she could find something to use to pick the door lock.

Despite being confined to the room, not knowing how she would ever get away, Delilah did feel better. The polished cotton dress she wore dragged on the floor when she walked, but it was clean. It looked homemade, as hers had been, and she wondered who had worn it before her.

"Jayme, it has pink and white flowers, little tulips. Is it yours?" she called out, describing the dress.

"No," the girl downstairs answered. "It must have belonged to one of the other girls."

"The dead ones?" Delilah gulped at the thought.

Jayme didn't answer at first, and then just mumbled, "I guess so."

Thinking about the two girls who'd disappeared, Delilah's mood darkened. "I don't think we can escape." Her voice cracked, and she wished she had something to dry her cheeks. She didn't know when she'd get another clean dress, and she didn't want to dirty the one she wore. But her tears came so fast, she finally gave in and used the hem to mop her eyes. Considering all she knew, Delilah confessed, "I think we're going to die here, like he says."

She wished Jayme would tell her not to worry, that they'd be okay, but she heard only one sound from downstairs, a muffled weeping.

CHAPTER THIRTY-NINE

The conference room resembled a shop that only sold blue dresses. We had them hanging all around us, carefully covered by long evidence bags. Some had white collars and sashes, small flowers, others plaid, solid shades of blue, and gingham. The CSI unit had seized everything they thought presented any possibility. On our way back to the sheriff's department, I'd called Naomi and asked her to bring Mother, Sariah, and Lily to look through the dresses. She said she didn't know if Mother would come, but she agreed to try.

While I waited, I thought back to Evan Barstow's shed, the horse lead and the chains. I wondered yet again if we'd left the real evidence, the important evidence, on the ranch. I understood Max's reasoning, but my frustration made my stomach churn and my nerves bristle. Although it had been only hours since the body was found, it felt as if everything moved in slow motion.

Needing to stay busy, I laid out photos of the girl in the field's dress. Some focused on the once-white collar. Others zeroed in on the small flowers that formed the stripes. Those taken a bit farther away showed the fabric's original light green color. Ivory buttons ran down the front, the thread that anchored each one cured the color of milky coffee.

"What are you looking for?" The sheriff stood over my gruesome photo gallery. "You think the answer's in one of those?"

"I'm hoping so."

"Clara, you've studied those photos," Max said as he walked in. "They aren't changing."

"I know," I said. "It just seems like there should be a clue here."

Max's phone dinged. "An email. Doc Wiley's sending more photos."

"I'll have one of the clerks print them," Sheriff Holmes offered, as he turned to leave. "Maybe this batch will have what you need, Detective Jefferies."

The new images didn't feature the dress. Instead, Doc had photographed a small gold ring in the shape of a flower he removed from the dead girl's right hand. Once we had prints, I lined them up on the table with the others. "That looks like the rings my father gave each of us girls for our sixteenth birthdays," I said to Max. A ball of anxiety lodged in my chest as I inspected the ring more closely. "But that can't be. We know this isn't Delilah."

"How similar is it?" he asked.

"I'm not sure. I have mine in a box in my apartment. I haven't looked at it in years. But this certainly reminds me of it." Holding a photo of the ring in my hands, scrutinizing how the band swirled into the flower, I wondered if we could be wrong. Was there any way that the dead girl could be Delilah? But that was ridiculous. Nothing matched. This girl was taller, her hair a different color, Doc pegged her as older, and she'd been dead for months.

Max picked up a few of the photos and took a closer look. "Clara, I don't think this is an unusual design for a ring."

"You're right, I'm sure. It can't be Delilah. We know that," I said, as I pushed the photos together into a stack. "Plus, she's only twelve. Father, my mothers, wouldn't have given her a sweet sixteen ring yet."

"I'll email some photos of the clothing and the ring out to the media," Max suggested. "The Amber Alert's been out a little more than an hour now. The TV stations are carrying the story about the girl in the field. This could help ID her."

"Sure," I said. "Good idea."

We'd already sent the two flashlights to the lab to be compared. The one from Evan Barstow's house would also be dusted for fingerprints and tested for DNA. I sat in a chair and looked at photos of them again, lined them up, side by side. They had to be identical. And if they were, Evan had to be our guy. He had to have Delilah. But if not at the house, then where? Preoccupied with the photos, I didn't hear them until they shuffled into the room.

"Mother, you came," I said, as she marched in the door with her two sister-wives and Lily.

"Only because Sariah asked me to." The stoop I'd noticed before looked more pronounced, as if she carried the weight of the family on her back. Her face hung wearily. I sensed she had all her remaining energy focused on retaining control.

"I'm glad you're here," I said. Mother didn't respond.

Sariah handed me two paper bags. The first held Delilah's hairbrush and some of her dirty clothes. Inside the second, I found a doll—a pudgy toddler with curly blond hair and blue glass eyes that flapped open and shut. In places, the doll's vinyl skin had discolored and worn thin from years of cuddling.

"Delilah's doll?" I asked.

Sariah nodded. "Her favorite."

I gave everything to Max to send to the lab to try to pull DNA.

"All these dresses," Naomi said. "They're from Evan Barstow's house?"

"Yes, take your time and look through," I said. "I need to know if any of these could be the one Delilah had on that night."

"We won't find Delilah's dress," Mother predicted, and I saw the anger in the downturn of her lips. "The Barstows are good men, sons of the prophet."

It was useless to argue with her, so I retired to the hallway where I had a view back into the room through a floor-to-ceiling window. Mother, Sariah, Naomi and Lily circulated one by one through the dresses. We had fourteen, various sizes, all the traditional, long prairie style. A crime scene officer held up each one as my mothers and Lily inspected it. When they reached the last dress, a solid blue that had flowers embroidered across the bodice, I returned to the room.

"Do any of them look like Delilah's dress?"

"None of these are Delilah's," Mother said. "I told you it wouldn't be here."

Sariah appeared relieved. "Clara, that could be good, couldn't it? That might mean he doesn't have her."

"Maybe, or not. We don't know," I said. "We're going to just have to keep on investigating and figure it out."

"This was a waste of time," Mother scoffed.

When I turned around, she stood across the table from me, flipping through the stack of photos I'd left out. "Then explain why Evan has Delilah's flashlight, Mother," I challenged, unable to keep the irritation out of my voice.

Mother ignored my question. When she reached the end of the stack, she started at the beginning again, this time pulling a handful out and laying them end to end. Her brow knit in worry. "What are these?" she asked.

"Those are of the girl we found in the field," I explained. "Her dress and jewelry."

Mother's face grew long, and she whispered, "Sariah, Naomi, come look at these pictures."

My mothers gathered in a line. I said nothing, just watched them. Minutes passed, and tears formed in my mother's eyes. Sariah put her hand on Naomi's shoulder. "It can't be," Sariah whispered. "It can't be."

Naomi lowered her body into a chair. Her face frozen in agony, she cried out, "Lord, please help us!"

Lily didn't appear to understand what upset them any more than I did but watched intently. I moved closer and skimmed over the images my mother had chosen, photos of the dress where it was unstained, of the buttons on the bodice, and a close-up of the ring.

At that instant my mother focused on me, and I felt as if she truly looked at me for the first time since my return. "Clara, tell me again. Is this the dress from the girl found in the field?"

"Yes," I said. "Why?"

"The girl they found dead today?" Sariah asked.

When I again said yes, Mother screamed, such a scream as I had never heard in my life, a shattering, torturous cry that threatened to strangle my heart. I ran and held her, wrapped my arms around her. In her agony, she didn't push me away. "Who is it, Mother?" I whispered. "Who is that girl?"

"The ring, too? That was on the dead girl?" Naomi asked, choking out each word.

I whispered, "Yes," and my mothers nestled together, held one another and wept. Again I asked, "Who is it?"

"I made this dress," Naomi said in a voice so wrought with emotion it came out as a hiss. "I sewed those buttons."

Lily examined the photos, as if trying to decide what so troubled our mothers.

"I need to know what you all know," I said. "Tell me!"

"I bought the fabric in St. George. And I took the buttons off an old dress of my own. See the last one near the waist?" Naomi asked.

I picked up a photo that showed the front of the dress, the placket with the buttons. I looked at it carefully. At first, I didn't see anything unusual. Then I noticed that the last button didn't match the others. Slightly larger than the rest, it looked more beige than ivory.

"I was short one button," Naomi said. "So I reused one from an old dress."

"The girl in the field isn't Delilah," I said. "It can't be."

"No," Mother whispered. "It's not."

"But it is one of my sisters, isn't it?" I said.

Lily turned to our mother, her face stricken. "Is this Sadie?"

CHAPTER FORTY

While the man was gone, Delilah and Jayme tried to come up with a plan that they believed had a chance, the only option they thought might work. One girl couldn't tackle the man alone, but maybe two could. "We have to convince him to let us room together," Jayme said. "Then we'll hide behind the door and jump him when he walks in."

"Maybe it would be better if we both took off in opposite directions," Delilah said. "He can't chase both of us."

"He might kill the one he gets his hands on," Jayme said.

"I don't think so," Delilah reasoned. "I think he'll tie her up and try to get the other one. He wants both of us."

"He wanted the other girls, too, but when he got mad, he got rid of them," Jayme said.

Delilah thought about that. "I don't care if he kills me. I won't let him do whatever he wants to me. I'm not going to give in and let him hurt me."

Jayme didn't respond at first but then, her voice thick with remorse, said, "I felt the same way, but I gave in. I'm scared."

"I am, too," Delilah admitted.

So they waited, hoping to work on the man to get him to do what they wanted. Instead, when the man returned, everything changed. He went to Delilah's room first, and when he opened the door, he held the chain and handcuffs.

"You said I wouldn't have to wear those anymore, not unless I was bad," she said. "I didn't do anything. Nothing at all."

"Shut up and come here," he said. "Now!"

Delilah's hands shook when she held her arms in front of her. He jerked them together, so rough it hurt her sore shoulders. "Please, don't make them tight," she whimpered. "Please, don't do that to me again."

The man didn't listen. The heavy chains pulled on her arms and wrists, and the handcuffs cinched so snug her little fingers went numb. She started to sit down on the mattress, assuming he'd again cuff her legs and chain her to the wall.

"Get up," he said. "You need to walk."

The man held the end of the chain and trailed her down the stairs. "This way," he ordered, and he took her to a door. He pulled out a key and unlocked it. A girl Delilah assumed had to be Jayme sat off to the side, so far into a corner she appeared to be trying to disappear inside it. The two girls exchanged wary looks, fighting to understand what was happening.

Delilah wondered if the man had tricked them, if he'd come back to the house on foot, hid and heard them plotting.

"We're going to be good, mister. You don't have to do that to us," Jayme pleaded. "We won't try to run away."

"Over here, girl," the man said. From his pocket, he pulled a second set of handcuffs. Jayme edged forward, cautious and frightened. When she reached him, he grabbed her left arm, tightened one cuff around it and ratcheted it in place. He then twisted the chain that held the cuffs together around the longer chain, the one he'd handcuffed Delilah to. Finally, he cinched the second cuff around Jayme's right wrist.

"That'll hold you two," he said, looking pleased. "We're taking a hike. I don't want any whining. I've got a place for us and no one knows it's there."

"In the mountains?" Jayme asked. "Why are we—"

"Don't complain to me, it's that woman's fault. She's behind all this." The man turned to Delilah. "That damn sister of yours should have stayed in Dallas. Clara Jefferies thinks she can find you? She gets close, anywhere near me, and it won't be pretty for you girls."

"We've done everything you said," Delilah protested. "Why would you hurt us?"

"Not 'cause I want to," the man said. "But if that sister of yours gets close, any of them gets wise and comes after us, I won't have a choice. You two will have to disappear."

At that, he grabbed the long end of the chain. "Let's go. Outside. Now!"

As she followed orders, Delilah thought about how the man said that she and Jayme might have to disappear. She tried not to cry. She didn't want the man to see how frightened she was. She walked slowly, dreading every step. It was the first time she'd seen Jayme, and she looked different than Delilah expected. The older girl had long dark blond hair held in a single rubber band at her nape, and wore a dress that bagged on her bony frame. Her cheekbones jutted out, making her gray-flecked blue eyes appear big and round.

Not long before sunset, in the west the sun had begun to dip in the sky. Jayme followed Delilah, and the man paced behind them, holding the chain. Delilah felt a slight breeze on her cheeks as they approached a dilapidated barn and corral not far from the house.

"Over there," the man said.

A horse waited tied up at the corral gate. As they approached the barn, an overpowering odor engulfed them, heavy and rancid, stomach-churning. It felt thick and solid, like it permeated the air with fine particles. Jayme coughed, and Delilah felt as if it seeped through her nostrils into her throat. She thought about the time a squirrel fell between the walls in the big house in town they used to live in. It took months to rot away, and the whole house reeked until it did.

The aged, dapple gray mare had a blanket thrown over its bony hips, and over the blanket a yellowed sheet knotted to form pockets that bulged with something heavy. A rifle in a long tan case was slung on one side, and a leather bag hung from the rear of the saddle. The man climbed onto the horse and wrapped the end of the chain around the saddle horn.

As they set off toward the pine forest and the mountains, Delilah glanced back at the house. It was as she'd pictured it, a ramshackle old place. Everything looked in need of repair, from the roof tiles the wind had blown askew to sections of the log fence that had fallen. As much as she hated the room inside the house, the prison she'd been locked in for four days, she feared what waited for them on the mountain even more.

CHAPTER FORTY-ONE

"Sadie left almost a year ago, soon after Father died," Naomi said. Mother held her hand, and Lily had her arms around Sariah. All four had tears spilling from their eyes, none bothering to wipe them away. I did as well. I didn't care. For this moment, I wasn't a big-city cop. I was a woman with one sister missing and one sister murdered.

Strangled, Doc had said. My sister Sadie had been strangled.

Naomi's oldest, Sadie celebrated her nineteenth birthday just days before she disappeared. When I left Alber, she was a nine-year-old with long dark brown hair, who collected insects in jars. She came by the hobby naturally. Like Mother's career as an herbalist, Naomi had a home business. She raised bees in hives she kept on a field outside of town and sold their honey to neighbors. A beekeeper since before she joined the family, she'd inherited the hives from her grandmother.

"Explain what you mean by 'Sadie left,'" I said.

"Well…" Sariah said, "it wasn't like Delilah. Sadie didn't disappear. She'd been seeing someone. We all picked up on the signs. She would be gone in the afternoons, come back for dinner. Aaron tried to follow her once, but she lost him. Sadie was always a tomboy, but then she changed. She started wearing perfume."

"I found a small bottle in the bathroom cabinet taped behind the extra rolls of toilet paper after she left," Naomi said. "Ardeth was the one who found—"

"Sadie's diary, where she talked about some man," Mother explained. "Sadie described him as older than she was. She said his family had money. He lived somewhere outside of town."

"She didn't name him?" I asked.

"No, and that description could fit many men in Alber," Naomi said. "After she left, we held a family meeting and questioned the children. All of them denied knowing anything about the man or Sadie's plans."

"So she didn't tell anyone who…" I looked over at Lily, who stared at the photos on the table with a look of incredible sadness, but something else too—regret.

"Lily, did you know anything about the man?" She shook her head, but I pushed. "If you do, now is the time to tell me."

Lily squeezed out an uncomfortable half-smile and shrugged, like she'd been caught. "I didn't know his name. But Sadie told me what they planned. Like that he said he'd remodel the house he lived in for her, and that she'd be his only wife. Sadie didn't want…" At that, Lily stopped and looked at our mothers.

"Go ahead, girl," Mother said. "Your mothers have read Sadie's diary. We know she turned her back on the Divine Principle."

Despite Mother's assurances, Lily turned her back on our mothers and spoke as if only to me. "Sadie didn't want to share a husband, Clara. She said it shouldn't be that way, to have one man with so many wives and children. Sadie said, 'Lily, the man I marry will love only me and our children.'"

I thought about that. "So this was a man who didn't have any wives? He wasn't already married?"

"I guess not," Lily said.

Mother looked up at me. "It couldn't be Evan Barstow then, Clara. He has wives."

"Maybe Sadie didn't know he was married," I pointed out. "Evan lives far enough outside of Alber that Sadie might not have known about his wives."

Mother didn't voice any agreement, but she didn't contradict me either.

"And Sadie said this man came from a family with money?" I questioned them. "As Evan does?"

"Yes, a wealthy or powerful family. Something like that," Mother said. It hurt to see the incredible pain etched on her thin face. I wondered if she considered the possibility that her actions contributed to Sadie's death. The house enforcer, Mother would have been the one Sadie feared most, the main reason she hid her relationship. Mother glanced at me, her voice laced with sadness and resignation. "Clara, it's been a while since we read Sadie's diary. There may be more in there that we've forgotten. We could get it for you, if it would help."

"Call Aaron and ask him to bring it," I suggested. Sariah stood up and slipped a cell phone out of her dress pocket. She turned her back to us and walked a short distance away to talk. Hoping for more information, I asked the others, "Did Sadie give any physical description of this man?"

"Only that he was a big man," Naomi said. "Oh, and Sadie wrote that when they left, they planned to hike up the mountain to look down on Alber."

At that, I thought of Christina Bradshaw, who'd disappeared nine years earlier. The way Sadie disappeared, on the pretense of running away with a lover, seemed eerily similar. I thought of the letter Christina's family said they received from Chicago. "Did you ever hear from Sadie?"

"Just once," Mother said. My heart sank when she said, "A card that was postmarked Seattle. Sadie wrote she'd fallen in love and married. She told us not to look for her."

Two women allegedly ran away with lovers, and both sent letters home from faraway places. Now one was dead. Murdered.

"But that must not have been true," Lily said, looking from one of us to the next. The girl was smart. She'd thought the clues through in an instant. "Sadie never left the area, or she wouldn't have been buried behind the cornfield, right?"

"Maybe not," Naomi said, her voice aching with pain.

Off the phone, Sariah came back and sat with the others. All three of my mothers appeared shaken, but Mother looked nearly destroyed. Her shoulders sagged and her breathing sounded labored, as if she was forcing her body to take in oxygen. "Before you leave so I can get to work on this, I have one more question," I said. As sorry as I felt for her, there were things I needed to know. "Mother, who did you tell about Delilah disappearing? Who did you think was looking for her?"

My mother stared up at me, her face as I'd never seen it before. She looked haunted, remorseful. Mother rarely let her guard down, but I heard shame in her voice. "I did what I have always done, what we were told to do for generations in Alber. What my grandparents and parents did before me. The Barstows have always been the family the faithful turn to in times of trouble. When Delilah disappeared, I asked the prophet for help."

"But your prophet, old man Barstow, is in prison."

"Yes," she said. "But the elders have a way of contacting him when something happens in the community."

Of course they would have found a contact within the prison who carries messages and keeps him involved. I should have known. I thought about what Hannah and Max had said, that little in Alber had truly changed. "What did the prophet tell you to do, Mother?"

"Our prophet sent a message that I wasn't to worry. He said his sons would look for Delilah."

My heart felt like butterfly wings fluttering within my chest, perhaps because I already suspected the answer when I asked, "Which sons?"

Mother hung her head and murmured, "Evan and Gerard."

I plopped down in a chair across from her. Mother's words hit me like a physical blow. My mother had trusted my prime suspect, Evan Barstow, to find Delilah. Livid, I ached to chastise her, to force her to accept responsibility for the folly of turning to men like the Barstows. But when I looked over at her, I lost any appetite for retribution. I saw that I couldn't punish Mother any more than she punished herself. Her hands locked in a death grip on her lap, her chin trembled and her eyes reflected the terror of someone truly lost.

I leaned toward her and asked, "So both of them, Evan and Gerard, were supposed to look for Delilah?"

"Yes." Mother examined my face, and I'm sure saw the disappointment there. "Clara, how could I have known? I mean, it made sense. They're both policemen."

"Did you talk to either one of them personally about Delilah?" I asked.

Her chest heaved with a swallowed anguish. "Only to Evan. He promised that he would explain the situation to Gerard and that they would work on this as a team, as their father ordered."

Only to Evan. I drew in a deep breath and tried to remain calm. "Why didn't you tell me this sooner?"

Mother wiped a tissue over her eyes, blotting tears. "Evan insisted we keep Delilah's disappearance a secret. He promised me that he and Gerard wouldn't tell anyone. And Evan said our family had to act as if nothing had happened, to protect Delilah."

"To protect Delilah?" I asked.

"Yes, to protect Delilah." Her voice dropped so low I could barely hear her when she swore, "I promise you, Clara, everything I did was to protect Delilah. She was my only concern."

Mother's words chilled me to my core like a harsh winter wind. "I don't understand. How did concealing the fact that Delilah had been abducted protect her?"

"Clara, you know what Alber is like," Mother said, as solemnly as I remembered she counseled me as a child. "In the eyes of the faithful, a girl despoiled by a man is ruined. No man wants a tainted woman as a wife."

"Mother, no." I couldn't bear to hear what I knew she would say. "Please, no."

"Clara, it's true. This is the way of our people," she insisted, her voice gravel. "Evan Barstow warned me that if people found out that Delilah had been taken by a man, she would be deemed unfit for marriage. Our Delilah would become one of the fallen girls."

CHAPTER FORTY-TWO

My heart ached as I watched Lily prop up Mother as they shuffled out the courthouse door. Sariah wrapped her arm around Naomi, who like Mother struggled to move forward. Once they reached the trailer, they faced the grim task of telling the rest of our family about Sadie. I found Max in his office, filled him in on what I'd learned and asked him to call Alber PD. "If Gerard is there, tell them that we're on our way. If he's not, ask where he is. We need to find out what he knows."

When Max circled back to my makeshift office, I was buckling my gun belt. As I slipped my Colt in the holster, he explained, "Gerard never returned to the station. They haven't heard from him. The dispatcher has been calling him all afternoon on another matter and he hasn't responded."

"Put a BOLO out," I said. "Anyone who sees Gerard should detain him for questioning."

"You sure about that?" Max asked. "We're talking about Alber's police chief."

Frustrated that he still pushed back, I pointed out, "We're talking about the brother of a kidnapping suspect who may have inside information."

Max looked concerned but agreed. "Okay. Will do."

"Strange time for Gerard to go AWOL," I remarked. "Let's send backup to help keep Evan under surveillance, just to be safe."

"I already did," Max said. "The squad we left there hasn't seen any unusual movement at the ranch. Just kids playing in the yard."

"We're not ready to confront Evan yet. We need more evidence." I thought about the chains in Evan's shed and wished yet again that we'd taken them. "The most important thing is that we need to figure out where he's keeping Delilah. Do we know if Evan owns any other property?"

"I haven't heard that he does, but it's possible."

"Can you check?"

"Sure, I'll call the county clerk." Minutes later Max rushed back through the door. "Evan has an old horse ranch in the far northwest corner of Alber, near the mountains."

Finally a break, I hoped. "It sounds like the perfect place to hide a hostage."

Then Max said something that immediately registered on my radar. "I put in a call to Mullins. He's going to lead us out there. It's off one of the old mining roads, hard to find."

I stopped and looked at Max, alarmed at what I'd just heard. "You told Detective Mullins that Evan Barstow is a suspect and we want to question Gerard?" Having Mullins on board could be a good thing, but I worried that he might not be on our side. I remembered what he said about Gerard being the boss. "Mullins could warn Gerard that we're trying to find him. Maybe he already has and that's why he's made himself scarce."

"Mullins won't do that," Max said. "I explained that we've got multiple abductions and one murdered girl. I told him that Evan had Delilah's flashlight and that Gerard may be aware of his brother's involvement. Mullins insisted it's some kind of mistake, but we agreed that he wouldn't alert anyone, especially Gerard."

"You trust him?"

"Yeah." Max looked over at me. "I've worked cases with him. Mullins is a good cop."

Although I was skeptical, it did no good to argue. I couldn't undo what Max had already done. Swallowing my doubt, I said, "Okay. Let's go."

On our way out the door, Helen, the sheriff's secretary, shouted for me and pointed at the waiting area. "Detective, your brother just arrived."

Aaron stood near the window holding a small beige book. I'd forgotten that I'd asked to have him bring Sadie's diary.

"Thanks," I said, as I grabbed it. I slipped it under my arm, and turned to leave.

"Clara," he shouted. I glanced back at him. "Can I help?"

"Not unless you know where to find Delilah." Aaron shook his head, and I ran out the door.

Moments later, Max and I drove out of the parking lot in his car, followed by two squads. "Where are we meeting Mullins?"

"We're swinging by the PD," he said.

"Okay," I replied, although doubts about Mullins still gnawed at me.

The siren on, we made good time to Alber. Mullins and someone else waited in a black-and-white outside the station. They took the lead, and we wound through town to the northwest, the sky now rapidly darkening. A ten-minute drive, and we turned onto a country road. We passed a few farmhouses, and off to my right I saw the dirt road that led to Mother Naomi's bee shed and hives. My throat tightened, and I coughed to clear it.

"You okay?" Max asked.

"Just thinking about Sadie."

"You think that was her in the field?"

"Yes, I do. We'll need to make sure, but the body has her hair color, her height, it's clothed in her dress and wears her ring."

"I'm sorry, Clara." He aimed straight ahead and we followed Mullins onto one of the old dirt mining roads leading toward the mountain. "I wish I'd stood up for you, when the sheriff and the Barstow brothers... Clara, if I could do it all over again..."

I still didn't completely trust Max. Just hours earlier, he'd kept me from following my instincts when I wanted to take Evan's chains into evidence. As Max drove, he kept glancing at me. I knew that he wanted me to say I forgave him. I should have been able to. But when I thought of Delilah, I couldn't.

"Max, just get me to Evan Barstow's ranch. I can't lose another sister today."

His jaw tightened, and Max pressed harder on the gas.

Three miles down the road, Mullins took a hard left and drove through a gate with a "B" in a circle at the top. It led to a two-story farmhouse, the wood siding weathered silver gray. I picked up Max's radio. "Detective Mullins, when we reach the house, hang back. We have our backup, and we'll go in."

"Miss Jefferies, with all due respect, I don't work for you," Mullins argued. "I'm going in with you to help, but as much to make sure this is all on the up and up."

"We don't know what we're walking into, Mullins," I said. "Stand back."

"You're not going to find squat here," Mullins scoffed. "I know Evan Barstow. I worked for him. He's a good man. He wouldn't—"

"I'm ordering you to stand down, Mullins," I said again. "This isn't your show."

"Shit, this is ridiculous," he mumbled. "Hell of a waste of—"

Max took over. "Detective Jefferies is right. You've got the wrong attitude for this, Mullins. We're going to handle it. It's our case, not yours."

"Okay, Max. You two win. You take the lead. But I'll be observing. This better be by the book." At that instant, Mullins pulled to the side and Max sped past him, followed by our backup. We parked in front of the house.

The sun was below the horizon, but the fading sunlight combined with the emerging moon to prolong the dusk. As soon as the car stopped, I jumped out. Max followed, leaving the headlights trained on the building. I wondered if Evan had an accomplice, someone guarding Delilah. We had our guns out, and I scanned the windows, leery that someone could be watching us. The other units pulled in and two deputies ran to guard the back door, while the others took cover behind their cars' open doors, rifles pointed at the house. I looked back and saw Mullins park near the barn. He and the guy with him stayed in the car.

My heart slammed against my ribs, pumping hard, as I walked up a few steps to the front door. No doorbell. I pounded on the heavy oak door. It felt solid and didn't budge. I wasn't waiting for permission. I put my hand on the knob and turned it. The unlocked door opened.

"Police! Anyone home?" I shouted. "Detective Jefferies and Chief Deputy Max Anderson here."

Max followed me in with two deputies behind us.

"Police! Anyone here?" he shouted.

No answer.

We split up and I took the kitchen. I tried the light switch and a bare bulb flickered into life in the center of the ceiling. The place was disgusting. We dodged bags of garbage, boxes piled up, dirty clothes. Clumps of food on dirty plates rotted on the table, more in the sink. A rat watched me as it nibbled on something in a corner. I kept walking. I heard the others, the sound of their feet slapping on the floorboards, the squeak of opening doors, as I circulated through the room. I held my breath, and slowly edged open the pantry.

Empty.

While the others finished combing the first floor, I joined Max in the hallway and we headed upstairs. The second-floor hallway had four doors. Four rooms. We walked in the first. A bed, rumpled sheets, piles of clothes. It looked like one Evan used when he slept at the house. I opened the closet door, half expecting someone to jump out. Plaid shirts and faded jeans hung haphazardly from hangers. Next was the bathroom, where wet towels soaked the floor. We circulated through another bedroom. Bare. Not even furniture.

The closets gaped open with nothing but cobwebs inside. We tried the last door, at the top of the stairs, and it creaked open. This room was darker than the others. I flipped on the light. Someone had boarded up the only window.

A frayed and stained cushion lay on the floor, a bucket beside it. A single chair sat in the center of the room. The room smelled of urine.

"What's that?" Max asked, pointing at the wall above the cushion.

A wave of disquiet surged through me. I thought once again of Sadie's body and the bruises Doc had shown me. He'd thought they were caused by a chain.

"It's an anchor," I whispered to Max. It felt as if everything had clicked into place. I understood. "Evan chains them to it. He keeps them locked up. That way he doesn't need any help, anyone to guard them."

Max shook his head, as if it were too depraved to comprehend.

"Chief Deputy, we found something in a room down here," one of the deputies called up.

The first-floor room appeared a near copy of the one we'd just left—a filthy mattress on the floor, a bucket, a boarded-up window, and a steel anchor screwed into the plaster wall.

My anger was building, but I reeled in my emotions. I couldn't think at that moment about the chains and the anchors in the walls. I couldn't let myself be overwhelmed by my growing sense of dread about what the monster who had the girls did to them. Finding Delilah required that I keep my cop face on. "There's urine in the bucket upstairs and some down here. Two buckets."

"Two hostages?" Max asked.

"Yeah. That's what I'm thinking. Two hostages."

"But where are they?" Max asked.

I shook my head. I didn't have an answer.

As soon as we stepped outside, Mullins approached. He introduced the guy he had in the car with him as Officer Bill Conroy.

I hadn't met him before, but I felt sure that his face wasn't usually ash gray.

"We checked out the barn, Detective Jefferies," Mullins said, surprising me by dropping the Miss and without instruction addressing me by my title.

"Did you find anything?" I asked.

Mullins spoke, and I thought perhaps my heart might stop. "Yeah. And I put in a call for Doc Wiley."

"We have a body?" I asked, afraid to hear his answer.

Every muscle in my chest contracted when he answered. "A woman. It's bad."

Twenty feet from its open door, the unmistakable stench of decomposition emanated from the barn. Max grabbed a hand-kerchief from his pocket. I took off my jacket, bunched it up and held it over my nose and mouth. It took our eyes a moment to adjust to the murkiness inside the barn. When mine did, I saw the decomposing body of a slender young woman. She hung by her handcuffed wrists suspended from a hook designed to move bales of hay. She had long dark hair, and wore a stained white prairie dress.

I took a closer look. Dried blood formed rows of irregular stripes down her dress. Thinking about how Doc said Sadie had been strangled, I examined her neck. She had a thin wound, ear to ear. Her throat had been slashed.

"Do you think it's Delilah?" Max asked.

I felt ashamed to look at such an outrage and feel any relief, but I did. The girl's body was bloated, her skin a ghastly greenish-brown. I would have bet she'd been dead for at least a week. In any case, I felt fairly sure this wasn't my sister. "I don't think so. Remember, Delilah has Sariah's auburn hair."

"That's right." He, too, sounded relieved, yet we were both looking at the girl as if we wanted to scream.

Another body. Another dead girl. Staring at the awful tableau, I couldn't think of anything but Delilah. Evan Barstow was confined on his ranch, but he had to have her stashed somewhere. Did he have yet another hiding place? Or was my sister dead? I wondered if we'd ever find her or her grave.

Max must have understood how lost I felt. He took over. "I'll send a few units to Evan's ranch to make the arrest. Once the forensic folks arrive and we turn the scene over to them, we can head to the office to question him. Let's not panic until we know more."

The CSI unit came quickly, but by then, the last of the light gone, the sky had transformed to a deep navy blue and the stars shimmered. Outside the full moon shone, but inside the barn the dimness turned to pitch dark. The team set up a generator to power floodlights. The resulting ring of light gave the macabre scene an eerie glow.

I was leaning against Max's car, waiting for him to tell me Evan had been arrested, when Doc arrived. "I hear you found another girl. Thought about your sister. Is it Delilah?"

"No. I'm sure that's not her." I'd been in such a rush that I hadn't yet called him to tell him what I had discovered. "But Naomi, one of my mothers, gave us a DNA sample. It's at the office. I didn't have time to have it sent to the lab before we ran out to come here."

"Why did you get a sample from her?"

"We need to compare it to the girl from the field."

"Why would we do that?" Doc looked confused. "Why would you—"

"Doc, I'm pretty sure the girl in the field is my half-sister Sadie – Mother Naomi's daughter."

"Oh, Clara, I—"

He looked stricken and moved forward as if he might embrace me. I appreciated the kindness, but I couldn't bear to see the sympathy in his eyes. "I can't talk about this now, Doc," I said, holding up a hand. "I just can't."

He appeared to understand, nodded and walked off.

When I saw Max approach with his cell phone to his ear, I got in his squad car for the drive to the sheriff's office. I couldn't wait to confront Evan, to push and prod, to manipulate and use everything I'd learned as a cop to get him to confess. Whatever it took, I would find my sister. And I would tie Evan Barstow up so tightly that no defense attorney would ever free him.

I knew immediately when Max slipped into the car beside me that he had bad news. "They found Delilah?" I asked. "She's dead?"

"No, not that, but this isn't good."

"Just tell me," I said.

"Okay." Max closed his eyes just a second. "When our deputies circled the house to make the arrest, Evan wasn't at the ranch."

"But we had surveillance," I said. "How is that possible?"

"His wives say Evan left the ranch not long after we did. He snuck out the back way, on a horse."

I smiled. Max looked at me, wondering. "Don't you see?" I said. "That makes it more likely that Delilah's alive. Evan had time to come here and take her."

Max looked worried. "That's possible, sure. But we can't be sure that's what he did." His eyes focused hard on me. "Clara, you can't pin your hopes on what's no more than speculation."

"I understand that," I said, a lump of anxiety lodged in my throat that made it difficult to speak. "But you're not understanding." I took a deep breath, and then confessed, "I have to believe we can save her."

Max nodded.

I paused, struggling to collect my thoughts. "Okay, so what we need to do is find Evan. And to do that, we need to find Gerard," I said. "No one knows Evan better than his brother. If what Evan told my mother is right—that he told Gerard about Delilah—then there's the real possibility that Gerard has first-hand information that might be useful. But one way or the other, Gerard is our best bet."

"How do we find him?" Max asked. "I know this sounds crazy, but no one seems to know where he lives. He had an address in St. George a couple of years ago, but nothing listed in or near Alber. I had officers check out the St. George apartment, and someone else lives there now. The dispatcher has called his cell, I've called, and Gerard's not answering."

"This is ridiculous," I said. "Why would Gerard suddenly disappear now? At this precise time? Unless…"

I walked over to where Mullins and his young partner, Officer Conroy, sat at a beat-up picnic table talking to the sheriff, who'd just arrived. "I still can hardly believe it, though I saw it with my own eyes," Mullins said. "If this ain't the damnedest thing, I don't know what—"

"Did you warn him?" I blurted out.

"What?" Mullins sputtered. "You don't think I—"

"Gerard Barstow has disappeared, nowhere to be found, at the precise moment that we need to ask him questions. I'm willing to bet someone gave him a heads-up."

Mullins looked like I'd slapped him, and I noticed the scar on his cheek had turned a dark shade of purple, as if his heart rate climbed.

Officer Conroy glanced from his partner to me. "Detective Jefferies, I was with Detective Mullins when he got the call to bring you and Max out here," the kid said. He was skinny as a scarecrow, straw-colored hair but dark brown eyes, and he looked scared. He scratched his right wrist, like his nerves were getting to him. "I didn't see him make any phone calls, not until he called for the sheriff and the doc."

Not yet ready to give the possibility up, I said, "I don't know, Mullins. Maybe you didn't, but if I find out you warned that piece of—"

"Clara, not now. Now we need to work together. And you're right, we need help to find Gerard," Max said as he turned to the others. "Mullins, you know him better than any of us. Where would the chief have gone?"

Mullins bit his lip and stared at me, furious. Then he turned to Max. "I heard that the chief left the station in a huff, upset about Detective Jefferies heading up the investigation. Sometimes when he's in a bad mood, he talks about going to Salt Lake. He has family there."

Sheriff Holmes sat on the opposite side of the table from Mullins, and I turned to the sheriff and asked, "Can you look into that? Find out where his family lives and get Salt Lake PD to send someone out. If he doesn't accompany them willingly, they can bring him in as a material witness."

"Got it," the sheriff said, and he walked off to make the call.

While he checked on the Salt Lake connection, I turned to the others. "In the meantime, we need to move ahead. Any ideas?"

Mullins shrugged, uneasy, and Conroy looked at me as if unsure what to say.

"Clara, they couldn't have gone too far," Max said. "Evan's squad and personal vehicles are at his house, and he came here on horseback. His wife said he only had the one horse with him. If he has a hostage or two someone is most likely walking."

I considered the landscape, the trees spreading out thin behind the ranch, growing thicker up the mountainside. "He's taking them into the woods, most likely up onto the mountain."

"Yeah, that's what I'd do, if it were me," Max said. "The Barstow boys were like the rest of us. We all grew up hunting on that mountain. We played in the caves and the miles of old mining tunnels."

"If they're up there, this won't be easy," Mullins said. "That mountain's got more hiding places, more twists and turns than a maze."

CHAPTER FORTY-THREE

The climb up the mountain through the pine forest hurt Delilah's legs. The trail, overgrown with scrub brush and thistles, looked like no one had traversed it for decades. Delilah was in the lead, and had to pick her way through the darkness. The man aimed a powerful flashlight ahead of them, casting a blue-white light on the ground and trees, but it bounced with the rhythm of the horse.

It turned out that the man liked to talk. Ever since they'd left the house, he'd babbled on about the mountains, the hunting he'd done as a boy with his brothers. "The miners used to use this trail, but they haven't been around in years. Follow it all the way and it dead-ends at an abandoned mine."

"Is that where we're going?" Delilah asked.

The man's eyes grew round and he smirked at her. "*Is that where we're going?*" he mocked. "Don't think you can figure me out. I'll always surprise you."

It scared Delilah that the man's mood worsened so fast. "I didn't mean to…" she stammered.

Scowling at her, he warned, "Don't ever think I don't know what I'm doing. I got another place in mind. Even better. A place no one knows about. It's not on any maps."

Delilah swallowed hard. "Yes, sir."

The sweat that trickled down her back dried in the cooling night air. Her ankles kept twisting on the rocks; she wore her sandals and old white socks the man had given her with holes in the heels. She wished she had a pair of tennis shoes to protect her feet. A round, deep-red bloodstain saturated the right sock where a stone must have cut her. The chain pulled on her arms. The dress too long, it dragged in the dirt, got under her feet and threatened to trip her. The hem caught on branches as they made slow progress up the mountainside.

Something darted across the path in front of her, and Delilah stopped, startled. "What's that?"

"A damn jackrabbit, nothing that'll hurt you," the man said. "But watch out for rattlers. There's a lotta them around here. They're active just after dusk. Don't put your feet under anything."

Delilah looked at the scattered rocks and wondered what hid beneath them.

"Move on!" the man shouted.

Carrying the heavy chain with them, Delilah and Jayme huffed and puffed farther up the mountain, heads down, the man effortlessly riding behind them on the horse.

"Are we going to stop and rest soon?" Delilah asked.

"We got a ways to go," the man said. "No stopping."

"My legs hurt something terrible," Jayme said.

"Keep going," he answered.

Delilah tried, but her legs wouldn't cooperate. They felt wobbly. She hit a patch of loose rock, and her feet slid out from under her, skidding across the dry earth. She tried to grab a scrawny pine's trunk to break her fall, but couldn't with the handcuffs. The man tugged at the chain and she went flying, taking Jayme with her. When they landed, Delilah lay flat on her stomach with Jayme beside her. Slowly, they sat up, dazed. Delilah pulled up her skirt to see why her knees burned. Badly skinned, they seeped blood.

Jayme had a deep cut on her forehead. She put her hands down to push up, but immediately pulled up her right arm and screamed in pain. "My elbow. It hurts bad."

"It ain't nothin'," the man said.

"Maybe you broke it." Delilah thought back to a time one of her brothers broke a finger. Mother Ardeth mashed up comfrey from the herb garden and tied it over the break in a cotton wrap.

"Damn it, you girls! Shut up!" the man grumbled. "We gotta get moving. Get up."

It was awkward with the handcuffs, but Delilah stood and gave Jayme her arms to brace on. "I'm trying," Jayme said. "It hurts real bad, though."

The man shook his head. "Maybe you girls are more trouble than you're worth."

Delilah thought about what Jayme had told her about the other girls. She considered how Jayme heard the man screaming at them, and then they disappeared. The older girl, the one who vanished right after the man took Jayme? The man had said that he left her on the mountain. Now he was taking them there.

"Are you going to kill us?" Delilah asked.

"Nah, I wouldn't…" he stammered.

"You would." Jayme looked at him out of the corners of her eyes, almost daring him to tell the truth.

The man pulled on the chain. "You two do what you're told, and nothing will happen to you, except you'll be happy. You'll be my wives, and we'll have a family. But we gotta go. Now!"

Delilah shot him a distrustful look, then turned and started back up the trail. She'd walked fifty feet when she heard a horse's hooves hitting the hard earth behind them.

Someone was coming.

"Behind that rock," the man ordered. "Over there!"

The man jumped off his horse, pulled it alongside him and hustled the girls toward a vast boulder, taller than the man. In a panic, he pulled them with the chain, making them run between the pines, jumping over shallow roots. He pushed them behind the massive rock, and then took his rifle out of the sling on the mare's side.

"Not a sound," he warned as he backed in beside them, the rifle aimed around the side of the boulder.

Delilah's pulse pounded and pounded until her body shook.

An unfamiliar male voice surrounded them. "You out there? If you're there, come out. I don't have time for this."

The man looked at Delilah and Jayme, and then answered. "Over here."

The stranger on horseback stopped on the path and dismounted, tied a tall black stallion onto the scrawny trunk of a half-dead tree. "What the hell are you up to?" he asked. "Get out here, and bring that Jefferies girl with you."

The man turned to the girls, frowning. "Damn it," he said. "You heard him. Git out there."

Jayme ambled around the side of the boulder at Delilah's side, and they retraced their steps to the path. A big man waited there; he bore a resemblance to the man who had taken them.

"You've got two girls? *Two?* Goddamn it, you twisted son of a—"

"What business is it of yours?" The man scowled at him. "This hasn't got anything to do with you."

"You girls okay?" the stranger asked.

Delilah started to answer, to scream that they weren't anything like okay, but before she could, the man cut her off.

"I asked what you're doing here."

"Where else would you go?" the stranger asked. "As soon as I hung up the phone with you, I knew you were gonna run and head to the cave. We must'a talked a hundred times when we were kids about how it was the perfect hideout."

The man tightened his eyes, angry. "But why did you come? I don't need you here."

The stranger's face looked like he was chewing on something sour. "You haven't got a choice. You've gotta come with me. We're going to take those girls back. And you're going to confess."

"Why, I'm not gonna... Why would I do that?"

"Because that woman cop isn't giving up," the stranger said. "Because before long she's gonna figure out that I knew you take girls, what you do to them. It's over. I need you to come with me back to town. This is done."

"Well, I—" the man tried to interrupt.

"They aren't just going to go after you," the stranger said. "They're gonna prosecute me for murder just like you, as an accessory. I should have turned you in years back, the first time you took a girl, instead of covering up for you. You did all this, but it's gonna fall on me, too. And I won't have that."

"I'm not—"

Delilah fixed her eyes on the barrel of the long, black handgun the stranger pulled out of his belt, silencing the man. He held it up and pointed it at him.

The man winced. "Take it easy there. Don't do anything rash."

"I'm sick of covering up for you," the stranger said. "I'm not going to do it anymore."

"Okay," the man said. He set down his rifle and held his hands up high. "I'll go with you. I understand."

"I hope you do. Now get the key. Unlock those girls," the stranger ordered.

"It's in the saddlebag on the back of the horse."

"Move slow," the stranger warned. He lined up where he could get a better look at the man and the saddlebag. "I'm not taking my eyes off you."

Jayme reached over and grabbed Delilah's hand, the ends of her mouth tugging up into the slightest hint of a smile. The girls watched, excited at the prospect of freedom, as their captor turned toward the gray mare. He slipped his left hand into one of the brown leather saddlebags under the sheet that held supplies. He pulled out the ring with the keys on it. The stranger moved back and seemed to relax, just as the man slid his right hand under his shirt. When he pulled it out, he held a small black pistol.

The shot went off before Delilah could finish shouting the warning. Jayme screamed. One bullet hit the stranger in the chest. A second sliced directly through the center of his forehead. His legs collapsed under him, and he toppled over, dead.

Silence for a heartbeat, and then the girls' screams and sobs filled the night air. Delilah's chest heaved so hard she thought she might never be able to stop.

Jayme and Delilah huddled together, crying, while the man walked over and nudged the stranger. Nothing. No movement. The man did it again. The stranger didn't respond.

The man hesitated, as if considering what to do.

"You've got no right to tell me what to do," he whispered. "And you ain't gonna need that horse. So it might as well be mine."

The man untied the knotted sheet filled with supplies from his old mare and carried it over to the stranger's mount. While Delilah and Jayme watched, he tied the sheet on the back of the stallion. He took the end of the chain and looped it around the saddle horn. Once he finished, the man pushed the body off the trail, a short distance into the woods.

Then the man went back to his own horse and took off the reins.

"Get the hell outta here, you flea-bitten hag!" he shouted, whipping the horse with the leather straps. The horse neighed and backed up, hemmed in by the forest. It clomped backward, then turned and ran down the trail.

"Okay," the man said to the girls. "We need to get moving."

CHAPTER FORTY-FOUR

I stared up at the black sky and the thousands of stars overhead and wondered if my instincts misled me. I couldn't forget Max saying that I pinned my hopes that Delilah might still be alive on no real evidence. Two girls found dead. The one in the field? Sadie. The one in the barn? Doc thought we'd found Eliza Heaton. On the right side of her face, just a touch above her upper lip, he saw a mole like the one in her picture.

"We'll do DNA, of course," Doc said. "But my guess is that someone's going to be delivering very bad news to the Heatons."

In the barn, I pitched in to help Doc remove the body. It's not what I wanted to be doing. I wanted to search for Delilah. Every breath I took screamed, "Go now! Before it's too late!" But we couldn't.

The sheriff confirmed through Salt Lake PD that the Barstows' relatives hadn't heard from Gerard. Unless he suddenly reappeared, it seemed unlikely that we would be able to find him to question him about what he knew and Evan's whereabouts.

Instead, we focused our attention on our theory that Evan had fled with Delilah to the mountains. That gave him tens of thousands of acres of forest to hide in. Our only advantage: If he did have Delilah, and maybe a second hostage, he would have to travel slowly. But none of us knew how big a head start Evan had or where he'd go.

The darkness complicated our situation. Traditional tracking methods would be far less effective at night. Ground and vegetation disturbances could be too easily missed.

It made no sense to simply head into the wilderness and hope we'd find Evan. Instead, Max and I drew up a plan. To carry it out, we called in specialized equipment and people to operate it.

I handled the call to the state police. We needed state-of-the-art equipment, helicopters and drones equipped with thermal imaging cameras. Since Evan had a horse, he'd be a big target, generating a lot of body heat. If he had Delilah or any other girl with him, they would give us multiple targets. The disappointing response came first: the drones were unavailable. The agency had three, but they were spread across the state and in use for other cases. The news on the choppers was better; two left immediately to join us, but both were an hour out.

While I worked on getting the choppers, Sheriff Holmes tracked down a K-9 search unit. The dogs, housed at a state prison, would take a couple of hours to reach us. He also contacted one of his SWAT units and requested radio equipment, tactical vests and assault weapons.

Meanwhile, the forensic folks combed through Evan's house and barn. Once we had the body on its way with Doc Wiley, much of the attention centered on the two rooms fitted with the wall anchors. My heart nearly jumped from my chest when luminol sprayed on a stain on the upstairs pad glowed blue. I understood the results before the tech conducting the test turned to me and said, "Looks like we've got blood. Lots of it."

After the initial testing, they logged the pad and the downstairs mattress into evidence. On the cellar floor, we found a blue dress with a white sash. Delilah's, I guessed. It looked the way my mothers and the others had described it. We boxed it and sent it to the lab.

The forensic work going well, I looked at my watch. It was closing in on midnight. "How far out are the choppers?"

"Half an hour, tops," Max said. "The dogs won't be here for another hour, though. What do you want to do?"

"Let's speed this up and get in position under the mountain."

Mullins had called a neighboring ranch, the owner a friend of his, and secured five horses. He had them saddled up—growing up in rural Utah, we were all comfortable on horseback. Since Mullins and Conroy knew Evan—they'd both worked with him when he was Alber's chief—Max and I decided that bringing them might give us an advantage. We needed the fifth horse for a professional tracker, a contact of the sheriff's, who'd driven flat out to join us from a town on the other side of Pine City.

I'd just finished suiting up in my bulletproof vest when another car arrived, this one a beat-up red Camry. Stephanie Jonas climbed out carrying two big brown paper bags.

"Stef, why are you here?" I asked.

"I heard about what's going on," she said, holding up the bags. "I brought sandwiches, and I want to help."

She'd risked her job to show me the file room. If she hadn't, we might not be as far along as we were. I owed her.

I thought about what we needed, and a second set of eyes on the laptop seemed like a good idea. We were all wearing transceivers, so our positions would be visible to the techs on the helicopters, and on the laptop the sheriff would monitor on the ground. "You can compare coordinates on the map with the info coming in from the choppers. Track us to verify that we're heading in the right direction."

"Great," she said.

My morning hard-boiled egg less than a memory, my ham-and-cheese sandwich disappeared in a few bites. As soon as the others finished, I said, "Okay, let's go."

We climbed onto our mounts, handguns in our holsters and rifles hanging in leather scabbards on the sides.

"One last reminder," Max said. He looked around at all of us, making sure we were listening. "Evan Barstow is undoubtedly armed. He'll be watching for us. Remember, he's a cop. He's had the same training we have. Be careful."

"You got it," Conroy said. All of us were high on adrenaline, but the kid looked more scared than excited.

"Just listen to orders and keep alert," I said.

Conroy gave a brave nod.

In a moment, we'd be on our way. But as I pulled the reins and turned my horse toward the mountains, Sheriff Holmes shouted, "Detective Jefferies. There's a call for you. A woman. Won't say who she is."

"Now?"

"Yes," he said. "She says it's important."

He handed me his phone, and I walked my horse a short distance away from the others.

"It's Jessica Barstow," the woman on the phone said. "I overheard the deputies you have here at the ranch talking. They said you're going up into the mountains to look for Evan."

It surprised me to hear from her, but then I realized that she undoubtedly understood the man she'd married, and what he was capable of. Perhaps she had a vested interest in stopping him. Yet, I couldn't assume her motives were friendly. "I can't comment—"

"Detective, there's a cave up there where Evan and his brothers used to play as kids. They had a fort in it. Kid stuff, but they were really proud of it. Talked about it sometimes, about how no one but them knew where it was."

"Where in the mountains?" I asked.

"I'm not sure, but I had the impression it was a long hike, pretty high up, where the trees thin out and stop," she said.

"Anything else that might help us?"

For a while she was silent, and in the end said, "I don't think so. But if I think of anything, I'll get in touch with the sheriff."

I had something I wanted to ask her. "One question, Jessica, about your sister Christina," I started.

"Christina?"

"Yes. Who was the man stalking her?"

"I don't understand. Why are you asking about Christina?"

"I just need to know, was it your husband?"

Silence while she apparently considered my question. "Yes, it was Evan," Jessica said. "That was the one time there was trouble between Evan and Gerard. My sister was beautiful. They both wanted Christina. She didn't want either one of them. She saw how Evan treated me, and she told my parents that she'd run away before she married into the Barstow family."

"How did the brothers react?" I asked.

"Evan was furious," Jessica said. "He and Gerard fought. Not long after that, Gerard was forced out of Alber. I always figured Evan had to be behind it. But how is this related?"

I thought about Sadie's Seattle letter. So much was beginning to make sense. "Did your family ever hear from Christina after that letter from Chicago?"

"No. Never. Why are you asking about this now?"

I didn't answer, but made an excuse and hung up.

When I returned to the horses, I approached the tracker, a lanky guy with an angular face named Joe Rodgers. He had a long, thin mouth that tucked high into his cheek on the right.

"Joe, I know this isn't a lot of help, but we have a source who believes Evan may be heading for a particular cave. One he played in as a boy."

"Where's it at?"

"That's the bad news. Our source doesn't know, except that it's rather high up."

Rodgers chuckled. "Well, that is a problem. There are dozens of caves up there, and a lot of them fit that description. Add in the deserted mines…"

"Shit, a cave high up? That's no tip," Mullins murmured. "That's no more help than throwing a dart at a map."

*

We took off, the tracker in the lead. I'd hoped to get night-vision gear, but the sheriff only had two sets and both were out for repair. That left us with flashlights and the full moon. We searched the ground looking for trampled grass and broken branches, hoof prints, shoe prints, debris left behind, anything that gave a clue about which way to head. The drought was our enemy. The sun had baked the earth to concrete, withered the underbrush and grass.

"Looks like there's an indentation in the lower tree line to the right. It could be a trail," Rodgers said, staring through a pair of binoculars. "Let's head there, forty degrees to the right."

We followed, seeing nothing that confirmed he'd chosen the right direction. No one talked. All of us focused on the ground beneath us and the landscape ahead of us, as we wound between the scraggly pines. The sounds of the horses' hooves hitting the ground, their steady breathing, gave our quest a rhythm. If it hadn't been for the circumstances, it would have felt good to be on horseback. It had been years since I had taken the time to ride. We caravanned toward the mountains. Before long the dry brush surrounding us grew denser, and as we approached where the woods thickened, Rodgers pointed out the opening in the forest he'd noticed earlier.

"It's a trail," he said. "Could be where they'd head."

Mullins's lips curved into a doubtful arc. "These mountains are scarred with them. Lots of old miners' trails. You go a couple hundred yards down, and there'll be another. You get farther up, and sometimes they run together. Sometimes they just dead-end and disappear."

"Mullins is right. I used to go three-wheeling around here," Max said. "But let's go. At least this'll get us into the woods.

"Sure, let's take it," I decided. "The choppers should show up soon. The pilots can use the path as a center divide, to plot sections to search."

We headed up the path, and fifteen minutes later we heard helicopter blades beating overhead.

"They're here," Conroy shouted.

"Quiet down," Mullins warned. "You want to let the whole blasted forest know we're here? Keep it low."

The kid, embarrassed, nodded.

"Chief Deputy Anderson," a voice came over our headsets.

"Here," Max said.

"We've got sights on your party. We're going to start scanning with the thermal equipment."

Finally, I thought.

While the choppers searched for the bright images of body heat on their monitors, we continued up the mountain. We moved slowly. We didn't want to be too high if they spotted Evan east or west of our position.

"We think we've got them," an excited chopper tech radioed. "We can see a group, looks like a horse, maybe three other figures…"

I held my breath. The seconds dragged.

"Not them. A clutch of elk," the man said. "Sorry, folks."

Half an hour passed. We had more false sightings, ones that turned out to be a small herd of mule deer and two black bears foraging.

The helicopters kept spreading out. As we traveled higher, the woods grew deeper. The trees massive, shafts of moonlight illuminated the ground between them. Our tracker stayed in the lead. He saw no sign that the trail we were on had been used in more than a year. The forest had begun to retake it, sending up young pines. Nothing in front of us looked disturbed. To our disappointment, Joe announced, "This can't be the way. I would have seen something by now, broken branches, crushed vegetation."

I'd made a mistake. Anxious to get started, I'd jumped the gun. "We should have waited for the dogs," I said to Max. "Find out where they are."

Max tapped the button on his radio's mic. "Sheriff Holmes, has the K-9 unit arrived yet?"

"Yeah, they're here. You want them?"

"Looks like we need them. We're not picking up anything out here," he said. "We'll head back down the mountain to meet them. You can truck them to our position on the three-wheelers."

"We're on it," the sheriff said.

The ride down the path seemed longer than the ride up. I chastised myself for wasting time. The choppers flew above us, little radio chatter because we kept noise levels low, and they flew high to keep from tipping Evan off with the sound of their engines and blades.

In the distance, a pack of coyotes howled at the full moon. Without the sun to warm it, the thin air turned cool. It smelled of pine trees and dust. We emerged from the woods, and I glanced at my watch. Ten to one. My weary eyes burned. The day long, exhaustion weighed me down like a heavy shroud. And we were back where we started.

CHAPTER FORTY-FIVE

The bloodhounds had jowls and ears that drooped, giving them as dour an expression as I'm sure I wore. Wide black mesh harnesses circled their chests. Two trainers held onto the ends of heavy rope leashes, letting the animals root around. The dogs in charge, we followed. They'd been exposed to the scent inside of Evan Barstow's squad car. The dogs' training had only one purpose – to hunt people.

This wasn't something I'd encountered in my years in Dallas. I hadn't used dogs on any of my cases. "What if Evan's on horseback? Will they still be able to follow him?"

"Yeah," Mullins said. "Out here in the boonies, we have to use dogs off and on, missing persons and such. The scent drifts down and settles. It'll be harder with the scent of the horse mixed in, but they'll get it."

I looked over at the Alber PD detective and thought about how his attitude had changed. Finding the hanging body of a young girl with her throat slit had apparently been enough to convince him that we had evidence, not some misguided hostility against Evan Barstow. Was I too hard on Mullins? Perhaps. I wasn't in a particularly forgiving mood.

We sauntered on the horses at the rear, while the trainers worked up front. The dogs scouted, noses to the ground, darting off into the trees and then circling back. We tracked them with our flashlights, and it gave the dogs a firefly appearance as they darted about in the shafts of light flickering between the trees. Twenty minutes passed. An hour. Nothing.

But then the dogs, one after the other, took off down a trail that cut into the forest, not unlike the one we'd traveled earlier. "We've got something," one of the trainers shouted. We followed, hanging back, letting the dogs lead us in.

"Detective Jefferies, can we hold the dogs up?" Rodgers asked after we'd traveled a hundred feet or so into the woods. "Let me go a little ahead, see if I can find anything on the path."

"Whoa," I shouted to the trainers. "Pull them back."

Reluctant, the dogs stretched their leashes taut. They considered this playtime. At the end of the trail, when they found their prey, there'd be praise and treats. But the trainers held the leashes tight, and our tracker rode his horse ahead. He scrambled down and walked in a ways. Wielding his flashlight, Rodgers knelt to examine the foliage and then called back. "Someone's been on this trail. Broken branches. The grass is packed down. Looks like a horse, some footprints. Smallish ones. Women or kids."

"Can you tell how long ago?" Max asked.

"Recently," Rodgers said, holding up a broken branch. "This cut is still seeping sap."

"Okay, let's go," I said.

The dogs took over again. Meanwhile, I radioed the helicopters. "We're heading your way," one of the pilots said. Five minutes later, we heard the faint beating overhead. We rode on for another hour or so, the dogs darting into the woods off and on, and then coming back to the trail. Rodgers followed directly behind them, watching for more evidence that signaled we were on the right track.

"Hold up!" he shouted.

"Stop!" I called out.

Rodgers got off his horse again, looked around. He motioned toward us, and we all got off our mounts. "There's something that looks like blood here, ground disturbances, something happened."

"How long ago?" Mullins asked.

"Blood's dry, but, from the state of the vegetation, compacted recently, I'm thinking not more than a few hours ago."

Just then, Stef broke in on our radios. "Detective Jefferies?"

"Yeah, Stef. I'm here."

"The pilots have a hit on something large up ahead. Could be a man on a horse."

"Got it," I said.

"Hold the dogs back," Max ordered, and the trainers did. We gripped our weapons and doused our flashlights. All we had to light our way were the thin beads of moonlight from above, the dawn still nearly four hours off. I whispered a thank you for the full moon. "Radio silence. Let's go in slowly, see what we've got."

We scanned the woods as we ambled in on the horses, picking our way on the trail. The tracker and the trainers with the dogs took a position behind us. We watched, waited, suspicious of what was hidden in the woods. The landscape dark, the moonlight illuminated the trees in silhouette. Then I spotted the outline of a horse ambling listlessly fifty feet ahead. The mare had a saddle on. No rider.

"Wait here."

The others fell back, and I moved forward. I dismounted and approached the horse. It had a sloping back, one that befitted an animal that had worked hard all its life and earned the aches and pains of old age. It neighed as I ran my hand over its neck. "What's going on?" I whispered, as if the horse could answer. I searched around, saw no one.

"Just the horse. No rider. I'm not seeing anyone from here," I said into the mic. I kept nervously scanning the trees. I half expected to hear a shot ring out from the shadows. "Keep watch. He could be nearby, hiding."

I needed more eyes on the woods. "Stef?"

"Yeah," she said.

"Do the helicopters see anything, anyone else around the horse? Anything at all close to our position?"

A pause while I presumed that she checked the screens and double-checked with the chopper pilots. "Nada. Just you, the horse, and the rest of your party behind you."

"Looks like we're clear," I told the others.

Just then, one of the dog trainers called out, "Back here!"

Instead of the others riding up to join me, we turned our horses and retraced our steps about sixty feet. As I approached, I saw that the dogs had meandered off the trail, a short distance into the woods. Rodgers, the tracker, stared down at something hidden in the brush. I dismounted, as did the others. Conroy took the reins of all the horses and kept watch. Mullins and I walked in behind Max. My heart quickened when I realized that Rodgers stood over a dead body. I thought of the blood we'd seen a short distance down the trail. Was it Delilah?

Rodgers called out, "We've got a dead man."

My mind grasped the most likely scenario. We had one man missing. "Is it Gerard?"

As I walked up, Max rolled the body over. We all stared at it, stunned and silent until Mullins wandered close enough to get a good look. "Who the hell shot Evan Barstow through the damn head?" he said.

Deep-red blood trailed down Evan's broad forehead from a smoky black circle of ruptured muscle and tissue where the bullet had entered. His eyes open, he stared out unseeing into the darkness. I wished I could have asked him questions, wondered what he would have told me, but his voice was silenced, forever.

A minute earlier, I'd assumed the body would be Gerard's. Now I had to rethink. What had I missed?

"I bet Gerard rescued the girls and he's bringing them down the mountain," Mullins speculated. "That would be just like the chief, to come up here on his own to rescue them. Let's head back down, see if we can meet up with them."

All three of the men looked at me expectantly. Meanwhile, the dogs milled around in the woods. I saw one dog amble up higher, as if still following a scent.

"No, I…" I paused, thinking it through. "Mullins, that can't be right. If Gerard found them and had to shoot his brother to save them, he would have called for help. If he took the girls back down the mountain, it would have been on the path we took. We would have run into them on our way up."

Mullins took off his bill cap with CRIME WATCH—ALBER PD on the crown and scratched his scalp through his thin, graying hair. "Well, I guess," he said. "You've got a point there, Detective."

"It's Gerard we're trailing," Max blurted out. He appeared angry, perhaps with himself, when he added, "How could I have missed this? Why didn't I ever consider that it could be Gerard who took the girls? Even when he went missing, I never thought… We've been chasing the wrong brother."

Max had to be right. "Don't be so hard on yourself," I said. "I never considered it either. He always seemed like—"

"The better Barstow brother," Max said, finishing my thought.

"I don't understand," Conroy said. "The flashlight was at Evan's house. He owns that ranch where the girls were kept. How does this make sense?"

"I don't know," I admitted. "But Gerard has to be involved. Either the two brothers did this together, had a spat and one shot the other. Or Gerard has had Delilah all along."

"Look at that," Mullins said, pointing at the bloodhounds pulling their trainers up the mountain.

"Looks like we might have been chasing the wrong suspect, but we're on the right trail," Max said.

"That's all that's important," I said. "Somewhere up ahead, we may find the girls."

"Detective Jefferies, should we leave anyone here to wait for the ME?" Mullins asked.

"No. We're sticking together. Evan is long dead. No one can help him. And it's too dangerous for the CSI folks and Doc Wiley to come up here until we've got Gerard." I looked down at the body sprawled out below us, Evan's hulk spread across the ground. "He'll be here when we're ready."

"So…" Max started.

"We keep moving," I said. "And we end this."

CHAPTER FORTY-SIX

"We've arrived, girls," Gerard Barstow said, relief in his gruff voice. "Time for you to see your new home."

Hidden behind the trees, the vast cave's opening yawned, a crude half-moon cut into the mountainside, black even against the dark night. Gerard dismounted from his dead brother's stallion. "First things first," he said. "Let's get you two secured."

The entrance looked scary, and Delilah didn't want to go in. "I bet there are bats in there," she whispered to Jayme. "Maybe rats. Could even be coyotes."

Jayme had her arms up against her chest, bracing the one she'd hurt. "Maybe he'll take the chains off."

Delilah gave her the slightest of smiles, but she didn't believe it. She felt the same dread as the evening he'd carried her through the cornfield, as much anxiety as waking up blindfolded and chained to the wall in the house.

The man walked over with the end of the chain in his hands. "Go inside."

As frightened as she felt, Delilah didn't argue. She led the way, Jayme behind her. Once inside, the man aimed his flashlight around the interior. As it flicked back and forth, Delilah glimpsed an old mattress flat on the ground, a pile of camping equipment, a stove, and three sleeping bags in rolls.

The flashlight landed on the gray rock wall above the mattress. The man stopped it there, lighting up something that glinted. Something metallic.

"Over there," he ordered.

Delilah did as told. She marched twenty feet or so into the cave, her head crunched down to her shoulders, fearing an onslaught of bats. As she got closer, she realized the object in the wall was a metal loop, another anchor like the one she'd been shackled to above the pad in the room. "You don't have to chain us up, mister," she pleaded. "We'll be really good. We will."

"Yeah," Jayme said. "If you don't chain us, we can help you. We'll set the sleeping bags up. Warm up some dinner."

"I'm not gonna have to worry about you girls running off," he said. "Stand on the mattress, close enough so I can lock this chain to the wall."

"But, please, mister. Jayme's right. We could help," Delilah insisted.

"Do as you're told," he ordered.

Delilah edged forward, stood on the mattress and waited, Jayme beside her. The man strung the chain through the anchor's loop, then retrieved a padlock out of his pocket, pushed the shackle through two links and clicked it shut.

Out of a dark corner, the man pulled two lanterns and switched them on, sending a warm glow through the chilly cave. He put them down, one near the girls and the other in the center of the cavern. "I'm getting the supplies. Don't try anything. I'll be right back."

Drained from the hike, Delilah sat down on the mattress. "You think he'll unchain us when he's done bringing in the supplies?"

Jayme's frown sunk lower as she eased down next to her. "Not likely."

They watched warily as the man carried in bread and fruit. In the corner, he had a cooler he slipped the perishables into, including a half-gallon of milk. Delilah saw water bottles and twelve-packs of beer stacked beside canned goods. She spotted blankets next to the mattress. "We're cold," she said. "Is it okay if we use these?"

"Sure." He walked over, grabbed a blanket and threw it at them. "We're gonna be really cozy here."

"How long are we staying?" Jayme asked.

"Long as we need to," he replied.

Once he had the supplies unloaded, Gerard led the stallion in and tied it off to an anchor on the opposite side of the grotto, just inside the opening. "They'll have the helicopters with the heat equipment out. Can't have the horse visible," Gerard said. "See, girls, I know what they'll do. I know how to hide out until they give up and go home. Even that damn sister of yours, Delilah."

"That's good," Delilah said, as if pleased. All she could think of was what she and Jayme talked about when they made their plan. They had to convince the man to trust them, so he'd unchain them. Only then could they find a way to escape. "We could make you some dinner."

The man sized up both the girls, as if unsure. "Nah, I'll cook. I got some canned chili I'll heat up. Give you girls a treat."

"Jayme, how's your elbow?" Delilah asked, loud enough so she was sure the man would hear.

"Swollen," she said. "I think it's broken."

He walked over toward them. "Bad, huh?"

Jayme grimaced. "Mister, it's real bad. Did you bring anything for pain?"

"No. Never thought of it. Just some Band-Aids and stuff." He pushed her right sleeve up on her reed-thin arm. Delilah nearly gasped, seeing how near-starvation made the older girl's bones stand out. Right below her elbow, Jayme had a bruised lump the size of a quail egg. The man rotated her arm, and Jayme let out a shrill cry.

"That really might be broken," he mumbled.

"I could help," Delilah whispered. Gerard looked over at her, questioning. "I can make a poultice of mashed herbs, especially comfrey if I can find any," she explained. "Mother Ardeth always used it to stop the pain and help things heal. We can wrap it on Jayme's arm and find a piece of wood for a brace."

Gerard stared down at her. "You know how to do that?"

"I watched our mother Ardeth make poultices. She's like a doctor," Delilah said. "She taught me."

"OOOOWWWWWW," Jayme cried again, her eyes filling with tears. "It hurts bad."

"Shit." Gerard stared down at Delilah. "I'll think about it. Maybe, if you two behave, in the morning we'll look for those herbs and stuff. Too dark out there now."

"Thank you, mister," Jayme said, and she smiled up at him.

"Right now, after dinner, bed," he said. "Tomorrow we'll have a big day."

"How come?" Jayme asked.

He grinned. "My dad, the great prophet, never trusted me with a wife. Now he's in prison, and I don't need his permission. I got the two of you without him."

"But what's happening tomorrow?" Delilah wondered if she really wanted to know.

"Tomorrow, you and me are getting hitched, little one. You'll become my wife in every way. And we'll be sealed for eternity." Gerard smirked at her, and Delilah felt nauseous. "I'll teach you what it means to be a wife."

CHAPTER FORTY-SEVEN

The helicopters flew to St. George to refuel about 4 a.m. They'd return in the morning. We'd had a few more false alarms, but no more sightings. Not long after, we tied off the horses on the trail to rest and wait for sunrise. The dogs had apparently lost the scent. Somehow, we must have gone past where Gerard left the trail. In the daylight we'd be able to look for clues. We had a few hours to go, and an overwhelming fatigue plagued all of us. It had been a grueling day and as taxing a night. I felt like I'd aged decades since the previous morning. My bones and joints ached as if we'd hiked to Salt Lake and back. The men slumped in their saddles. I thought of Delilah and feared stopping, but we couldn't go on.

"The dogs are confused. We exposed them to Evan's scent, but now we're after Gerard," one of the trainers explained. "I'm surprised they could trail him without being given anything of his to smell. The only thing I can come up with is that they've been picking up the scent of his horse."

In our hours together, I'd learned that Officer Conroy was a pragmatic kid, one who had a tendency to see through it all and get to the bottom line. Maybe he'd inherited the tendency, since both his parents were cops. "It doesn't really matter why the dogs lost the scent, or whose scent they were following. We just need to find the chief," he said.

The horses dozed, the dogs slept, and we threw out ideas. Mullins and Max had their rifles out, keeping watch. We wondered who Gerard had with him, mentioning again the two mattress pads in the bedrooms and the two petite sets of tracks Rodgers found. I reassured myself that Delilah, the most recently kidnapped, was probably one of the girls, but who was the other? Could it be Jayme Coombs?

As we talked, I took deep breaths, in, out, in again. *Calm. Be calm.* I felt sure that Gerard had Delilah somewhere on the mountain, not terribly far away. Yet I could do nothing to save her. Although unavoidable, I resented the delay, and I felt helpless.

"Gerard doesn't seem to be moving all that fast. I think our assumption is right and the hostages are slowing him down," Max said, giving some comfort that all wasn't lost. "We're getting fairly high, and the trees will start thinning soon. It'll make it harder for him to find cover. My guess is that wherever he's hiding isn't much farther up than we are now."

"Most likely that cave," I mused. "If we only knew where it was."

We talked it through. As we got closer, I worried about the dogs tipping Gerard off by barking. Mullins suggested that once we found the spot where Gerard and the girls left the trail, we let Rodgers take over the tracking. The decision made, we agreed that from that point on we'd leave the dogs back with their trainers on the trail and forge on without them. If we needed them, we could radio and have them rejoin us.

"The choppers make a lot of noise, too. Could make it tough to take the chief by surprise, right?" A rhetorical question; none of us responded to Conroy. "Maybe we shouldn't use them?"

"What do you think?" Max glanced over at me and asked.

"Yeah, they're noisy. But do we have another option?" I asked. The men shrugged, and offered no opinions. "I think we're stuck with the helicopters. We need the thermal imaging to find Gerard. What else can we use?"

"Even the choppers won't help us if Gerard has the girls hidden in a cave," Max pointed out. "If they're inside layers of rock, the equipment is useless."

No one said anything, but we all knew Max was right. From here on out, the choppers could hurt more than help. But I still didn't see that we had a choice.

"What about the horses? They're pretty noisy, too," Conroy mentioned. A brief discussion and we agreed to hike the final trek up the mountain.

Our plan set, all we could do was wait for morning. I knew I'd never sleep so I took over the watch. The others napped but with my mind on Delilah, I couldn't quiet it enough for even a moment's peace. It was then that I remembered Sadie's diary in the saddlebag on my horse.

"*These mountains that surround us confine us,*" my sister wrote in a precise hand. "*They keep out those who disagree with the way we live, but they keep us locked in, too. I wish I could fly over the mountains, or down the highway and escape. Somewhere there is another world.*"

It turned out that Sadie was a chronicler, and something of an artist. Unhappy with her regimented life, journaling apparently gave her an outlet to reveal her feelings and thoughts. I wondered if there were other such books hidden in the trailer, for this volume covered only her final two years. In the margins she'd drawn playful caricatures of our family. My tension eased enough that I chuckled at one of my mother. It bore a striking resemblance to the wicked witch in *The Wizard of Oz*.

On other pages, Sadie sketched her mother's beehives, the boxes surrounded by buzzing bees, the drawers filled with intricate building blocks of honeycomb. She excelled at drawing their small occupants, honeybees colored in with black and yellow markers. Her bees had whimsical faces and playfully positioned antennae, drooping in sadness, straight up in anger, and stretched out sideways in surprise. She fashioned detailed drawings of cardinals and bluebirds, vultures, warblers, swifts and sparrows. On one page, she drew an eagle. I pushed up my sleeve and compared it to my tattoo. They could have been siblings, as we were.

"*When I stand alone outside the bee shack, I see the birds on high branches, preening their feathers and watching me,*" Sadie wrote. "*What do they think of a girl who dreams of escape?*"

Two dozen pages in, I noticed my name. "*Could I find Clara? Does she remember me? Would she help me if I ran away?*"

"Yes, I would have," I whispered, a tear forming in my eye. "Oh, dear Sadie, if you had only come to me."

What did our mothers think when they read Sadie's words? On page after page she expressed disdain for our family's way of life, especially the church hierarchy, who assigned women as property. "*I'll never marry an old man with a harem, to live my life only for his pleasure,*" she swore. "*Whatever I have to do, I will find a way to avoid such an existence.*"

I skimmed through the book, looking for anything that might help. In an entry dated a few months before Sadie disappeared, she wrote that a man drove up to the bee shack in a pickup truck. As Sariah had said, the description offered few clues. "*He's tall and big. Why would he seek out me? His family has money and influence. At first, I worried. I didn't understand why he'd come. What he intended. But he brought me presents, flowers and perfume, and he stayed and talked.*"

I understood why my mothers saw no hints to the man's identity when they read the diary, but in hindsight, Sadie's descriptions fit Gerard Barstow. She talked of his position in town, that he had the ability to keep her safe. As the prophet's son, as the police chief, he could have done that. Instead, he buried her in a rock-covered grave.

"*I don't love him, but he touches me and something deep inside me moves. And he says he loves me. We'll live on his brother's ranch at the foot of the mountains. I'll join him there, and we'll rebuild the old house. One day, it will be a good home to raise our children. I do want children. On their walls I'll draw princesses and pirates.*"

So Gerard lived at the ranch where the girls were held. One answer fell in place. I felt a devastating rush of disappointment, questioning again how I could have zeroed in on Evan Barstow and never considered his brother. I'd been fooled.

I wished I had time to read the entire diary. When I fled, I'd lost so many years with Sadie, time I could never get back. Her words brought her to me. But the day would break soon, so I concentrated on mentions of Gerard, anything that might help.

In the very last entry, dated a day before Sadie disappeared, I found it.

CHAPTER FORTY-EIGHT

Sunlight crept through the darkness and day arrived. The woods transformed slowly, channeling light between the trees. I woke the men. I handed out energy bars and water, and told them what I had planned. "We're going to ground the helicopters and find Gerard on our own."

"How?" Mullins asked.

"Using this." I held up Sadie's diary. "There's a notation that could refer to the location of a cave." I opened to the page and read it to them. "*He whispered his plans to me at the bee shack. When he came to me, he said that I should be his wife, his only wife for eternity. I again confessed that I don't love him. Sometimes I see things in him that frighten me, but then I have never known a man in this way. Perhaps that's why I am afraid. I know he wants me. I see it in his eyes.*

"*I am to tell no one of our plans. We will meet where we have before. From high on the mountain, halfway between Samuel's Peak and the hump, we'll look down on the world we've known. By the time our families discover we're gone, we will be man and wife.*"

For a moment, the men remained quiet. Then Max asked, "Samuel's Peak and the hump, she's talking about the camel's hump on the east, the one closest to the peak, right?"

"I think so," I said. "In our family, Father told the legend every Christmas Eve, explaining how the two lesser mountaintops resemble humps and Samuel's Peak the head of a camel. We'd stand out in the cold while he traced the mountains with his hand. He said one of the three wise men, Balthazar, carved his camel there for us to see."

"Halfway between," Conroy mused. "You think…" He paused and raised his hand up and pointed east of where we stood. Most of the mountaintops were obscured by the trees; we could barely see the ridges. "Right about there?"

"It's too hard to plot a course from here," I said. "I'll cancel the choppers but ask them to stand by in case we need them. If the dogs are able to lock onto the point where Gerard took the girls into the woods, we'll be able to call Stef and get our bearings based on our position and the mountain."

My nerves on edge, fearful I'd misread the clues and we'd squander more time, I took some comfort from the men. They all seemed more hopeful as we hiked back down the trail, the dogs and Rodgers in the lead. About twenty minutes later, one dog appeared to pick up the scent on a narrow dirt path. The other kept ambling down the trail.

"I don't know," one of the trainers said. "When it's a sure thing, they both lock on. Not happening here."

Max and I scanned the waking forest with binoculars, while Rodgers ventured a few dozen feet into the woods. He walked back to whisper to us, not risking a shout. "Looks like this might be it, but I'm not one hundred percent. Lots of rock. The ground's hard as cement from the drought, and I can't see human footprints, but there are broken branches and a handful of indentations that may be horse prints. Since the one dog likes this, I'd say it might be right."

I looked at Max, who shrugged and said, "Clara, this is your call."

The others waited for me to decide. I got on the radio. "Stef, can you see us on the computer screen?"

"Yup. I've got you."

"Figure out what direction we need to hike from here to get to the upper tree line at a point where we'll be halfway between the peak and the closest hump, the one farthest east."

"Hump?" Stef questioned. I'd forgotten that she'd just moved to Alber a year earlier.

"Ask someone, maybe the deputies who grew up around Alber. They can show you where the camel's humps are. We need to set a course that'll end up approximately halfway between the eastern hump and Samuel's Peak."

For a while, silence. Then Stef clicked back on. "I've never heard of this camel thing, but I found someone who did. It looks like you want to hike so that you end up about twenty-five degrees east of your location. The sheriff's looked it over, too. He agrees."

"Okay, thanks," I said. "Monitor us and let us know if we wander off course, or if it looks like we're heading in the right direction to hit our mark."

"You've got it," she said.

We tied the horses' reins on trees and said goodbye to the trainers and the dogs. "Keep your guns handy. We don't know where this guy is," I warned them. "And listen in on the radio, in case we need you."

Then I asked Rodgers if he would continue on with us. "We need you to keep looking for signs indicating what direction Gerard took. We know that you're not a cop. If you'd rather not, we understand."

Our tracker put his hand on his side and patted his firearm. "I'm coming."

The opening in the woods slender, we formed a line. The trees spread out around us. We carried our rifles at our sides, and more soft morning light filtered through as the sun rose higher. Off and on Rodgers made us retrace our steps, readjusting. "I'm not seeing much, but I think this is right," he said. "A few broken branches, and where the ground is soft enough some partial prints that could be from the horse. I don't have a clue how old they are though. What if it's not them?"

Max told him, "Joe, don't worry. None of us can do any better. Just keep looking."

We kept angling up the mountain, bearing slightly east. Off and on I whispered to Stef. "Headed in the right direction?"

"Yeah. That looks like it might work. The spot where you want to come out is just a little to your left," she said.

The trees thinned, the sun climbed higher, and the heat built.

We marched slowly forward, weaving around trees, following Rodgers, who kept his eyes on the ground, charting our course based on a few snapped branches thinner than a pencil.

Time passed, and we covered more ground. My legs burned from the climb, steeper as we hiked higher. Our binoculars around our necks, I sometimes gazed through mine, searching for anything that looked out of place, anyone hiding in the woods. I wondered what lay ahead. I worried about what we might find.

Where are you, Delilah?

I'd told myself for the last decade that no one listened when I prayed. But in that moment, I needed to believe someone with power watched over us. *God, keep my sister safe and help me find her. Please.*

An eagle flew overhead, screeching, as if to greet the new day. I instinctively glanced down at my sleeve. Hidden underneath, my good luck charm reminded me of where I'd come from and all I'd endured. Perhaps it was more a testament to my journey, and that the pain and disappointments of my past had made me stronger.

CHAPTER FORTY-NINE

"How much farther?" I asked.

"Slightly to your right, maybe two hundred feet up the mountain, and you'll be halfway between the hump and the peak at the tree line." Stef's voice rose an octave. "Detective?"

"Yeah?"

"Are you sure you don't want a chopper? The sheriff thinks it's a good idea. The SWAT team can drop down to help."

As reassuring as that sounded, I thought again about the chopper's noise, and that Gerard, with a bird's eye view from his cave, might shoot at the officers as they rappelled down the ropes. If he had advance notice, Gerard could use the girls as shields. "We can't risk it," I said. "We have to take him by surprise."

"You got a plan?" Max asked.

"I do," I said.

"Let's hear it," Mullins said.

"Rodgers, you'll stay here," I said. He looked relieved. "Take that gun out of your belt and keep watch. Before you pull the trigger, though, you need to make sure you know who you're shooting at. It could be one of us falling back. But be ready in case it's Gerard. Understand?"

"Got it," he said. "If it's one of you, wave at me or something. Give me a sign. Okay?"

"We'll try, but you watch for us, too. Don't be trigger-happy. Okay?" I took a slight bob of his head as agreement.

I scanned the other faces, Max, Mullins, and the kid, Conroy. They looked as tense as I felt. Even my teeth were nervous. These were the bad moments, the ones before we put ourselves aside and took action, when we had time to consider what could go wrong.

Everything.

"We'll take it slow. There are four of us, so we have him outnumbered and outgunned. We'll spread out, stay in contact with our mics," I said. "Anyone sees the cave, Gerard, Delilah, or anyone else, radio us your location, and wait for backup. Unless you have to, don't try to take Gerard alone."

"Okay," Max said. "How about Mullins swings far left, Conroy far right, and you and I track up the center?"

"How far apart?" I asked. "I'm thinking maybe a hundred feet between each of us?"

"Yeah," Mullins said. "Depending on the woods, we might be able to see who's next to us. That way, we can signal, if we have to, instead of use the mics."

"Okay. Keep the noise down. Careful where you walk. When we get within fifty feet of the tree line, everyone stops and gets low, stays hidden but puts on binoculars. Look for the entrance to a cave. For any signs that someone is in the area. I don't think Gerard is stupid enough to leave anything out in the open, but we can hope."

Almost in unison, the four of us moved forward and fanned out. I couldn't see Mullins on the far left, but had eyes on Max closer on my near left, and Conroy just visible through the trees on my right. As we climbed higher, we became increasingly careful, tried not to step on branches, anything that would make a noise, but we couldn't hide the crunch of our feet on the dry grasses. When I saw bright sunlight ahead, the trees thinning out and the mountainside becoming clear in front of us, I knew we were close. By then, I'd lost sight of the others.

"Slow and easy," I whispered into the radio. "Anyone see anything?"

"Not yet," Max said, and then the others repeated his news.

I searched through my binoculars and saw nothing that resembled a cave. I worried that by basing everything on Sadie's diary, I'd led us astray. That we were wasting our time, while Gerard had his hostages acres away in a cave we'd never find. What if the reference to looking down from the mountain meant nothing, and I'd jumped on it as a lifeline out of desperation?

"Something here, Detective," Conroy whispered. "Not sure, but there's a dark area in the mountainside."

I made a snap decision. "Max, you and Mullins maintain your positions. I'll check on Conroy."

"Okay," Max said, "You got that, Mullins?"

"Got it."

I picked my way over and around the dry brush. I had to walk a good distance before I thought I saw Conroy in the distance, crouched down, his rifle out, aiming straight ahead. But I wasn't sure. Was it him? I tapped my lapel mic. "Stef, are you listening in?"

"Yup," she said. "I can see all of your transceivers. Conroy's not far ahead."

At that, the kid gave me a wave of his hand. When I reached him, I knelt next to him. He pointed at something dark to our right, barely visible between the trees. I nodded at him and whispered, "Let's work our way up there."

We stayed low, hid as much as we could behind trees and tall brush, moving forward. As we did, the dark area spread wider. A cave opening? My pulse hammered so hard I heard it in my ears as I motioned for Conroy to stay back and I eased gingerly forward, watching each step, but not taking my eyes off the goal. When I stood fifteen feet away, I had a clear bead on it. There was nothing there, no opening in the mountain's wall. The darkness was merely a shadow cast by an outcropping. "Not our cave," I said into the mic. "I'll work my way back to my position."

"Check," Max said. "We'll maintain until we get new orders."

I waved at Conroy and he gestured back, then I walked carefully, scanning the mountainside through my binoculars. Nothing but more shadows, dry grass, and rock. My detective work had led us to the wrong place.

"Let's regroup. I'll call in the choppers," I said into my mic. "Once we get eyes from above, we'll reposition."

"I agree," Max said. "Let's do it."

"Stef," I said into the mic, when I reached my original position. "Send the helicopters up. Have them scan the mountainside. Thermal imaging but also watch for that cave."

"On their way," she said.

Just then Mullins whispered into his radio. "I hear something. I think it's voices."

"Where are you?" I asked.

"Two hundred yards west of Max. I walked off a bit. I know that's not what you ordered, but—"

"Stef, hold the choppers," I said.

"Got it," she answered.

"Mullins, stay where you are. Max, Conroy, and I are on our way."

As soon as I walked up, I heard murmurs not far ahead, a high, small voice I thought could be that of a girl. Mullins hid behind a tree, his rifle out, pointing at an opening in the vegetation. Thirty feet up the mountainside, I saw someone low to the ground, moving. I wanted to go in closer, but I waited for the others. Once Max and Conroy arrived, I motioned for us to spread out. Then I whispered into the mics, "Let's fan out again and surround them. From now on, no radio except in an emergency. No talking. They'll hear us. Don't take a shot unless the girls are clear. Be careful. We don't want anyone caught in crossfire."

The others did as I ordered and moved forward toward the voices. We walked up in a line, and then spread out to hide behind brush and trees.

At first, nothing but the hum of voices and a shadow cast by something or someone moving. Then something glowed golden-red ahead. What was it? I eased closer, and saw sunlight reflecting off auburn hair. Delilah stooped on the edge of the clearing, one knee down, pulling weeds from the forest floor. I eased farther ahead and took a position concealed behind a stand of pines.

Gerard stood above Delilah, a rifle at his side. He had binoculars on, watching the sky, looking for helicopters, I guessed. Max was right; Gerard had guessed the tactics we'd employ. Satisfied nothing circled overhead, he next scanned the woods, then let the binoculars drop to his chest. I slipped in closer, hoping the others did as well. I stopped breathing when he turned his head in my direction, as if listening. I didn't take another breath until he moved past me.

"Haven't you found the right weeds yet?" Gerard prodded, his voice impatient, his right hand gripping his rifle. "How much of that damn stuff do you need?"

I slid a bit forward and hid again, this time nestled in a thick cluster of saplings. From there, I could better see and hear them.

"It has to be the right kind of herbs." Delilah pushed the dirt back with her hands, rustled through grass and whatever else grew at the base of a thin-trunked pine. "I'm looking for comfrey. Like I told you, Mother Ardeth says it's the best thing for pain."

"I told you to quit talking about your mothers," he said. "You sound like a baby when you do that."

Delilah shot him a glance and scrunched up her nose. "You know, I am just a kid. I'm only twelve."

"You're old enough," he said. "Now finish up out here. We need to get back inside the cave."

Gerard paced, nervous, watching Delilah but stealing glimpses into the forest, off and on studying the sky. Max and the others must have been closing in, too. Gerard didn't know it, but they were surrounded. I advanced closer and stopped behind the trunk of another pine, one that gave me a straight shot at him. I raised my rifle, took aim at his chest, left center, at his heart. My finger eased onto the trigger.

Delilah stood and blocked my shot.

I took a breath.

"Is it okay if I go a foot or two into the forest to look?" she asked.

Gerard frowned. "Only a step or two in. No farther."

"Thank you." Delilah walked a short distance into the woods. She dropped to her knees, a spindly bush at her side. The brush was dense around her, and to her left a pine soared high above the other trees, its trunk wider than the rest.

I refocused my shot, targeting Gerard's heart.

In a split second, Delilah crawled toward the pine. She stood and slipped behind the tree trunk. Gerard rushed toward her. A tree blocked my shot. He stopped walking, raised his rifle and stared toward her.

"Goddamn it, get out here!" he shouted. "You think that tree will hide you?"

Delilah didn't move.

I didn't know where Max and the others were. If I shot, I worried I'd hit one of them. I slid two feet to my right. Again I lined up a clear shot at Gerard with the mountain behind him. He moved, this time to the left of the tree, and peered at Delilah. "I can see you. This isn't some stupid game of hide-and-seek. I told you get the hell out here!" he demanded. "Now! Or I'll put a bullet through that empty head of yours, like I did that damn brother of mine."

In that moment, another girl ran out of the cave, her hair long and dark blond. My brain flashed up the photo Genevieve Coombs brought to the station. It was Jayme. Distracted, Gerard didn't see her. In a single leap, Jayme jumped on Gerard's back, wrapped her legs around his waist and her handcuffed arms around his head. She dug in, gouging at his eyes, and he screamed.

He grabbed the cuffs' chain, but she held tight, dropped the chain lower and tried to use it to strangle him. He pulled at her arms, then lurched back and rammed her into a tree. Frail, painfully thin, she refused to let go. He bashed her against a second tree, and she fell.

Jayme rolled and came to a stop in front of the cave.

Gerard turned and brushed a hand over his burning eyes. "Goddamn it, you ain't worth it. None of you two's worth it. I can get new girls anytime I want. I don't need the likes of you."

As he aimed his rifle at Jayme, Delilah flew at him from behind the tree. I couldn't get a clear shot. I stepped forward, but stayed hidden. I needed that element of surprise. Delilah and Gerard wrestled, and his rifle discharged. The bullet struck rock, blasting off splinters of mountainside. Delilah fell, landing on her back. Gerard stood over her, smiled, and took aim.

I squeezed the trigger and took my shot as I heard others ring out from the behind the trees.

At first, Gerard looked startled, as if he didn't understand what had happened. He stared down at his chest, stunned. Blood spread out, saturating his shirt. I marched toward him from behind the trees. We stood twenty feet apart, eye to eye. He looked at me as if surprised. I smiled. Clumsily, he attempted to raise his rifle. I lined up a shot and pulled the trigger.

Gerard spun a quarter-circle to his right, and then dropped. Blood oozed from a wound in the center of his forehead, the same spot where he'd shot his brother.

Max, Conroy and Mullins emerged from the forest. Jayme lay where he'd thrown her, sobbing.

Dazed, Delilah had shuffled to rest at the foot of a tree. She watched in silence as we approached her. She looked at Conroy's uniform. I had my badge on my shirt. Her hands were dirty from scrounging for weeds, and her tears smeared a sooty brown as she tried to wipe them away. She gazed up at me.

Max checked on Jayme, holding her as she sobbed. "He unlocked Delilah, and he forgot to lock me back up to the wall," she whispered. "He forgot, and I couldn't be scared anymore. We had a plan. I had to help Delilah."

A few steps away, Conroy watched as Mullins felt for a pulse on Gerard's neck. A pool of blood collected around his head.

I sat in the dirt beside Delilah. I reached over and took my sister in my arms. I held her as she wept. Her words came in stutters. "He-he told me that you were looking for me."

"You're so brave," I whispered. "But it's over now. And he can't hurt anyone, not ever again."

Delilah pulled away and her eyes ran over me. "You look like Lily all grown up."

"I think I do too," I said. My eyes filled with tears but my lips climbed up slightly at the corners.

"Are you really my sister?"

"I am," I said.

"Clara?" Delilah asked.

"Yes, I'm Clara."

EPILOGUE

When we drove into Alber, Lily and my three mothers were waiting for us at the police station. Delilah ran to Sariah, and they sank together onto the floor, sobbing and laughing, holding each other and whispering.

Mother Naomi raised her hands to the heavens and cried, "Praise to the Lord for his goodness. He's brought our daughter home!"

The others chimed in: "Praise the Lord, for he is good."

I stood alone, watching, and Mother walked over. At least for this moment, her features had softened, and when she spoke I heard sadness and regret. "Clara, I am sorry for the way I acted. I should have believed that you'd come to help, not harm."

"It's okay." I wished that she would have reached out to touch me. I thought that perhaps she could have said she was sorry for other things, the events that separated us for a decade. She didn't. Our culture had strong talons, like the eagle. It held tight. I'd brought Delilah home, but I remained an errant daughter, an interloper whose very presence she believed threatened our family. "I'm glad Delilah is safe."

Only Lily hugged me, whispering, "Thank you" through her tears.

Despite all we had been through together, despite all I'd done, the distance between me and my mothers persisted, a canyon that separated me from those who were mine. Mother's sadness touched me, but I wondered if she truly understood how wrong she had been and that her actions could have cost Delilah her life. No permanent bridge had been built between us. No true understanding had been reached. Perhaps this would be our fate, to never again truly be mother and daughter.

The official inquiry took a few days. We had three scenes to document: the cave, the location on the mountainside where we found Evan Barstow's body, and the spread where Gerard kept the girls. During our investigation, we were able to determine that Evan had loaned his brother the ranch house to live in not long after Gerard returned to Alber.

On the kitchen table, we found an envelope addressed to the postmaster in El Paso, Texas. Inside was a stamped, sealed envelope addressed to Sariah and a note to the postmaster asking him to postmark the letter and put it in the mail for delivery. When we opened the inner envelope, we found a handwritten note from Delilah, telling our family that she'd run away.

As Doc predicted, the body in the barn turned out to be Eliza Heaton, and we had a DNA match on Sadie for the girl in the field.

The morning after the investigation officially ended, I drove out to tell Jessica Barstow of my belief that Christina was another of her brother-in-law's victims. Too much was the same for it to have been a coincidence, most glaring her strange disappearance and the letter. Jessica cried in my arms and asked if I would look for Christina's body. "I want to bury my sister," she said.

"I have to go home to Dallas," I told her. "But I'll talk to Max Anderson and the others about it. Maybe they can try."

She appeared disappointed, but said nothing.

Something still bothered me. "One question," I said, and her eyes locked on mine. "That orange flashlight we took into evidence. When did Evan bring it home?"

"He didn't," she said. "Gerard stopped in one afternoon. He gave it to Evan. My husband seemed surprised. It wasn't his birthday. I remember him being happy about it, that Gerard had shown him respect by bringing him an unexpected gift."

On my drive back to Alber, I wondered why Gerard had given the flashlight to Evan. That one piece of evidence started everything. Perhaps it was what Evan thought—Gerard's grateful gift to a brother who kept his secrets. Or could Gerard have been trying to offer his brother up as a suspect? If so, he succeeded.

A few hours after I visited Jessica, my family buried my sister Sadie. The sky turned overcast that afternoon, and we felt a whiff of moisture in the air. Halfway through the ceremony at the gravesite, the clouds opened and heaven cried as Sadie was finally laid to rest in a proper grave, not the stone mound where Gerard Barstow hoped she'd spend eternity.

I wasn't officially invited to the service, so I stood under an umbrella near the rear with Max and the sheriff, watching as Naomi placed a bouquet of lavender on her oldest child's casket. I thought of the sister I'd left behind and would never see again. I had her diary in my suitcase. Mother hadn't asked for it back, and I hadn't offered it. I counted our siblings in attendance. Father had twenty-one children at the gravesite that day, and it appeared seven grandchildren. None of the others looked my way except for Lily and Delilah, who snuck peeks at me until Mother put her hands on their faces and turned them back toward the grave.

Still, it wasn't completely over.

The story made for sensational headlines. Two girls murdered, two more abducted by a police chief in a polygamous enclave in the mountains of Utah. It had what the media calls legs, enduring interest, and the Internet carried it everywhere. I got requests for interviews from reporters all over the world, and I turned them all down.

That didn't stop the coverage. Here and there people talked to reporters: one of the dog trainers, Jessica Barstow, and one of Gerard and Evan's brothers. Coming and going from the Smith County Courthouse, photographers snapped my picture.

Before long, my face stared back at me from front pages, the evening news.

Ten days after I arrived in Alber, I packed my suitcase in my room on the second floor of Heaven's Mercy Shelter. Chief Thompson had understood my absence, but he had a case he wanted me to take over in Dallas, a series of burglaries of high-end jewelry stores. He thought I needed a break from murder investigations.

"Give yourself a few weeks to put this behind you," he'd said on the phone.

"Thanks," I'd replied. "That sounds good."

The chief never mentioned the press coverage, but he'd said, "That little town, Alber, is your home? You grew up in a polygamous family?"

"Four moms, but Mother Constance died years back. My father is gone, too," I'd told him. "I'm not sure how many siblings, but there are a bunch."

He'd paused. "Well, you know, Clara, we all come from somewhere. But this is pretty complicated."

I chuckled. "If you only knew."

"We don't care where you came from," he'd said. "You're one of us. Come home."

I thought about the word home.

I had my sleeves pushed up, and I looked down at my eagle tattoo. I thought about how the majestic birds build their nests high in trees, on cliffs, far away from humans, to protect their young. I'd read once that Native Americans considered bald eagles spiritual envoys who carried messages to and from God. I thought about that moment in the woods, when I prayed for the first time in many years. I asked God to keep Delilah safe, and to help me find her. Moments after I sent off my plea, an eagle cried out.

In the end, God must have heard me. He granted both my prayers.

*

"You all packed?" Hannah stood in the open doorway looking wistful at my imminent departure.

"Yup," I said. "I'm stopping at the police station on my way out. Alma Heaton is dropping in. She wants to talk to me. And Max is coming to say goodbye. Then I'll head to Vegas to hop on a plane home."

Hannah appeared interested. "Max, huh? You two have any plans?"

I turned away to slip the final items into my suitcase. If I'd been truthful, I would have said that I felt drawn to Max. We had such history. I could still close my eyes and remember how his lips felt against mine that day at the river. But life hadn't been kind to either one of us, and we both came with heavy baggage. I sensed Max held more secrets beyond what he had said about his daughter. Ones as painful as mine. "I don't know, Hannah. I guess we'll have to wait and see what's ahead."

I thought she might push, but instead she asked, "How's Jayme?"

"Still in the hospital in St. George, but improving. They've set her arm, but they're building her back up before they release her. She's skin and bones. I asked Max to investigate the allegations Jayme made about the abuse before they send her home."

"Good." Then Hannah sighed, the kind of sigh that starts deep in the soul. "I wish you weren't leaving, Clara. I will miss you. Whether you realize it or not, we need you here."

"I'm not wanted here," I reminded her. "You'll have to come visit me in Dallas. I'll take you to restaurants, plays, and show you what the rest of the world is like."

A slight shake of her head, and I knew that would never happen. "This is my world. I belong in this house with these women and children. They need me."

"Of course," I said. "Then there will be phone calls."

"And letters," Hannah agreed. "I enjoy receiving letters."

I gave her a last hard look and considered the beauty of a woman content in her world, someone who understood where she belonged. That would never be me. For the rest of my life, I would be an outsider.

Stef buzzed me in at Alber PD. Alma Heaton waited inside.

"I wanted you to have this." She held a copy of Jane Austen's *Sense and Sensibility*. "Hannah told me that you and Eliza both loved this writer. My daughter had this next to her bed the day she disappeared."

I held the book in my hands and felt the weight of it. I ran my hand over the title, stamped in gold on the rough cloth cover. Inside, I found a bookplate. Under a spray of delicate blue flowers, Eliza had signed her name. Alma Heaton reached out and embraced me. "Thank you for bringing my daughter home so I can bury her," she whispered. "Without you, we might never have found her."

After Alma left, Mullins popped in the door and asked, "You still here?"

"I'm waiting for Max."

"Well, me and Conroy are heading out to a call. Probably won't see you again." He extended his hand. I shook it. He looked a bit embarrassed. He nodded, turned and left.

I'd brought the secret files back, and I carried them in from the SUV and gave them to Stef when we were alone. "Someone should really go through all those files back there," I said. "No telling what they'd find."

"Yeah, but we both know that won't happen," she said, her voice matter-of-fact. This wasn't something she held any doubt about. "I haven't been here long, but I figure this isn't a town where folks put much stock in rocking the boat."

I let out a short huff in agreement. "That's true."

At that, the door opened, and Max looked in. "Sorry I'm late." He turned and kept the door open with his back while he pulled in a wheelchair holding a young girl with long strawberry-blond hair, the one whose picture I'd noticed on his desk my first day in Alber.

"Alice couldn't stay with Brooke. She had something she had to do today, so I brought her along." The girl's legs twitched a bit with some kind of spasm. A beautiful child, she had inquisitive hazel eyes that locked onto me.

"So this is Brooke." I reached down and took her right hand and shook it. "Pleased to meet you."

"Dad says you're a Dallas police officer." Grinning up at me, she added, "And Dad told me you came here and really shook things up."

I laughed. "I guess I did. I know he hasn't been home much lately. Thanks for lending your dad to me. I couldn't have done it without him."

"That's funny," Brooke said. When she smiled, dimples creased her cheeks.

"What is?"

"Dad told me he couldn't have done it without you."

Max shrugged and flashed me a smile. "I think Clara needs to go now, Brooke. She has a plane to catch in Las Vegas."

"I'm going to go there someday," Brooke said. "And Dallas, too. When I walk again, I'm going to see the world."

"I bet you will see the world. Maybe, one day, your dad will bring you to Dallas to visit me. I'd like that." I picked up Eliza's book and handed it to Brooke. Some things are meant to be shared. "In the meantime, it might be a little early, but keep this. When the time comes, you will find a world inside its covers."

Brooke put the book on her lap and opened it. "These are really pretty flowers," she said, running her hand over the bookplate. "What are they?"

"I'm not sure," I said.

Max's voice tinged with melancholy, he said, "Those were your mother's favorites, Brooke. They're forget-me-nots."

We stood quiet, lost to our own thoughts. I watched the way Max looked at Brooke, the love in his eyes, and I wondered if I'd been unfair to him. In hindsight, Max had been right about much of it, especially that I was stepping over the line, but I hadn't been in a place where I was willing to listen. I looked at my watch, and considered the departure time for my flight. That talk would have to wait. I had to drive to Vegas and check in the Pathfinder at the rental counter. "I need to go," I said.

"Is it okay if you wait here with Stef while I walk Clara out?" Max asked Brooke.

Brooke looked at Max, as if uncertain.

A grin stretching its way across her face, Stef emerged from behind her desk. She placed her hands on the wheelchair's arms and looked down at the girl. "How about we play some wheelchair tag?"

Brooke shouted, "You're it!"

Giggling followed us out the door, as Stef tried to touch Brooke, who swiveled her chair to get away.

Max held the door for me, and we took our time rounding the corner to where I had the SUV parked. "Clara, thank you for coming."

"Thank you for calling me," I said. "If you hadn't…"

"Delilah and Jayme may never have been found. We wouldn't have known what happened to Eliza and Sadie. And Gerard may have never been stopped. There would have been more victims." He held out his hand and I took it. Then he released it, leaned close and whispered, "Again, I'm sorry. When you needed me, I should have backed you up."

He was thinking back to the day he'd sided with the others and told me to go home. At the time, I didn't understand why Max worried so about losing his job. I thought about Brooke waiting inside, and all he'd told me about her, losing her mother, the accident, that she might never fully recover. Without medical insurance to pay for her care, she had no hope.

In that moment, I forgave him. "It's okay, Max. We all have our priorities. Brooke has to be yours. I understand."

"But I shouldn't have let that get in the way of my work when a life could be at risk," he said. "I was wrong. I won't do that again."

"I know you won't," I said, meaning it.

Moments passed, before he said, "Clara, I have missed you."

I didn't know how to respond. He moved toward me and wrapped his arms around me. At first, I didn't react. Then, slowly, I slipped my arms around him, and I laid my cheek on his chest, where I could hear his heart beating. We held each other for mere moments, but it felt like a lifetime. For that brief instance, we were teenagers again, and he was my first love. When we parted, I ran my fingers down his cheek, letting them come to rest on his lips. He put his hand gently over mine and lightly kissed my fingertips.

I reclaimed my hand and stepped back, turning toward the Pathfinder.

"You know, you don't have to go." I felt his eyes on mine, traveling deep inside of me to places I'd buried long ago. I realized it would take every bit of determination I had to get inside the SUV, especially when he said, "I don't want you to leave."

"I have a job in Dallas. My chief has a case waiting."

"You have a job here, if you want it," Max said. I shot him a curious glance. "Alber needs a new police chief. I talked to the mayor today. The job's yours if you want it."

"No. I need to…" I started to object.

Max smiled at me, questioning, waiting for an answer.

From him, my eyes traveled down the familiar street, the sidewalk I'd taken as a young girl. The buildings I'd passed as a child. And I wondered what lay ahead.

A LETTER FROM KATHRYN

I want to say a huge thank you for choosing to read *The Fallen Girls*. If you did enjoy it, and want to keep up to date with all my latest releases, just sign up at the following link. Your email address will never be shared and you can unsubscribe at any time.

www.bookouture.com/kathryn-casey

Now, I'd like to tell you a bit about the inspiration for the Clara Jefferies series.

As Clara has in the book, I have a history in a polygamous town, albeit admittedly a very brief one. Many years ago, as a magazine writer, I covered an adoption case involving a polygamous family. For that piece, I interviewed people who lived in Colorado City, Arizona, and Hildale, Utah. Those towns lay in what's known as the Short Creek area, and, as in the fictional Alber, many of the residents belonged to a fundamentalist Mormon sect that practiced polygamy.

I found my time there fascinating. High in the mountains, I saw huge houses where men had many wives, some dozens, and more than a hundred children. The people I talked to seemed very open about their unusual lifestyles. Some avowed a deep faith and expressed satisfaction with their lives. Others described a stifling culture where young women were married off to old men and teenage boys were driven away.

That experience never left me.

I've thought of it often, especially in the past decade when polygamous enclaves made international headlines. Their leaders were taken away, some imprisoned. Videos of the women in prairie dresses surrounded by scores of children became fodder for the nightly news. *The Fallen Girls* and the Clara Jefferies books to come are pure fiction. None of the characters are depictions of anyone I met during my time in the mountains. Alber is a fictional town not found on any map. None of these events are based on any events that actually took place. Yet the books are inspired by my travels to a world very different from my own.

In closing, I hope you loved *The Fallen Girls*. If you did, I would be very grateful if you would write a review. I'd love to hear what you think, and it makes such a difference helping readers discover my books.

I truly enjoy hearing from my readers—you can get in touch on my Facebook page, through Twitter, Goodreads or my website, kc@kathryncasey.com.

Thank you again, and happy reading,
Kathryn

kathryn.casey.509

@KathrynCasey

www.kathryncasey.com

ACKNOWLEDGEMENTS

Based on my time in Colorado City and Hildale, I first want to thank all of the people I encountered during my days there. You told me your stories, and I appreciate your candor. My time with you enriched this book and those in the Clara Jefferies series to come.

Thank you to my dear friend author Gregg Olsen, who has been so kind to me for so many years. I cherish our friendship.

Thank yous to retired detective Tracy Shipley, Texas Ranger Lt. Wende Wakeman, and forensic pathologist Elizabeth Peacock MD for sharing their expertise.

Thank you Anne-Lise Spitzer, my agent, and her dad, Philip Spitzer, who was my very first literary agent.

A big thank you to all the wonderful people at Bookouture: my editor, Jennifer Hunt, who took such great interest in the book; Alexandra Holmes, Fraser Crichton, Jenny Page, Hannah Bond, Lucy Dauman and Jenny Geras.

Thank you to my husband and my entire family for their constant support. I love all of you. And to all our friends who drag me out of my office and keep me from slipping completely into my fictional world.

Finally, thank you to all of you who read my books. Without you, I wouldn't be able to do what I love. A special thank you to all who recommend my books to others. You make a world of difference.

The Fallen Girls is the first book in the Clara Jefferies series. I've loved writing it, and I look forward to many books to follow.

S

PROPERTY OF MERTHYR
TYDFIL PUBLIC LIBRARIES

Printed in Great Britain
by Amazon

59435702R00194